"You may not have much reason to trust me, Belle, but I wish you'd give me the benefit of the doubt for a few minutes. I'm not quite the crook you imagine—"

"I don't *imagine* you're a crook, Sandro. I know for a fact that you're a criminal low-life sleazeball." She gave him a smile that was all teeth and no emotion. As long as she didn't look at him, she could function pretty well.

"You have every right to be angry with me, but you're in a hell of a lot of trouble, and I want to help." He moved toward her, and she jumped back, shattering the illusion that she was calm and in control.

He ignored her reaction and took her hands, pulling her toward him. "Belle, please, you have to look at me. I want you to see that I'm not lying. *Look at me, dammit.*"

Incredibly, despite everything he'd done and everything she knew about him, she wasn't smart enough to grab the phone and call the police. Instead, she looked up and gave a tight little smile. "I wouldn't believe what you said if the archangel Gabriel appeared in a flash of light and swore every word was true. In fact, I'd be searching for the holographic equipment you'd used to produce the angel."

"Cresswell's woman-in-jeopardy plots are tightly woven with no loose ends."

—*Publishers Weekly*

THE
INHERITANCE
JASMINE CRESSWELL

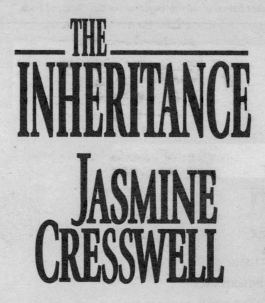

ISBN 1-55166-511-5

THE INHERITANCE

Copyright © 2000 by Jasmine Cresswell.

Visit us at www.mirabooks.com

Printed in U.S.A.

To the Ladies of the Lounge,
who never fail to brighten my day.

One

Her father was dying, and Isabella Joubert was so angry that she hadn't spoken a word since she'd boarded the plane at O'Hare Airport three hours earlier. She was afraid that if she opened her mouth to speak, she would start yelling at anybody unlucky enough to be within earshot. Either that, or she would start bawling and not be able to stop. She wouldn't be crying because she loved her father. Of course not. She would be shedding tears of rage because she was so damn angry at how he'd chosen to squander his talents and waste his life.

According to her mother, Marc Joubert's life expectancy could be measured in days, perhaps even hours. It would soon be too late for him to make amends, too late for anything except regrets. God knew, she had plenty of those, whereas her father most likely had none. With his usual reckless aplomb, he would face the prospect of meeting his Maker without a twinge of guilt or apprehension. Why would he be fearful? He had always enjoyed a flexible conscience and a supreme confidence in his ability to charm the stripes off the meanest tiger. He'd bargained with Saddam Hussein and come out the winner. He'd dealt with one of the bloodiest splinter groups of the IRA and made a tidy profit. When the

Soviet army was being routed in Afghanistan, he'd sold Stinger missiles to three different factions of Afghani rebels and walked away unharmed. In her father's mind, talking himself through Saint Peter's pearly gates would barely present a challenge.

Belle paid off the cabdriver, adding a generous tip as an apology for not having spoken a word, and, in the sweltering air, crossed the few feet of pavement that separated her from the air-conditioned entrance to Miami's Good Samaritan hospital. When she'd left her Chicago office, it had been unusually cool for late September. Here in Miami, it was hot and steamy enough to wilt her gray linen skirt and stick her tailored jacket to her back. She hoisted her hastily packed travel bag higher onto her shoulder and willed herself not to feel frazzled. For a woman who prided herself on keeping her emotions on an even keel, her coping techniques had been conspicuously unsuccessful since her mother's phone call.

The hospital was vast, and Belle realized she was going to have to ask for directions to the Intensive Care Unit. Was she capable of sounding civil if she spoke? Belle closed her eyes, drew multiple deep breaths, and managed to shove her anger back down into the deep hiding place she'd custom-built for it during two years of expensive therapy.

"I'm here to see Marc Joubert," she said to the gray-haired volunteer at the information desk. "He's had open-heart surgery and he's in Intensive Care." She was relieved to hear that her voice sounded calm and perfectly pleasant. She left high drama to the other members of her family. Her parents and siblings could transform a piece of burned toast into a tragic opera in four acts.

The volunteer glanced down a list on the clipboard in front of her. "Yes, Mr. Joubert is in the hospital, but his visitors are restricted to immediate family only."

Thank God, he wasn't dead already. "I'm his daughter. Isabella Joubert." Her voice suddenly sounded thick with tears. Belle gave a tiny shake to clear her head and held out her Illinois driver's license to prove her claim, waiting patiently while the volunteer searched for her name on the list of approved visitors. Instead of increasing her tension, the delay actually calmed her. Belle understood the need for rules and approved of security measures in public places. In fact, Belle appreciated rules and regulations in general, since they made life more civilized and orderly. She only wished the other members of her family shared her point of view.

The volunteer smiled as she handed over a plastic card. "Thanks for waiting, Ms. Joubert. I've found your name, so you can go right up. Here's your pass. Intensive Care is in the west wing." She pointed to her left. "You can take these elevators here. Go straight ahead and follow the maroon arrows when you get to the fifth floor."

The Intensive Care Unit turned out to be a considerable distance from the elevators. Belle strode briskly along the corridors, trying to outpace the images crowding into her head from the last time she had seen her father, seven years earlier. Marc Joubert had been a vigorous sixty then, still at the height of his powers, a master of manipulative charm. It troubled her to remember that if it hadn't been for Sandro Marchese and her desperate need to get away from their failed love affair, she probably would have suc-

cumbed to her father's blandishments and remained
in Miami. How ironic to think that a crook like Sandro had been responsible for pushing her out of the
soiled family nest and into the world of honest, legal
work.

Belle hated that memory and all the others involving her father. Not because Marc had been cruel and
vindictive, but because he'd always seemed to be the
ideal father. Why couldn't he have been a monster
who beat his wife and tortured his children? Why did
he have to be so damn lovable...so seductively rea-
sonable in his self-justification?

As usual, she could find no answers to her questions. Marc Joubert was living proof that it was possible to be both a devoted family man, a friendly
neighbor, and a ruthless merchant of death. Belle's
footsteps faltered under the weight of painful and
guilty memories. What was she doing here? Despite
seven years of trying, she'd never come to terms with
her past—only found ways to keep it buried, where
it couldn't hurt. This trip was opening up old wounds
and making them bleed hot, fresh blood.

But it seemed that emotion was stronger than reason, and she kept walking, although when the nurses'
station came into view she almost turned tail and
marched straight back to the elevators. In the end she
was propelled forward by a primeval urge to see her
father once more before he died.

"I'm Isabella Joubert," she said to one of the
nurses, flashing her pass. "I'm here to see Marc Joubert, my father."

"Yes, of course. He's in room 506. Your mother
is with him, but your brother and sister just went
downstairs to the cafeteria. They'd been sitting with

your father for five hours straight, ever since my shift started.'' The nurse gave her a sympathetic glance and handed her a tissue. To her chagrin, Belle realized that despite her best efforts, she was crying—from frustration and confusion and the ache of old wounds, she decided. It couldn't be from grief. She wouldn't *allow* it to be from grief.

She blew her nose, straightened her shoulders and walked to the door the nurse had indicated. Tapping softly, she walked in.

Her mother was sitting on one side of the bed, holding Marc's hand. Carole Joubert had none of her husband's warmth or wit, but she had an unlimited reserve of volatile emotions. Although she and Belle had never been close, and hadn't seen each other for seven years, she emitted a flood of tears the moment she saw her eldest child, scooping Belle into her arms and sobbing gustily, as if every second apart had been sheer torment for her.

''I thought you were never going to get here,'' she said, mopping her eyes. ''Your poor father has been asking for you ever since he came out of surgery. I didn't know what to say to him. I was afraid you wouldn't come. You were so cold and hostile on the phone. You never did love any of us, did you?'' She dissolved again into tears.

Belle felt the sharp stab of old hurts. She drew in a shaky breath. ''I'm sorry, Mom. I caught the first plane I could. I didn't mean to sound hostile when you called, but I was in a meeting and it wasn't easy to talk.''

Carole's only reply was to sob into her wad of tissues. Feeling guilty—no surprise there—Belle untangled herself from her mother's embrace and cast a single, swift glance toward the shrunken figure in the bed. She had to swallow hard before she could speak. "How's Dad doing?"

She shouldn't have asked. Her mother's tears intensified to the point that she could barely speak, which was all the answer Belle needed. She poured her mother a drink of ice water and gently led her to a chair. "Rest for a few minutes, Mom. Maybe you could even try to catch a few minutes' sleep now that I'm here. You must be exhausted."

"I couldn't possibly sleep," Carole said with sudden composure. "For heaven's sake, your father is dying. The doctors say he's hanging on by sheer willpower, and he might go at any minute."

"Dad always had plenty of willpower, that's for sure," Belle said with wry appreciation. "He's got to be the most stubborn man I've ever met."

Carole frowned. "Really, Belle, you're impossible. Now isn't the time for rehashing old scores, especially since you were the person at fault."

"I'm sorry." Belle didn't attempt to defend herself. She and her mother had such different personalities that they frequently misunderstood each other. But having agreed to come home to Miami, she was determined not to fight with her mother or anyone else in the family.

She walked over to the bed, her anger and frustration melting into a sorrow so intense that her stomach clenched in pain. She wondered if it had been easier to confront death in the old days, when people died at home, without monitors and blinking digital numbers displaying the inexorable failure of the body's systems. She'd thought she was mentally prepared to see her father laid low, but she found she was far from ready to endure a visible, second-by-second count-down to death.

Turning her back on the telltale electronic graphs, Belle eased herself between the machines and the bed so that she could take her father's hand. It felt dry and paper-light in her clasp, tethered to life only by the needles and tubes running in and out of his bruised flesh. Belle blinked hard and stared at the wall, because it suddenly hurt too much to look down at this dying man who was her father. The man who had been the idol of her childhood and the lodestar of her adolescence.

Her mother's voice came from behind her. "Look, your father is opening his eyes. I don't know if he'll be able to speak to you. Sometimes he has the strength and sometimes he doesn't."

Marc Joubert's gaze wandered for a moment, then fixed on Belle's face. It took a full minute before recognition dawned, then his mouth trembled into a smile. "Isabella, my beautiful girl. You came."

Helpless and aching, she returned his smile. "Hello, Daddy. I came as soon as I knew you were sick."

"I couldn't go without seeing you again." His smile faded into a grimace. "Don't...cry, pumpkin."

She could feel the tears rolling down her cheeks, faster and faster. She looked around for a box of tissues, but couldn't see one amidst all the high-tech clutter. She rubbed her eyes with her knuckles. "All right, I won't."

He tried to stroke her cheek, but he lacked the strength to lift his hand with its accompanying welter of tubes and needles. Heart aching, she grazed her knuckles gently against his cheek and he closed his eyes, drifting off into another few seconds of unconsciousness.

When he opened his eyes again, his gaze was momentarily confused. "Isabella, my girl. You're still here. I was afraid I'd dreamed you."

"No, I'm really here. It's good to see you again, Daddy."

"So why are you crying?"

Belle shook her head. "I'm not crying. I'm just glad you're feeling well enough to talk."

"Talk has always been my strong suit." With visible effort, he brought his gaze into focus, the pain- and drug-induced confusion conquered by his infamous willpower. The commanding Marc Joubert she remembered was in charge again, at least for a moment. "You deserved a better man than me for your father, Belle."

The old Marc Joubert would never have apologized, never have admitted to any possible failure on his part as a parent. Pulses pounding, Belle closed her eyes, not knowing how to handle this unexpected apology. In the end, she gave up fighting the truth and leaned across the bed to rest her head on his shoulder, as she had done so many times when she was a child. "I love you, Daddy, and when I was little I thought you were the best father any child could have."

"I love you, too." His fingers brushed her hair with shaky strokes. "God, I've missed you, Belle. You were such a happy child. Always laughing—even when you were a teenager, full of hormones and rebellion. You've no idea how much I've missed the sound of your laughter."

Had she once been a girl who laughed easily? It

was difficult to remember a time when she'd been carefree enough to laugh. The darkness of her early twenties lay between the happy child her father recalled and the solemn, hardworking woman she had become. Since she didn't know what to say, Belle remained silent. It was a coping mechanism of hers that had been overworked in recent years, she thought grimly.

Even on his deathbed, Marc Joubert was a smart enough negotiator to know when to change the subject. He gave a final brief caress to her hair, then spoke abruptly. "Belle, I need your help."

She tensed, instantly wary, pulling herself out of his embrace as she sat up. Her father looked at her with an expression full of regret and self-reproach. "Don't worry," he said. "I'm not asking you to offend against those tiresome suburban moral values of yours."

"*Suburban* isn't a curse word, you know." The rebuke had been reflexive. Belle pulled herself up short and started over. "What do you want me to do, Dad? I'll help if I can."

Before answering, her father looked across at his wife, who smiled at him anxiously. "Marc, honey, don't tire yourself. You know what the doctors said—"

"Sure, I know. They said I'm dying."

"No." Carole's smile dissolved and she gave way to a fresh bout of noisy tears. "No, they said you had to rest to regain your strength—"

"And I will as soon as I've spoken to my daughter." Marc sighed, sounding weak and exhausted.

Belle gestured to her mother, indicating the monitors that were spiking ominously. Carole subsided into her chair, sobbing, and Belle took her father's hand. "I'm listening, Dad. If it's legal, I'll try my best to do whatever you want."

"It's legal. Right up your alley, in fact." His voice grew so hoarse and shaky that Belle had to put her ear almost against his mouth in order to hear what he was saying. "There's a computer disk in my office at home. It's hidden behind your photograph, labeled Charitable Donations. Take it, Belle."

"Yes, I'll find it. Do you want me to bring the disk here for you? Or I could print out the information."

"No." His voice shook with anxiety. "Don't let anyone know what you've got. Not anyone, understand? Keep it safe, and use it after I'm dead. I need you to make everything come right, Belle."

"By making charitable donations? Haven't you taken care of that in your will?"

Her father's eyes were hazy again, their momentary power and focus fading. "Make it come right, Belle. I'm counting on you. You're the only one I can trust to do this. There's someone using my name…"

His voice faded away, and Belle remained silent so that he could catch his breath. She was relieved that he'd asked her to do something that seemed unlikely to pose any ethical dilemma for her. Although, even if her father planned to leave every penny he possessed to worthy causes, that wouldn't compensate for a lifetime spent selling stolen U.S. technology to the highest bidders. But since the past couldn't be unwritten, Belle was grateful to know that he was planning to give a portion of his ill-gotten gains to charity. The gifts must be substantial, she reasoned, or he wouldn't need a computer disk to itemize his instructions. As far as she was concerned, the more of his illicit fortune that was given away, the better.

She squeezed his hand gently when she saw that he was watching her again. ''I'll take care of it, Dad, I promise. You can count on me.''

''That's my girl. I'm sorry, Belle, for everything. Always loved you bes...'' His eyes closed and almost at once the monitors started to buzz an insistent ominous warning.

From the corner of the room, Belle heard her mother scream. She looked down at her father, panic sending her stomach into a sharp nosedive. She wanted to scream at him to hang on, to fight for life as he'd fought for power and success and money, but her voice was stuck somewhere behind the huge swelling that closed her throat.

''Marc!'' Her mother's cry spiraled into a high note of hysteria. Pushing Belle aside, Carole fell across her husband's body, begging and pleading with him to talk to her one more time.

The flat-line on the monitors explained why the once-mighty and powerful Marc Joubert couldn't answer.

Two

More than four hundred people crowded the church for Marc Joubert's funeral, which rivaled that of a nineteenth-century robber baron in grandeur and hypocrisy. So many eminent friends and neighbors requested the privilege of eulogizing the dearly departed that Carole collapsed into hysterics at the prospect of making a choice among the contenders, and Belle found herself appointed to save the day. This she did by the simple method of putting the names of the competing dignitaries into her father's fishing hat and pulling out four winners.

Her impromptu selection system worked well, given that few people attending the funeral had any interest in hearing the truth. The eulogies couldn't have been more full of accolades if Marc Joubert had been America's answer to Mother Teresa.

The bishop praised him as a loving husband, wise father, loyal friend and generous contributor to the church. Miami's chief of police called him a model citizen, whose efforts on behalf of the less fortunate in the community had become legendary. The mayor, who was running a tight campaign for reelection, seized the opportunity to deliver a homily on Marc's old-fashioned family values, taking care to speak in short sentences that would provide convenient sound bites on the evening news. And the president of the Chamber of Commerce wrapped up the paeans by waxing eloquent on Marc's vital contributions as a pioneering entrepreneur in the field of international trade.

Belle reflected that there was no whitewash so effective as money.

In contrast to her cynical daughter, Carole showed no sign that she felt some of the praise for Marc might be a tad exaggerated. Supported by her son and younger daughter, as well as her son-in-law, she cried throughout the funeral mass, her arms wrapped around Tony and Marisa for support. Her sobs, which had been virtually unending for three days, punctuated the anthems of the choir with noisy pathos. Evan, her son-in-law, had appointed himself keeper of the tissues. He handed out clean ones at appropriate intervals, along with soft murmurs of comfort—but nothing stanched the flow of Carole's tears for long.

Belle, one of the few dry-eyed people in the church, sat at the end of the family pew and stared unblinkingly ahead, disoriented by this lavish expenditure of emotion over the demise of a merchant of death. She wished she could offer her mother some consolation, but she could find no words to articulate her own feelings, let alone provide comfort to anyone else.

She envied her family's tight-knit closeness and their ability to grieve with such uninhibited fervor. Her father had embraced life with a warm, Mediterranean gusto, and he'd taught his three children to do the same. Unfortunately, Belle had lost the knack of easy tears and careless laughter right around the time she discovered that her father was one of the world's richest and most successful criminals.

Her relationship with Carole and Tony had never quite recovered from that shattering discovery, although she'd remained on fairly close terms with Marisa. The fact that her younger sister had flown the family nest at an early age meant that the two of them were able to maintain a semblance of a normal relationship, although they still danced clumsily around any and all issues related to their father and the family business.

Denied the comforting release of tears, Belle had no outlet for the heavy weight of pain that squeezed her heart and made her stomach churn. Sardonic detachment, she discovered, was no substitute for tears as a method of alleviating grief.

The cortege of cars escorting Marc's remains from the church to the cemetery took twenty minutes to drive through each intersection, and required half a dozen motorcycle cops to control the resulting traffic jams. After the interment, two hundred of Marc's closest and most influential associates came back to the house to eat expensive canapés and offer their condolences in person.

Belle managed to last for over two hours of socializing, her polite smile frozen in place, her throat dry with the effort of finding words to acknowledge the overt sympathy—and the covert curiosity—at her return. Sorrow jostled with anger, swelling until there didn't seem to be room for her lungs to draw breath. Finally, the tears she refused to shed threatened to blow off the top of her head. Choked by the cloying aroma of lilies and insincerity, she ran upstairs in search of silence and space.

She walked into the first empty room she found, which happened to be her father's study. Once inside, she leaned against the door, gulping air. Now that the din of voices was shut out, she realized that she had a pounding headache. There was no way she could rejoin the guests without taking a break.

She walked to the window and let down the shades, shutting out the fierce afternoon sun. The filtered light was soothing, and the pounding in her head eased almost at once. She had always liked this small office more than any other room in the house. It had been her father's real workplace, unlike the imposing library downstairs that a decorator had filled with leather-bound editions of the classics and imported antique chairs too uncomfortable to sit in for longer than it took to glance at the day's newspaper.

The sense of her father was stronger in this room than anywhere else, and Belle kept waiting for him to burst through the door, demanding to know why his wife was having a party to which he hadn't been invited. Marc had always loved to entertain, and it seemed vaguely indecent to be holding such a lavish affair without him.

Belle drifted around the study, memories that she'd kept at bay for years rushing back to taunt her. She let her fingers trail along the edge of the battered desk that her father had refused to replace or refurbish because it was the only piece of furniture that *his* father, Grandfather Joubert, had managed to save from their Paris apartment during the Second World War. She'd heard the story a hundred times of how Grandfather Joubert and Great-Uncle Pierre had carried the desk down the service stairs on their backs while Gestapo officials pounded at the front door of the apartment with a warrant for their arrest.

As a child, she'd accepted the exciting story at face value. As a young adult, she'd asked her father why Grandfather Joubert and Great-Uncle Pierre had risked their lives to salvage a piece of furniture. Her father had explained that not only was the desk a cherished heirloom that had been in the Joubert family for four generations, but it had also been stuffed full of secret documents and blueprints for enemy weapons. Grandfather Joubert and Great-Uncle Pierre, who were members of the French Resistance, had stolen the blueprints at incredible personal risk. They'd even infiltrated Nazi headquarters and photographed maps and diagrams of German troop movements.

According to Marc, the documents in the desk had been so valuable that his father and uncle had rowed the twenty-two miles across the English Channel from Calais to Dover, dodging German submarines and patrol boats, in order to deliver them personally to the Free French army in England. The papers had been reviewed by General Charles de Gaulle himself before being put to use helping the Allies defeat Adolf Hitler.

Belle had loved to listen to her father tell stories about her ancestors' daring escapades during the darkest days of the Second World War. It was only after she went to work for the family firm that she learned the part of the story her father had left out: when her grandfather and great-uncle joined the French Resistance and bravely fought the occupation of their country by foreign invaders, they also acquired all the basic skills and contacts they needed to set up their post-war business of selling stolen war materials to a world that seemed determined to squander the hard-won peace.

The partnership of the two older Jouberts had flourished until Great-Uncle Pierre died abroad under mysterious circumstances, when Belle was in grade school. It was years before she understood that Pierre had been murdered when negotiations with a particularly bloodthirsty African dictator turned sour.

Belle jerked away from the desk, cutting off the flow of memories before they could become too painful. She drew in a couple of deep breaths and carefully refocused her attention on her surroundings. Even this favorite room had changed a lot in the past seven years. The wallpaper was now silvery-green, the carpet Chinese silk. The expensive leather chair looked brand-new, and the computer equipment on the credenza was state-of-the-art. Her father had been sentimental only up to a point, and he'd never allowed his sentimentality to interfere with the efficient operation of his business. Marc had kept Grandfather Joubert's desk, but not his old-fashioned working methods.

Belle sat down in the high-backed chair and caught a faint whiff of the imported French cologne-water her father had worn ever since she could remember. Hot tears rimmed her eyes but didn't fall. She blinked hard. Damn him, anyway. And herself, too, for being such an overemotional idiot.

Enough already with the maudlin regrets. She'd come to this room for a reason, she realized, not just to escape the crowds downstairs. Her father's last words had been about a computer disk and a list of charitable donations he wanted her to make on his behalf. Even if she couldn't alter the fact that Marc had spent his adult life selling weapons to rogues and terrorists, she could at least accommodate his belated attack of conscience and see that a hefty portion of the profits from those sales went to charity.

Her father had indicated that she would find the disk wedged into the back of a photograph in his office—which, she realized, was a very odd place for it to be stored, given that in matters of business her father had been orderly to the point of fixation.

For the past three days Belle had been too busy to think about her father's dying words, and there certainly hadn't been time to feel curiosity about the details of his instructions, or why he'd chosen her instead of Tony or Marisa to take charge of his final bequests. Now that she had a moment to sit and think, she was full of questions. Most of all, she wondered why he'd hidden the disk behind a picture, when he had a custom-built storage system for computer disks right here in this study.

Grandfather Joubert had displayed a Gallic indifference to the U.S. government and its tax code, but Marc had treated the IRS with great respect. From the day he inherited the family business, he had taken steps to ensure that he didn't provide the government with an excuse to jail him for failure to pay taxes. To that end, he'd always kept extensive records of his personal finances filed away in his desk. The records were fraudulent, of course, but they were mind-numbingly detailed, and even before Belle left home, they had all been computerized.

Just to make sure this wasn't one of the things that had changed in the years since she left Miami, Belle checked the credenza. As she expected, the drawers were filled with row upon row of hanging plastic pockets for computer disks, all labeled and stored by subject in meticulous alphabetical order.

She was surprised to see that among the disks was an entire set that dealt with charitable donations, each one labeled for a separate year, with neat handwritten notations as to the institutions and charities that had received gifts. Frowning, Belle riffled through the plastic folders. If her father had been making charitable donations for the past several years, why had he exhibited so much anxiety when he asked her to handle the bequests to be made after his death? Wouldn't such bequests form part of an ongoing program that already had some person or organization in charge?

Belle pulled out the disk labeled Charitable Donations 1999, and turned it absently in her hands. According to the label, her father had donated eight million dollars to institutions as diverse as South Florida University and the Salvation Army during fiscal 1999. Charitable donations were easy for the IRS to trace, so it seemed unlikely these gifts were fakes. Which merely added to the puzzle. Were the gifts Marc wanted to make after his death so huge that he felt there was a danger his wishes wouldn't be carried out? Belle grimaced. If that was the case, she sure hoped he had prepared ironclad legal documents to back up whatever instructions were contained on the disk. She and her family had enough issues to fight about without adding this one to the list.

First things first, Belle decided. Before she got too worried about the legalities of the situation, she needed to locate her father's instructions. There were family photographs scattered all over the bookshelves, as well as on the desk and nearby credenza, but there were only two pictures of her, which would make the search easy.

Belle collected the two photos and set them on the desk. One had been taken as she climbed onto the school bus for the start of first grade. She was laughing straight into the camera, her eyes sparkling with mischief, her long dark curls caught up in a ponytail that had already started to come loose from its moorings. She was clutching a *Star Wars* lunch box and carrying a neon-bright purple sweater that she had insisted on taking to school, despite her mother's plea that she wear something pretty in pastel-pink.

The other picture was a formal studio portrait taken with her father a couple of days after she started working for the Joubert Corporation—weeks before her excitement at being part of the family firm had turned to foreboding about the precise nature of the family business.

In this picture her hair was cut short, but the dark curls still tumbled around her face and her eyes still laughed confidently at the world as if she had been amused by the solemn pose the photographer wanted her to adopt. She wore a scarlet suit with oversize brass buttons and a neckline that looked mighty low-cut for business attire.

It seemed that her flamboyant taste in clothes hadn't changed much between first grade and first employment, Belle thought wryly. The contrast between then and now could hardly have been more stark. Her hair was long again these days, but she wore it pulled back tightly enough to banish nearly all trace of curl, and her normal expression nowadays was one of bland detachment. As for her current wardrobe, it was a carefully planned mix of neutral colors and conservative styles designed to avoid catching anyone's attention.

She ought to have felt satisfaction at how greatly her tastes had matured. Surprisingly, she felt a pang of fierce loss for the carefree girl who had been bold enough to wear purple sweaters and bright scarlet suits.

The emotion caught her off guard. Belle reminded herself that she liked her current life-style. She liked Chicago, with its challenging climate and stimulating cultural life. She liked living peacefully alone, liked being inconspicuous, and she especially liked having a boring boyfriend like Donald Gates. No, not boring, she corrected herself hastily. Worthy. Reliable. Considerate. Good-looking, even.

Boring.

Belle sighed. Okay, so things weren't going exactly as they should with Donald, but this wasn't the moment to analyze why her character was so defective that she couldn't appreciate a man who was ideal husband material. Handsome thirty-nine-year-old engineers, gainfully employed, with no children and an ex-wife who lived in Mexico, weren't exactly stacked three-rows-deep in singles bars. She ought to be grateful for what she had, and stop crying for the moon. Donald Gates was a good person, unlike the men she'd dated earlier in her life. Men like Sandro Marchese, for example, who had certainly been endowed with all the charisma Donald lacked. Unfortunately, Sandro had also been a criminal, and flagrantly unfaithful. So much for charisma.

This trip down memory lane needed to stop, Belle realized. She hadn't thought about Sandro since she'd completed her counseling, and that was one piece of hard-won tranquillity she didn't plan to relinquish. She returned her attention to the two pictures. Since the studio portrait was more recent, she decided to open it first.

She fiddled with the little clips that held the velvet backing in place against the silver frame, and took less than a minute to discover there was nothing behind the photo but dust.

She reassembled the frame and set the picture in its original place on the credenza before taking apart the other photo. She immediately hit pay dirt. Taped to a sheet of cardboard, she found the CD-ROM her father must have been talking about in his final moments of life. It was labeled Charitable Donations 2000, and in every respect it seemed identical to the disks she had found in the credenza drawer, except that its date suggested it was the most recent in the series.

There was no way to know what was so special about this hidden disk without putting it into a computer and reading it. Belle returned the second photo to the bookshelves and was on the point of booting up her father's computer, when she was interrupted by the sound of somebody opening the door.

Acting before she had time to question her own motives, she slipped the disk into the side pocket of her dress. Leaning casually on the desk, she swiveled the chair around to face the entrance.

Tony stood in the doorway, his expression forbidding. Her brother was strikingly good-looking, Belle reflected, even when he was scowling. He had inherited their mother's handsome features and their father's charm—a formidable combination. Add to that a keen intelligence and the best education money could buy, and there should have been no limits on what he could achieve. Regrettably, he'd chosen to join the family business and had never expressed the slightest qualm about the way the Joubert Corporation made its money. On the contrary, he'd told Belle during one of their endless arguments that the only difference between Joubert money and Rockefeller money was that the Rockefellers had made their millions long enough ago that the smell of its rotten origins had faded. Belle had pointed out acidly that two dunghills didn't make one bed of roses. Tony hadn't bothered to respond.

Now that Marc was dead, Belle hoped—fervently—that Tony would put a stop to the family tradition of criminal behavior, and run the Joubert Corporation as a fully legal operation. She was tired of living with the nightmare that one day she would turn on the six o'clock news and see her handcuffed brother being marched off to jail for selling stolen weapons technology to some group of wild-eyed domestic fanatics or international terrorists.

Now that they were alone for the first time since she'd arrived in Miami, she wondered if there was any tactful way to exert some sisterly pressure and encourage Tony to seize the chance that their father's death offered. If ever there was a time for her brother to move away from a life of crime, this was it. But much as she wanted to improve the hostile relationship that existed between the two of them, Belle wasn't sure that she would be able to keep silent on the topics that divided them. The family's deadly and illegal business loomed between them like the tiger that kept roaring just when everyone had agreed to pretend it was an acrylic fur rug.

Hoping for the best, she greeted him with a smile. "Hi, Tony. Come in and enjoy the quiet. Are you trying to escape the crowds, too?"

Her brother didn't respond to her smile. He strode angrily across the room. "What are you doing searching through my father's private files?"

"I'm not..." Belle started to say, then realized that she was, in fact, doing just that. "Well, I guess I am looking through Dad's files. But that's because he asked me to."

"Dad asked *you* to go through his personal files?" Tony's voice was heavy with sarcasm. "And that must have been because the two of you had such a terrific relationship, right? The daughter who sat all through his funeral mass and didn't shed a single tear. Yeah, sure, you're exactly the person he'd choose to paw through his personal files."

Belle gripped the edge of the desk and willed herself not to say something she would later regret. Her relationship with her brother had been so fraught with misunderstanding for so many years that they could never manage to spend more than a few hours together without precipitating at least a minor fight. "I'm not going to get into a shouting match with you, Tony. Just because I didn't cry at Dad's funeral doesn't mean that I didn't care about him."

"Have you any idea what it did to Dad when you walked out on him like that?" Tony stopped abruptly, as if regretting that he'd brought up the subject. "You cut yourself out of our family, Belle, and I don't believe Dad would have chosen to welcome you back in again."

"You can believe me or not, as you please. But for whatever reason, just before Dad died he asked me to find a disk containing some special charitable bequests he wanted to make. He told me I'd find the disk here in his study, and that's what I've been looking for.''

"What special bequests? I'm the executor of Dad's will, and I'm not aware of any special bequests.''

Belle shook her head. "I've no idea. I didn't get a chance to put the disk into the computer before you arrived. But the last words Dad ever spoke were about these bequests, so obviously they must have been important to him.''

Tony's mouth tightened. "Mom never said anything to me about Dad giving you last-minute instructions right before he died. According to her, you only arrived fifteen minutes before...before the end.''

"Mom probably didn't hear what Dad said to me. She was exhausted, and he was having difficulty speaking clearly. I had to bend very low to catch what he was saying—''

Tony snorted. "How convenient for you that nobody heard these all-important last words. Except you, of course.''

The ends of Belle's temper were fraying fast. "It's not convenient at all. There's nothing I want less than to be drawn back into the middle of this family's dysfunctional antics—''

"Rest easy,'' Tony snapped. "If I have anything to say about it, you won't have a damn thing to do with this family's *dysfunctional antics* now or ever. It's bad enough that we've lost Dad, without having to put up with you as a replacement.'' He snatched up the disk labeled Charitable Donations 1999 that was lying on the desk where Belle had left it. "Is this the disk Dad supposedly asked you to find?''

Belle was appalled to realize that she was going to flat out lie. "I guess so," she said. "Although I didn't have time to check it out before you came in."

"Well, since I'm the executor and in charge of Dad's affairs, I'll take care of it from now on." Tony took the disk and put it into the pocket of his jacket. "In the unlikely event there's anything on here that concerns you, I'll let you know."

Belle clenched her teeth so hard that her jaw ached. "Okay, Tony, you've made your point. You're the son and heir, and you're in charge. Now, do you think we could start this conversation over? Dad has been dead for less than seventy-two hours. By tomorrow afternoon, I'll be flying back to Chicago. Could we manage to be civil to each other for the short while we'll be together?"

"I doubt it."

"We could at least try. It would be nice if we could look back and say we got through Dad's funeral without a major family row."

"You haven't mellowed, have you, Belle? You're still the same self-righteous pain in the ass you always were." Tony swung away. He pulled on the window blind and it rolled up with a violent clatter. "For your information, there have been no arguments in this family since you took yourself off to Chicago. Mom and Marisa and I get along just fine. Evan, too, when he's in town. You're the one who's so busy trying to legislate morals for the entire family that you drive us all crazy."

He slammed out of the room before Belle could respond. His words hurt because she feared they were true. Everyone in her family seemed to jog along quite happily, provided she didn't come around and butt into their affairs. Was she wrong to keep demanding that they should confront the reality of how the Jouberts made their money?

Belle rubbed the center of her forehead, trying to banish the headache that had returned in full, pounding force. She was still sitting at the desk with her head in her hands when Marisa spoke quietly from the doorway. "Hi, Belle. You look as if you could use some company. May I come in?"

"You sure can." Belle gave her younger sister a smile that was a lot warmer than the one she'd managed for Tony. "I was just trying to work up the energy to go downstairs and be polite to the visitors, but talking to you is the perfect excuse to stay up here."

"The crowd finally seems to be thinning out a bit," Marisa said. "If we hang out here for ten minutes, we might even be lucky enough to miss the mayor giving another campaign speech as he says goodbye."

"That's certainly a goal worth working for." Belle and her sister exchanged grins.

Marisa tucked her feet under her in the chair. "It's really good to see you again, Belle."

"It's wonderful to see you, too. And looking more gorgeous than ever, if that's possible."

Marisa had been a skinny, plain child who developed into a raving beauty at thirteen, when most of her classmates were fighting zits, bad hair days and lumpy thighs. A taller, thinner, blonder version of their mother, her mouth was too wide for classic beauty, but photographed with sultry sexiness. Her complexion was flawless and her hair magnificent enough to provoke serious envy. She had been snatched up by a modeling agency when she was still in high school, and had left home to pursue a career in New York City not long after Belle fled to Chicago.

Marisa had been very successful in her career, making the cover of *Vogue* before she was eighteen, and flying on photo shoots to exotic locations around the world. Then she'd met Evan Connor when she was only twenty, fallen madly in love, and married him three months later.

Their fifth wedding anniversary was coming up in November, and Marisa had changed a lot from the outgoing teenager Belle had known before she left home. Her sister had suffered three miscarriages in the first two years of her marriage, and eventually needed surgery before she could manage to carry a baby to term. Spencer, so eagerly awaited, was now a boisterous eighteen-month-old, and obviously the light of Marisa's life. Evan seemed, if possible, an even more doting parent. He had been endearingly proud of his son's vocabulary yesterday at lunch, and he'd insisted on taking Belle outside so she could see how fast Spencer ran—Belle would have said toddled—around the garden.

"These past few days must have been especially difficult for you," Belle said as Marisa leaned against the chair back, yawning. "Spencer's old enough to know you're upset, but not old enough to understand why you have to keep leaving him."

Marisa pushed at a heavy swath of to-die-for hair that had fallen into her eyes. "Yes, he's been a bit cranky, but he's cutting teeth, so he could be feeling out of sorts over that. Today is really the worst in terms of leaving him. We've been gone for seven hours already."

"You're lucky to have a nanny living in," Belle said. "She seems very competent even though she's so young. What did you say her name was? Anita-something?"

"Anita Gillespie. And she's twenty-four, which is only a year younger than me." Marisa pulled a face. "Thank goodness she's not any older, or I'd be really intimidated. Evan found her for me on one of his buying trips to England. She's been trained at one of those famous English colleges for nannies, and I swear she's a walking encyclopedia of rules and regulations for the proper care of babies."

"That must be reassuring in a crisis," Belle said. "Better than somebody who has no experience, anyway."

"I guess so. But Anita's so highly qualified she terrifies me."

Marisa sounded as if she meant what she said, and Belle felt a niggle of unease. Her sister had once been confident to the point of brashness. It was sad to think that her miscarriages had battered her self-assurance so much that she was intimidated by her own hired help. "You manage Spencer so well, and he's turning out to be such a sweet child that I can't imagine even a highly trained nanny has much to teach you. Besides, who cares if Anita has oodles of professional expertise? After all, you're Spencer's mom. So if Anita thinks a baby ought to eat mushed peas three times a day and you don't—well, you win."

Marisa looked shocked, then laughed. "You know, you're right. I'll have to remember that next time I give Spencer a cookie and Anita treats me to one of her stern lectures about infant nutrition."

"If she gets too annoying, you can always fire her."

Marisa rolled her eyes. "Honey, I don't mean to sound rude, but you're speaking as a carefree single woman who has never spent hours on the phone trying to locate a baby-sitter because your husband has arrived home with surprise tickets for the theater."

"I envy you," Belle said quietly. "Having a baby like Spencer would be worth missing a lifetime of impromptu visits to the theater."

"Yes, he's worth everything." Marisa jumped up from the chair and strolled over to the window, squinting at an angle so she could see the end of the driveway where the valet parkers were busy. "Hey, good news. The mayor is getting into his limo. Windy old fart. Let's give it another five minutes, then we should go and help Mom with the last of the goodbyes. She's so exhausted she's going to collapse if she doesn't get some rest soon."

"I know, but she insists that it's worse if she tries to nap. She says the bed feels too empty without Dad lying next to her."

"She'll make herself ill if we're not careful." Marisa moved away from the window. "Maybe Tony can persuade her to take a sleeping pill now that the funeral is over. She might listen to him, since he's a man."

"And of course, we all know that being male guarantees total wisdom."

"According to Mom it does. You know what she's like."

"Yes." Belle sighed. "I know. Gosh, Marisa, how is she going to cope without Dad to tell her what to do thirty times a day? She'll be totally lost."

"We'll have to hope that she transfers her dependency from Dad to Tony."

"Poor Tony!" Belle said with sincere feeling. "I wouldn't want to be in his shoes. Mom's been so cushioned from everyday life that I don't think she has a clue about how to handle routine household management, let alone major financial investments. Do you think she understands that someone has to pay all those bills she runs up on her charge accounts?"

"No, I'm sure she doesn't, but Tony is very patient with her," Marisa said. "And then she has Dave Forcier and Ray Hillman acting as trustees for her shares in the company."

Belle grimaced at the mention of the Joubert Corporation's senior accountant and in-house legal counsel. "Is that supposed to reassure me?" she asked dryly. "I wouldn't trust either one of them. Did you know that two of the reasons I first suspected that the family firm was armpit-deep in illicit activity were because of Dave and Ray? They might as well walk around with labels saying *Sleazeball* attached to their foreheads."

"They've changed since you knew them," Marisa said quietly. "In fact, the whole firm's changed since you left Florida. Dad was too stubborn and too proud to tell you, but he was deeply affected when you left. Especially when Tony joined the company a couple of years later and said virtually the same things you had."

"I never knew that Tony protested," Belle said, astonished. "Whenever we've talked about the firm, Tony has always insisted that he sees no problem with skirting the law if it helps increase profits."

"Surely you've realized by now that Tony is jealous of you and didn't want you to come back? He wasn't going to do or say anything that would heal the rift between you and Dad."

"Why in the world would Tony be jealous of me?"

"Oh, come on, Belle." Marisa sounded impatient. "Dad tried hard not to show it, but Tony and I both knew you were his favorite."

Belle wanted to protest, but honesty kept her silent. In her heart of hearts, she had always known that she shared a special bond with her father. That was why it had hurt so badly when she discovered that her golden idol had feet of very dirty clay.

"Dad loved us all," she said lamely. "You know he did."

"Sure he did," Marisa agreed. "He just loved you a bit more. I guess it didn't bother me too much, because I kind of opted out of the competition for his attention early on in life. But Tony is only eighteen months younger than you, and he kept trying to be the best so that Dad would be impressed. Except that whatever he tried to achieve, you'd always been there and done that first. When you and Sandro Marchese split up, and you took off for Chicago, Tony seized the moment, so to speak, and was finally able to come into his own."

"I didn't leave Miami because of Sandro," Belle claimed, then realized that she'd reacted much too vehemently. Her sister sent a curious gaze in her direction.

"I saw him a couple of weeks ago," Marisa said. "Sandro, I mean. He was right here in Miami. I happened to spot him at the airport."

"Did you?" Belle intended to sound casual. After

all, Sandro had meant nothing to her for the past seven years. She saw that her fingers were drumming on the edge of the desk, and she quickly hid them on her lap. "I was under the impression that he'd taken a job in the Washington, D.C. area."

"I don't know what happened to him. He left here quite soon after you did. But that didn't surprise me, because Dad got rid of a lot of the old employees around that time. He kept Dave and Ray, because they'd all been together for so long. But he fired most of the old guard. Then he hired a lot of eager young kids, fresh out of business school, and built up the legitimate side of the company. For the past two years there hasn't been a crate leaving the warehouse without a valid export license."

Belle was so shocked that she could only stare at her sister in silence, feeling relief, hope and regret in almost equal proportions. Regret that she'd wasted the last few years of her father's life in a quarrel over a situation that no longer existed. Hope that there was still time to put things right with her brother. And overwhelming relief that the long nightmare seemed to be over. She would never again shiver with dread when the phone rang, wondering if the call was to inform her that Tony had been arrested, or that her mother was under suspicion as an accomplice in the illegal activities of the Joubert Corporation.

The relief was so strong that Belle felt a burst of renewed energy. She could cope with funeral guests, prying neighbors, even an extended family dinner with her weeping mother and hostile brother. Anything was possible in a world that suddenly seemed a much less frightening place.

"Are you sure?" she asked Marisa. "Please tell

me the truth, not what you think I'd like to hear. Is
the Joubert Corporation really limiting its trade to legal weapons and approved military technology?''

"Absolutely," Marisa said. "You can stop worrying, Belle. Dad's given away most of his fortune,
and the family business is now strictly, one-hundred-
percent legitimate.''

Belle realized she was shaking. She drew in a deep,
calming breath. "Thank God," she said. "Thank
God.''

Three

On the morning of Belle's return to Chicago, the unusual harmony that had reigned during family dinner the night before broke down completely. Carole succumbed to hysterics because her cruel daughter was abandoning her less than twenty-four hours after Marc's funeral. Tony, still furious with Belle despite her attempts to apologize, barely managed to snarl goodbye before driving off to the Joubert Corporation offices. And Marisa called from her home in Boca Raton, upset and only semi-coherent because baby Spencer had caught some sort of bug and had been wailing on and off for five hours straight. She apologized for not coming to say goodbye in person, then gave a panicked shriek and hung up in midsentence when she realized she was going to be late for Spencer's appointment with the pediatrician.

Belle reflected wryly that her father might no longer be around to orchestrate the melodrama that passed for everyday life in the Joubert family, but her mother and siblings were doing their best to keep up his tradition of exaggerated emotions for every occasion. She could feel herself withdrawing, becoming outwardly cooler and inwardly more agitated as her mother's outpourings of grief became increasingly extravagant.

The tension level in the house was so high she was actually relieved when Dave Forcier and Ray Hillman turned up with various papers for her mother to sign. Ray, the company lawyer, had about as much genuine warmth as a piranha pretending to be a dolphin. But Dave, the accountant, was a kind man at heart, despite his dubious professional past and a tendency to trade in his wives more frequently than other men traded in cars. Having discarded four or five wives during the years he'd worked for the Joubert Corporation, he probably knew Carole better than any other woman in the world. With remarkable patience, he managed to chivvy and cosset her into a calmer state of mind, chiefly by telling jokes of outrageously bad taste about funerals, a method of cheering her mother that Belle would never have thought to adopt in a thousand years. She was grateful enough to "Uncle Dave" that she barely winced when he insisted on giving her a wet and far from avuncular kiss goodbye.

One way or another, it was a definite relief to return to the peacefulness of her small house in Crown Park, a family-oriented enclave near Evanston in the suburbs of Chicago. The subdivision dated from the sixties, and its name was a lot grander than its architecture. It was filled with modest homes that lacked adequate kitchens and closets by the standards of the new millenium, but the sidewalks were lined with flourishing oak trees and the small front yards blossomed with the results of forty years of careful tending by proud home owners.

Belle paid off the taxi she'd taken from the airport and waved to old Marge Bruno, who lived directly across the street from her. Marge and her husband had been the first people to move into Crown Park and they were the acknowledged guardians of the neighborhood. Weather permitting, Marge spent every daylight hour working in her garden, keeping a rheumy-eyed tally of her neighbors' comings and goings.

Marge was an inveterate gossip, and when Belle had first moved in to Crown Park, she had been so determined to protect the secrets in her past that she'd taken obsessive care not to provide any interesting tidbits for the gossip mill. Eventually she'd realized there was nothing so intriguing to busybodies as a neighbor nobody knew anything about, so nowadays she went out of her way to be Ms. Friendly. She made sure people knew that she worked as an information systems manager at Mutual Life Insurance Company of Chicago, and she mentioned Donald's name often enough for everyone to understand that he was not only her current boyfriend, but a serious candidate for the role of husband. By sacrificing a little of her current privacy, she was able to throw a thick blanket of protection over her past.

Realizing that a brief conversation with Marge would save her from hours of neighborhood speculation about where she'd been, Belle took a couple of minutes to walk across the street and admire the spectacular display of fall daisies and chrysanthemums in the Brunos' front yard.

"I've been looking for you these past few days," Marge said as soon as the preliminary courtesies were out of the way. "I've got some more zucchini to give you, if you want 'em."

The offer of produce from the Bruno garden was never refused by any Crown Park home owner with a grain of common sense. Belle managed a smile. "Er, yes...thanks. I'd love them. Home-grown vegetables always taste so much nicer than store-bought ones. If you're sure you can spare them, that is.''

Marge didn't bother to respond, and Belle knew why. By this time of year, Marge's vegetable garden had produced sufficient zucchini to feed a small European nation. ''Did you have a chance to try that recipe for zucchini bread I gave you last week?'' she asked. ''That's one of my Wally's favorites, especially when I make it with cream-cheese frosting.''

Wally was Marge's husband, and from the size of him, Belle reckoned that zucchini bread with cream-cheese frosting was only one of his many favorite foods. ''Your recipe was great, Marge. It's delicious and very simple to follow. Thank goodness, because I'm not much of a chef.''

''It's never too late to learn. If you make my special bread for that Donald of yours, he'll be popping the question before you know it. Remember, the best way to a man's heart is through his stomach.'' Marge had stored up a lifetime supply of clichés, and never hesitated to pull one out at the slightest provocation.

''I don't think I'm ready to marry Donald,'' Belle said, surprising herself with the admission. ''Maybe I shouldn't bake him anything that tastes too good.''

Marge seemed to ignore the comment as unworthy of reply. She set down her rake and stripped off her gardening gloves. ''If you can wait a minute, hon, I'll get those zucchini for you now. They're right on my kitchen table.''

''Maybe we could hold off until tomorrow—if that's okay with you?'' Belle gestured to her suitcase, which she'd left sitting on her front doorstep. ''I need to unpack, get some laundry done, and straighten up the house. I don't really have time to start baking for a couple of days. You know what it's like when you've been away, even for a short trip.''

Marge's interest was piqued at once. "Ah, so you've been away, then? I didn't see any lights for the past few nights, and I told Wally you must be gone. You should've warned me you were leaving and put some lamps on timers, you know. That way, when it gets dark, the house don't look so empty. It just encourages burglars when there's no lights.''

"You're right, I know. I would have made better preparations, but I was called out of town unexpectedly. There wasn't even time to let you know I'd be gone.''

Marge's eyes gleamed with avid curiosity. "There's nothin' wrong, I hope?''

"I'm afraid there was. It was my...grandmother. She died." Belle hated to lie, and she stumbled badly.

Fortunately, Marge interpreted the faltering as a sign of grief. "I'm real sorry to hear that." She reached out to pat Belle on the arm, her curiosity giving way to genuine sympathy. "That's too bad, hon. I'll say a prayer for her tonight. I hope she went peacefully?''

"I think so. The family was all there, even though it was unexpected. That was important to hi—to her, I'm sure." Belle cleared her throat. "Anyway, I'm very glad I arrived in time to say goodbye.''

"That always helps to ease the loss," Marge agreed. "It's real hard if you've got things to say and you don't get a chance to say them. Your grandmother hadn't been sick, then?''

"No. It was a real shock to everyone, but especially to me, I guess. I live so far away, whereas the rest of the family is all in Florida and they were more in the know.''

"What was it that took her, then?"

"Just age more than anything else." Belle hated to invent lies about her father's death, but since she was supposed to be an orphan, she couldn't tell the simple truth. "Gran was eighty-five. She had a heart attack, and the doctors couldn't save her, even with surgery." She fell silent, unable to embroider her story any further.

"Eighty-five?" Marge snapped her fingers, so unimpressed that she forgot to be tactful. "Hon, eighty-five these days, that's nothin'. I'm seventy-six and I've told the good Lord he needs to wait at least another twenty years before he can call me home. I'm way too busy keeping my Wally in line to quit the world now—not to mention what our kids would get up to without me to keep 'em in line. You won't believe the latest about George. Lord love us, but that son of mine is a true knucklehead if ever I met one."

Belle hid a smile. Marge considered everything her sons did foolish unless they consulted her first. From buying new curtains to changing jobs, all three Bruno boys were expected to stop by their parents' home and justify their plans. "What's happened to George this time?"

"He's gone off to Vegas and married some woman who's got four kids already, and the eldest isn't no more than thirteen." Marge huffed a few times for emphasis, but she clearly took a perverse satisfaction in being able to report such alarming news.

"Good grief, that's quite a handful to take on! George already has two children of his own, doesn't he?"

Marge nodded dourly. "Yep, a boy and a girl. Eldest just turned eleven."

Belle had no need to feign awe. "Wow! That'll be six kids between the two of them! That's quite a houseful."

"You betcha. And all my husband can say is that George is in love and I should leave him be. Let 'em be happy, Wally says." She snorted. "I ask you, how is he gonna be happy? Love and marriage only go together in the song. In real life, what you need to make a marriage work is money. George should get his head examined, if you ask me. I can't believe he's takin' on four kids what don't belong to him in addition to the two he got dumped on him from that nogood ex-wife of his."

Belle tried to be upbeat although she couldn't help thinking Marge had reason to be worried. "George wouldn't have got custody of the kids from his first marriage unless he was a really good father," she suggested.

Marge gave another snort. "He'll need to be, that's all I've got to say. He told me it worked out okay on the *Brady Bunch,* so it should work out just as good for him. I reminded him the *Brady Bunch* was a TV show, for gosh sakes. His new wife and her kids are for real. They're moving into his house and it's only got two bathrooms. Two! Count 'em—one, two! Can you imagine what it'll be like mornings when they're all getting ready for school?"

Marge was so outraged that Belle laughed. "No, to be honest, I can't." Belle gave up on trying to be encouraging. "But I couldn't imagine getting six kids ready for school and staying sane even if they had a bathroom each."

"You said it, hon. Now we just have to hope Cherry—that's his new wife—don't get pregnant. She's only thirty-eight, so she could pop out half a dozen more babies before she's through."

Once Marge got started on the problems of her children she could keep going for hours, although this time Belle had to admit that George seemed to have provided genuine cause for alarm. Fortunately, she wouldn't have to wonder how the marriage turned out. She could count on Marge to keep her informed of every triumph and every crisis.

Pleading tiredness and her long list of waiting chores, she said goodbye to Marge and crossed the street to her own house. The strain of the past several days shed like outgrown snakeskin as she unlocked the door and walked in, letting the silence wrap her in restful welcome.

Her home offered none of the elegance that had surrounded her when she was growing up. Belle cherished every modest square inch of space, however, because the mortgage was paid with her own money—honestly earned and painstakingly saved. Bit by bit, whenever her bank balance wasn't too precarious she tackled a home-improvement project, and she'd discovered that it was a lot more fun to have grass in the front yard that she'd grown from seed instead of grass being laid down by a landscaper, and a paint job that looked spiffy not because she'd summoned the decorators, but because she'd spent three weekends in a row perched on a stepladder wielding a paintbrush. And last year she'd splurged, using her Christmas bonus to get custom shelving built in the living room. Now her TV fit neatly behind sliding maple doors, and her collection of books formed splashes of vibrant color on either side of the set.

Belle found herself smiling as she made her way upstairs and into her bedroom. Pulling up the blinds and opening the window, she breathed in a satisfying gulp of crisp fall air, feeling a sudden regret that her father had never seen the home she'd made for herself. Somehow, she suspected he would have liked both her house and the friendly, gossipy neighborhood. At least it wasn't too late to invite her mother and sister to visit. Tony, too, if he ever stopped being mad at her. Now that the Joubert Corporation was operating legally, there was no reason why she couldn't resume normal contact with her family.

Feeling a renewed surge of relief, mingled with regret for the estrangement of the past few years, Belle turned abruptly from the bedroom window and started her unpacking. The blinking light on her answering machine indicated that she'd had eight phone calls during the time she was away. She pressed the play button and listened to two hang-ups, five sympathetic messages from co-workers about the death of her "grandmother," and one from Donald Gates.

"Hi, Belle, honey. I hope you had a good time in Miami." He paused. "Well, I guess that's a dumb thing to say, since you were at your grandmother's funeral and she was your closest surviving relative. No offense intended, as I'm sure you realize. I'm just calling to let you know that I'll pick you up this evening at the usual time. I wish you'd agreed to let me come to the airport to meet you, but since you didn't, I'll pick you up at your place right after work. We'll have dinner, okay? One of the division vice presidents took me to a great new restaurant yesterday. It's ex-

pensive, but we'll go there to celebrate.'' He stopped
again. ''Aw heck, honey. I don't think any of this is
coming out right. You know I'm not good at these
conversations with a machine. I didn't exactly mean
'celebrate.' I just want you to know that I sure do
miss you. See you tonight at the usual time. I guess
I said that already, didn't I? Bye.''

Belle switched off the answering machine and
stared broodingly into space. Donald's awkward attempt at sympathy brought home the urgent need for
her to tell him the truth about her father's death—a
confession that she dreaded. She could only hope he
would understand why she'd chosen to conceal her
past. When she'd arrived in Chicago she'd been determined to start afresh, with no Joubert strings trailing in her wake. So she had introduced herself to
everyone she met as an orphan without brothers or
sisters. She'd invented a tragic hotel fire in Puerto
Rico to kill off her parents, and given herself a grandmother and some scattered cousins so that she
wouldn't seem suspiciously bereft of relations. Having told Donald the standard lies at their first meeting,
there had somehow never seemed an opportune moment to explain the truth, not even when they finally
became lovers.

When her mother had summoned her home to Miami, Belle had been in no fit state to call Donald and
start making complicated explanations. So she'd
phoned him from O'Hare airport and told him she
couldn't keep their date because her grandmother was
very sick and she was flying to Florida. Fortunately,
the boarding of her plane was announced before Donald had time to ask any difficult questions. She had
called again from her parents' home when she knew

he'd be at work, and had left a message on his answering machine saying that her grandmother had died and that she was staying for the funeral, but that she would be home late on Friday afternoon and would look forward to seeing him sometime over the weekend.

In retrospect, her lies seemed tawdry. She had been sharing Donald's bed once or twice a week for almost two months, so why had she never found the right moment to share the truth about her past? If the best sexual relationships always involved the sharing of intimate personal details, no wonder sex with Donald left her feeling empty and dissatisfied. Perhaps the problem with their lovemaking wasn't her fear of passion, or her reluctance to surrender control—which was what she'd assumed until now. Belle made a mental apology to Donald for all the times she'd silently blamed his unimaginative sexual techniques for the lack of spark in their lovemaking. The root cause of their humdrum sexual life obviously lay in her failure to be honest with him.

From their first meeting, Donald had come across as a man with no tolerance for moral ambiguity. Perhaps that was part of his appeal when her own moral code had all the firmness of a wet noodle. His former wife had cheated on him for years, then run off to Acapulco with his best friend. Not surprisingly, Donald now valued honesty even more than did most people, so it was daunting to visualize his reaction when she revealed that her father had once been the mastermind behind a major international criminal enterprise.

Belle decided that she was way too tired to start on complicated explanations tonight. In fact, she was

really too tired to see Donald at all. She would have
preferred to skip the meal in the fancy restaurant and
curl up in bed with a bowl of cereal and a good book.
Except that she never did anything messy like eating
in bed, and Donald was her lover, so of course she
was pleased to go out with him, even if it did mean
that she would have to overcome her tiredness and
get dressed up. Donald didn't go for the casual look.
Which was just fine with her, of course. Belle gave
herself a mental shake and started to plan her time-
table for the evening.

The Snoopy clock beside her bed showed a couple
of minutes after five. Donald always picked her up at
seven and made dinner reservations for seven-thirty,
which meant she had more than an hour before she
needed to start getting ready.

Belle found her gaze wandering to the comfortable
old robe hanging from a hook on the back of her
closet door. She firmly turned away and began to unpack her suitcase, separating her clothes with brisk
efficiency into two wicker hampers—one for dry
cleaning, the other for home laundry. Sorting swiftly
through the papers that had accumulated during her
trip, she hesitated with her hand poised over the disk
that was her father's legacy to her.

Belle turned it over in her hands, staring at the
label: Charitable Donations 2000. She felt a twinge
of guilt, she still hadn't admitted to Tony that he'd
removed the wrong disk from their father's study. Despite Marisa's revelations about the Joubert Corporation's conversion from criminal enterprise to legal
corporation, she had wanted to take her first look at
the disk without anyone else around. Her father had
been obsessively concerned that she keep the exis-

tence of the disk secret, but that probably reflected his mental confusion caused by approaching death. Plus, a love of melodrama was so much part of Marc Joubert's character that she couldn't really conclude anything from the strange hiding place he'd chosen. Still, she hadn't been able to shake the feeling that he must have had some good reason for his secrecy. After all, if it contained nothing more than a straightforward list of charitable bequests, why hadn't he handed it over to Tony, whom he saw every day?

With sudden decisiveness, Belle pulled the disk from its case and took it to the spare bedroom that she used as a combined office and guest room. She had fifty minutes to review the disk, she calculated, pulling up her chair. Plenty of time to study the bequests her father wanted to make and discover if there was any valid reason for him to have circumvented Tony and the other executors of his will.

She flipped the master switch on the surge protector, and the computer hummed into action. As soon as she slipped the disk into her CD-ROM drive, the prompts on her screen alerted her to the fact that this wasn't a standard CD-ROM. Her father had used a DVD disk, with the capacity to store not only huge quantities of printed data, but also high-resolution film, backed by stereo sound. Fortunately, she was enough of a Joubert to love high-tech gadgets, and her computer was equipped with a DVD drive.

The monitor stopped flashing and opened to a neatly typed cover sheet. "'Marc Joubert,'" she read aloud. "'Charitable Donations To Be Made After My Death. Strictly for the attention of my beloved daughter, Isabella Joubert. Everyone else, BUTT OUT!!'"

Belle swallowed a chuckle that turned into a lump

in her throat. Blinking, she clicked to the next screen.
A long list of alphabetized names and addresses followed, each one showing a sum of money on the line
right after the zip code. Oddly, the names all seemed
to be of individuals rather than of organizations, and
a prestigious list it was. Several judges were to receive memorial donations from her father, not to mention two senators, a regional chief of the FBI, and
half a dozen senior Treasury officials. There were nu-
merous police officers and IRS accountants named as
beneficiaries, most of them located in the greater Miami area, but some living as far away as Utah.

The sum mentioned was always sizable. In the case
of Judge Albertson, the first name on the list, the be-
quest was for a hundred thousand dollars. Belle found
such a large gift surprising. She vaguely remembered
meeting the judge right after she finished college and
joined the family firm. He was a distinguished gentleman of the old Southern school, but she hadn't realized he was such a good friend to her father.

One name jumped out at Belle, hitting her with
enough force to make her breath come faster. *Sandro
Marchese.* Unlike most of the other beneficiaries,
there was no profession listed after his name—simply
an address in Washington, D.C. and a sum of money:
two hundred and fifty thousand dollars.

Belle stared at the screen in silent amazement. Her
father wanted to make a memorial gift of two hundred
and fifty thousand dollars to *Sandro?* A quarter of a
million dollars? That made no sense at all. In fact, it
was nuts. Marc's relationship with Sandro had been
a business one, and Sandro had left the Joubert Corporation years ago, in October of 1993. Belle remem-

bered exactly when he'd quit, because she had been the person who'd warned Sandro to get out of Miami.

It wasn't a memory that made her proud. After years of trying to catch Marc red-handed, a multi-agency federal task force had finally accumulated enough evidence to issue indictments not only against Marc, but also against other employees of the Joubert Corporation. Belle, shocked and horrified by what she'd discovered after joining the family firm, had initially worked with law enforcement to build a case against her father. At the last moment, she had developed cold feet. Instead of helping the feds to close down the Joubert smuggling operation, Belle had ultimately blown the whole investigation by warning her father—and Sandro—about what was going on.

The choices she'd made at that time still had the power to give Belle nightmares. It was bad enough that she'd been so morally deficient that she'd saved her father from the punishment he deserved. It was a hundred times worse that she'd allowed Sandro to escape as well. She had been a lovesick fool, so captivated by Sandro's careless sexual charm that she'd broken out of the motel where U.S. Customs officers were keeping her in protective custody and fled across town to warn Sandro that the feds were on to him. Her reward was to discover him in bed with a woman whose major attraction seemed to be a pair of breast implants only slightly smaller than twin footballs.

These were buried and forbidden memories, and their resurrection was painful. Belle drew in a deep breath and forced her thoughts back to the present. She clicked to the next screen, resisting the urge to jump ahead and find out why her father wanted to bequeath money to Sandro Marchese. The monitor flickered, then displayed an entry for Judge Albertson, the first name on her father's list. She skimmed the copious notes under the judge's name, comprehension warring with shock and revulsion as she realized what she was reading.

Rubbing her arms to get rid of the goose bumps, Belle silently acknowledged that what she had in front of her wasn't a list of bequests her father wanted to make in the future. It was a detailed record of bribes he had paid in the past. All these judges, senators and IRS officials weren't worthy recipients of Marc Joubert's deathbed generosity. They were the despicable creeps he had paid off in order to keep his illegal activities safe from investigation.

Four

Belle pushed her chair back from the desk, quelling a sudden sharp wave of nausea. Sometimes the poison from the past wouldn't stay safely covered where she had buried it. When she was confident that she wouldn't throw up, she clicked to the next screen.

She discovered that her father had been as meticulous in chronicling this record of bribery and corruption as he had been in keeping records of all his other business transactions. Judge Albertson, it seemed, had been the presiding judge when four of Marc's associates came up for trial on smuggling charges. Marc had paid off the judge at the rate of $25,000 per indictment to make sure that the cases were all dismissed for technical reasons before they ever came to trial.

Marc had backed up his written data with a series of photos, obviously taken from a hidden camera. The first photo showed Marc handing Judge Albertson a package. Subsequent photos showed the judge opening the package and extracting a wad of cash, which he tucked into the breast pocket of his jacket, a pristine affair tailored in expensive white linen. The jacket, Belle thought acidly, was a great deal cleaner than the judge.

Her fingers were icy cold on the keyboard, but

sweat was trickling down her spine by the time she'd viewed similar photographic records for Gerald Berman, a United States senator, and Christopher Busch, a senior aide to the Governor of Florida. Sandro Marchese's name was still some way down the alphabetized list, but Belle couldn't wait any longer to find out why he had been included in this infamous roster of bribe recipients. What in the world had Sandro done to earn a quarter-of-a-million dollar payoff from her father?

Scrolling to the appropriate screen, Belle realized her teeth were clenched so hard that her jaw ached, which was ridiculous given that she hadn't seen the man in seven years and had no reason to care about him. So what if Sandro had been one of the many people her father bribed? She already knew his ethics were nonexistent; otherwise, he wouldn't have been working for the Joubert Corporation back in the bad old days when at least ten percent of the technology shipped out was stolen, and another third was on the government's list of forbidden exports.

Ignoring the sick churning of her stomach, Belle unclenched her jaw, moved her mouse down the list and highlighted Sandro's name. A new file opened.

Unlike the judge, the senator, and the governor's aide, her father's indictment of Sandro Marchese didn't open with a written record of bribes offered and taken. Instead, it opened with film taken in Marc's office. Mesmerized, Belle watched as the man she had once imagined she loved beyond all others strolled into the middle of her screen.

Sandro stopped and smiled quizzically at her father—and straight into the hidden camera. ''Hi, Marc, you wanted to see me? Your secretary said it was important.''

She'd forgotten how attractive Sandro was, Belle thought dispassionately. That combination of black hair, gray-green eyes and hard-muscled body was sexual dynamite, even on screen. In real life, it had been lethal. No wonder she'd fallen so hard for him. At twenty-two, fresh out of an all-girls college, she had been ripe for romantic disaster, and Sandro might as well have been custom-ordered to play the part of destroyer.

On screen, Marc coughed and stubbed out his cigar. ''Yes, it's important. Sit down, Sandro. We need to talk.''

The camera was hidden somewhere that provided no view of her father except his hands, but the sound of his voice sent an arrow of grief straight through Belle's heart. She blinked fiercely and forced herself to concentrate on the date scrolling at the bottom of her monitor. The film had been taken almost seven years ago, on September 15, 1993, only days before her affair with Sandro ended so abruptly.

Sandro eased into the chair facing her father's desk. His movements were casual, almost languid, and his expression was somewhere between polite and sleepy, but Belle wasn't deceived. Sandro was one of the most ruthlessly focused men she'd ever met; he just hid his ambition better than most.

''Is this going to take long?'' Sandro asked politely. ''I'm flying out to Paris tonight and meeting with Zauriac tomorrow afternoon. I'll need to leave for the airport within the hour.''

''Yes, I remembered your appointment with Monsieur Zauriac,'' Marc said. ''In fact, he's the man I want to speak with you about. I've received some disturbing information about him.''

Sandro looked up. "You have? His credit checks out, and he's willing to pay the price we're asking for the merchandise. What's the problem?''

"One we can't overcome, I'm afraid. I've learned that Mr. Zauriac isn't an agent for the Algerian government, as we both believed. In reality, his operation is a sophisticated front for brokering arms to various rebel armies around the world. The shoulder-held missile launchers we've promised to send him are destined for the rebel army operating in Rwanda.''

Sandro raised an eyebrow. "And so?''

"And so we can't go ahead with the deal. Shoulder-fired SAMs are on the list of forbidden exports to that country.''

Sandro gave a quiet laugh. "Okay, Marc, don't keep me in suspense. I'm waiting for the punch line.''

"There is no punch line.'' Marc's voice was clipped and cool. "The sale is off. Cancel your flight to Paris. The Joubert Corporation can't deal with a man like Zauriac who isn't operating within legal parameters.''

Sandro stood up and leaned across the desk. "What the hell is going on, Marc? We both knew that Zauriac was lying from the moment he first made contact with us. That was cool. We don't expect our customers to tell us the truth.''

"You may not,'' Marc said blandly. "But I do.''

"No, you don't.'' Sandro slanted a derisive gaze toward his employer. "You don't expect anyone in the world to tell the truth, much less your customers. But that's beside the point. Zauriac has produced all the documentation we need in order to get export ap-

proval, so why the hell do we care who he really
works for? His money's good. Trust me on that, I've
triple-checked. Do the deal, and the Joubert Corporation is going to be half a million bucks richer, this
time next week. That's net profit, after overhead. And
my commission on the sale is fifty thousand. I don't
intend to give up fifty thousand dollars of my hard-
earned money just because Zauriac is planning to kill
Hutus or Tutsis hiding in refugee camps, instead of
Muslim fundamentalists hiding out in Algerian villages. As far as I know, this company has never been
in the business of making moral judgments about our
customers. That's one of the reasons I chose to work
here.''

"I don't make moral judgments, and I'm not asking you to make them either. I'm simply reminding
you that the Joubert Corporation can't make sales that
contravene the Military Critical Technologies List.
That's got nothing to do with morality. It's simply
good business practice. As an organization dealing in
the sale of high-tech weapons and strategic materials,
we have to be especially careful to stay within the
government's legal limitations.'' Marc's words were
coated with audible irony. "Sorry, Sandro. You'll
have to make that fifty-thousand dollar bonus on some
other deal. I can't have my employees involved in
anything illegal.''

Sandro didn't reply. He turned abruptly and walked
around the perimeter of the office, peering at the decorative molding on the walls, bending down to examine the skirting boards and staring up at the central
light fixture. Finally he came back to the desk and
tore apart Marc's phone.

"Okay, where's the bug?'' he demanded, pieces of

the phone fisted in each hand. "Who's monitoring this conversation?"

"I've no idea," Marc said. "Is there a bug? If there is, maybe *you* could tell *me* where it's hidden. You're more likely to know than I am."

Sandro tossed the dismantled phone onto the desk. Electronic innards clattered across the glossy surface. "Tell me what game we're playing here, Marc, and I'll be happy to join in. If your office is bugged, then you must have done it, because I sure as hell didn't."

"If you didn't bug the office, maybe you're wearing a wire."

"Are you crazy? What's gotten into you?"

"A useful dose of reality." Marc reached for another cigar. His voice was without emotion and icy cold, a startling contrast to the exuberant father Belle knew. "I had breakfast with an old acquaintance from the Treasury Department today—a very senior person who is kind enough to remember past services I've performed for him. He had some interesting information to pass on to me. He informed me that in February this year, U.S. Customs got off its collective ass long enough to decide that they would target the Joubert Corporation for yet another undercover investigation. A task force was formed and personnel assigned. The upshot is that my company has been under federal surveillance for the past five months."

Sandro shrugged. "As I recall, you told me when I signed on that the feds target you every few years and invariably come away empty-handed. The fact that some feds are bumbling around doesn't have to shut the Zauriac deal down. I realize there's no point in taking unnecessary risks if we're being watched, but the documentation Zauriac provided was first-rate, and our systems at this end are foolproof. Trust me—this shipment isn't going to get stopped by Customs."

"You should know," Marc said.

Sandro turned slowly, all pretense of lethargy gone. Not a single muscle flickered, but Belle had once known his body language so intimately that his very stillness betrayed to her the tension that gripped him. "What the hell does that comment mean?" he demanded.

"It means that I know what you are, Sandro. You're the hot-shot undercover operative Customs sent into the Joubert Corporation as point man for their investigative task force."

Sandro gave an impatient shake of his head. "For Christ's sake, Marc. You can't believe everything your informants tell you when they're trying to make a quick buck—"

"Don't insult me by lying." Marc's voice warmed with temper. "For your information, I don't work with cheap informants out to make a quick buck. My man inside Treasury is senior enough to know exactly what's going on, and I pay him enough to make sure his information is golden. You're out of luck, Agent Marchese. You have no compelling evidence that this company ever made illegal sales of armaments or technology in the past, and the deal with Zauriac is off for the reasons I gave you earlier. And by the way, you're fired."

Instead of leaving, Sandro sat down. "Okay, let's start this conversation over—"

"I'm a busy man, Agent Marchese, and you're an ex-employee. Goodbye."

"You're reacting instead of acting smart. Okay, Marc, you're right. I'm a United States Customs agent. I've had a lot of experience working under-cover. I was sent in by the director to build a case against you—''

"I already knew that at breakfast this morning," Marc said curtly. "If you have anything interesting to say, you'd better talk real fast, because I'm about to have you thrown out of here."

"You're in trouble, Marc. Deep trouble. In fact, you're about to be busted. Is that interesting enough to get your attention?"

"No, because it isn't true." Marc reached for the intercom. "I'm calling Ray Hillman to escort you from the building. We'll go through your desk and send you any personal belongings."

"Not so fast." Sandro stopped Marc from pressing the intercom button. "You're getting overconfident, and you of all people should know how dangerous that is. Customs sent me in here because I'm the best undercover operative they've got. If I want to make trouble for you, I can. You may be good at covering your ass, but I'm even better at exposing it. The main reason you're not under federal indictment right now, this minute, is because I've chosen to cover for you."

"That's horseshit—"

"No, it's the simple truth. For the first two months of my assignment, I didn't turn you in because I only had access to pissant stuff and I was waiting to get you for something bigger, something that would put you away for longer and look great on my personnel file. Then—well, I changed my mind about who had a greater claim to my loyalty."

Marc laughed. "Don't try and convince me you can be bought off, Sandro, because you won't succeed. I make my living knowing who can be bought and who can't. You can't."

Sandro's gaze narrowed. "Bad judgment call, Marc. Before you decide who I've really been working for these past few months you need to come back to my condo and take a look at some of the material I've collected about you and your company. Collected and not forwarded to my superiors in Washington, by the way."

"That doesn't prove a damn thing. It's easy enough to hold back a few tidbits as insurance for just this sort of emergency."

Sandro leaned forward, his gaze almost sympathetic. "We could argue this all day and not get anywhere. Let's cut to the chase. You think you're such a great judge of character, but you're not. In my case, you totally fucked up. The really damaging stuff is stored in your personal computer, and that's in your office at home. In theory, I have no access to any of it. So how do you suppose I got my most incriminating information against you?"

Marc's eyes narrowed. "You seem eager to tell me."

"There's only one person in this organization you trust. Only one person who could really bring you down. Only one person who could access your private files at home."

"What the hell are you talking about?"

"Not what, Marc. *Who.* I'm talking about your daughter, Marc. The lovely Isabella."

Belle's breath froze in her lungs and her eyes blurred. She had to halt the program for a moment and then click back to recapture several crucial seconds of film that she'd missed. Her father had dealt with threats all his working life and he was a master dissembler when he needed to be. His only visible reaction to Sandro's remark was to blow a perfect smoke ring, but by watching his hands Belle could see that although his hold on his cigar remained relaxed, his fingers were shaking.

Marc tapped ash from his cigar to hide the tremor and spoke coolly. "If you're trying to piss me off, you just succeeded. If you're trying to frighten me, you failed. Isabella is completely loyal to me."

"Don't you wish you could be sure?" Sandro's smile was mocking. "You should never have sent her to that convent, Marc. Your daughter loves you, but she has this rigid moral code that the nuns drummed into her. It crops up at the most damn annoying moments."

"Isabella knows nothing about me that would bother her conscience. I've made sure that every project she's involved with is one-hundred-percent legitimate. What's more, at her own request she never deals with the sale of weapons, even when those sales are entirely legal. She doesn't know anything that could be used to build a case against me, and she has no reason to suspect that there's anything to look for."

"You're being willfully blind, Marc." Sandro sounded almost sympathetic. "You may have assigned your daughter only to strictly legal negotiations, but she's as smart as you are. Maybe even smarter. She realized pretty quickly that this organization operates at two levels, and she set about uncovering the truth. She found plenty, and I'm telling you that she's a hairsbreadth away from turning over everything she's got to the feds."

"How do you know what my daughter is planning to do?"

Sandro shrugged. "I'm sleeping with her, Marc—"

"Goddamn it!" Marc rose to his feet.

"I'm sleeping with your daughter," Sandro repeated with cruel emphasis. "She tells me a lot more than she realizes."

"You son of a bitch!" Marc's voice finally betrayed his rage. "Did you seduce my daughter so that you could persuade her to betray me?"

"Not entirely," Sandro said. "Your daughter is a very desirable woman, Marc."

Belle's cheeks flamed with humiliation. Seven years had passed since this film was made, but that didn't cool the anger she felt at having given Sandro the power to degrade her so completely.

Her father lost his self-control for a fatal moment. His fist crashed down onto the desk and the dismantled phone slid to the floor. "Isabella would never betray me. Never."

Sandro's mouth twisted into a tiny, mocking smile. "You want to bet your life on that?"

Marc drew in an audible breath. "However you may have twisted my daughter's emotions, I don't believe you have enough evidence to convict me in a court of law, or you already would have arrested me. You needed the Zauriac deal—and you're not going to get it. But if you want to take a shot at bringing me down, go ahead. It's been tried before, and the feds ended up looking stupid. More stupid than usual, that is. My criminal defense lawyers are the best money can buy. So send your evidence to Washington, and be damned. See if you can earn yourself a nice promotion."

Unexpectedly, Sandro laughed. "Sure. That's just what I'm looking for in my life. A promotion to Civil Service Grade 16. That way, with expenses, I might pull down eighty grand next year if I got real lucky. No, Marc, it's like you said. If I wanted to help the feds make a case against you, I'd have come in here with a warrant weeks ago. Far from rushing to get you convicted, I'm the man saving you from the actions of your own flesh and blood."

"What, precisely, do you want, Agent Marchese? Spell it out."

"Okay, here it is in plain language. I like the good life, Marc. I like earning a hundred grand before we start counting my bonuses. I like the racing yacht Dave Forcier has, and I want one of my own. I like the way women behave around a man who has money to spend. Since I started working for you, I've discovered that what I don't like is government rules and regulations that prevent American citizens from making a legitimate profit from international trade."

Marc was too wily to be instantly trusting. "You're slick, Agent Marchese, but I know when somebody is trying to entrap me. The reason I'm here today smoking a nice fat Cubano instead of reading books in the prison law library is that I've never trusted dicks like you."

"I'm not trying to entrap you." Sandro ripped open his shirt and unzipped his pants, dropping them to the floor. He swung around to show Marc his naked back. "Now are you convinced I'm not wearing a wire?"

"No. I make my living from advanced technology, remember? I know how small recording devices can be. It could even be a subdermal implant, if you wanted to be sure you could escape detection."

Tugging his pants back on, Sandro gave an impatient exclamation. "Listen, Marc, I'm not wearing a wire and I don't have a subdermal implant. I'm not interested in getting you convicted. Period. Face facts, Marc. I'm not your problem. Isabella is your problem—unless you let me take care of neutralizing her."

"I refuse to believe that my daughter is secretly in league with the feds."

"Then let me help you see the light. I'll take you to the motel where she's meeting with one of my colleagues tomorrow evening. I'm going to be monitoring their conversations, so you can see and hear for yourself what she's telling them."

Marc's voice was suddenly weary. "What's your angle, Sandro? What do you want from me?"

"Money." Sandro said bluntly. "Why is it so hard for you to accept? Working for you has opened my eyes to a lot of things. Take Zauriac, for example. If we refuse to sell him the missile launchers he wants, it doesn't mean he'll do without. He'll simply turn around and buy what he needs from the Russians. Or from the French, even more likely. I've decided that scumbags have the same right to buy American as anyone else."

Marc shook his head. "You're glib, but I'm not convinced. My source inside Treasury says you've been feeding your boss cartloads of damaging information about the Joubert Corporation's operating systems."

"I've been feeding them cartloads of junk," Sandro said. "Trivial stuff that suggests you skirt the edge of the law occasionally, but nothing major. I had to give them enough to make sure that the investigation didn't get shut down before I had a chance to build my retirement fund.''

"Isabella thinks she's in love with you," Marc said with seeming irrelevance.

"Does she?" Sandro shrugged. "Yes, I guess she does."

"I'll work out a deal with you, on one condition— make sure she falls out of love with you real fast. There's no way I want my daughter involved with a lying son of a bitch like you."

"Flattery will always win me over," Sandro said. "How soon do you want me to dump the divine Isabella?"

"Tomorrow wouldn't be too soon."

"Let's talk terms," Sandro said. "Belle may deserve a better man than me, but I'm the one she wants. And since you and I are being honest with each other, Marc, you can see that I'd be a fool to give her up without adequate compensation. Trust me—if I pop the question tonight, we could be flying off to a wedding chapel in Vegas tomorrow morning. And then I'd be *real* expensive to get rid of.''

"*In the circumstances,* I'm willing to make it profitable to ensure that the subject of marriage never comes up between the two of you."

"How profitable?" Sandro asked.

"A quarter of a million bucks profitable."

Sandro began to close the buttons on his shirt. "But if I married her, I'd make a lot more money than that."

Marc spoke softly. "No you wouldn't, boy. Because if you marry Belle, I'll kill you. And you would be wise to believe that I'm not making an idle threat. Don't get greedy. You're too smart to make that mistake. Accept my offer of a quarter of a million, and you can leave Miami a happy man.''

"Are we talking lump sum payoff?''

"No. I want some guarantee that you're going to keep your side of the bargain. I'll pay you at the rate of fifteen thousand a month, provided you don't make contact with my daughter. That gives her more than a year to get any foolish feelings she has for you out of her system. Of course, if I end up in jail, you won't get your fifteen thousand bucks, so you'd be smart to see that the case Customs is building against me never comes to trial.''

"A quarter of a million isn't enough to persuade me to give up Belle and keep my mouth shut.''

"Take it or leave it. Your other option is to make sure your family knows whether you want to be cremated or buried.'' Marc didn't sound as if he were joking.

Buckling his belt, Sandro gave a tight smile. ''*In the circumstances,* I guess a quarter of a million dollars sounds like a real appealing payoff.''

"A hell of a lot more appealing than the alternatives,'' Marc agreed.

The monitor went dark, then flickered to life again with columns of figures. Before Belle could begin to decipher their meaning, she heard Donald calling her from the foot of the stairs.

"Belle, honey, are you there? I let myself in when you didn't answer the doorbell. Is it okay for me to come up?''

She was shaking so hard that her fingers could barely click through the simple commands to close the program and shut down the computer. "Yes, I'm here,'' she said, but her voice was no more than a squeak. She had to clear her throat and try again. "Come on up, Don."

He arrived at the door of her office just as her computer shut down, and she'd managed to shove the disk into her purse, which she'd left lying on her desk. She stood up, pushing the chair back from her desk and feeling so disoriented that she couldn't think of a single thing to say to him. Fortunately he didn't seem to notice.

"Hi, honey, it's lovely to have you back." He took her into his arms and kissed her warmly on the lips. She stood limply, no more capable of responding than if she'd been under anesthetic.

Don smiled lovingly. "Mmm...you taste so good. I sure have missed you, honey."

She finally found her voice. "I've missed you, too."

He beamed and chucked her under the chin. "Can you find a smile for me, honey? You don't look too cheerful."

"It's been a rough week."

"Of course it has, and I feel terrible for you. But I'm ordering you to stop thinking sad thoughts, at least for now. Your grandma lived a good life and a long one. I'm sure she wouldn't want to see you mourning her like this. You haven't even changed into something pretty for our dinner date."

"I'm sorry. I didn't expect you before seven. There hasn't been much time since I got home."

"No need for apologies, honey. I got off work a little early and came right over." Don dropped another kiss on her cheek, leaving his arm tucked lovingly around her waist. "Okay, do we have a deal? Tonight we're just going to relax and enjoy great food and forget all about sad things. Come on, hon. Let me see you smile.''

Belle turned the corners of her mouth upward, and Donald beamed his approval. ''That's my girl.''

As so often happened when she was with Donald, Belle found that it was easier to agree than to explain what she really felt. She experienced a familiar twinge of irritation, quickly overlaid with guilt. What right did she have to be irritated by Donald's heavy-handed attempts to cheer her up? She couldn't blame him for his lack of sensitivity—he had no idea that she was mourning the death of her father.

''Are you ready, then?'' he asked. ''You look fine in what you're wearing. I've made reservations for seven-thirty, and we'll be late if we don't leave right away.''

''Just let me put on some lipstick.'' In a way she was grateful that Don's presence required her to behave as though nothing were wrong. Because, in a way, nothing was wrong. Sandro Marchese had been out of her life for seven years. She'd always known he was morally bankrupt. Was it worse to learn that he'd been outright corrupt? And why should it hurt more to learn that he'd been bought off by her father, instead of just two-timing her once he got bored?

''Come on, hon.'' Donald put his arm around her waist. ''You'll feel better once we're at the restaurant. Is that purse on your desk the one you want to take?''

''Yes, it is.'' She smiled, grateful for his unfailing good humor. ''Thanks, Donald.''

''Whatever for?''

''For being so understanding.'' Even as she paid him the compliment, she realized it was a lie. He didn't understand her at all. But that wasn't his fault, since she'd given him almost no real opportunity to get close. It suddenly occurred to her that she was dating a man whose chief attraction was that she could lie to him and he never noticed. Not exactly the sturdiest foundation on which to build a relationship.

At least it was an improvement over wanting to marry a man because he was so sexually attractive that she lost all power of rational thought when he was anywhere within touching distance. Especially when the man in question obviously hadn't given a damn about her.

The more Belle thought about it, the more insulted she felt that her father had managed to buy off Sandro Marchese for a measly quarter of a million dollars. Sandro had struck a lousy deal.

When she turned him in to the feds for corruption, she'd make sure she had an opportunity to confront him in person. That way, she could tell him that he'd sold himself cheap. To keep her away from slime like him, Belle was quite sure her father would willingly have forked over several million dollars.

Five

Donald had made reservations for dinner at The Winter Garden, a restaurant Belle had heard good things about but never tried. Located on the corner of an upscale shopping mall, an enclosed area outside the windows had been landscaped to create the illusion of a garden. From their table, Belle and Donald looked out onto an attractively lit flower bed of yellow chrysanthemums, mauve asters, and dark red dahlias, surrounded by evergreens. Inside the restaurant, a low hum of voices provided the festive sensation of other people enjoying their dinners, and an attentive wait staff worked unobtrusively to ensure that they were efficiently served.

Despite the pleasant surroundings, Belle fought against an almost overwhelming sense of impatience. She didn't want to be here, she wanted to be home, examining the rest of the disk and brooding over what her father had intended her to do with it. Rushing to the nearest FBI office didn't seem like a good option. In view of the number of senior government dignitaries Marc Joubert had managed to bribe, she would be naive to count on the honesty of any public official she hadn't thoroughly checked out.

Unfortunately, she had hours of being sociable still ahead of her before she could return to full-time brooding. Donald viewed dining out as akin to holy ritual, and there was no way she would be able to cut their reunion short without hurting his feelings. She had a gloomy suspicion that he would expect to spend the night as well. Belle sighed. Right now, she definitely wasn't in the mood for sex. While they ate their salads, she silently invented excuses that she hoped would send Donald home to his own bed without wounding his pride too badly.

At first he didn't seem to notice that she was unusually quiet. To celebrate her return, he had splurged on a bottle of Château Potensac Bordeaux to go with their filet mignon and porcini mushrooms. During the summer he had taken a tour of the French wine country and he'd been trying to teach Belle about fine wines ever since, patiently educating her palate and never complaining about her continuing inability to distinguish between eminent French imports and upstart California imitations. Happily, he was so pleased with his selection tonight that he entertained himself for the entire first course, explaining how soil changes in the Medoc region contributed to subtle variations in the quality of the vines that were noticeable only to a connoisseur's palate.

Belle listened with less than half an ear, expressed amazement that deep gravel beds in the Margaux region did something or other to the grapes, and kept sipping her wine, in part to satisfy Donald that she was duly appreciative of his expert selection, but mostly because she hoped if she drank enough she would eventually blot out the memory of Sandro Marchese's mocking smile as he sold himself to her father for a quarter of a million dollars. Unfortunately, she was already well into her third glass, and so far the only noticeable effect seemed to be a mounting desire to pick up her plate and empty it over Donald's head.

Either her gritted teeth or her monosyllabic replies finally alerted Donald to the fact that something was wrong. Contrite, he stopped in midsentence and reached across the table to pat the back of her hand. "Gee, honey, I shouldn't have forced you to come out tonight. It's too soon, isn't it? You're still really upset about losing your grandmother." He gave her fingers an affectionate squeeze. "She must have been a very special woman to affect you so deeply."

It was the perfect opening—the ideal opportunity to tell him that it was her father who had died, not her grandmother. Belle searched for the least shocking way to explain that she was the daughter of a man who had made millions of dollars on illegal international arms deals. She knew she had to do this some time, so why not now? She drew in a deep breath— and wimped out.

"The whole trip to Miami was harder than I expected," she said, taking another gulp of wine to wash away the bad taste of her own cowardice.

Donald shook his head in mock disapproval. "Belle, honey, you're too tenderhearted, that's your trouble. After all, we're talking about an old woman here—"

Given that her grandmother had been custom-crafted to conceal a lie, Belle was surprisingly irritated by Donald's casual dismissal of her supposed death. "Because she's old, does that mean I'm not allowed to grieve for her?"

"Of course not, honey." Donald sounded appalled that she'd misunderstood him. "I hadn't realized you were so close to your grandmother or I'd have been more sympathetic. But you never went to visit her, or even talked about her, so I guess I concluded that the two of you didn't have much in common and that you went to her funeral more out of respect than anything else. My mistake. I apologize."

"No, I'm being oversensitive. You've been great." Her irritation switched to instant guilt. It was crazy that they were picking a quarrel over a woman who had, in reality, been dead since Belle was in kindergarten. She tried once again to inject a note of at least partial truth into their discussion.

"I loved my…grandmother, but we had some complicated issues still unresolved between us and I've avoided talking about her because I didn't want to get into all the crazy background stuff about my family." She tried to look rueful. "The truth is, my relationship with my relatives gives new and deeper meaning to the word *dysfunctional*."

"That's too bad, honey. Although you only have cousins left now, so it shouldn't be too difficult to work things out with them."

"Perhaps not, although we still seem capable of having knock-down-drag-out fights about nothing at all." Belle felt an unexpected flash of affection for her noisy, combative family and the exuberance they brought to daily life. "My…cousins…work on the principle that there is no event too trivial to turn into a three-ring circus. With marching bands on the side."

Donald winced in commiseration. "Poor you," he said. "I know how much you must hate that. You're so wonderfully in control all the time, and I sure do admire that, especially in a woman. It's such a rare quality.'' He stroked her hand tenderly. ''You're a woman who needs privacy, Belle, I realize that. I don't want you to think I'm butting into your personal affairs, but it's not always good to bottle things up inside. You know I'm always here for you when you decide you're ready to share any concerns or problems you might be having with your family.''

''I'm not anticipating any new problems, thank goodness. You mustn't think I'm cutting you out of my family life, Donald. I'm really not—it's much more that I've cut myself off from my own past. Until this week, I hadn't seen a single member of my family in seven years.''

She was rewarding Donald's sincere offers of sympathy with a bunch of weasely half truths, Belle thought, angry with herself. To make matters worse, instead of taking the hint and changing the subject— even the soil of the Medoc would have been better— Donald set about reassuring her that he didn't feel in the least excluded from anything important in her life. Avoiding his gaze, she looked around the restaurant, hoping that she might magically find either the courage to tell him the truth, or at least inspiration for some fascinating new subject of conversation.

She found neither inspiration nor courage.

What she *did* find was Sandro Marchese sitting at a table in the corner, apparently deep in discussion with another man whose back was turned toward her.

Belle's hand jerked so violently that she knocked over her wineglass. Fortunately the glass was once again empty. While the waiter mopped up a few droplets of wine and brought her a fresh napkin, Donald fussed and asked concerned questions until she was ready to scream. She drank some ice water, which did absolutely nothing either to calm her down or to improve the clarity of her vision. When she sneaked another glance, Sandro Marchese was still there in the far corner of the dining room, looking older and more cynical, but otherwise disturbingly unchanged.

He must be an alcohol-induced illusion, she decided. Admittedly a very solid illusion, but the coincidence would be too great if it really were Sandro. She reminded herself that three million people lived in the Chicagoland area, and at least a few hundred of them were likely to be tall, dark, handsome men with sardonic expressions. She was tired, she'd consumed half a bottle of wine, and her eyes were obviously playing tricks. Yes, that was it. Combine excess alcohol with the shock she'd felt over watching the film of Sandro negotiating a contemptible deal with her father, and she was primed to fall prey to just this sort of optical illusion.

"Will you excuse me?" she said to Donald, realizing only after she'd spoken that she'd interrupted him in midsentence. She would have apologized, but she saw Sandro—or whoever the man was—getting up from his table along with his companion. He was leaving! She had the impression that he had seen her, even that he inclined his head in a tiny salute, but she couldn't be absolutely sure. Belle hurried across the dining room, dodging one waiter who was pouring flamed cognac over a brace of quail, and barely missing another who was carrying brimming cups of espresso. She registered them only at the outer periphery of her consciousness.

When she reached the corner table where Sandro had been sitting, it was empty and he was nowhere in sight. She swore beneath her breath, cursing her high heels as she ran through the lobby and into the parking lot. A Buick sedan was just exiting onto the highway, but in the dark it was impossible to see how many people were inside, much less confirm whether one of them was Sandro Marchese.

Now that she'd lost sight of him, Belle couldn't seem to move. The parking valet asked if he could get her car, and she shook her head. She remained outside until she started to shiver from the cold. Her mind blank but her emotions rioting, she finally turned and walked slowly back into the restaurant.

Donald was pacing up and down the lobby. "What happened?" he asked. "Belle, whatever is the matter with you tonight?"

"We've had this conversation already," she snapped. "Nothing's the matter with me." Immediately remorseful, she put her hand to her forehead and massaged the throbbing pain pounding between her eyes. "I'm sorry, I should have stayed home. I'm in a weird mood, and I know I'm being rotten company."

Donald's irritation never lasted for more than a minute or two. "You could never be rotten company," he said, smiling as he tucked her hand into the crook of his arm. "It's only that I worry when you aren't your usual sweet self."

He'd been dating her for months. Hadn't he noticed how far removed from *sweet* she really was? Belle knew she ought to be grateful for his kindness, but forbearance wasn't what she needed from him tonight. This was one of the rare occasions when her flamboyant Joubert genes were getting the better of her and she was spoiling for a fight. An unregenerate part of her wished that Donald would lose his temper so that they could indulge in a rip-roaring shouting match that would only end when he flung her on the bed and they made love. Rough, hot, passionate love.

But there was no point in wishing that Donald would turn into Sandro— Belle put a stop to the treacherous thought before it led her too far down a path she definitely didn't want to follow. Seething with sudden energy that could find no legitimate outlet, she let Donald escort her back to their table. Once there, she nibbled on bread until he finished his entrée, simply so that her fingers would have something more acceptable to do than drum on the starched tablecloth.

The bread, combined with her earlier dose of cold night air, seemed to sober her up enough to carry on a pretty good imitation of a normal conversation without actually having to listen to what Donald was saying. She even ordered coffee and forced herself to drink it. The fact that she could swallow sip after sip of coffee seemed proof that she was in control of her imagination. She wasn't going to rush home so that she could start obsessively replaying her father's disk and inventing wild stories to explain why Sandro Marchese might be in Chicago, eating dinner at the same restaurant she was. No way. She didn't even care if Sandro was in Chicago.

Her act must have been more successful at deceiving Donald than it was at fooling her. When they arrived back at her house, Donald escorted her to the front door and stopped on the top porch step, smiling down at her. "Well, it sure is nice to have my own cheerful Belle back again. You had me worried there for a minute or two, honey. I'm glad you're feeling your old self again."

Belle was so relieved to be home that she didn't attempt to disabuse him about the state of her emotions. "You were right as usual, Don. I just needed to get my mind off the events of the past week, and now I feel fine again. Thanks for a lovely evening."

"My pleasure, as always."

"Your boss has impeccable taste," she said. "The Winter Garden is not only a great restaurant, but the setting is lovely, too. I'm glad you chose it for us tonight."

They would go into fructose overload if they didn't soon quit with the exchange of compliments. On edge with the desire to be rid of him, Belle reached in her purse for the key and unlocked the door.

Donald was supremely oblivious to her tension. He gave a beaming smile, making no move to return to his car. "We have to go there again sometime soon. Their wine list is quite remarkable."

"I'd love to go back whenever you feel in the mood." She would have agreed to eat dinner in a ditch if that was what it took to get rid of him. The door was unlocked but she didn't push it open. Instead, she turned to give him a swift good-night kiss, praying he would take the hint. *Kissing on the steps means no coming inside.*

She should have known better than to expect Donald to take such a subtle hint. He put his arm around her waist and tilted her head back so that he could turn her casual kiss into something a lot more passionate. Too late, she realized that faking cheerfulness had been a really bad mistake. For the past hour she'd pretended everything was fine to such good effect that Donald had no idea she was counting down the seconds to be rid of him.

Belle broke free from their embrace to suck in a gulp of air, but Donald still didn't get the message. He opened the door and started to edge both of them through it, her body clamped hard against his, while one of his hands inched under her coat in search of her breast. Good grief, couldn't the wretched man tell that she felt about as eager to make love to him as she would have been to spend the night with a grizzly bear?

Belle faked a huge yawn, then pushed him away before he could get too far inside. Ever the perfect gentleman, he let go at once. "Honey, what's wrong?"

If he asked her that one more time, she would run demented and screaming into the night. Oddly, she wasn't entirely sure why she was so anxious to get away from him. She'd been tired before, and she'd faked pleasure in their sexual encounters often enough. Why couldn't she do it one more time? What was so different about tonight?

Realizing that she'd unwittingly brought herself face to face with the problem that lay at the core of their relationship, Belle tucked herself behind the door, determined to put a solid barrier between the two of them. "Donald, I'm sorry, but I really want to be alone tonight. I've been surrounded by hordes of cousins and old family friends for days, and I'm running on emotional overload. I need some space. Tomorrow, too. I'm sorry. Maybe we can get together on Sunday...spend the whole afternoon and evening together."

"That would be great." Nobody could accuse Donald of being quick to take offense, or of having an oversensitive ego. "As for tonight, there's nothing for you to be sorry about. I understand that you're feeling drained and too tired to enjoy making love. I sure will miss holding you in my arms, but if you want to be alone, of course I respect that. I should have been more considerate of what you've gone through this past week.''

"Thanks, Donald, I appreciate your sensitivity." It occurred to Belle that she and Donald spent an awful lot of their time together tenderly apologizing. It was nice that Donald was so willing to accept his share of blame for any discord, but it would have been even nicer if they didn't always have so many misunderstandings to deal with.

Despite her refusal to invite him in, Donald seemed quite happy about the way the evening had gone. Why wouldn't he be happy? Belle thought grouchily. He hadn't seen visions of past lovers, or lied through his teeth about whose funeral he'd been attending. He hadn't been forced to listen to her deliver pompous lectures about wine for hours at a stretch. He had every reason to be happy.

She held herself stiff and unresponsive when he leaned forward and kissed her forehead. "Sleep well, honey. I'll call you tomorrow afternoon, and we'll set a time to meet on Sunday. Think about what you'd like to do with the day. It's your choice."

"Yours, too."

Donald smiled. "True, but I guess I'm the easy-going one in this relationship."

She was absolutely not going to analyze what he meant by that remark. Belle returned his smile with a high-wattage one of her own. "Don't worry, I'll pick somewhere I know you like. See you Sunday.

'Night, Donald.'' She closed the door behind him as fast as she could.

The moment she was alone, she pulled the bolt into place and kicked off her shoes, sighing with relief as she slumped against the inside of the door. Thank God, he was gone! Energized by the thought of her father's disk waiting to be viewed, she picked up her shoes and walked quickly toward the stairs. As she passed through the living room, a man got up from the chair where he'd been sitting. ''Hello, Belle. It's good to see you again.''

She froze at the sound of Sandro's voice. Incapable of movement, only her emotions continued to function, leaping instantly from shock to white-hot fury without stopping anywhere along the way. ''What are you doing here?'' she demanded, glaring at him. ''How dare you come into my house! How did you get in?''

The combined effect of intense rage and mind-numbing shock seemed to be that her voice sounded clipped and ice-cold, as if she were in total control of herself and the situation—the exact opposite of the truth. Inside, she felt hot and fragile enough to explode.

''I came here because I need to speak with you,'' Sandro said. ''And I got into your house through your back door. It was open.''

''I suppose you can't help lying since it's a congenital disease with you.'' Her voice layered scorn on top of the ice. ''But please, don't treat me as brainless, Sandro. I checked the house before I left. The security lights were on, and I'm a hundred-percent certain that the back door was locked.''

''I'm sure it was—''

"Then how did you get in? Have you added break-ing-and-entering to your list of criminal activities?"

"No, of course not. Just as I was parking my car, I saw somebody run out of the house and take off through your backyard. I tried to catch him, but he had too much of a head start. I lost him at the corner and had to guess which way he'd turned. Obviously, I guessed wrong, because I never caught sight of him again."

"You're claiming there was a burglar in my house?" Belle didn't attempt to disguise her skepticism.

"I don't know if he was a burglar. Nothing seems to be missing, but I didn't want to check the place out without asking your permission."

"Your thoughtfulness is overwhelming."

"I came inside because the door was standing wide open and I was afraid the intruder might have left one of his friends behind to attack you."

She didn't for a single instant believe that Sandro had found her back door unlocked, much less that he'd seen an intruder running off into the night. He'd broken in for some nefarious purpose, then searched her house, and now he was trying to lie his way out of trouble. The only mystery was why he'd hung around long enough for her to find him.

What could she possibly have in her house that Sandro Marchese wanted? The moment Belle asked herself the question, she knew the answer. *The disk.* He had broken into her home in order to search for her father's disk. Somehow he had found out that there was a record of his illicit dealings with Marc Joubert, and now he was frantically trying to steal back the evidence and cover his tracks. Which explained why he was still here, waiting for her to come home. He hadn't found the disk and now he hoped to trick her into revealing its whereabouts.

Hah! Belle thought. *In your dreams, buster.* Just in time, she prevented herself from glancing down at her purse, where she'd put the disk before leaving for the restaurant with Donald.

"As soon as you get out of here, I'll check through the house myself." She looked away, swallowing hard. For some reason, if she looked at Sandro for too long, an annoying quiver came into her voice. "If it turns out that anything's been stolen, I'll be sure to let the police know that my number one suspect in the crime is Sandro Marchese."

"You may not have much reason to trust me, Belle, but I wish you'd give me the benefit of the doubt for a few minutes. I'm not quite the crook you imagine—"

"I don't *imagine* you're a crook, Sandro. I *know* for a fact that you're a criminal lowlife sleazeball." She gave him a smile that was all teeth and no emotion. As long as she didn't look at him, she could function pretty well.

"You have every right to be angry with me, but you're in a hell of a lot of trouble, and I want to help." He moved toward her, and she jumped back, shattering the illusion that she was calm and in control.

He ignored her reaction and took her hands, pulling her toward him. "Belle, please, you have to look at me. I want you to see that I'm not lying. *Look at me, dammit!*"

Incredibly, despite everything he'd done and everything she knew about him, she wasn't smart enough to grab the phone and call the police. Instead, she looked up and gave him a tight little smile. "I wouldn't believe what you said if the Archangel Gabriel appeared in a flash of light and swore every word was true. In fact, I'd be searching for the holographic equipment you'd used to produce the angel."

He frowned, obviously frustrated. "Dammit, Belle, there are no special effects. No holograms. And certainly no angels. Just you and me being honest with each other."

She gave a short laugh.

"You're right," he said, as if she'd spoken. "I wasn't honest with you in the past, but that wasn't from choice. I wasn't free to reveal the truth."

"And what might that be, Sandro? At least your version for today's meeting."

"The truth is that I work for the investigative branch of the United States Customs Service. I've been with them for the past nine years."

"You need a drumroll to get the full dramatic effect of your announcement," she said scathingly. "Too bad, Sandro. I already knew that."

"Do you also know that when I worked for the Joubert Corporation, my job was a cover? That during the time I was in Miami, I was the lead operative for a multiagency task force investigating your father's smuggling operation?"

Her body wasn't numb anymore. It was painfully alive. She twisted her hands free of his grasp and pushed him away. "Yes, I knew that," she said. "But let's be accurate, shall we? You may be *employed* by Customs, but you don't really work for them, do you? I assume you make your money the same way you always did—with payoffs from the people you're supposed to be investigating.''

If she'd hoped to embarrass him, she was disappointed. Sandro's eyes narrowed, but he displayed no other reaction. "Is that what your father told you? That I took payoffs from him to keep quiet about the Joubert Corporation's smuggling activities?''

"Yes, that's what my father told me." Her voice cracked, no longer sounding gratifyingly cool.

"Then your father lied," Sandro said flatly. "Apart from the salary I took from the Joubert Corporation, your father knew I never accepted a penny of his money.''

How typical that he should attempt to cover up his criminal past by blaming a dead man, Belle thought acidly. She had to knot her hands behind her back to prevent herself from taking a swing at Sandro's arrogant face. Not that she would have any compunction about hurting him, but she didn't want to demean herself by touching him.

She had been angry from the moment she came home and first saw him in her living room, so it was astonishing to discover how much more intense her anger could actually get. It was on the tip of her tongue to scream at him that she had irrefutable, living-color proof of his corruption, but common sense intervened just in time to keep her silent. Her father's final request to her was fraught with danger, she realized. Sandro could find himself spending years in jail as soon as she placed the disk with the appropriate authorities. Obviously, the fewer people who knew for certain that she had the disk, the better her chances of getting it into the right hands.

If she was going to fulfill her father's final request,

she couldn't afford to give way to the anger fizzing and bubbling inside her. Belle walked to the front door and opened it, forcing herself to act as if Sandro's presence merely bored her. "You're trespassing. Get out."

He crossed the room and stretched around her to shut the door, leaning against it to block her access. "I can't leave yet. We need to talk—"

"We have nothing more to talk about," she said, making a dash for the kitchen. She grabbed the phone, but he caught up with her in seconds, snatching the receiver and disconnecting before she could dial 9-1-1.

"You may not like what I have to say, Belle, but you'd damn well better listen because you're in big trouble. An informant—one who ought to know exactly what he's talking about—notified us that your father left you in charge of his final project. If that information is true, then you should be smart enough to realize that you've taken on a very dangerous task. Your life is seriously at risk."

She was more angry than frightened, even though the way he loomed over her should have felt menacing. "Are you planning to kill me, Sandro? I didn't realize you'd sunk quite so low."

He stepped back, visibly shaken by her question. "Jesus, Belle, that's a crazy question. Why would you think I'm planning to kill you?"

She shrugged. "You're a criminal. You broke into my house. You threatened me. Seems like three pretty good reasons to me."

Sandro looked as if he badly wanted to punch something or somebody. Instead, he shoved his hands into the pockets of his pants and sucked in a gulp of air. "I apologize for entering your house without permission, but I thought I had good cause," he said finally. "And when I pointed out that your life was in danger, that wasn't a threat, for God's sake! I was trying to warn you."

"Gee, my mistake. But with a man like you, threats and warnings often seem interchangeable commodities."

Sandro spoke through gritted teeth. "I know we have a lot of history to overcome, but we have to put that behind us. Right now, we need each other. I need your help, and you need my protection—"

She gave him a smile that was sharp enough to cut glass. "What history do we have to overcome? Speaking for myself, I believe I got over my feelings for you—oh, about ten seconds after I found you in bed with that blond bimbo whose breasts were only slightly smaller than the peaks on Mount Everest."

"She was amazing, wasn't she?" To her absolute fury, Sandro looked amused. "But I didn't sleep with her, you know. Despite her astonishing attributes."

"Even I wasn't naive enough to imagine for one minute that you *slept* with her," Belle snapped.

"I meant that I didn't have sex with her." Sandro paused. "Her only purpose was to lie on the bed until you came into the motel room and saw her. I'd made a deal with your father to break up with you and I had to live up to my side of the bargain. At that point, keeping on the right side of your father was more important than anything else."

Belle chose not to express even a spark of interest in Sandro's story, despite the fact that the film clip she'd watched suggested that he might be telling the truth. Whether or not he'd actually slept with Bimbo

Boobs, the part of her life she'd shared with Sandro was dead, killed by his lies, and she had no intention of artificially resuscitating the corpse.

"What were you doing at The Winter Garden tonight?" she asked. "Why are you following me?"

Sandro hesitated before answering. "I wasn't following you," he said at last. "I was following Donald Gates."

"You were following *Donald?*" Belle would have been less astonished if Sandro had said he was in hot pursuit of the Tooth Fairy. "Why in the world are you following Donald Gates?"

Sandro sent her a look that she couldn't interpret. "Customs suspects him of smuggling technology stolen from his employers, using the Joubert Corporation as his conduit."

"You suspect Donald of smuggling?" Belle said. She felt dizzy, and reached behind her to grab the edge of the kitchen table, needing to feel something solid in a world where familiar boundaries suddenly seemed to be dissolving.

"You're lying," she said, her voice harsh with the force of her denial. The world was full of coincidences, but she wouldn't believe that she had fled Miami only to end up dating a man involved in the same criminal enterprise as her father. What would that make her? At best a fool; at worst the sort of corrupt person who was instinctively drawn to other criminals.

It was easier to believe that Sandro was trying to mislead her. "Donald is an engineer, with a solid job at Century Engineering. He designs irrigation systems, for heaven's sake! Why are you accusing him of smuggling? What's your game, Sandro?"

"No game," he said quietly. "We first became suspicious of Donald Gates when he was identified coming away from a meeting with your brother—"

"I can assure you that Donald Gates has never met my brother!"

"We have photographs of the meeting," Sandro said. "Do you want to see them? I could arrange for that."

"No. I wouldn't believe them anyway. These days, anyone with a computer and a scanner can fake a photo. Why are you lying to me about Donald and my brother?"

"The photos aren't fake," Sandro said quietly. "Donald met with your brother on at least three occasions in the past six months."

"How did Customs happen to have an operative in place to take the pictures?" she demanded. "How did you know Donald and my brother were planning to meet?"

"I didn't. Your father and his senior associates were under surveillance for several weeks before he died, so when Donald Gates turned up at company headquarters early in August, he was photographed. Pure routine. Same procedure for all visitors. It took us a while to put a name with the face, but eventually we discovered that Donald worked for a company called Century Engineering—"

"Yes, that's true. Donald does work for Century, but he designs irrigation systems. He's not involved with anything that would interest my brother—"

"Donald doesn't work on irrigation systems," Sandro said. "Century is a high-tech firm with government and military contracts. Donald Gates works on guidance systems for short-range missiles."

The notion of Donald working on high-tech weapons as opposed to watering systems for public parks was so crazy that Belle would have laughed—except that she was too angry. And, it had to be admitted, too scared. Could Sandro possibly be telling her the truth? If he was, then she and Donald had been engaged in a farcical game of mutual lies and deception.

"There's no way you'll convince me that Donald Gates ever met my brother." Belle spoke too loudly, and her staunch protest sounded hollow even to her own ears. She quickly changed the subject. "And why were you keeping Tony and my father under surveillance? If you were any good at your job, you'd know that the Joubert Corporation hasn't made a single illegal export in almost five years."

Sandro didn't reply. His silence frightened her even more than had his earlier accusations. Belle realized that she was furiously angry with him at least partly because that was a lot easier than facing the appalling possibility that his statements about Donald might be true. The fact that Customs had kept Marc Joubert under surveillance in the weeks prior to his death was even more worrying. They must have had some evidence that smuggling was going on in order to justify the expense of full-scale covert observation. Belle couldn't bear to consider the possibility that Marisa was wrong and that the Joubert Company was still operating illegally. If her brother was still smuggling stolen technology out of the country, how could she go to the authorities with a computer disk that was going to focus their attention on the Joubert Corporation?

Suddenly weary to the point of exhaustion, she turned her back on Sandro and walked out of the kitchen. "This interview is over," she said. "I have absolutely nothing more to say to you. For the last time, I'm asking you to leave."

"Okay, I'll leave. But let's be clear about why I came, Belle. I'm offering you a warning—an official warning, if you like. If your father left you in charge of any final projects, reject them. Don't get caught up in a wave of sentiment and start thinking that you owe it to your father's memory to pick up the family business where he left off. That's an easy route either to prison or to the graveyard. You're too young and too pretty for either of those places."

The arrogant, patronizing *rodent*. Belle didn't answer for the simple reason that she couldn't trust herself to speak.

Fortunately, Sandro didn't appear to expect a reply. He opened the front door and let himself out. "Bolt the door behind me," he said. "I wasn't lying about the intruder."

He walked away without looking back.

Six

The phone rang, interrupting the *whir* of the printer churning out copies of the material contained on her father's disk. Belle was jolted out of her glassy-eyed fixation by the images of her sister and baby Spencer scrolling on the computer monitor.

Letting the phone ring, she frowned as she watched Spencer playing with his mother in a meadow lush with flowers, although some mountains in the background still had snow on the peaks. In the distance, signs of new construction were everywhere. The sound track indicated that Evan, Marisa's husband, was the person operating the video camera, and that the film had been taken in May, around the time of Spencer's first birthday.

Off to the side of the picture she caught a glimpse of Dave Forcier, who seemed to be alternately chatting with Evan and tossing a ball to Spencer. Dave's remarks were limited to comments about the price of new homes in the area, which Belle gathered was somewhere near one of the ski areas in Utah, but it wasn't clear whether he was recommending that Evan should invest in a vacation home, or whether he thought the houses were overpriced.

This was the third time Belle had played the same segment, and she still couldn't fathom what message it was supposed to convey, other than that Spencer was a cute baby with an adorable smile who had an indulgent surrogate uncle in Dave Forcier. Her father had been meticulous in putting much of this disk together, but there was evidence throughout the disk that he'd been working in haste, with reminder notes to himself scattered everywhere. Belle was beginning to think this snippet of home movie had been included by mistake.

The answering machine picked up the incoming call, and she listened to Donald Gates deliver his second warm, caring message of the day. Warm, caring, and probably insincere, Belle thought, pressing the message-delete button with far more force than was necessary. Insincere, that is, if she chose to believe Sandro Marchese's accusations of the previous night. Which she would be crazy to do.

Except that she found it disturbingly easy to believe that her relationship with Donald was riddled with mutual deceptions. At some level she had never quite trusted his unfailing patience and perpetually tender smiles, Belle realized. She was beginning to wonder if her reluctance to confide in him had reflected a subconscious awareness not only that he was too eager to please but also that he had some unspoken agenda.

Refusing to let her thoughts slither down a path that had already become far too well-trodden, she pushed her chair back from her desk and stretched her cramped muscles. While she waited for her printer to finish regurgitating the final few pages, Belle wandered across to the window. She waved down at Marge Bruno, who was digging energetically in her garden, oblivious to the wind and gray skies. Probably uprooting another hundred or so zucchini to inflict on her neighbors, Belle thought, unable to contain a wry smile.

A car drew up in the Polaski driveway next door to Marge, and a trio of giggling teenage girls clumped up the driveway, wearing boots that looked as if they'd been designed to correct serious orthopedic deformities. Marge looked up at Belle, pointing to their boots and shaking her head. Belle grinned back, giving the thumbs-down in silent agreement.

She leaned against the window frame, soothed by the familiar neighborhood scene without really watching it. She couldn't stop fretting about her father's disk. Now that she had viewed it all, the problem of what to do next seemed even more difficult. Last night everything had seemed relatively simple—until she saw Sandro. Poor deluded woman that she was, Belle realized part of her had been waiting for him to provide some magical justification that would explain why he'd negotiated a quarter-of-a-million-dollar payoff from her father. She was infuriated by her own ambivalence. Why was it so hard for her to accept that Sandro was involved in the worst sort of professional corruption?

To compound the murkiness of what she ought to do about the disk, the snippet of film with her sister and Spencer really bothered her. Her father had never been a man who made sloppy mistakes. Why had he included those innocent family pictures on a disk he'd created to serve as a criminal indictment? Was he suggesting that she needed to take great care because Marisa and her family would be threatened if she handed the disk over to the authorities?

Much as she wanted to see the people who had

accepted bribes from her father punished, Belle didn't want to hand the disk over to the government until she completely understood the contents. When the chips were down, it seemed she wasn't ready to see justice done at any cost. If they ever handed out awards for moral vacillation, Belle thought, she'd win the grand price.

She resisted the urge to scream and pound walls. After her father's funeral, when Marisa had claimed that the Joubert Corporation now operated strictly within legal parameters, Belle had assumed her problems were over. In retrospect, her optimism seemed quaintly naive.

Enough already. Belle scooped pencils into her desk drawer, then slammed it shut. Her printer finally stopped, and she added the last few sheets to a stack that was now several hundred pages thick. The amazing sharpness of the DVD film and pictures couldn't be copied onto paper, of course, but the scanned images of documents such as checks and bank records had reproduced with crystal clarity. This printed material alone, even without the disk as backup, was probably enough to secure convictions of three-quarters of the people on whom her father had compiled files.

Belle took her father's disk from the CD-ROM drive and shut down the computer. She needed to forget about smuggling, bribery and corruption for a few hours. It was Saturday afternoon, with low clouds obscuring the sun and a biting wind blowing off the lake—perfect conditions for a trip to the mall. Not to buy clothes, but to search for household gadgets, her preferred form of therapy on days that really sucked. Days like this one. There was no good reason to stay at home, wrestling with problems that had no acceptable answers, when she could be out at a giant home-improvement store, buying herself an electric glue gun, or a nifty new pair of wire-cutters. Next time Martha Stewart came on TV and suggested that her viewers might like to make a holiday centerpiece out of empty coffee cans and sequined pinecones, Belle would be ready.

She stowed her father's disk inside the zippered lining of her purse and hesitated for a moment, deciding what to do with the printout. It was probably crazy to worry about the intruder Sandro had claimed to see, but there was always the faint possibility—very faint—that he'd been telling the truth. Feeling foolish, she shoved the papers into a box before going into her bedroom in search of a jacket.

On Monday she would ask Wayne, the resident geek at her office, what equipment she needed to make a duplicate of a DVD disk. Once she had a spare copy of the disk to work with, she could decide if she wanted to excise the puzzling snippet of film with Marisa and Spencer. Quite apart from the problem of protecting her family, she would feel a lot safer handing the disk over to the authorities if she knew that she had another copy of the actual disk in her possession. She would make it very clear to whoever took possession of the disk that she had made duplicates as well as retaining a hard copy. That way, there would be less temptation for a corrupt official to conveniently ''lose'' the original in an attempt to make prosecution impossible.

In the meantime, she wasn't about to leave the disk or the printout lying around in her house. The material her father had bequeathed to her had explosive po-

tential. The officials and the politicians cited on the
disk were not only facing indictment on charges of
corruption, but were also acutely vulnerable to blackmail. An unscrupulous person could use the disk to
make a comfortable living, extorting payment for his
silence. Between the twin risks of prosecution and
blackmail, Belle figured that a lot of people had powerful reasons to want the disk. Sandro probably hadn't
been exaggerating when he suggested her life would
be at risk if the wrong people discovered that she had
inherited it from her father.

*If Sandro really had been warning her, and not
making a veiled threat.*

Belle shut her closet door with a *bang*. This endless
mental gnawing had to stop. She tugged on her jacket,
grabbed the box holding the printout and ran downstairs. She was already in the garage when she was
struck by a sudden inspiration. She didn't really believe that some mysterious invader was watching the
house, waiting for her to leave so that he could steal
the disk—but better to be safe than sorry.

Returning to the living room, she searched her music collection for a CD made by The Black Watch, a
group of folksingers she had heard in concert a few
years ago and had admired ever since. She gave a
little murmur of satisfaction when she saw that she'd
remembered correctly what the CD she'd bought at
their performance looked like. It had been privately
made and, unlike disks from the big commercial pro-
ducers, was stamped with nothing more than the name
of the group and the title of the recording, *September*.

The name The Black Watch came from a Scottish
tartan, but it sounded vaguely sinister, and *September*
was about as neutral a title as she could hope to find.

It created the illusion of a disk bearing the date of the current month and might be enough to fool a would-be thief. Presumably, anyone who broke into her house in search of her father's disk would not expect to find it labeled Detailed Record of Important People Bribed by Marc Joubert.

Anyway, since she had no blank DVD disk to use as a decoy, this would have to do. Belle removed The Black Watch recording from its plastic case and slipped it into a sandwich baggie. Then she taped the bag to the underside of a low cupboard shelf where she stored her canned goods, and stepped back to make sure that it wasn't visible to anyone who didn't take the trouble to bend down and look.

So far, so good. The hiding place would be found by anyone making a serious search of the house, and yet it wasn't obvious enough to create suspicion that she wanted it to be found. As a decoy, a music CD seemed pretty forlorn, but it was the best she could manage on short notice. There was even the delightful possibility that the thief would be deceived into thinking the music was some elaborate form of code that had to be broken before the true contents of the disk could be accessed. Belle grinned and gave the CD a farewell pat. She could only hope. Not that she seriously believed anyone was about to break into her house. She was fairly sure Sandro's warning had just been a way of making excuses for his intrusion last night. And she absolutely was *not* going to start thinking about Sandro Marchese again.

The shopping expedition proved a balm to her soul, although hazardous to her charge card. She managed to buy several totally unnecessary gadgets, along with a remnant of imported linen fabric that was on sale for sixty percent off, which reduced its price from laughable to merely ridiculous. Replete with bulging shopping bags and a cheerful new attitude, Belle drove home, looking forward to a relaxing evening spent recovering her dining room chairs, bought at a garage sale the previous month. So much for their rock-bottom price, which was going to increase dramatically by the time they had their new Irish linen seat covers. Belle sighed without any real regret. She should have learned by now that there were few things as expensive as a bargain.

Mentally planning how she could cut the fabric to best advantage, she turned the corner onto Maple Street, paying little attention to her surroundings—until she saw a trio of police squad cars parked outside her house. She pulled into her driveway, heart racing. Good grief, had she actually been robbed?

One of the squad cars was parked so that it blocked access to her garage. A young uniformed cop waved at her to stop, indicating that she should get out of her car.

Damn, Belle thought, still incredulous. *Someone really must have broken into the house.*

Stomach knotting, she tumbled out of the car. ''What's wrong?'' she asked the cop. ''Why are you blocking my garage?''

The police officer was young, but he looked tired and harassed. ''Do you live here, miss? Could I see your driver's license, please?''

For some reason she'd carried an armful of shopping bags with her when she got out of the car. Belle dropped them onto the driveway and fumbled for her purse. ''Yes, I live here,'' she said, holding out her license. ''Why all the squad cars? What's going on?''

The cop examined her license with the help of a flashlight. "Thank you, miss," he said. "I'm Officer Robert Kresky, by the way. Sorry for the inconvenience, but we're trying to control access to the crime scene area. If you'll just wait a minute, miss, one of the other officers will escort you inside."

Belle resisted the urge to grab him by the shoulders and shake him. "What crime scene, for heaven's sake? Has my house been robbed?"

"We're not sure, miss, but it's been vandalized for sure, and your neighbor's been shot."

"Shot?"

"Yes, miss. It looks like she was shot straight through the heart at close range. We're treating her death as a homicide. I'm real sorry."

Her *death?* Belle whirled around, belatedly registering the fact that one of the squad cars was parked in the Brunos' driveway. "You mean that *Marge Bruno* is dead? She was shot?"

"Yes, miss. But she wasn't shot in her own house. She was found lying just inside the entrance to your house. I'm sorry."

Horrified, Belle glanced toward the door of her house. It was open, she finally noticed, with yellow tape across the gaping entrance. She quickly looked away again. She stared at the cop without seeing him, then turned abruptly and walked back to her car. She leaned against the hood, her legs suddenly too wobbly to support her.

"I'm sorry for the bad news, miss." Officer Kresky sounded wooden, as if he had not yet become accustomed to consoling the friends and family of murder victims.

Belle felt a rush of angry disbelief, as powerful as

the earlier shock. "Marge can't be dead. It's not possible. You've made a mistake. She waved at me when the Polaski girls came home, and we both laughed about the boots they were wearing. Besides, she was working in her garden when I drove out, so she knew I wasn't home. And even if she forgot and came across to visit me, I locked the front door when I left, so how did she get in?"

It was hard to imagine how police officers could make a mistake about a dead body on the floor of her house, but Belle wasn't willing to be rational. She dodged around her car and ran out into the road, determined to go to the Brunos and prove to herself that Marge was still alive.

Officer Kresky grabbed her arm, dragging her out of the path of an ambulance that was turning into the Brunos' driveway. "Watch it! We don't want another tragedy here tonight."

Belle ignored his warning, didn't even really hear it. She tugged her arm free and marched across the road. "I have to talk to Wally. How in the world is he going to cope without Marge to boss him around? He'll be totally lost. Jesus, this is awful—"

"Sorry, miss, but you can't talk to him—"

"Of course I can. Let me go!"

"No, miss, it's no use going over there. Mr. Bruno has suffered a heart attack. The shock of finding his wife was too much for him, I guess, and he collapsed only a couple of minutes after we got here. The ambulance is for him, to take him to the hospital."

"Oh, my God!" The fire went out of Belle, leaving her limp and sagging. Wally Bruno suffered from angina, and she found his heart attack easier to accept as real than Marge's death. "Poor Wally! Is he going to be all right?"

"I'm not a doctor, miss, I couldn't say." Whatever skills young Officer Kresky still lacked, he had already acquired the police knack of not answering simple questions, Belle thought acidly.

It had started to drizzle rain. A few icy droplets trickled inside the collar of her jacket, and once she realized how cold she felt, she couldn't seem to stop shivering. Officer Kresky was talking to her again, but she didn't listen. Another policeman, older and not wearing a uniform, came up and introduced himself.

"Ms. Joubert? I'm Detective Sergeant Patrick Brady. We're ready for you to come inside now, miss."

"Have you moved—" Belle had to clear her throat before she could continue. "Has Marge's body been taken away?"

"Yes, miss, although there's still some blood on the carpet just inside the door. And I have to ask you not to touch anything until our technicians have finished making a complete record of the crime scene. I'd also like you to walk me through the house and indicate anything at all that's missing."

She would have to go back into the house some time, so maybe it was better to get it over with right away. Belle drew in a deep breath of fresh air to steel herself, then followed the detective. He escorted her into the house via the garage, so she wouldn't trample on the bloodstains by the front door.

She thought she was prepared to face the worst, but soon learned her mistake. It was one thing to see the white outline of a dead body on the television, another thing altogether to see it on the floor of her home, with sticky pools of real blood spilling over the edges.

It didn't help much to turn her gaze resolutely in another direction, because her living room was in chaos wherever she turned. Every book had been pulled from the shelves, the sofa cushions had been slit open, and pieces of pink foam stuffing drifted in the draft coming through the front door. Her kitchen was even worse. Milk, jam, rice, flour, sugar and pickles had been upended into the sink in a revolting puddle, with coffee grounds floating on top of the congealed mess. Her canned goods were scattered over the floor, mixed with shards of glass from jars that had smashed as they fell when they were swept from her cupboard shelves.

"Walk carefully, miss." Sergeant Brady stayed close to her side as she picked her way toward the dining area. Without thinking, she reached into the small pantry as they passed by and felt under the shelf for The Black Watch CD. It was gone.

She made no effort to hide what she was doing from the detective, but he didn't seem to notice, so she didn't tell him. Shock numbed her brain as well as her body, keeping her silent.

"We can give you the names of a couple of professional cleaning crews you can call to get this mess taken care of," Sergeant Brady said, stopping so that they could wipe a revolting muck of pickle vinegar and jam from the soles of his shoes with a wad of paper towels. "Your home-owner's insurance will pay for them, I expect, so it could be worse."

Belle reflected that the cost of the cleanup was the absolute least of her worries at this point. "Thanks," she said, wondering whether to laugh or cry as she automatically searched for a trash can to throw away the soiled paper towels. "Some phone numbers would be useful."

"You're welcome." There was no audible irony in Sergeant Brady's response. "The crime lab technicians will be finished here in another couple of hours," he said. "So you can start the cleanup as soon as you can arrange for a crew to come in. You'll be surprised what a good job they do of making the place look like home again. A few hours, and you'll never know this happened."

If she'd had the energy, Belle would have told him that it took more than tidy rooms and clean floors to make a place feel like home, but the effort of stringing words together in a coherent sentence was beyond her. The smell was nauseating; she found it impossible to focus.

"I've got to get out of here." Belle groped her way past the detective, heading toward the dining room. Absurdly, about the only pieces of furniture that seemed to have survived unscathed were her garage sale chairs. Their shabby, stained seat covers were no more damaged than they had been before.

She opened the window and hung her head outside, sucking in cold, rain-misted air until she was reasonably sure that she could speak without gagging.

"Is the mess this bad upstairs?" she asked.

"Not quite as bad. There was no food for them to throw around, and they seem to have been a bit more methodical up there. We think maybe they started upstairs and worked their way down, getting more frenzied the longer they searched."

"Searched?" Belle asked, her attention caught by the word.

"Yes, miss. This doesn't look like a typical home invasion or a regular burglary. Whoever did this was searching for something specific. And if we knew what they were looking for, it's likely we'd find it easier to identify Mrs. Bruno's murderer. That's one of the reasons we need your help. Since we've no idea what they wanted, we can't tell if they found what they were looking for."

The disk, Belle thought. Whoever killed Marge had been looking for her father's disk. She pushed the realization away, not wanting to take on the burden of knowing that she was at least partly responsible for her neighbor's death.

"How can you be sure they were looking for something specific?" she asked, hoping the detective was mistaken. "Don't thieves often mess up the homes they rob?"

"Sometimes," he agreed. "If they're high, or if they have a reason to dislike the home owner. But this place hasn't been vandalized, it's been searched. The walls haven't been defaced, and your belongings haven't been smashed just for the hell of it. The TV is still here. The VCR, the stereo—"

"Marge Bruno must have interrupted them before they could steal anything."

"Not likely, miss. A regular burglar would have started with your electronic equipment, because that's the easiest stuff for him to sell. He would have had a truck parked at the back, and he'd have loaded up real fast, starting with your TV and VCR. That's not what happened here. Whoever did this job was looking for something of a particular size—"

"How can you be sure of that?"

"The perpetrator smashed your giant jar of dill

pickles, and a big container of jam, but he didn't touch your bottle of ketchup, or your small jar of mayo, or the fancy pot of mustard, or anything else small. The logical explanation is that he was in a hurry and knew what he was searching for couldn't have been hidden inside anything as narrow-necked as a ketchup bottle.''

"Those smaller items might have survived by sheer chance,'' Belle protested.

She must have sounded too vehement. Brady looked at her with sudden speculation. "Could have been chance, miss, but I don't think so.'' He made a rough circle with his thumbs and forefingers. "I'm guessing the perp was looking for something about this big in diameter. Any idea what it might have been?''

The size the detective indicated was smaller than a CD, but not by much.

She couldn't keep quiet about the disk, Belle thought, stomach churning. She had no right. Marge Bruno had been murdered. She owed it to her neighbor to share any information that might help to identify the person who had killed her. How many people knew she had the disk? Her brother, possibly. Her sister, maybe. Sandro, for sure, given his behavior last night.

As soon as she named them, the police would immediately consider all three of them suspects. But that wouldn't matter in the long run. Belle couldn't believe that any of them were killers—not even Sandro. She and Sandro had been lovers for three idyllic months and, despite the devastating revelations on her father's disk, she refused to believe that he was capable of murder. The only time in her entire life that she had felt truly happy had been during the hours she spent alone with Sandro. If he was a cold-blooded killer, what would that say about her?

"If you have any idea what the person who murdered your neighbor might have been looking for, miss, I need to know." Sergeant Brady interrupted with a subtle echo of her own thoughts, a reminder that she had no right to keep silent if she held any clue to solving Marge's murder.

He was no fool, Belle reflected. He already knew precisely which buttons to push to get a response from her. She looked down and realized her fingers were twisting in nonstop nervous motion. It wouldn't be too difficult for Sergeant Brady to deduce that she was stressed, she thought derisively, shoving her hands into the pockets of her pants.

"I think whoever did this might have been looking for a computer disk," she said.

"Ah." Brady's gaze narrowed intently. "Did they find it?"

She had less than a second to decide how she would answer.

"Yes," she said.

"I see." Brady drew out a notebook and a pen. "Is that what you were feeling for when you ran your hand along the underside of the cupboard shelf in the kitchen?" he asked. "I wondered."

It would be a definite mistake to underestimate this particular cop, Belle decided. She looked at him with rueful respect. "Yes, that's what I was looking for."

Brady gestured to encompass the wreckage strewn around them. "Must be an important disk for someone to want it this bad," he said. "Exactly what was on the disk?"

"I'm not sure." Belle searched frantically for some explanation she could give that would protect her family, and yet set the cops looking in the right direction for Marge's murderer.

Brady sent her an incredulous glance. "You're not sure? What does that mean, miss?"

"It was technological material," she said, inventing rapidly. "I didn't understand any of it, but I knew it was very important and valuable because my father gave it to me just before he died, with instructions to take care of it."

"Ah." The detective's response was so bland that it sounded skeptical. "Did your father die recently, miss?"

"A week ago."

"I'm sorry." Brady barely pretended to pause before continuing with his questions. "What sort of technological information was on the disk, miss? Relating to what subject? Computer technology, military technology...the design for a new plane? You must have some idea."

She shook her head. "I'm sorry. It was all symbols and numbers. Nothing I could understand at all."

"Well, if you couldn't understand the material, how did you know it was valuable enough to need hiding in your kitchen cupboard?"

"I already explained that. My father warned me to take care of the disk and not to let anyone know that I had it. But I can't tell you precisely why it was so important to him, because he died before he could explain what he wanted me to do with it. I wish to God he *had* given me some explicit instructions."

If she had hoped to elicit sympathy, she failed. Brady's stolid expression never wavered. "And what was your father's line of business, miss? Maybe one of his colleagues will be able to help me with some more specific information."

So, for all her squirming and evasions, Sergeant Brady had still arrived at the inevitable question. She was actually relieved when she saw Officer Kresky come inside and head toward them, obviously intent on delivering a message.

"Yes, what is it, Bob?" Brady didn't bother to hide his exasperation at the interruption.

"Sorry, sir, but I thought you would want to know that Mr. Bruno died en route to the hospital."

"He didn't regain consciousness?"

Kresky shook his head. "No, sir, I'm afraid not."

Brady muttered under his breath, then looked up. "Don't let the Bruno son leave the hospital before we get a statement from him."

"Which one, sir? George or Frank?"

"The one who came home from bowling with his Dad and found the woman's body."

"That was Frank."

"Okay. Don't let him leave until I've spoken with him. No excuses, you hear?"

"Yes, sir. And there are two TV news crews out there with cameras ready to roll. You want to handle that, sir?" He coughed. "Or I could do it, if you're too busy."

Brady gave a sudden, totally unexpected grin. "Want to get your handsome face on TV, do you, Bob?"

"No, sir. I just thought, if you were busy—"

"I am," Brady said. "Which reporters have they sent?"

"Sally Reton and Josefina Garcia. Channel 2 and Channel 22."

Brady wrinkled his nose. "Oh, them. They're just pretty faces, both of 'em. You can take care of it, Bob. And if you tell either one anything even remotely confidential, I'll personally make sure that you're on traffic duty from now until Christmas. Name of the victim, suspected homicide, and we're investigating. That's it."

"Yes, sir." Kresky tried not to look too delighted at his opportunity to shine on TV.

"He's got a new girlfriend to impress," Brady said, watching him leave. "Before he met her, he used to have a functioning brain." He lumbered to his feet. Belle had a suspicion that the detective's ponderous physical movements were as much a sham as was his stolid expression. She sure wouldn't like to be a fleeing suspect if Detective Brady were chasing her.

"Do you want to check upstairs next?" he asked, as if he didn't remember the precise point in their conversation Kresky had interrupted. Belle wasn't counting on it, although the change of subject was a tremendous relief. "The sooner we've gone through everything, and you've told me all you know, the sooner we can get out of your way."

Belle followed him upstairs and into her bedroom. As she walked past the bed, feathers lifted into the air from the ripped pillows. She swallowed over a sudden lump in her throat, and hot tears welled in her eyes. For the first time she felt rage on her own behalf, and loathing toward the person who had destroyed the home she had worked so hard to make for herself.

"Is anything missing in here as far as you can see?" Brady asked, a hint of sympathy creeping into his voice.

"No, nothing." Belle closed the lid of her jewelry box. "Although the only valuable jewelry I have was left to me by my grandmother, and I keep it in a safety deposit box."

"Very wise. You've no idea how careless some home owners are with their property. Sometimes you wonder if they *want* to keep the criminals in business." He pushed open the bathroom door. "What about in here? Any more hidden disks?"

"No." Belle did a cursory check of the bathroom which was as messy as the kitchen but smelled of shampoo and perfume—an improvement over pickles and coffee. "Do you know what time it was when Marge was killed?"

For some reason, Brady decided to be free with his information. "Mr. Bruno came home from bowling with his son at around five-thirty. According to the son, when they couldn't find Mrs. Bruno in their own house, they came outside to look for her. Mr. Bruno Senior noticed that the door to your house was open, and his son noticed what looked like one of his mother's gardening boots protruding. They rushed over here and discovered her body."

"Was she...dead already?"

"Yes, according to her son. As soon as they got over the initial shock, they called 9-1-1. The medical examiner got here at six-fifteen, and she was certainly dead then."

"How long had she been dead?"

Brady shook his head, stepping aside so that she could precede him into her office. "It's only in the movies that the doctor looks at the body and claims to know at a glance how long ago the person died. In real life, you need an autopsy. And even then, it's a lot more difficult than people think to pin down the exact time of death.''

Belle didn't comment, because the condition of her office left her speechless. The dove-gray carpet was invisible beneath a covering of what looked like several thousand pieces of paper. The wreckage downstairs had been vile, but this mess affected her far more deeply. One of the ways she'd tried to compensate for the chaotic drama of Joubert family life was by being compulsively organized. She kept more paperwork than she should, and she filed everything. Now seven years of paperwork—her entire life since she arrived in Chicago—was scattered randomly over her office floor. From Sergeant Brady's point of view, this might seem less of a disaster than the kitchen. From her perspective, she saw hundreds of hours of tedious work ahead of her, restructuring her files; she also saw a brutal violation of the order she had struggled so desperately to impose on her life.

With an instinctive need to reclaim her space, she moved her chair back to her desk and started to close drawers and pick up plastic organizer trays. Belatedly, she noticed that although her computer monitor and keyboard were still sitting on her desk, the processing unit was gone.

"They've stolen my computer," she said to Brady.

"Ah. Do you have any data stored in there that would be worth stealing?"

She shook her head.

He gave her an assessing look. "No more of your

father's technological information that you don't understand? You're sure?''

"I'm quite sure," Belle said curtly. She'd printed out the material from the DVD disk, but she hadn't taken the time to download the information onto her hard drive. She was beginning to think her omission was fortunate.

She gave the room another quick search. "I think they've taken my entire case of CD-ROMs as well. It's hard to tell with all this litter on the floor, but I don't see it anywhere, and it's big enough that it ought to be fairly easy to spot."

"What does it look like?" Brady was already scooping up armfuls of paper, searching for the missing case.

"It's dark gray nylon, zippered. About half the size of a traditional briefcase. When you open it, there are plastic sleeves inside to hold the disks. I had twenty or thirty disks in there—"

"Any of them important? Worth stealing?"

Belle shook her head. "There was absolutely nothing in there that you couldn't buy at the local computer store. Nothing that wasn't clearly labeled—" She stopped, but not quite soon enough to prevent Brady from making a connection.

"That's a good point," he said. "What about the disk that was taken from downstairs? What did the label on that say?"

Damn. If she relaxed even for a second, she gave him ammunition for another question she didn't want to answer. What the hell was she going to tell him now?

"It was labeled The Black Watch. *September,*" she said after a pause that lasted a tad too long.

Brady raised an enquiring eyebrow. "Care to tell me what that means, miss?"

"I haven't any idea. I don't think it means anything."

Brady looked openly skeptical. So much for her pathetic attempts to be clever, Belle thought. Still, she had to try to convince him that she was being as helpful as possible. She shrugged with what she hoped was a convincing touch of irritation. "I've told you already, I didn't understand the material on the CD-ROM, so it's not surprising that I've no idea what the label meant. I assumed that *September* was some sort of date code."

"Okay, miss, let's give this one more try. Let me see if I've got this straight. What it amounts to is that your home has been torn apart and the only things that have been taken are your computer and a bunch of CD-ROMs, most of them standard issue, but one of them containing what you think is important technological information. You have no idea who might have stolen this disk because you have no idea what information it contained."

"Yes, that's right. Unfortunately."

"Very unfortunate, miss. And although you didn't understand the information contained on the disk, you understood enough to be afraid somebody might try to steal it, or you wouldn't have hidden it."

"I told you. My father warned me—"

"Ah, yes. That was what we were talking about when Bob Kresky interrupted us." Belle didn't believe for one second that Brady had forgotten his question. "What line of business was your father in, miss? How did he happen to have a disk somebody else wanted bad enough that they were willing to kill your neighbor for it?''

Brady was going to discover the answer soon enough, so it was foolish to withhold it, Belle decided. With a family name as unusual as Joubert, and with all the obituaries that had been written about her father, a computer search would reveal the connection with no trouble at all.

''My father inherited the family company twenty years ago,'' Belle said. ''It's called the Joubert Corporation, and it's been active in the import-export business since World War II.''

''Import-export, eh? Does the company specialize in any specific line of imports and exports?''

''The Joubert Corporation brokers international sales of weapons and high-technology items,'' Belle said stiffly. ''A lot of the high-tech sales are to foreign governments, for military use.''

''Ah, I see. So you weren't at all surprised that your father had a disk full of high-tech information?''

''No, that didn't surprise me. And it doesn't surprise me that other people might find the disk worth stealing. I was only surprised that my father chose to give the disk to me.''

''Ah.'' That seemed to be Brady's favorite all-purpose response. This time there was a wealth of satisfaction in the small sound. ''Now we're finally beginning to get somewhere that makes sense. Your father's dying and he gives you a CD-ROM containing the blueprints for a high-tech product that probably has military uses. Someone finds out you have the disk and comes in search of it. They're interrupted by Marge Bruno. They kill her and make off with the disk. Does that sound like a plausible scenario to you, Miss Joubert?''

"It sounds plausible." Belle walked around her office, picking up papers as an excuse to avoid making eye contact with the detective. She wished he would leave so that she could think. Sometime tonight, she would call her brother and warn him that the police would most likely come to interview him in the very near future. Once Brady left and she finally had five minutes of solitude, she would decide whether she should also tell her brother that the thief hadn't succeeded in stealing the real disk. The trouble was that if she told Tony that she still had her father's disk in her possession, he would demand that she return it. And she would refuse. Was she ready for the huge family fight that would follow?

Sergeant Brady asked rapid-fire questions until he established that her brother was now CEO of the family company, that it was located in Miami, and that Belle had nothing to do with the day-to-day running of the business.

"Since your brother worked in the family business and has taken over the company now, have you any idea why your father decided to bypass him and give you this all-important mystery disk?" Brady asked.

"I happened to be the only person in the hospital room when my father realized he was dying," Belle said. "Except for my mother, and she was so upset that she wasn't in a fit state to listen to instructions about computer disks."

"Instructions, miss? I understood that your father died before he could explain anything about the disk."

"He did," Belle said. "The instructions concerned

where I could find the disk. Obviously my father didn't have it with him in the hospital, so he told me where I could find it.''

With his apparently unerring instinct for asking the most unwelcome questions, Brady pounced on her statement. ''And your brother, who is now in charge of the company, didn't object to you walking away with this extremely valuable piece of company property?''

Belle hesitated for a moment before acknowledging the truth. ''He doesn't know I have it.''

''Ah.'' That damn non-reply again.

''My father asked me not to tell anyone,'' Belle said defensively. ''Until I understood what was on the disk, I didn't feel that I had any right to ignore my father's dying wishes. He said not to tell anyone that I had it, so I told nobody.''

''Pity. Your brother might actually have understood what it said, and that would have given us a head start on finding out who might have stolen it.''

''You're right. It's a pity my father didn't give the disk to my brother. But he didn't—he gave it to me. And now Marge Bruno is dead. So is Wally. And my home is trashed into the bargain. All because somebody badly wanted a disk that I understand nothing about. Now, if you don't mind, Sergeant, I guess I'm through with answering questions. I'm heartsick about Marge's murder and Wally's death, but I don't want to talk about them anymore. I'm tired and I'd like to get started on cleaning my house.''

Brady surprised her by agreeing without protest. ''Have you got friends you could stay with tonight?'' he asked as they returned downstairs. ''Since the thief seems to have gotten what he came for, you're probably not in any danger at this point. But you'd most likely sleep better if you had company. Besides, you shouldn't clean up too much until the insurance people have had a chance to take a look at the damage, and you won't want to look at this mess for the rest of the night.''

Since the thief got what he came for. Belle thought she'd run the entire spectrum of negative emotions already this evening. Now she realized that she'd missed at least one. Until this moment, she had felt no personal fear. She'd been so busy lying to Sergeant Brady, she'd conveniently forgotten that the thief had been unsuccessful tonight. She still had a disk that somebody was willing to kill for.

And sometime quite soon the murderer was going to realize that.

Seven

"**I** came as soon as I heard the news on TV! This is so terrible, honey, I can't believe it!" Donald burst into the house in Officer Kresky's wake, but stopped in his tracks when he saw the state of Belle's living room.

"My God!" he said, his gaze resting with furtive fascination on the bloody mess by the front door. "This is even worse than I imagined."

He swept Belle into a hug that she didn't have time to sidestep. "Poor little you," he said, ruffling her hair. "What a nightmare you've been through! But don't worry, I'm going to take you back to my condo for the night, so you'll be out of here in a jiffy. Let's go upstairs and throw a few essentials into a suitcase right now. Come on, honey. The sooner we get started on your packing, the sooner we can leave."

Belle decided that she was a difficult woman to please. Yesterday she'd complained that Donald wasn't masterful enough. Tonight he'd taken charge, and all she felt was a surge of resentment at his arrogance. But, dammit, he had no right to assume he could bounce into her home and start making decisions for her.

None too gently, she disengaged herself from his

embrace. "I can't leave right now, Donald. The police are still here. Besides, there are things I have to do."

He gave her a playful squeeze. "What could be more important than taking care of yourself, sweetie?"

"Cleaning up in here, for one. Making an inventory of everything that's damaged or broken. Then I need to call the insurance company—"

Donald shook his head. "Jeez, honey, there's no sense in starting a major cleanup tonight—not when you've had such a terrible shock. And if there are phone calls you can't avoid, you can make them much more comfortably from my condo. Is the phone even working here? I couldn't get through when I tried to call."

"It's probably just off the hook somewhere. I'll check it out. Anyway, thanks for your invitation, Donald. I know you mean well, but I'd prefer to stay home tonight."

He began to explain all over again that she was in shock, that she wasn't being rational, and that she needed to let him pamper her. Since he showed no sign of pausing to draw breath, much less allowing her time to speak, she cut across him in midword. "Donald," she said pleasantly. "If you don't shut up right now, this second, there's going to be a second murder committed here tonight."

He stared at her with an air of injured bewilderment, as if his pet poodle had suddenly turned into a pit bull. He quickly explained to Sergeant Brady, who was listening to their exchange with interest, that "poor little Belle" was too traumatized to realize what she was saying.

The detective sent her one of his bland glances. "Is

that right, miss? I'd never have thought it. Are you so upset that you didn't know what you were saying to your friend here?''

''No, it's not right,'' she snapped. ''Donald, please go away. I'm in full possession of all my faculties, and I don't want to spend the night with you at your condo. Not tonight. Not ever again.''

She certainly hadn't planned to break up with Donald in full view of Sergeant Brady, but the words slipped out, leaving behind an astonishing sense of freedom and release. How easy it suddenly seemed to end a relationship that had dragged on for nine uninspired weeks. Belle grimaced in rueful self-mockery. All it took was her father's death, her neighbor's murder, and the trashing of her home, and she finally had sufficient perspective to see Donald for the dishonest man he was, and their relationship for the pathetic mistake that it had been.

She should have known there was no hope that Donald would accept his banishment without protest. Wagging his finger at her, he gave an infuriating little chuckle. ''Belle, sweetie, however hard you try to maintain that independent facade of yours, I'm convinced this tragedy has you too upset to think straight. We're such a perfect match in every way—''

''We're a terrible match,'' she said, resisting the urge to grab his wagging finger and bite it. ''We have totally different tastes and opinions about almost everything that matters.''

''We agree about politics,'' he said at once.

She refrained from pointing out that politics ranked low on her list of things that really mattered. Donald had no sense of irony. He would take her comment seriously, and launch into a long lecture about the importance of civic participation in the democratic process.

"Why do you always make excuses for me when I behave badly?" she asked, sufficiently riled to speak the thoughts she only now realized she'd been nursing for weeks. "Most men would have dumped me ages ago for being way too high maintenance, so why haven't you? What's your real agenda, Donald? I'm beginning to think you must have one."

Donald was obviously more worried about their audience than she was. His gaze flickered uneasily from her, to Sergeant Brady, to the technician packing away test tubes at the front door. "Honey, that's a terrible thing to say. You're not your own sweet self tonight—"

"I'm not sweet!" she yelled. "I—am—*not*—sweet!"

"Honey, of course you are—"

"No, most of the time I'm a demanding, perfectionist pain-in-the-butt. That sweet, boring woman you keep talking about exists only in your imagination."

"You're never boring, honey—"

Belle couldn't stand to listen to his condescending flattery any longer. "Why did you visit my brother in Miami two months ago?" she demanded. "Why didn't you tell me that you'd met him?"

"Your brother?" Donald's face took on the haunted expression of a teenager caught reading *Playboy* magazine. "Er...I don't understand what you mean, honey."

"Yes, you do. Let's stop the pretense, can we? You must have known it was my father who died last week, and yet you listened to me tell you it was my grandmother—'' Belle stopped abruptly, alarmed to realize that Sergeant Brady was still listening, with ears almost visibly flapping. Maybe Donald was right about her state of mind, after all, she thought wryly. She must be a lot more upset than she had realized to bring up a contentious subject such as her father's death when a detective as smart as Brady was sitting a couple of feet away from her, making no effort to conceal his interest.

''Well, I guess it doesn't matter anymore,'' she said, picking up an armful of the books heaped around her feet.

Donald took the books out of her hand and put his arm around her waist. ''Of course it matters, honey—''

Belle grabbed the books back and stacked them randomly on the nearest shelf, a more mature choice than throwing them at Donald. ''Please go,'' she said through clenched teeth. ''I'll call you in a couple of days.'' She wasn't sure if she was more anxious to be rid of Donald, or to prevent him from revealing anything that would clue in Sergeant Brady about Marc Joubert's criminal activities.

Donald's smiles finally disappeared. He stalked toward the door, back straight, the picture of outraged dignity. But Belle's hope that he would leave without any more fuss was short-lived. Instead of going quietly, he paused in the doorway, drawing a heavy, dramatic breath as he swung around to confront her.

''I don't know why the hell you're sounding so damn self-righteous,'' he snarled. ''So what if I didn't mention visiting your brother? You're not exactly a truthful person yourself. It isn't as if those crazy lies about your grandmother's funeral were the first you ever told me. You lied to me about your family from day one, telling me that stupid story about your parents being killed in a hotel fire in Puerto Rico. Poor little orphan girl—*hah!* You were real anxious to stop me finding out about your father, weren't you?''

Sergeant Brady latched on to that remark with the speed of a starving dog attacking a juicy bone. ''Is there something more that I should know about your father?'' he asked Belle.

''Only that Marc Joubert was one of the richest men in America!'' Donald said heatedly. ''Don't be fooled by this crappy little house Belle's living in. Now that her father's dead, she stands to inherit a multimillion-dollar trust fund. When the estate gets settled, she'll be one of the richest young women in America.''

Belle stared at Donald, mute with shock. *He thought she was an heiress.* Whatever motives she'd mentally ascribed to Donald's secret visit to Florida, fortune-hunting hadn't been one of them. How...humiliating—if the explanation for his unflagging interest in her turned out to be something as basic and sordid as money. Had he weaseled an acquaintance with her brother to reassure himself that even though she never mentioned her family, she was still included in Marc Joubert's will? Belle shivered with distaste, although there was a certain satisfaction in knowing how disappointed Donald would be when he discovered that she'd made arrangements for every penny she inherited from the Joubert estate to go straight to charity.

Belle was on the point of telling Donald to leave before she personally threw him out, when a female cop stepped into the house from the garage. ''Excuse me, miss, there's a friend of yours here to see you. He says the phone isn't working." Smiling and fluttering her lashes, the cop beckoned to summon the unseen visitor.

Sandro Marchese walked in.

Now we've hit rock bottom, Belle thought. *This night can't possibly get any worse.*

Sandro's glance swept around the room, but his only reaction to the chaos was a slight narrowing of his gaze as he registered the bloody outline of Marge's body at the door. Without commenting, he made his way across the cluttered floor, nodding briefly to acknowledge Sergeant Brady and Donald Gates.

He stopped a couple of feet away from Belle. He didn't smile, didn't touch her, but she felt his presence in every cell of her body. "You look exhausted," he said.

Immediately energized, she flashed a ferocious smile. "Do I? Next time there's a dead body in my living room, I'll try to find time to touch up my makeup before receiving visitors."

Sandro returned her smile, looking genuinely amused. "I'm glad to see that you're still fighting fit, despite everything that's happened."

"Oh, sure. My neighbor's dead and so is her husband, my house is trashed, and you're here for the second time in two days—but I'm just *peachy keen.*"

"Good. But if you want to get away tonight, I've booked a room at the Ritz-Carlton downtown. I thought it might seem like a refuge after all you've gone through here. And before you bite my head off, it's easy to cancel the reservation if you'd prefer to stay home or go to a friend's house."

He turned to Sergeant Brady without waiting for her to reply. "Hi," he said, holding out his hand. "I'm Sandro Marchese, an old friend of Belle's. How much longer is it likely to be before Belle can leave?"

"A few minutes, that's all. We're almost done here. I'm Detective Sergeant Pat Brady, by the way." The detective shook Sandro's hand. A gleam came into his eyes as he gestured toward Donald.

"And this is another friend of Ms. Joubert's. Do you two know each other already?" He tipped his head enquiringly toward Donald. "You know, I don't believe you ever got around to telling me your name."

"I'm Donald Gates." Donald had used the interruption to get control of his temper, and he greeted Sandro with a friendly smile. "Hi, nice to make your acquaintance. It's always a pleasure to meet one of Belle's friends."

His manner was bizarrely social, as if they'd bumped into each other at a cocktail party. "Do you live in the Chicagoland area, Sandro? I don't believe Belle ever mentioned your name."

"I just transferred here," Sandro said. "I've already discovered that Chicago's an interesting city."

"It sure is. Magnificent architecture, too. Did you move here because of a job transfer?"

"Yes. I came from Washington D.C. I work for the federal government."

Donald gave a hearty chuckle that set Belle's teeth on edge. Or maybe it was just Sandro's admission that he worked for the government that was making her nervous. Why hadn't he told Sergeant Brady that he worked for Customs? Law enforcement officials usually liked to pull rank on each other.

"Oh, no!" Donald exclaimed. "I thought the Midwest was still a safe haven for private enterprise. Don't tell me the feds are shipping their excess bureaucrats out here nowadays!"

Sandro gave a tight smile. "Not all of them. Only the ones that caused too much trouble back in Washington."

"Donald was just leaving," Belle interrupted. "Don't let us keep you, Donald."

If he was irritated by her renewed dismissal, he decided not to show it. He came and stood very close, speaking to her in hushed tones that he obviously hoped would not be overheard by Sandro or the sergeant. "I'll get out of your hair, honey, but I want you to know that I realize we both got overexcited just now. No harm done, though. In fact, it's probably better that we cleared the air. I'll call you tomorrow and we'll straighten everything out. If you remember, we're supposed to have a date."

She wanted to ask him if there were any limits to how much he'd grovel in order to assure himself of access to her mythical trust fund, but with Sandro in the same room, possibly within earshot, she felt constrained to keep her tongue locked behind her teeth. Trapped, she reluctantly agreed that Donald could call her. Anything to get rid of him.

The female cop escorted Donald out through the garage, not without casting a final appreciative glance at Sandro, who was prowling the living area, turning furniture right side up.

Belle didn't bother to contain a sigh of relief when the door closed behind Donald. Brady looked at her with droll sympathy. "This is one of those times when I'm glad I've been married to the same woman for twenty years," he said. "Dating isn't for the faint-hearted these days."

"It sure isn't," Belle agreed. She didn't acknowledge Sandro in any way, but she was acutely aware of him nonetheless. "I'm beginning to think nuns have the right idea. Get together with some compatible sisters and throw up a wall to keep out the men. Chastity seems like a small price to pay for the resulting peace and quiet."

Brady actually laughed. "My great-aunt is a nun, and she'd agree with you, I'm sure. But my daughter wouldn't, unfortunately."

"No, I've noticed we women get smart a bit too late in life. Your daughter's probably still at that sweet, naive stage where she thinks men are regular human beings."

Belle heard a muffled snort from Sandro's part of the room, but he didn't speak. From the corner of her eye, she saw that he already had the major pieces of furniture back in place and was stuffing ripped cushions and foam filling into a giant plastic garbage bag. Donald had offered hypocritical sympathy and done nothing practical to help. Sandro had offered no sympathy at all, but already had the living and dining areas looking halfway normal.

It was crazy to pursue this sort of comparison, Belle knew. Sandro had always been clever at pretending that he was an honorable man who really cared about her. That was why she'd been so crushed when she'd found him in bed with Bimbo Boobs, and why she'd been hurt all over again when she saw the devastating piece of film on her father's disk.

Doggedly, she refocused her thoughts. "It's getting late, Sergeant, and I've decided that I badly want to get out of here. Is there anything else we need to discuss before I can leave?''

Brady shook his head. ''Later we'll have to talk at length so as to compile a list of all the people who might have an interest in this CD-ROM of your father's that's been stolen—''

Belle was acutely aware of the fact that Sandro had stopped his cleanup and was listening intently to her exchange with the detective. ''I really don't think I can help you with any names. I don't know anything about the contents of the disk—''

''No, miss, so you said earlier. But it's surprising what people manage to remember if they're asked the right questions.'' Brady's smile didn't begin to hide the threat implicit in his mild words. ''But I won't bother you any more tonight. The technicians are done with their DNA samples and fingerprints. Photographer's been and gone. I'm off to interview your neighbors before they go to bed and forget something useful they might have seen or heard. However, in case anything pops up tonight and I need to get in touch with you right away, are you planning to stay at the Ritz-Carlton as Mr. Marchese suggested?''

Was she? A room at one of Chicago's most elegant hotels sounded like the perfect refuge right now, except for the annoying fact that Sandro had suggested it. However, irritating as it was to fall in with Sandro's plans, she would be crazy to punish herself by insisting on going somewhere else just to thumb her nose at him.

''Yes, I'll be at the Ritz-Carlton,'' she told Brady. Sandro must have heard what she said, but he just kept on stuffing foam chips into the garbage bag. Unlike Donald, he was smart enough to know when to keep his mouth shut.

"That's fine, then," Brady said. "And here are the names of those cleaning companies I told you about. They're all in the phone book." He tore out a page from his notebook and handed it to her with an unexpectedly friendly smile. "Hope they work out for you, miss."

"Thanks. Do you know if they take calls over the weekend?"

"At least a couple of them do, but I don't remember which ones. Try 'em all and see who can get out here soonest." Brady paused at the door leading into her garage. "I just remembered another important question. How many people have keys to your house? Other than you, that is."

"Nobody except Donald Gates," she said. "He gave me the key to his condo, and I didn't see how I could avoid—" She broke off, not wanting to reveal what a wimp she'd been in her relationship with Donald, especially when Sandro could hear every word. "You surely don't think whoever did this let himself in with a key, do you?"

"Either that, or he picked the lock expertly enough that it isn't damaged," Brady said.

Her opinion of Donald was pretty low at the moment, but Belle wasn't willing to believe that he had trashed her house, much less that he'd murdered Marge Bruno. "The person who did this must have picked the lock," she said with conviction. "Apart from anything else, Donald could never have created this much mess. He's way too fastidious."

Brady shrugged. "People do very out-of-character things when they're acting under pressure," he said.

"Still, we already decided whoever searched your house was a pro, so it wouldn't be a surprise if he picked the lock without any trouble. As locks go, the ones on your doors are real simple to manipulate. In fact, you might want to call in a locksmith so that you can get them changed for something a bit more challenging. And add a deadbolt while you're at it— one that's mounted into a steel plate inside the wall. That won't keep out anybody who's determined to get in. But it'll keep out your run-of-the-mill burglar who tries to bludgeon his way through the lock and then pry the door open with a crowbar."

Under the circumstances, the image of a nameless, faceless intruder smashing down her door was too vivid for comfort, especially since she knew—as Sergeant Brady didn't—that the murderer hadn't found the CD-ROM he'd come searching for. Belle had never been a person who obsessed about personal safety, but standing in the middle of her wrecked living room, with the outline of Marge's body right in front of her nose, she acknowledged that it might take more than a cleaning crew and a couple of replacement locks to make her house feel safe again.

Upon reflection, her stubborn silence about her father's CD-ROM seemed foolish. Maybe she ought to tell Brady the truth about the disk—about the people whose careers and livelihoods would be totally destroyed if the contents of the disk became public knowledge, about the possibility that one of them might care enough about protecting his reputation to come in search of the disk and to kill Marge Bruno....

While she hesitated, Brady was getting ready to leave. "Good night, miss. I'll be in touch. I hope you manage to get a decent night's rest despite all this upheaval. Goodbye, Mr. Marchese.''

Sandro propped the bulging garbage bag against the window ledge. "Goodbye, Sergeant."

In a second or two Brady would be gone. This was her last chance to tell him the truth and thereby not only increase her own personal safety but also ensure that Sandro got the punishment he deserved. Belle drew in a deep breath. "Sergeant Brady—"

"Yes, miss?"

"I—I hope one of my neighbors saw something that will help you to identify the killer." She despised herself for the cop-out, but it wasn't just Sandro whose freedom was at stake. Her brother and even her sister might be at risk, too. Why did she feel this stupid, dumb loyalty to her family, even though they had done little or nothing to deserve it?

"I hope we get lucky, miss. We need to get this murderer locked away where he can't cause any more trouble." Brady opened the door to the garage. "I'll keep you informed, and if you think of anything at all that might be relevant, I'm counting on you to let me know."

"Yes, of course. Sure, I'll do that."

She sounded way too eager, and she could tell from the look Brady sent her that he picked up on her insincerity. Fortunately, one of the TV reporters was waiting inside the garage, right on the other side of the door, and between hollering at the hapless Officer Kresky and refusing to talk to the reporter, Brady seemed to forget about Belle.

As soon as the door closed behind him, Belle was furious with herself for remaining silent. She took her anger and directed it straight at Sandro. "Why did you come here tonight?" she demanded.

"To make sure that you've learned your lesson," he replied grimly.

"What lesson might that be? In your opinion."

"That taking on your father's final project is not only dangerous and illegal, it's likely to get you killed. If your neighbor's murder doesn't teach you that these people going against you are ruthless killers—"

"*These people!*" she exclaimed, fizzing with outrage. "You're a fine one to talk! The person who killed Marge Bruno is probably an immoral scumbag just like you. Same sleazy motivations, same determination to cover his slimy tracks—"

"If I'm immoral, what does that make you?" Sandro's voice was hard. "You're the one whose morals and emotions are so screwed up that you've never been able to separate what's right and wrong from the love you have for your father—"

"Don't you dare lecture me about morals." Belle was foot-stomping mad with frustration, especially since Sandro was exasperatingly correct in his assessment of her twisted family relationships. "You sold yourself for a paltry quarter-million dollars—"

"Only a spoiled Joubert brat like you would consider a quarter of a million dollars *paltry.*"

"Go find a deep hole and jump in it!" Belle seized the garbage bag and threw it at Sandro's head. It burst open, and foam cascaded over him, choking him when he opened his mouth to respond. She stared at him, scarcely able to believe that she'd been so incredibly childish.

And exhilaratingly delighted that she'd had the final word.

Eight

Alternately blowing fluff out of his mouth and cursing in a creative mix of Italian and English, Sandro brushed foam chips from his sweater, his pants, his nostrils and his eyelids. So much for being prepared to tackle this assignment with cool professionalism. Jesus, he'd forgotten what being around Belle was like. How was he going to see this through? Two encounters with her were more than enough to convince him that he would be a gibbering lunatic before this operation was wrapped up. There were limits to how long a man could be expected to survive in alternating states of lust and body-shaking fury.

To hell with professional detachment. Sandro stormed up the stairs and followed Belle into her bedroom. She slammed a suitcase onto the bed, ignoring him as she opened dresser drawers and pulled out various wisps of silk and lace, stuffing them randomly into the case. He tried not to stare. Belle's taste in clothes and hairstyles might have changed from flamboyant to severe since the days when they'd been lovers, but it seemed she still wore underwear designed to reduce susceptible morons like him to the mindless state of a bull moose in heat.

"You have pink foam in your hair," she said, marching past him into the bathroom. "You look ridiculous,'' she added as she came back out carrying a handful of toiletries.

Sandro managed—just—not to explode. Running his hands through his hair and reaping a crop of foam puffballs, he reminded himself that he'd faced down some of the most powerful and vicious criminals in the world and emerged the winner. He was not going to let this woman get under his skin and render him ineffectual. He was thirty-eight years old, and smart enough to know that he functioned a whole lot better when he reasoned with his brain instead of his penis.

"Belle, listen to me for a moment, will you?" He interjected himself between her and the suitcase on the bed in an effort to catch her attention.

"No." She shot him a glance of acute contempt and walked around to the other side of the bed, zipping her toiletries into a plastic pouch and tossing it into the case. She shut the lid with a bang.

"I'm ready to leave now," she said, hitching her purse over her shoulder and picking up the suitcase. "Goodbye, Sandro, thanks for stopping by." Sarcasm dripped from her words. "I sure hate to cut your visit short, but you need to leave so that I can lock up after you."

"I'll drive you downtown to the hotel. I'm headed in that direction."

"Thanks, but I'd prefer to drive myself."

"Fine. Whatever you want." Sandro briefly contemplated the pleasures of shaking Belle until her teeth rattled. He shoved his clenched fists into his pockets, fuming. Why the hell was he going miles out on a limb when she wasn't prepared to give him even a jot of cooperation? He glared at her. "Be warned, however, that if you're not willing to talk with me informally, you will be required to come to my office downtown so that I can take an official statement from you.''

''An official statement? About what, for heaven's sake?''

''Your neighbor's murder—''

''Marge Bruno's murder has nothing to do with Customs. Zilch. Zero. *Nada.*''

''It has everything to do with Customs. We both know your neighbor was murdered because of the CD-ROM your father gave you before he died.''

''I don't know any such thing.'' She shot him a contemptuous look. ''Don't threaten me, Sandro. You have no leverage, and I'm not even marginally impressed by your attempt to impersonate an honest, hardworking public official.''

''Jesus, Belle! Can you stop tossing off insults long enough to realize how much danger you're in? I know the Jouberts have been bred for generations to believe that law enforcement is the enemy, but trust me just this once. Right now, Customs and the cops are the least of your problems.''

''I agree. In fact, they're no problem at all, because I've done absolutely nothing illegal.''

''Complicity in a crime can get you indicted just as fast as actually committing it, as you know very well.''

''I'm not complicit in anything. In case you've forgotten, I'm the *victim* here.''

''Criminals are often the victims of their fellow criminals. The solution is to stop your criminal behavior.''

''Has anyone told you that the past seven years have turned you into a lying, hypocritical pain in the ass? No? Then let me be the first to give you the news.''

She looked as if she was longing to take a swing at him. Sandro heartily reciprocated the feeling. "I'm not going to lose track of the subject we were really talking about," he said with grim determination. "I have no idea what's going on with family politics inside the Joubert Corporation, or why your father turned to you rather than your brother or one of his usual cronies, but I was reliably informed that you'd taken over the Cronus assignment when your father died.''

She blinked, appearing confused. "The Cronus assignment?"

"Yes." Her pretense of ignorance fueled Sandro's impatience. "We have a very reliable informant. He informed us that word is out all over that Marc gave you the only copy of the CD-ROM that contains details of the Cronus organization. If you still have that disk, you're either going to end up a very rich woman or a very dead one. Right now, I'd say the odds are in favor of the latter."

"Word is out *all over* that my father gave me the…Cronus CD-ROM before he died?" Belle stared at him as if he'd suddenly started speaking in an obscure foreign language.

"It's too late to try your bewildered innocent act," Sandro said, wondering for a split second if she really could be as confused as she appeared. He dismissed the possibility, annoyed that he was still vulnerable to her manipulations. He'd heard her admit to Sergeant Brady that a CD-ROM given to her by Marc Joubert was the only thing that had been stolen tonight, and yet she could turn those incredible smoky hazel eyes in his direction, bat her lashes a couple of times, and he wanted to believe that she'd never heard the words *Cronus project*.

Engage brain, he ordered himself. *Disengage libido.* "Try being honest with me," he said. "It would not only be a novel experience for you, but it would produce really great results, I promise."

"You're a fine one to talk about lies," she said, sounding weary. "As it happens, I haven't lied to you."

She was ghost-white, no longer able to hide the toll the night's events had taken. Sandro felt a spurt of compassion that was instantly transmuted into anger toward Marc Joubert. The man had been a genius, with a sweeping grasp of both the theoretical and practical uses of modern technology. On a personal level, he could charm the socks off virtually every human being he ever met, and Sandro didn't doubt that he'd truly loved Belle in his own way. Yet this entrepreneurial genius had lacked the smarts to understand that he was destroying his daughter's life by involving her in his criminal enterprises.

"I wish I could believe you," he said. "When I came to see you yesterday, I was trying to convince myself that you weren't involved in the Cronus project despite everything that indicated the contrary, but it's not possible for me to ignore the evidence any longer. What happened here tonight convinces me that your father handed off the Cronus project to you before he died. The alternative is to accept that Marge Bruno got killed by sheer chance because your home was randomly invaded by a homicidal burglar who doesn't steal anything except computer disks."

"That's not impossible. Coincidences happen.

You, of all people, ought to know that my father would never have involved me in any of his…business affairs.''

"The Cronus project isn't a *business affair*," Sandro said harshly. "You still can't bring yourself to say the words out loud, can you, Belle? Your father didn't conduct *business affairs*. He masterminded criminal projects that put vital American technology in the hands of terrorists and brutal governments that oppress their citizens. People got slaughtered in huge numbers because of what your father did. And he sat back, basking in the glow of community approval, raking in the multimillion-dollar profits. Don't feel that you have an obligation to carry on the family tradition, because it isn't exactly glorious.''

She flinched and the tiny bit of remaining color drained from her cheeks. Then her expression hardened to rocklike impenetrability. "However you choose to describe my father's commercial activities, the fact remains that he had no chance to pass off any Joubert business projects to me, legal or illegal. Until thirty minutes before he died, we hadn't spoken to each other in seven years.''

"That's what you want everyone to believe. It may be true. Or not. We'll talk about it some more when you make your official statement. And you'd be smart to bear in mind that I know you a hell of a lot more intimately than Sergeant Brady does, which means that the more sincere and virtuous you look, the more suspicious I get.''

"You can save your insults, Sandro, they're not effective.''

"Is it an insult to remind you that we were once lovers and that I know you—intimately?''

He would have been smart to shut up about that. Fortunately, Belle declined to be sidetracked down the slippery byways of memory lane. She froze him with a look, but otherwise ignored his reference to their past. "I refuse to talk to you about Marge Bruno's death or the robbery that took place in my home tonight. In fact, I wouldn't make an official statement to you about the items on my grocery list unless you arrested me first. And then I wouldn't speak unless my lawyer was in the room recording every word that we both say."

"Fine, go ahead and call your lawyer. And while you're talking to him, tell him I want to know whether the thief really succeeded in stealing the Cronus disk from you, or whether you still have it stashed away somewhere, waiting 'til the heat cools before you take charge of the network."

"I've never heard of the Cronus project," Belle said flatly. "I have no CD-ROMs connected to the Cronus project. I have no plans to take charge of any network. There, are you satisfied? Gee, I've made a statement, after all. Type it up, and I'll sign it and swear it's true."

Far from being satisfied, Sandro was fast approaching a state of boiling frustration. He wanted to believe that Belle was an innocent dupe and not her father's accomplice—in fact, it was disturbing to realize just how badly he wanted that. But the more she prevaricated, the harder it was to cling to hope that she was being honest with him. Worst of all, the strongest reason he could think of for her to remain silent was that the thief *hadn't* succeeded in stealing the Cronus disk. If so, her life was worth less than yesterday's breakfast donuts. And despite everything, he didn't want the outcome of this operation to be notification that Isabella Joubert's body had been found floating face-down in Lake Michigan.

She had to be fully aware of the dangers of assuming her father's mantle, but he tried one last time to warn her. "Doesn't it worry you even a little that your neighbor is dead? An innocent old woman was killed in cold blood because she poked her head around your front door and interfered with someone's access to the Cronus disk. Is it worth continuing to risk your life on the off chance that you can establish yourself at the helm before you get killed? Your father left an estate worth millions of dollars, so you don't need the money. What's driving you, Belle? Ego? Misplaced loyalty? Lust for power?"

"You're making the mistaken assumption that I know what you're talking about. You also have no proof whatsoever that Marge Bruno was killed by anything other than bad luck." Belle kept her back to him so he couldn't see her face, but for the first time her voice held a trace of uncertainty.

Sandro seized on that tiny crack in her facade. "You're only at risk if you keep silent," he said. "Tell me where the disk is, and most of your problems vanish."

"Do they?" She laughed without a trace of mirth. "Funny, it seems more complicated than that to me." She turned and looked up at him, her expression almost wistful. "Tell me something, Sandro. Why in the world do you expect me to trust you, when we both know that you're for sale? I'd be the biggest kind of fool if I confided anything to you."

She'd made the accusation before, and Sandro decided not to gloss over it this time. If she truly believed he could be bought, then she had every right to be afraid of confiding in him. He decided to gamble on the slim chance that she wanted to trust him and genuinely felt that she couldn't.

"You've accused me several times of being on the take," he said. "It's not true, Belle. I've never accepted a bribe, from your father or from anyone else. If Marc told you that I took a payoff from him, then he lied."

For a split second he could have sworn that the expression in her eyes was bitter disappointment. "My father didn't lie," she said. "You're the liar, Sandro. I *saw* you ask my father for a quarter of a million dollars the day the Zauriac deal fell through. I *saw* you agree to end your relationship with me in exchange for fifteen thousand bucks a month and the chance to buy a new speedboat. With my own eyes, I *saw* you boasting about the incriminating material you had on my father that you'd chosen not to send back to your colleagues in Washington—"

"No," Sandro said, his voice harsh with revulsion. "Belle, you can't always believe what you see. Hasn't it ever occurred to you that appearances can be deceiving—"

"It sure has," she said. "And you're my number one example. At first glance, if you don't get up too close, you look like an honest man."

"That's because I am honest," Sandro said quietly. "I have a hell of a lot of faults, Belle, but taking bribes is one you can't lay at my door."

"Don't you listen?" she said. "I saw you solicit the money. I saw you negotiate the terms of payment—"

"I don't know where you were hiding that day, or

why your father chose to make you a witness to that particular conversation, but what you saw wasn't me accepting a bribe—''

"No, of course not."

"What you saw was my desperate, spur-of-the-moment effort to salvage six months of painstaking investigative work that was about to slide right down the drain."

She looked at him with angry admiration. "You're good," she said. "Great recovery, Sandro. You think fast on your feet, which I bet is a real useful skill when you're a man who plays one end against the other, and then both against the middle. But you're out of wriggle room this time. A plausible lie from you isn't going to convince me that I didn't see what I saw."

For once she didn't hurl her insults with gusto. On the contrary, she sounded desolate, and Sandro found himself fighting the crazy desire to take her into his arms and comfort her. An odd reaction given that only a few minutes earlier he'd experienced an almost equally strong desire to gag her.

"How can you be so sure that your interpretation is the right one?" He was hurt that she didn't believe him, even though he realized he was being irrational. "You expect me to believe that you haven't taken charge of the Cronus disk, but you aren't willing, for a second, to give me the benefit of the doubt."

"You're right," she said after a tiny pause. "All right, Sandro. Convince me that I didn't really see what I know I saw."

It was as close to a concession as she was ever likely to make, and he grabbed his chance. "Just listen without interrupting, okay? Even if you think you know what I'm going to say."

"Yes, all right." She had finally stopped roaming the room, picking up papers, and was really listening to him.

"Seven years ago, I was assigned as lead operative on the biggest job of my career. The director of Customs was seriously pissed by a number of daring thefts that had ended up putting critical technology in very wrong hands. He decided to devote whatever resources were necessary to build a strong case against one of the most brilliant and effective smugglers this country has ever known—"

"My father?" Belle's question was scarcely more than a whisper.

Sandro nodded. "Yes, your father. I got hired on by the Joubert Corporation, which was a feat in itself and took almost three months of intensive preparation. I'd worked undercover before, with some success, but Marc was a lot smarter than any of the criminals I'd dealt with in the past. It took another five months before I finally won Marc's trust. In late July, he assigned the Zauriac negotiations to me, and I got to handle the entire deal on my own, unsupervised. It was a difficult assignment because Zauriac was no more of a fool than your father, and I had to make sure that the missiles we sold were inoperable, which meant coordinating with the military to ensure that I had defective stock. A pretty hazardous deception, considering that Monsieur Zauriac's way of getting rid of unreliable colleagues is to break their legs and put them in a small pond full of starving crocodiles. Fortunately, your father's reputation was golden in the international arms markets, and I was able to coast on the fact that Joubert Corporation products always live up to their promised specifications.

"In the course of my negotiations with Zauriac, I accumulated photos and documents that showed exactly how Marc Joubert operated, at least in this one particular type of transaction. It was good, solid evidence that I was sure would stand up in court, even against the top-notch defense lawyers Marc could afford to hire."

Belle's gaze was fixed on him with powerful intensity. For the first time, he had the feeling she was really listening to him instead of seeing him through the distorting filter of their shared past. "Go on," she said.

"My boss back in D.C. assured me that the Zauriac deal was big enough to get Marc and his criminal partners indicted, convicted and jailed for a good long time. So when your father summoned me into his office a few hours before I was due to fly to Paris to close the deal, I really didn't feel any alarm. I was feeling pretty damn smug, if you want to know the truth—convinced that I'd succeeded where a half-dozen other senior operatives had failed. Then Marc dropped his bombshell. The Zauriac deal was off, he announced."

"Because he'd been tipped off by a crony inside the Treasury Department that you were a Customs agent," Belle said.

"Yes." Sandro drew in a sharp breath. "Consider what happened next from my point of view. If you count the amount of time spent preparing to get hired on by the Joubert Corporation, almost a year of work was about to be blown out of the water. I needed to salvage something—anything, even if it was only the right to remain employed until I could accumulate more incriminating evidence. So I did the only thing I could think of on the spur of the moment. I pretended I could be bought.''

Belle was silent for a full minute. ''It's a compelling story,'' she said at last. ''But it would be more convincing if my father had been prosecuted. Why wasn't he?''

''Because it turned out that I'd been working against impossible odds right from the start.'' Sandro shrugged, feigning an indifference he didn't feel even after seven years. ''The son of a bitch who told Marc that I was a Customs agent was my own boss.''

Belle looked shocked. ''But why? That makes no sense. Why would he send you down to Miami if he didn't want the investigation to succeed?''

''Jim—that was my boss—didn't have much choice. The director was breathing down his neck, demanding results. It was the director's choice to send me, and Jim didn't protest too much, probably because he decided it would be easier to control an operative who was reporting directly to him. And who trusted him, of course. It sure made it easier for him to destroy a lot of the intel I sent back. And who knows? I've often wondered if Jim might have hoped that I would succeed. Putting Marc away for a few years was the only way my boss could hope to get out from under your father's domination. In the end, though, Marc turned the screws, and my boss caved.''

''How did my father turn the screws?'' Belle asked.

Sandro looked at her, debating whether he should tell her the truth. In the end, he decided it was perhaps time to shatter a few of her illusions. ''It was quite easy. Nothing physically violent or anything primitive

like that. Your father had some sexually graphic pictures of my boss with a male lover. He threatened to
send them to Jim's wife and teenage daughters.''

Belle pressed the back of her hand to her mouth.
She didn't speak.

"I'm sorry," Sandro said quietly.

She turned away from him. "There's no reason for
me to believe you," she said. "You've had seven
years to think up a convincing story, complete with
all the horrifying details about crocodiles and my dad
threatening a man's family—"

"Yes, but this convincing story happens to be the
truth."

She was silent even longer before replying. "It's
ironic, you know. You've told me this story and I
admit it's plausible, but I still haven't a clue as to
whether I can trust you. Either you tricked my father
by pretending to be corrupt when you're really honest, or you're tricking me now by pretending to be
honest when you're really corrupt. There are no facts
that I can use to decide which scenario is the true
one."

"You could trust your instincts. You loved me
once—"

"That isn't reassuring," she said dryly. "I've come
to the conclusion my instincts aren't very reliable
where men are concerned. I loved my father, you
know, and yet you've just told me that he was capable
of the most despicable sort of blackmail. And, yes,
for what it's worth, I loved you once. That doesn't
encourage me to trust you. On the contrary. I've recently come to the conclusion that I have some fatal
genetic flaw that causes me to be attracted to men
that other women would instantly spot as frauds,

cheats and liars. Look at Donald Gates, the latest addition to my list of slimeball lovers."

Much as he disliked being lumped in with Marc Joubert and Donald Gates, Sandro had to acknowledge that Belle was partly right. He'd lied to her from the beginning of their relationship right up to the end. He'd used her and deceived her, manipulating her emotions for five long months. From her point of view, he reluctantly conceded, she would be crazy to trust him.

Unfortunately, he would be equally crazy to trust *her* when she claimed to have no knowledge of the Cronus project. The evidence plainly suggested that she was lying. Against that, he could stack nothing except his gut instinct that the woman he had once seduced in the line of duty, and fallen in love with against all his better judgment, was incapable of setting herself up as the head of an international smuggling ring. Especially a smuggling ring that dealt in weapons for terrorists rather than fake Rolex watches, or contraband videos.

Picking up her suitcase once again, Belle gestured toward the bedroom door. She gave him a sad smile. "Trust isn't that easy to give, is it, Sandro?"

"I've told you the truth," he said. "You haven't told me anything."

"You're assuming I have something to tell. Goodbye, Sandro."

He could insist on taking her downtown to his offices, but he knew her well enough to be quite sure that she would tell him nothing. What's more, however tired and worried she was, like all the Jouberts she was much too smart to be tricked into revealing anything during a formal interrogation that she would prefer to conceal. The truth was that he would learn much more from covert surveillance than he would from direct attack.

He said goodbye without fanfare, but stopped at the bottom of the stairs, unable to resist one last warning. "If you have the Cronus project disk, take it to the FBI and turn it in. Among the lives you save will be your own."

And, dammit, that still mattered to him.

Nine

Overnight, the temperature dropped and the rain turned to sleet, producing a chill and dreary morning more appropriate to November than late September. Even so, the weather was more cheerful than Sandro's mood as he got out of his car and picked his way across the deserted parking lot to his office. Belle, it seemed, was living up to everyone's worst expectations.

Despite a direct accusation from Dave Forcier, their current informant inside the Joubert Corporation, Sandro had steadfastly refused to believe that Belle was the designated heir to Marc Joubert's criminal empire. Against concerted opposition from the other members of the task force, and scathing input from an FBI profiler whose specialty was studying the children of criminals, Sandro had stubbornly held to the view that Belle was incapable of taking command of a business that would require her to sell weapons to terrorists. Hell, when he'd known her, she'd even been opposed to the unlicensed sale of rifles for deer hunting.

Sandro's opinions had met with reactions that ranged from mild disbelief to outright derision. The FBI profiler, who'd obviously read Sandro's personnel file, pointed out with patronizing kindness that unresolved emotional conflicts invariably led to bad professional judgments. Even his boss had quietly taken him aside and asked if he would prefer to be taken off the Joubert task force. Trying to sound off-hand, Sandro had informed his boss that an affair, however torrid, wasn't going to affect him for seven weeks after it ended, much less for seven years. He'd known he was lying, and his boss had probably known, too.

The events of the past couple of days suggested he'd been seriously wrong in his assessment of Belle's character. The focus of the investigation was narrowing with disorienting speed, and for an experienced career professional, Sandro was having a hell of a time making the necessary mental switch. It was way past time for him to work on a major attitude adjustment in regard to Isabella Joubert. No more getting distracted by memories of exhilarating days sailing together and nights filled with warm laughter and hot sex. His role in this investigation was no longer anything as trivial as saving Belle from getting herself killed, much less proving that she was innocent of criminal activity. His role was now clear-cut: to prevent her father's international smuggling network from being smoothly reestablished with a third-generation Joubert selling high-tech weapons to low-life terrorists—and raking in the multimillion-dollar profits.

Ken Oliver, chief of the covert ops division of Customs, had been at the office since yesterday morning. Seated behind a desk buried under donuts and foam coffee cups, he wore yesterday's rumpled sweatpants and dirty sneakers, and sported a thirty-six-hour growth of beard.

Monday through Friday, Ken dressed like an upscale corporate lawyer and spoke in sentences that sounded as if they'd been lifted wholesale from a government rule book. For lunch he drank water and ate a tossed green salad—presumably to compensate for the dietary sins of the weekend. Saturday and Sunday, he did his best to look like a homeless person and spoke in short folksy sentences, liberally studded with four-letter words.

On all seven days, he was the most effective Customs agent Sandro had ever worked for or with.

Ken grunted when he saw Sandro, his only concession to a normal greeting. "You're lookin' mighty pretty for a man who's been up all night."

"I took a shower. You should try it sometime. Works great as a refresher."

Ken swigged putrid black coffee and ignored him. "Where's your suitcase? Soon as we've talked, you gotta get out of here."

"My bag's in the car, packed. This had better be good, Ken. I had a heavy date with a sailboat this morning, and I'm real unhappy to be missing it."

"It's smokin' hot. The Joubert woman called her brother. Didn't wait five fuckin' minutes after she checked into the hotel room." Ken gave a smug leer. "I told you she would."

"Why didn't you call me earlier? Belle checked into the hotel eight hours ago."

"She placed the call right away, but she didn't reach her brother until just before I called you."

Sandro tossed his jacket over the back of a chair. "Play the tapes," he said.

Ken grunted again and flipped a switch on the elaborate electronic panel behind his desk. Belle's voice filled the office, sounding harsh with urgency.

"Tony, this is Belle. If you're there, pick up, please. I really need to speak with you." She paused, but a *hiss* of static was her only response. "Tony, don't play games. If you're there, pick up." Silence. "Okay, but you have to call me as soon as you get in, whatever time it is. Please don't ignore this message, because it's vital for the two of us to talk. I'm in room 516 at the Ritz-Carlton in downtown Chicago." She gave the phone number of the hotel and hung up without saying goodbye.

Ken switched off the tape and smirked at Sandro. "She sure is anxious to talk to her baby brother, isn't she?"

"Yep, she sure is." Sandro managed to sound casual, although a feeling of intense disappointment was tying a knot in the pit of his stomach. He shrugged. "She just discovered her neighbor's dead body wedged behind the front door of her house, for Christ's sake. It's not surprising that she wants to talk with someone in her family."

Ken shot him a pitying look as he fast-forwarded the tape. "You gotta stop letting your dick rule your head, sonny boy. I know the Joubert woman is real sexy, but great tits and a cute ass can't be taken as proof of innocence."

Sandro had just enough smarts not to rise to the bait his boss was dangling. He leaned back in his chair, putting his feet on the desk between two boxes of discarded fast food. "I have to believe you didn't call me in at the crack of dawn on a Sunday morning so that I could listen to Isabella Joubert ask her brother to phone home."

"Nope. Got somethin' better for you than that. She called him twice more before midnight, and she called her sister once, asking if Marisa knew where Tony was. The sister didn't answer her phone, either, so Isabella left messages both places. No need for you to hear what-all she said. It was standard frantic. Then her brother finally called back at 5:57 this morning. Listen up and then tell me again how Isabella Joubert ain't had nothin' to do with the family business for seven years.''

Ken had a law degree from Harvard. When he started playing TV hick sheriff, it was invariably bad news for some unwary criminal. The knot in the pit of Sandro's stomach pulled tighter. ''Play the damn tape, Ken.''

''Here you go, sonny boy.'' He depressed the play button, and Sandro heard the *click* as Belle picked up on the first ring.

''Hello?'' Her voice sounded tired and anxious, but not in the least sleepy. She'd been on tenterhooks, waiting for the call, Sandro concluded.

''This is Tony. Why all the phone calls? What the hell is going on, Belle?''

''My neighbor was murdered this afternoon. My house was ransacked while I was out shopping, and she was shot, then left to die on my living room floor.''

''Jesus, that's terrible! I'm sorry.'' Tony seemed to hesitate for a moment, as if unsure what to say next. ''Are you okay?''

''No, I'm not okay. Marge Bruno was a kind old woman with a lot of good years still ahead of her. Her husband was so upset about her murder that he had a heart attack and died on the way to the hospital. I hate to think that two innocent people are dead because of me.''

"They aren't dead because of you." Tony sounded impatient. "Even with your exaggerated sense of responsibility, surely you can figure out that you aren't to blame for what happened."

"That doesn't seem to be the way the police are viewing the situation. They seem to consider me a prime suspect."

"What else would you expect?" Tony sounded bitter. "I hope to God you weren't anywhere near the house when your neighbor was shot. You know what law enforcement officials are like with our family. If you don't have an alibi, they'll make your life hell, even though any impartial observer would say that you're the person who's been victimized."

"Of course I wasn't anywhere near the house. I already told you I was out shopping."

"Yeah, well, take my advice and keep your receipts in case the police decide to come after you. And stop worrying, Belle. If you were out of the house, the cops can't pick on you—"

"I'm not worried because the cops are picking on me. I'm sad about Marge. I feel responsible—"

"You shouldn't. Anyway, why was your neighbor at your house if you were out shopping? How did she get inside?" Tony's voice took on a sharp edge. "Tell me you hadn't given her a key. Jesus, Belle, you didn't do anything that stupid, did you? Dad trained you better than that, didn't he?"

"Of course Marge didn't have a key. I guess she came over to bring me some zucchini from her vegetable garden. Every so often she would leave produce for me on the step by the back door. Maybe she heard someone inside the house and assumed I'd come home. I feel so damn guilty—"

"Belle, get a grip. You always behave as if you want to take on the moral obligations of the entire world. You can't blame yourself because a neighbor got killed as the result of random violence."

"Random violence? It's you who needs to get a grip. For heaven's sake, Tony, you know as well as I do that this wasn't random violence. Marge got killed because somebody has spread the word that Dad handed off his final project to me right before he died. It wasn't a regular thief who broke into my house. Somebody tore the place apart looking for Dad's disk, and I want to know who."

"Holy shit, Belle, watch what you're saying!" Tony sounded horrified, far more horrified than when he'd heard of Marge Bruno's murder. "You're in a hotel, for Christ's sake! How do you know the phone line's secure?"

There was a brief silence. Sandro could almost hear Belle's thoughts ticking over, registering the fact that *he'd* suggested the Ritz-Carlton, and recognizing that he would have had plenty of opportunity to arrange for a wiretap on her phone.

"Maybe there is a tap on the phone," she said finally. "But we still have to talk. Why did Dad give the disk to me, not you? You're the one who's been working with him on a day-to-day basis, not me. I need to know—"

"Go downstairs to the lobby and find a public phone." Tony cut her off. "Don't say another word, Belle. I'll wait for your call."

The tape ended in another *hiss* of static, and Ken clicked the off switch. "Well, wha'dya think, lover boy?"

"Is that everything we got?" Sandro asked.

"Yeah. Unfortunately, she took her brother's advice and went downstairs to one of the public phones in the lobby. We had a tail on her, but our guy couldn't get close enough to hear what she was saying. But we're doin' okay with this tape. We've got a tacit admission between the two of them that Marc Joubert handed off the Cronus project to Isabella."

"Actually not," Sandro said. "What we have is an admission that he handed off *a* project to her. She never mentions that it's the Cronus project—"

"She admits that Marc gave her a disk on his deathbed. She admits that the disk is important enough for a thief to ransack her house. She even wonders why her father didn't give the disk to Tony. If it isn't the Cronus disk she's talking about, what is it? How many vitally important deathbed disks was Marc handing out, for Christ's sake?"

"More than one, maybe."

Ken's answer was a disbelieving snort.

Sandro paced restlessly. "Okay, if that's such an unreasonable suggestion, explain this. If it really is the Cronus disk that Belle has, why did Marc choose her as his heir? And why is Tony going along with the arrangement? Why isn't he furious?"

Ken shrugged. "When you live by your wits, you gotta accept that the one with the most smarts wins. Tony musta realized by now that his sister can whip the pants off him, intellectwise. Besides, it isn't as if Marc went outside the family circle. He chose the Joubert who was most likely to succeed, and Tony is willing to go along with his father's decision."

"Tony doesn't sound as if Belle is in charge of things," Sandro protested. "The opposite, in fact. He's telling Belle what to do most of the time."

"So maybe that's Tony's way of challenging his father's arrangement. He bosses Belle around to make up for the fact that he has no real power. Typical male reaction." Ken swirled coffee around in a foam cup, but reluctantly decided it was too foul even for him to drink.

Sandro jumped on his boss's words. "Yeah, and that's precisely the reason Marc would never have designated Belle as his heir. She lacks two essential qualities for negotiating with terrorists and dictators."

"What's that?"

"No penis. No balls. Macho guys who go around killing babies like to deal with other macho guys, not wussy women."

"So Belle sends her baby brother to deal with the male chauvinist dinosaurs in the Middle East. No reason why Tony can't be salesman-in-chief even if she's the real boss. Plus, if she isn't doing any traveling, there's no reason for us to suspect her. Marc musta hoped that it would take us a while to get on to her. Which would give her some breathin' time to get the network reestablished. You gotta admit, if we hadn't heard from Dave Forcier, we wouldn't have any reason to suspect her."

"That's true," Sandro acknowledged. "Nobody was paying much attention to Belle during the funeral. She could have made contact with a half-dozen people who are really important to the ongoing success of the business, and we wouldn't have noticed."

"Yeah. Daddy Joubert musta known we'd been watching Tony." Ken shook his head in reluctant admiration. "You gotta give it to the son of a bitch. Marc was a fuckin' genius at sniffin' out when the feds were on his tail."

"We're lucky he never realized Dave was working for us."

"Give him another few days. If the ol' bastard had lived another coupla weeks, he'd probably have cottoned on to the worm in his woodpile."

Sandro played the tape again, listening with his eyes shut to cut out the distraction of Ken's presence. The conversation between Belle and her brother bothered him even more the second time through.

"We're missing something," he said when the tape ended. "Belle and Tony don't sound like they're working together. Tony's notorious for being obsessed with security. So why didn't he remind Belle right off the bat that there might be a wiretap on the hotel phone?"

"He didn't think of it," Ken suggested.

Sandro shook his head. "No way. The reason we don't have a tap on Tony's phone is because he sweeps his home and office every twenty-four hours, and his technology is more sophisticated than ours. He would never forget to warn Belle that the line wasn't secure if he expected her to talk to him about Joubert Corporation business."

"So why didn't he warn her? You obviously have a theory. Share it."

"Tony didn't warn her because he didn't expect Belle to say anything that would be of interest to people listening in. At the start of their conversation, he doesn't sound like a criminal partner. He sounds like a brother doing a not-too-good job of consoling a sister who's had a real rough night."

Ken's fingers drummed on the edge of his desk, the closest he was likely to come to admitting that he found some truth in Sandro's assessment. "Tony *is* her brother. He *is* consoling her. Why shouldn't he? There's no rule that says dickheads who sell military secrets to terrorists can't love their family. Marc Joubert's proof that they can.''

"Then here's a practical question for you. We both agree Belle is a smart woman. If she's taken charge of the Joubert smuggling operations, why is she hanging around her house with the Cronus disk in her possession? That isn't smart. In fact, it's damn stupid. She has to be aware of the risk. On Friday night I warned her that I'd seen an intruder running away from her house. That ought to have lit a fire under her—''

Ken grunted. "She didn't believe you. She assumed you were trying to trap her.''

"Maybe," Sandro allowed, not because he was convinced, but because he knew there was no way on earth to explain to Ken the subtle and complex signals that, taken together, had persuaded him only two nights ago that Belle would never involve herself in the Joubert Corporation's criminal activities. "But you haven't explained why she still has the Cronus disk in her possession, and why Tony isn't forcing her to store it in a dark vault, under armed guard. Why take the risk of keeping the disk a single day longer than she has to? Why the hell would Tony allow her to take that much of a risk?''

Ken shrugged. "She's got a lot to learn. Takes a while to digest all that information. Marc had most of the details already stored in his head. He didn't need the disk, except as an occasional reference. Belle has had seven days to absorb names, contacts, and systems that her father spent a lifetime putting together. For all we know, the Jouberts have some important shipment they need to get out, and she has to have the disk on hand to know how to keep it movin' safely. The fact that Daddy Joubert died doesn't mean trade can stop. In fact, they gotta bust their asses to make sure their first deal goes down real smooth.''

That made sense, Sandro conceded. Marc had died so suddenly that neither Belle nor her brother would have had time to ease gradually into leadership positions. Marc's customers would be watching closely to see if the new generation of Jouberts still had the magic touch. Belle couldn't afford to screw up. In the international arms trade, mistakes weren't allowed. Retribution was invariably swift—and it didn't take the form of a polite complaint to customer service.

"Somebody, for sure, thinks she has the disk hidden in her house,'' Ken pointed out. ''That's why Marge Bruno is dead.''

"The most likely person to try to steal it from her is her brother,'' Sandro said. ''In fact, there's a fair chance Belle is putting her life at risk if she trusts her brother too much. She could be arranging to meet her potential killer.''

Ken pondered for a moment. ''In most crime families, I'd say you were right, but not when we're dealing with the Jouberts. In three generations they've never had a real family fight, much less a murder. Loyalty to other family members is drummed into them from the minute they're born.''

"Loyalty can get stretched thin when you're involved in high-risk, high-profit crime. Belle was ready to become a federal witness against her father seven years ago—''

"That's what she claimed,'' Ken said mildly. ''When push came to shove, though, she warned her father and ran away. At the very least, the government's case was decimated by her failure to testify. At worst, she was tricking us from the beginning. How do we know whether she got cold feet at the last minute, or whether it was all a carefully calculated plot to make us think she'd broken with her father?''

Damn good questions. For years Sandro had felt guilty about the ending of his relationship with Belle. He'd relived their last meeting over and over again, wondering if there might have been a less brutal way to end an affair that was seriously threatening his ability to do his job. It was ironic to consider that Belle might have been deceiving him every bit as intentionally—and a lot more successfully—than he had deceived her.

Ken rummaged around in a box of donuts and chose one that oozed virulent pink cream. He bit into it with every appearance of pleasure. ''The Joubert woman is in deep shit, any way you look at it.'' He licked goo from his thumb, his expression either melancholy at Belle's fate or ecstatic over the synthetic cream—Sandro couldn't decide which.

Ken sucked sugar from his fingertips, then shuffled papers on his desk until he found a faxed printout of a plane reservation. ''This is yours,'' he said. ''O'Hare to Miami International. Leaving at eight-fifty, arriving at twelve-forty. You need to get a move on, or you'll miss your plane. Traffic's always a bitch when it rains.''

Sandro glanced down at the fax. ''I take it we're sure Tony Joubert isn't flying into Chicago, despite what Belle started to suggest on the phone?''

''No, she's going to him. We followed her to

O'Hare, and Bill Sosho confirmed that she actually boarded a seven o'clock flight to Miami. She'll be landing just after eleven. You need to move your ass if you're going to catch your plane."

"Okay. I'm out of here."

"Good hunting. By the way, that was a wise decision on your part not to bring in the Joubert woman last night. Much better to leave her out there with enough rope to hang herself."

Ken had ditched his country-bumpkin accent, an event so rare that it was a sure signal they were facing a major crisis. Acknowledging the rare praise, Sandro banished a lingering image of Belle's chalk-white face, along with the knowledge that his motives in failing to arrest her wouldn't bear even slight scrutiny.

"Who's covering Belle once she lands in Miami?" he asked, as Ken walked with him to the main office exit.

"Wendy Lister. She's been seconded from headquarters for the duration. Pete Hintz is gonna work the tail with Wendy. Do you know him? Born and raised in Miami, so he's real familiar with the city."

Sandro shook his head. "He must be after my time."

"You'll like working with him. He's a good guy. Young and enthusiastic, but not stupid. Call me as soon as you've contacted Wendy. She's expecting you to check in at the Hyatt by one-thirty at the latest. She'll fill you in on what the Joubert woman has been doing, and you can report back to me. Make sure you keep me informed. I want hourly updates."

Sandro had worked with Wendy Lister before on several memorable assignments. She was fifty years old, medium height, medium build, mouse-brown hair, the sort of woman you had to meet ten times in a social situation before you remembered her name. Belle, unfortunately, was an extremely observant person with an incredible eye for detail. Tailing her wasn't going to be easy, and Sandro hoped Wendy would be up to the task.

Ken Oliver shot him a shrewd glance. "What you thinkin' about, boy? You got that half-assed dreamy look comin' over you."

"I'm visualizing the cup of real coffee I'm going to buy the minute I get out of here."

"Sure." Ken clapped him on the back, abandoning his country-bumpkin act for the second time in two minutes. A *very* bad sign. "Get your head on straight, okay? Isabella Joubert is the daughter of a terrorist. Her father wasn't just a smuggler—he bought and sold weapons and technology that put the security of this country at risk. If Isabella has inherited her father's job, you've got to stop thinking about the fact that you once fell for her."

"I have no problem with that," Sandro said. "Isabella Joubert is a suspect to me, nothing more."

Ken gave a sour smile. "That's a real good attitude, boy. You say that often enough and you might even learn to believe it."

Ten

Tony was already over an hour late for their meeting. Craning her neck, Belle scanned the other occupants of the crowded café, hoping against hope that one of them was finally going to approach her with a message from her brother. Nobody stirred, except for a trio of Cuban men who left the restaurant hugging every waitress they passed and even giving one buxom server a cheerful slap on the bottom.

Her father had shown a similar lack of concern for the threat of sexual harassment suits, despite repeated warnings from his exasperated lawyers, and Belle experienced a surge of nostalgia, half-irritated, half-affectionate. Even dead, her father could evoke feelings in her that were more powerful than her reaction to most people who were still alive.

Right now, Tony was provoking all of the irritation and none of the affection previously generated by her father. Her brother had suggested meeting on neutral ground in the Havana Café, near the Joubert Corporation offices, and Belle had been more than willing to agree. The last thing she wanted was another frazzled encounter with her mother, or with former employees of her father who might still be neck-deep in illegal smuggling activity. Until she and Tony thrashed out a solution to the problems raised by her father's infamous disk, she didn't want to set foot on Joubert property, either home or office.

But, despite his promises, Tony was obviously not planning to put in an appearance at the café. Suddenly decisive, Belle pushed aside the chocolate fudge cake she'd been nibbling for the past half-hour, and picked up her check.

"Is there a phone I can use?" she asked the young woman at the cash register.

"Right next to the rest rooms." The girl pointed toward the back of the restaurant, indicating a narrow archway leading to a short corridor. "I hope everything was all right with your meal?"

"Everything was great, thanks," Belle said, scooping up change. She made her way to the phone and dialed the once-familiar number of the Joubert Corporation. Tony had told her he would be working at the office until she arrived in Miami, slogging through the multitude of tax and legal documents that had piled up since their father's death. There was a chance, albeit remote, that he was still there. Belle wanted to give her brother the benefit of the doubt. She supposed it was possible that he'd gotten caught up in some sadistic IRS form and lost track of the time. Possible, but not very likely, she thought morosely.

She navigated a voice-mail system that was new since her days as a Joubert Corporation employee, and managed to reach Tony's extension before her quarter ran out. He didn't pick up his phone, but she left a message, frustratedly aware that it was a waste of time. Calling his beachfront condo was no more successful. She left a brusque message on his answering machine, fuming as she spoke. Damn Tony!

This was so typical of him. As a boy, he had always coped with unpleasant situations by avoiding them, and the pattern seemed to be holding even though he was now old enough to know better.

What the heck was she supposed to do now? One possibility would be to bypass Tony and contact her sister, except that Belle was afraid to trust Marisa's judgment. Her sister had always distanced herself from the day-to-day running of the family business—that was part of the reason she and Belle had managed to maintain a decent relationship—and nowadays she had a baby and a husband to distract her still more. What if Belle handed over the disk to the FBI at Marisa's urging, and thus precipitated her brother's arrest? Was that an outcome she could live with?

The fact that Sandro had referred to the disk as part of the Cronus project was another bad sign as far as Tony's innocence was concerned. Belle's Greek mythology was a bit rusty, but as far as she could remember, Cronus was an ancient Greek god, one of the Titans who had ruled the universe until he was dethroned by his son, Zeus.

The father-son parallel was troublesome. Belle really hoped that her father's choice of name for his final project was meaningless, and didn't suggest that Tony had been involved in staging a coup to snatch the family business. Of course there was always the chance that she was buying trouble for herself by obsessing over the name *Cronus*. The disk her father had talked about on his deathbed was simply labeled Charitable Donations, and for all she knew to the contrary, Sandro could have invented the name *Cronus* out of thin air. In fact, he probably had. Based on experience, she had every reason to distrust anything and everything Sandro Marchese said to her.

Whatever name her father had given to his final project really made no difference to her problem, which was that she needed to consult with Tony before handing the disk over to the FBI. So back to square one. Where was her brother?

If her mother were a less-volatile person, Belle could make a simple phone call home and ask if Carole knew Tony's plans for the day. Unfortunately, she couldn't predict how her mother would react to the news that Tony had failed to turn up for a scheduled meeting. There was a good chance that her mother would instantly decide her precious son was in dire straits—if not stretched out in a hospital emergency room, then dead under the wheels of a truck, or tossed onto the roadside by carjackers, unconscious and bleeding.

Belle winced, just imagining the sobbing and wailing as her mother elaborated on all the dreadful disasters that might have befallen Tony. On the other hand, Carole had been accustomed to her husband's disappearing for days at a time on mysterious business trips, and she might casually dismiss Tony's not showing up as unavoidable, simply inviting Belle to wait at the house until he turned up. With Carole, it was impossible to guess her reaction.

Belle wasn't feeling resilient enough to take the risk that her mother would go the high-drama route typically preferred by members of the Joubert clan. The murder of Marge Bruno and Wally's heart attack, following hard on the heels of her father's death, had used up a hefty chunk of her emotional resources. Not to mention the draining effect caused by the trashing of her home and the totally unsettling reappearance of Sandro Marchese in her life. Before she approached her mother for help in locating Tony, she would check out the Joubert Corporation offices in person, Belle decided.

Feeling hot, tired and more worried about her brother than she cared to admit, she made her way to the corporate offices, which were housed in an art deco, two-story building, not more than five minutes' walk from the Havana Café. As Belle had hoped, the turquoise outer doors stood open; they permitted access to an art gallery that occupied most of the ground floor and did a roaring tourist trade, seven days a week.

Although the winter season hadn't yet started, the gallery and lobby were both crowded and the gilt-cage elevator had been locked to prevent tourists wandering upstairs to the various office suites. Belle located the emergency exit and took the fire escape stairs up to the second floor, aware that she was almost certainly wasting her time.

The fire stairs led her into the Joubert corporate offices via a deserted back corridor. The lights were dimmed and the air had a stuffy smell that suggested the air-conditioning was running on minimum, but the offices weren't empty. Belle could hear the faint murmur of masculine voices coming from what had, in her day, been the conference room.

Tony, she thought, indignation overcoming a wave of sentiment evoked by being once again in a place where her father's presence felt very strong. She set off in pursuit of the voices, deliberately stoking her annoyance. Trust him to get carried away with some business meeting and forget about her. He knew how worried she was and how badly she wanted to confer with him about Marc's disk. She'd swallowed her damnable Joubert pride last night on the phone and confessed how vulnerable she felt in the wake of Marge's murder. Dammit, she wasn't paranoid, and she didn't trust Sandro Marchese for a second, but she would be a fool not to acknowledge that Sandro's warnings to her had merit. Her father's disk was a dangerous thing to have in her possession, especially now that word had leaked out that she was the person who had inherited it.

Belle pushed open the door to the conference room, reminding herself to stay calm. She couldn't yell at Tony when other people were around. But when they were alone...boy, did she intend to let rip with her opinion of his selfishness.

Dave Forcier and Evan Connor, her brother-in-law, were the only two people in the room. They stared at her in astonishment as she walked in. Evan recovered himself first. He rose to his feet and walked around the table to greet her with a quick hug.

"Belle, this is a real surprise. I didn't know you were coming down again so soon." He ran his hand through his thinning hair, looking a bit embarrassed. "Maybe I shouldn't be surprised. Have I forgotten that you were scheduled to come back for another visit? Marisa is always telling me that I have the world's worst memory for everything except business deals and sports scores."

"No, I wasn't expected," Belle said, brushing her cheek against Evan's in a ritual kiss. "How are Marisa and Spencer? I hope Spencer's cold is better."

"Marisa's tired, but otherwise fine, and Spencer's on the road to recovery, thank goodness. The new medication the doctor gave us seems to have stopped his coughing finally.'' Evan smoothed out a worried frown. ''Well, I'm sure glad to hear your visit here is a spur-of-the-moment thing, Belle. I was gearing up for a real scold when I got home.''

''Relax, you're safe. Or at least, you're not going to get in trouble on my account.'' Belle smiled at him and he grinned back, appearing genuinely relieved that he hadn't forgotten some crucial family gathering. Marisa had her husband well-trained in humility, Belle thought with a brief but welcome spark of amusement. She wasn't surprised. Her sister had enslaved every boy she set eyes on from the time she turned from ugly duckling to raving beauty in the eighth grade. Evan was merely an adult addition to a decade-long tradition of humbly devoted boyfriends.

''Actually, Marisa's too excited to be mad at anyone,'' Evan said. ''We bought a puppy for Spencer yesterday. The baby and the puppy are both so happy, it's real cute to see them together.''

''Oh, that's great! Spencer will love growing up with a dog of his own. What breed did you choose?''

''Marisa had her heart set on a dalmatian, but I was afraid that might be a bit overpowering for Spencer, so we went with a golden retriever in the end. The breeder assured us that we'd picked a very friendly animal, so I'm hopeful it will work out.''

''You probably made a smart choice,'' Belle said. ''I've always heard that dalmatians need a lot of exercise. They were originally bred to run next to carriages, weren't they? Their coats have all those black spots because that made it more difficult to see the splotches of mud thrown up by the carriage wheels.''

''I don't know much about dalmatians,'' Evan said.

"I always had retrievers myself when I was growing up, and I know they're a very calm and friendly breed. Spencer and the new puppy spent the entire morning rolling around on the patio, licking each other. I couldn't decide who had more fun chasing the balls we threw, Spencer or Horatio."

"Horatio? That's what you decided to call the dog? It's a great name."

"My choice," Evan said proudly. "It sounds suitably self-important, don't you think?"

"I sure do." Belle smiled. "I'll have to come and meet him sometime soon."

"Marisa will be real pleased to see you. She's been a bit down ever since your father's funeral, and it's been worse since you left town. To be honest, she's finding Carole a bit of a handful. Your mother is so distraught that she can't bear to be alone even for five minutes. It's understandable, of course, but Marisa's feeling the strain of being constantly on call. With Tony working twenty hours a day and you being in Chicago—" Evan stopped abruptly, appearing uncomfortable at having made even such a mild complaint about the convoluted family dynamics of his in-laws.

Dave stepped into the breach, saving Belle from making excuses for herself or her mother. Dave stepped over and enfolded her in one of his much-too-close hugs, planting a smacking kiss on her cheek. "It's nice to see you, sweetie, but what are you doing here?" He stepped back and examined her with the critical license of a man who'd known her since she was a bulge in Carole's abdomen. "You're looking exhausted, Belle. What's brought you back to Miami?"

"I am a bit tired. I've been busy catching up since I got home to Chicago, and then the flight down here this morning was bumpy enough that the captain ordered the flight attendants to stay strapped into their seats for most of the journey. My stomach's still swooping."

Dave and Evan both expressed sympathy, but she cut them off. "Actually, I came here hoping to find Tony. It's fairly urgent. I don't suppose either of you happens to know where he is?"

"Well, yes," Dave said, frowning. "You've just missed him. He's gone out of town. You know how much he travels, Belle. You should have called."

"I did call. He knew I was coming." To her chagrin, Belle found herself fighting tears. She hadn't realized just how much she'd been counting on Tony's help until he failed to provide it. Why had he run away? Her family always accused her of being a changeling with a stiff upper lip and a steel spine, devoid of proper Joubert emotions. But her stiff upper lip had turned more than a touch wobbly during her phone call with Tony last night. Surely he must have known that she would never have begged for his help unless she was pretty close to desperate.

She drew in a deep breath, determined to speak calmly and avoid drawing Dave or Evan into a conflict that was hers and Tony's to resolve. "It's really important for me to speak with him. Did he leave word about where he's gone, or when he might get back?"

"You must have been landing at Miami International right around the time Tony was taking off," Dave said. "He's en route to Bangkok, but he should be home within a week. Is there anything I can help with in the meantime? If it's anything to do with your father's estate, I'm an executor as well as Tony—"

"Bangkok?" Belle almost choked. "Tony's gone to Bangkok, *Thailand?*"

"Well, yes," Dave said. "I'm real sorry, sweetie. It was an unexpected trip, I do know that, but there's no excuse for his taking off without a word to you."

"I was supposed to meet Tony myself this morning," Evan said. "I came into the office because there are so many financial documents to handle in the aftermath of your father's death that the administrative situation is getting out of control. The two of us had agreed to spend the entire morning working on papers related to the estate."

"So he stood you up, too?" Belle asked.

Evan shook his head. "No, he left a message that Dave would step into the breach and help me. In fact, from my point of view, it's turned out pretty well. Dave's so good with figures and government forms that we've managed to straighten out quite a few problems in less than four hours of work. I'm shocked that Tony didn't let you know. But he's been really upset by Marc's death, Belle, and you have to make allowances for him."

Belle paced the room, her mind wiped clean of any intelligent thought, not really listening as David and Evan made excuses for her brother's absence.

"The client in Bangkok called Tony at the crack of dawn this morning," Dave said, sounding apologetic, as if Tony's absence were his fault. "The client is one of these billionaire currency traders who thinks he owns the world, and he insisted the deal was off unless your brother got there for a face-to-face meeting within twenty-four hours. Of course, there's not much choice of planes and routes between Miami and Bangkok, so Tony was rushing around like a madman, trying to pull everything together before he had to leave for the airport. Still, I'm surprised he didn't remember to leave a message for you, Belle. He called me to let me know about Evan, so I don't understand how he forgot to mention that you were coming all the way from Chicago just to see him.''

"Maybe there's a message in Tony's office?" Evan suggested. "Or how about a message on your answering machine, Belle?"

She shook her head. "No, he knew I wasn't home last night. And my answering machine is brok— turned off.''

Dave shrugged, clearly not hopeful. "We can look in his office, I guess.''

She'd almost said that her answering machine was broken. And from there, she would have been only a few short steps away from explaining that her house had been trashed and her neighbor killed, and that she had a disk in her possession that people were obviously prepared to kill for.

Afraid of saying something she would later regret, Belle turned away until she could get control of herself. Dave had keys for all the office doors, and she followed him into Tony's office, even though she didn't expect to find a message and didn't care if they did. No message Tony left on his desk could make amends for the fact that, to all intents and purposes, he'd ditched her in favor of closing a business deal.

To hell with protecting the family, Belle thought. She was going to take her father's disk to the FBI. A week of almost sleepless nights was catching up with her, and she suddenly felt tired to the point of exhaustion. What was the point of worrying about whether her brother might be charged with smuggling, or bribery and corruption, when he couldn't even be bothered to call the hotel and let her know that he was flying to Bangkok instead of keeping his promise to meet with her?

In retrospect, she couldn't understand why she hadn't told Detective Sergeant Brady about the disk yesterday. She'd been afraid of putting her brother at risk, but she should have known he would demonstrate the usual Joubert disdain for law enforcement and blithely assume that the disk carried no personal threat to him. As for her fear that the disk would get conveniently lost if she turned it in to an unknown federal agent, none of the people accused by her father worked in the Chicago office of the FBI. Which wasn't proof of their honesty, of course, but it was at least reassuring.

She would fly back to Chicago as soon as she could get rid of Dave and Evan, Belle decided. First thing tomorrow morning, she would approach Wayne, the computer geek in her office, and ask him to make a copy of the disk—something she would have been better employed doing today, instead of flying down here on a wild-goose chase. Transferring data from one DVD disk to another would require specialized equipment, but even if Wayne couldn't make a copy himself, he would know who could. As soon as she had a second copy of the disk, she would put it in her safety deposit box and let the bank's security systems protect it. Then she would contact Detective Sergeant Brady. Once she explained the situation, he would almost certainly agree to accompany her to the Chicago FBI office. With representatives of two different law enforcement agencies present when she handed over the disk, the prospect of the disk being "lost" was minimized still further. An investigation would be launched, and the FBI would go all out to secure indictments against the corrupt officials and politicians her father had bribed. And Sergeant Brady would have an extra piece of the puzzle—a crucial piece that might help him to discover exactly who had shot Marge Bruno.

There would, of course, be fallout from her actions. Most likely, both the Joubert Corporation and the members of her family would be subjected to renewed investigations. But fortunately, Marisa was married to a man whose income didn't depend on the success or failure of any Joubert enterprise, and her mother had a trust fund of several million dollars that was safely invested in a diversified portfolio of blue-chip stocks. And Belle would lose no sleep if her mother forfeited a few more million because the Joubert Corporation was closed down by the feds.

Tony was the only person who was at real risk of serious jail time, which was why he was the person she'd tried to see. He didn't deserve her consideration, but Belle decided she would try her best to negotiate some sort of bargain with the feds in exchange for handing over the disk. Bottom line, she had made a promise to her father minutes before he died and she wanted to fulfill that promise. Marc had trusted her to "make things come right." She'd tried to atone for his past crimes without involving her family, and her attempt to go it alone had resulted not in justice, or retribution, but in the murder of Marge Bruno. She couldn't afford the luxury of any more procrastination, Belle concluded. Time to stop agonizing, and start acting. Without Tony's cooperation, turning the disk over to the FBI was the best she could do to fulfill her father's wishes.

"I don't see a message for you anywhere here," Evan said, riffling through the stack of papers on Tony's desk.

"Tony must have planned to call you from the airport," Dave said, flicking aimlessly through the calendar lying open on the credenza.

"Maybe," she agreed, just to be polite. "But it doesn't matter anymore. I've decided to go back to Chicago and handle things myself. Do you know where I could find a phone book? I need to look up the number for a cab company that services the airport."

Evan immediately insisted that she couldn't leave without joining him and Marisa for dinner, and Dave pointed out how hurt Carole would be if she discovered that Belle had been in town without stopping by to see her. "Your father has been dead barely a week, Belle. You have to see your mother, you know you do."

Yes, she did know it, and reluctantly agreed to stay for dinner. With almost no input from her, Dave and Evan made all the arrangements. Marisa was to leave Spencer with the nanny and drive in from Boca Raton, while Dave would go to pick up Carole from Fisher's Island. Meanwhile, Evan would drive Belle to one of his favorite Miami Beach restaurants so that she could relax over a cocktail while they waited for everyone to join them for an early dinner. Belle did manage to wrest a reluctant agreement that she would be driven to the airport by either Dave or Evan in time to catch the last flight of the night back to Chicago, but that was the limit of her control over the arrangements.

In view of her sudden state of almost catatonic fatigue, she was in no mood to parry difficult questions about why she'd come to Miami. Dave, thank goodness, was so busy rushing off to pick up Carole that he forgot to ask precisely why Belle had needed to see her brother so urgently. Evan did ask a couple of questions, but as soon as he saw that she didn't want to answer, he backed off.

Belle appreciated his tact, and wondered why Marisa had managed to find such a pleasant husband at the tender age of twenty-two, the same age Belle had been when she was breaking her heart over Sandro Marchese. Either her judgment in men was truly terrible, Belle thought, or life was big-time unfair. Her sister not only was smart, beautiful and possessed of the world's greatest hair, she had the perfect husband.

"Do you have a brother?" she asked Evan, rousing momentarily from her lethargy.

"No, I'm an only child. Why do you ask?"

"I was hoping to marry him," she said.

Evan laughed. "Thank you, I'm very flattered. But I didn't know you wanted to get married. Marisa always describes you as a dedicated career woman."

Belle thought about that for a while, then shook her head. "I'm not really dedicated. I like my job, and I would hate for society to go back to the bad old days when girls thought they were failures if they weren't married by the age of twenty. But I want to have children, and to do that right I figure I probably need a husband."

"I'll keep my eye out for suitable candidates," Evan said, sounding amused.

She smothered a yawn, too tired to invent a fresh topic of conversation. Evan took over, proving as congenial and low-key a chauffeur on this occasion as he had been when he drove her to the airport after her father's funeral. He talked about Spencer and his own attempts to cut down on the amount of travel he was forced to do. Almost all the toys his company sold were manufactured in the Far East, the majority in China and South Korea, and his travel schedule was grueling, but not without its rewarding moments, he explained.

"Everyone always imagines that the toy factories in Guangdong province are hellhole sweatshops," Evan said, driving off the causeway and heading toward the south end of Ocean Drive. "It's not true at all. Toys are so high-tech these days that the factories have to be high-tech, too. The Chinese workers who get jobs in one of my factories are the envy of all their friends. And each worker sends enough money to his home village that sometimes one worker is supporting five or six elderly relatives back home."

"I read an article in the *New York Times* that suggested much the same thing," Belle said. "They pointed out that toys nowadays often run on microchips, which have to be installed in conditions of pristine cleanliness."

"That's true. Even stuffed animals talk and squawk these days." Evan slowed as they approached the black-and-gold double doors of a very fancy Chinese restaurant. "We have nurses and a fully equipped clinic inside every factory my company uses as subcontractors, plus we have cafeterias with really excellent chefs." He grinned. "I have to say that I've gotten the impression that the employees appreciate the good food a lot more than the health care.''

''I've always heard that genuine Chinese cuisine is wonderful—something even the Communist government couldn't stamp out.''

Evan nodded as he handed his car keys to a parking valet. ''In the countryside, there are still far too many peasants eating rice every day, with boiled chicken feet as a treat once a week. But there are some magnificent restaurants for the people who can afford them. The owner of this place used to be the private chef for one of the most important officials in Beijing. I tried to persuade him to come and work at one of the factories, but I couldn't really offer him any position that was worthy of his talents, and he turned me down.''

''So you helped him immigrate to the States?'' Belle asked, murmuring her thanks as Evan held open the door to the restaurant.

''No. I didn't know he was coming here until the restaurant was already established and flourishing. I've never managed to find out how he got out of Beijing and ended up here in Miami Beach.''

''Maybe it's better not to ask.''

He grinned. ''I think you're right. China runs on bribery, you know. Not quite as bad as Russia, but the way you get things done is to pay off the appropriate officials. You'll love the food here, I'm sure. Joe—that's the English version of the owner's name—specializes in seafood dishes, but I'm sure he could make anything edible taste fabulous. His menu reads like an encyclopedia of Chinese cuisine.''

It was barely five o'clock and the restaurant was almost empty. Old folks in Florida tended to eat early, but apparently not in this restaurant, where the up-scale clientele kept more sophisticated hours. Evan was obviously a valued customer, and the maitre d' led them swiftly to a comfortable corner table, where they had an excellent view of the dining room and its central decorative feature—a giant fishbowl, at least six feet high, and full of exotic double-tailed goldfish.

Marisa, Carole and Dave arrived almost simultaneously, less than fifteen minutes after Belle and Evan. Marisa looked exquisite in a slender white sheath that was cut low at the neck and showed off every curve of her perfect body, but had intriguing long white sleeves that made the low neck and slender fit appear twice as sexy.

Carole looked tired and sad. She was so unnaturally subdued that she forgot to exclaim or throw her hands in the air even once while she greeted Belle, and when the server arrived to take their orders for a pre-dinner cocktail, she looked helplessly at Dave until he ordered a kir royale for her. To Belle's relief, this faux pas on Dave's part jerked Carole out of her abnormal state of meekness.

"Good heavens, Dave, you've known me for thirty-five years. I'd have thought you would remember by now that I can't stand kir royales. It's such a hideously blue-collar sort of drink."

"Sorry, sugar." Dave sounded contrite, but there was a gleam in his eye that suggested his mistake had been deliberate.

"I'll have a glass of champagne," Carole said to the server. "And please make sure it is champagne and not some ghastly California imitation that's all fizz and no flavor."

This was vintage Carole, dismissing the fruits of a

century of Californian viticulture with an imperious wave of her hand. Belle gave her sister an amused grin, but Marisa's nose was buried in the menu and she hadn't noticed their mother's return to traditional Joubert arrogance. Evan's hand rested on top of her arm, stroking lightly, the gesture so familiar that neither of them seemed to notice it. Belle felt a pang, not of jealousy but of wistfulness.

With her stomach still churning either from the stress of Tony's departure, or the aftereffects of her bumpy plane ride, Belle ordered Perrier. Then she turned to her own menu which, as Evan had promised, was not only comprehensive, but almost as large as a bound edition of the *Ken Starr Report*.

"Let me help you with that, miss." A waiter deftly opened the menu to the section labeled appetizers. As he returned it to her, she saw that he had a slip of paper folded small and held beneath his thumb.

"Thank you." She took the menu and, palms sweating, closed her thumb over the slip of paper. She tried to catch the waiter's eye, but he had already turned away and melded into the group of waiters standing next to the goldfish bowl. Belle realized to her dismay that she couldn't identify which man had actually passed the note to her.

"Will you excuse me?" she murmured to Dave. "Sorry to make you move when you just got settled, but I need to go to the rest room."

"Sure, sweetie. Hurry back." Dave stood up to let her pass.

Heart pounding, Belle made her way to the rest room. She entered a stall and locked the door before she opened up the scrap of paper and read the printed message.

Belle,
Don't tell anyone that you've heard from me.
Call 555-3031 for instructions.

Tony

Eleven

"Belle, are you in there? Are you okay? Evan sent me to find you. Mom said you looked as if you were going to throw up when you left the table."

"I'm here and I'm fine." Hands shaking, Belle crumpled Tony's note and tucked it into her bra. Trust Carole's maternal instincts to work perfectly at just the wrong moment. She gave herself another couple of seconds to calm down before she walked out of the stall.

"Mom's worrying for no reason," she said to her sister, crossing to the sink to wash her hands, which gave her an excuse to avoid eye contact with Marisa. "I'm feeling really tired, but I'm not sick."

Instinctively, she returned to the habits she'd learned when she'd been working as an FBI informant against her own father. Admit a little of the truth, mix in a lie, and hope the whole brew goes down smoothly. She met her sister's gaze in the mirror. "Can you keep a secret, Marisa?"

"Of course." Her sister sounded matter-of-fact. "I think Joubert babies are born keeping secrets."

Belle allowed some of the fear she was feeling to color her voice, hating the fact that the minute she got mixed up in Joubert family business she started to use the truth of her own emotions in order to de-ceive. Sandro Marchese was the only person she knew who had that miserable trick better perfected. "Please don't tell Mom, but my neighbor was murdered last night—"

"Oh, no!" Marisa gasped.

"But that's not all. Her husband was so upset when he found his wife's body that he had a heart attack and died on the way to the hospital."

"My God, how awful! Poor them, and poor you." Marisa reached out and took Belle's hand. "I'm so sorry," she said. "Were you good friends, or were they just people who happened to live next door?"

"We were friends. They were really kind people— salt of the earth, you know?" Belle dashed her hand across her eyes, rubbing away totally unexpected tears. "But I haven't told you the worst. Marge was killed right in my house."

"In your *house?*" Marisa paled, leaving two streaks of soft rose color painted across her cheekbones. Until that moment, Belle hadn't realized how carefully and exquisitely made up her sister was. "But why? What was she doing in your house?"

"I don't really know why she came over, but her body was found lying inside my front door."

"Jesus, that sucks." Marisa's voice cracked. "Were you the person who...found her?"

"No, thank goodness. The police were already there when I got home." Belle provided a carefully edited version of the police theory that Marge had been killed because she intruded at the wrong moment during a burglary. She left out all mention of her father's disk, but Marisa, unfortunately, put two and two together and came up with a perfect score of four.

"Is this why you wanted to see Tony so urgently?

I know you, Belle. You'd never have come rushing down here the day after your neighbor was murdered unless you thought the burglary of your house had something to do with Joubert Corporation.''

Belle scrambled to find a convenient scrap of truth in which to bury her lies. ''Of course I thought the burglary was something to do with the family business,'' she said. ''Wouldn't you, in my shoes?''

''Probably not.'' Marisa smiled wryly. ''I have a less suspicious nature than you—''

''You don't have to be suspicious to see a link in this case. Dad dies, I go back to Miami for the first time in seven years, and the day after I return to Chicago my home is invaded and searched from top to bottom, but the thief takes almost nothing—not even a TV or an expensive camera that was sitting on the dressing table in my bedroom. On the other hand, my computer has been stolen, presumably because the thieves suspect I may have interesting information on the hard drive. You don't have to be paranoid about our family's business activities to conclude there's probably a connection.''

Marisa thought for a moment or two, then nodded in agreement. ''Yeah, I guess you're right. But you have to remember that people's homes get robbed all the time, and if the burglars are high on drugs, they do totally weird things. We don't like to accept that something is coincidence, because human beings are programmed to see connections and logic where none really exist.''

Belle suppressed a sigh of relief that her sister wasn't pressing for details about precisely what Joubert property the thief might have been looking for. ''I sure would like to think it was a random burglary, because I don't want to spend the next several months of my life trying to convince a bunch of Dad's former cronies that I have absolutely nothing of his that they could possibly want.''

Marisa's eyes fixed on Belle with sudden intensity, assessing her with unexpected shrewdness. ''You're wondering if I was lying to you when we talked after Dad's funeral, aren't you? You're wondering if the Joubert Corporation is still smuggling stolen technology overseas, and this is some sort of fallout from an illegal deal they had in the works.''

''No, of course not. I accept your word—''

''Yes, you probably do, but you're asking yourself if I stayed close enough to Dad and Tony to know what they've really been up to for the past few years. The answer is that I *have* kept closely in touch, and I promise you, Belle, that Dad got out of the smuggling business years ago. The Joubert Corporation still sells military supplies to a bunch of foreign despots that you wouldn't approve of, but at least the sales are entirely legal.''

Belle wanted to believe her sister, but that was a lot harder to do now than it had been in the aftermath of her father's death. She didn't doubt that Marisa believed what she was saying, but Tony's note scratching against her skin was proof that her sister didn't have a clue about what was going on at Joubert Corporation. The reality was that neither her sister, nor anyone else outside the circle of secret inner management could say with certainty that Marc had abandoned his old ways—a fact she was acknowledging dangerously late, Belle now realized.

She tossed the paper towel she'd used to dry her hands into the trash. ''Do me a favor, Marisa? Don't say anything about Marge's murder to Mom, please. She has enough on her plate right now." She grimaced. "And, to be honest, so do I. You know what Mom's like. She'll have instant hysterics and send me home to live with an armed bodyguard until the police find the murderer. I couldn't cope."

Marisa grinned. "I don't know, a cute bodyguard might add an interesting spark to your life."

An image of Sandro Marchese flashed into Belle's mind. How odd that she should associate him, of all people, with her personal safety. "You're right," she said to her sister, forcing a smile. "I'll consider hiring one. I'm thinking blond and tanned, with biceps larger than his I.Q."

Marisa gave a mock sigh. "Sounds yummy to this old married woman."

"I'd have thought Evan was enough of a hunk for one woman. You're lucky, he's a really nice guy. I wish I'd had the chance to know him better over the past seven years."

"You did the best you could," Marisa said. "So did I. You wanted to keep a safe emotional distance from the rest of the family, and I spent two years obsessing about getting pregnant. That made meetings difficult for both of us."

"Still, I wish we'd done a better job of keeping in touch. When you think how close we were as teenagers, a phone call once a month really didn't cut it."

Belle's stomach ached with the tension of dissembling, and the frustration of not being able to reveal the true problem she was facing. "Anyway, we don't need to tell Mom about my neighbor's murder, agreed? Because that means we'll spend the rest of the evening alternately soothing Mom and rehashing every last detail of the murder. Which I absolutely, positively don't want to do."

"All right, I won't say anything. But you have to call me when you get home, okay? I want to hear how you're doing and whether the police find the killer."

"I'll call," Belle promised. "And now we'd better get back to the others. I'm surprised Mom hasn't come bursting in, demanding to know if I'm dying of food poisoning."

"You haven't eaten anything yet!"

"Since when did that ever stop Mom from fussing?"

Belle was trembling as they walked back to their table, totally drained by the effort of keeping silent about the message from Tony. Obviously he wasn't in Bangkok, but where was he? And why did he want everyone to think he was on the other side of the globe?

She was frantic to ditch Marisa so that she could call the number her brother had given her, but it proved impossible. Marisa wanted to chat about their mother and the brave efforts she was making to contend with her grief, and she never strayed more than a couple of steps from Belle's side. They passed by the phone with Belle still trying to think of any halfway credible excuse to stop and make a phone call. She was sure there had to be one, but her brain refused to work fast enough to come up with anything believable.

Back at the table, Belle ordered her meal in a state of mental fugue and was astonished when the waiter brought her an entrée of tiger shrimp and seaweed fried with honey-coated walnuts. How in the world had she managed to order this with no memory of having done so?

She attempted to choke down enough food to avoid provoking awkward questions, while at the same time trying to come up with an excuse to leave the table, but the double-pronged effort left her virtually mute. After a while, she realized that Marisa was covering for her, filling in gaping holes that Belle kept leaving in the conversation, and fixing attention on herself with cute stories about Spencer and the new puppy.

Belle was grateful to her sister, but as the meal progressed, gratitude vanished and her anxiety morphed into all-consuming panic. It was now almost an hour since the waiter had passed her that note. How long was Tony likely to stay in the same place? It seemed probable that he'd gone undercover because he was dodging pursuit by...somebody. Who? And how the heck had he known she'd be at this restaurant, to arrange for the waiter to slip her the note?

No, don't wander down that alley right now, Belle warned herself. *Concentrate.* The mechanics of how Tony had arranged to contact her didn't matter. What mattered was that he obviously didn't want the other family members to know he was still in town. But why not? Because he didn't want them to worry? Or for some other, even more ominous reason?

Belle decided she couldn't eat another mouthful, or listen to one more of Dave's bad jokes. He was currently telling some story in dubious taste about a Jewish meatpacker and the Pope. Dave usually managed to insult a minimum of two ethnic groups per joke. She was going to call Tony even if her excuse for leaving the table sounded hopelessly flimsy. Unfortunately, she couldn't simply announce that she needed to make a phone call, because Evan and Dave both had cell phones. They would immediately volunteer their phones and then would expect her to make the call without leaving the table—the exact opposite of what she needed.

Belle concluded that another trip to the bathroom was the only way she could guarantee a few minutes of privacy. "I'm really sorry," she murmured to Dave the second he reached his punch line. "Could you excuse me again, please?"

"What's up, sweetie?" Dave pulled her chair back, not really curious, but voicing a question she couldn't ignore.

Belle lowered her voice. "I have kind of an upset stomach—"

Dave frowned in concern. "Not something you ate here, I hope?"

"No, my entrée is wonderful. It must be all that turbulence on the plane this morning. I'll be right back, Dave."

Marisa looked up, brow wrinkled in concern. "Would you like me to come with you, Belle?"

Belle hoped her teeth weren't visibly gritted. "No, thanks. I'll be fine. Enjoy your dinner—the food here is so great."

She hurried toward the ladies' room. At the last moment, when she was sure nobody at the table was watching, she turned right instead of left and went to the phone.

She reached down the front of her blouse and pulled out Tony's note, twice dialing the number incorrectly because her fingers were stiff and clumsy with nerves. The third time, she managed to dial correctly and the phone was answered on the first ring—

but not by Tony. A male voice she didn't recognize said hello, but gave no clue as to who he was or where he was located.

"This is Isabella Joubert," she said, terrified that she would be told Tony had already left, and was no longer available at this number. "My brother, Tony Joubert, asked me to call him."

"You took a long time to get back to us, Ms. Joubert."

"I'm sorry. The note said not to tell anyone, and I had a problem getting away without drawing atten—"

"You've left us with very little time to complete our assignment. Here's the deal. Nonnegotiable terms. If you want to see Tony alive, bring the disk your father gave you to the Tropicana Hotel at Miami Airport. Room 823. Give us the disk, and you get your brother back, more or less in one piece. You have two hours to get here with the disk. Come alone, and don't tell anyone where you're going. Bring law enforcement with you, and Tony is a dead man."

More or less in one piece? Belle swallowed over the huge lump of fear in her throat. "Let me talk to Tony. I have to talk with him. How do I know that you have him, or that he's really alive?"

"Belle, for God's sake bring the disk." Her brother's voice was a hoarse, broken murmur, but unmistakably his.

"Tony, are you all right?"

"Come...soon. Do what they say. They're not...joking."

The phone clicked. Belle wasted several valuable seconds listening to the hum, then she dropped the receiver back into its cradle and started to run.

"Excuse, miss. Watch out for the hot dish. You okay?" A waiter stopped her just before she ran head-long into him.

"Yes, yes, I'm okay." Belle dodged around the waiter and started to run again, but the brief exchange had taken enough of the edge off her blind panic to return her to reality. She stopped running and started thinking. The voice on the phone had demanded se-crecy, and that meant she couldn't afford to draw at-tention to herself by wild behavior.

Belle tried to look untroubled as she approached the table, but just as she passed the giant fishbowl she came to a dead halt, her mind screaming out in panic.

What hotel room had the voice told her to go to?

She couldn't remember. What the hell room num-ber had the kidnapper given her? Jesus, her brother's life was at stake and she couldn't even remember a simple room number.

Belle felt herself coming unglued. Her knees buck-led, and she had to grab a nearby table to support herself. What had the kidnapper said? *822? 832? 823?* How could she possibly have screwed up al-ready on something that was literally a matter of life and death?

Please, God, let me remember. She had rarely of-fered such a fervent prayer, but her mind remained stubbornly empty of divine inspiration.

Okay, don't obsess. Move on. Do what has to be done now. Worry about the problem of the room num-ber later, when you get to the hotel. Belle glanced down at her watch and then had to look again because she hadn't registered the time. Six o'clock. Five minutes had passed since she hung up. She had to assume Tony's captors were counting their deadline down to the minute, which meant that she had until just before eight to get to the hotel and hand over the disk.

How was she going to do that without telling anyone what had happened? Panic spiraled again, bringing bile to the back of her throat. She forced it down.

One step at a time.

She was booked on the last flight to Chicago, departing Miami at eight-fifteen. The restaurant was about a half-hour drive from the airport, and Dave knew she had no bags to check, so he was probably planning for everyone to eat a leisurely dessert, enjoy coffee, and leave the restaurant in about forty-five minutes. Somehow she had to persuade him to change his plans and take her to the airport right now. That forty-five-minute window might be all she had to save her brother's life.

"You've been gone a long time," her mother said when she returned to the table. Strangely, Carole sounded more anxious than condemning. "Are you sure you're not sick, dear? Why do you keep jumping up and down like this?"

It wasn't much of an opening, but Belle seized it anyway. "Actually, I'm feeling pretty miserable." She managed a wan smile. "Not to go into gory details or anything, but dinner didn't go down too well."

Carole was already pushing back her chair. "We should go home. You should spend the night with me and allow yourself to relax. If you're not feeling well you can't possibly fly, and you know that, Belle. Planes are terrible places for sick people. You could take really ill, and there would be no way to get you medical attention."

Perhaps as a reaction to the suddenness of Marc's death, Carole had started to fuss over every cough and sniffle by any member of her family, and she looked genuinely panicked to hear that Belle was feeling unwell.

Belle hardened her heart and delivered a brusque, no-nonsense reply. She simply couldn't afford to let compassion for her mother put Tony's life at risk. "Thanks for the invitation, Mom, but I really do need to get back to Chicago. I have a very important meeting first thing tomorrow morning. I'm making a presentation to the president of my division, and I can't let a minor inconvenience like an upset stomach ruin my chance to shine."

"Nothing's more important than your health," Carole said. "When you're my age, you'll realize that jobs come and go, but your family and your health are important forever."

Marisa intervened unexpectedly, saving Belle from the need to ride roughshod over her mother's concerns. "Evan, you'll see that Belle gets to the airport safely, won't you?"

Evan looked a little surprised, but he rose to the occasion. "Sure, I'll take great care of her. Don't worry, Carole. Belle can snooze on the plane, and she'll be fine. Why don't we leave for the airport right away? Then you won't be rushed, and you can take everything nice and slow and easy. There's no point in being rushed if you're not feeling up to par."

"That would be great. Thanks for the offer, Evan. I appreciate it." Belle could barely believe her luck. She'd expected her brother-in-law to support the idea that she spend the night in Miami with her mother. She scrambled to her feet before anyone could suggest a different arrangement, and before Evan could retract his offer. She hugged her mother and sister and submitted to Dave's inevitable slobbery kiss, thanking them all profusely for the wonderful meal and promising that she would come back soon for a longer visit.

Evan watched the round of farewells with a sympathetic gaze, not saying much until they were in the car and on the way to the airport. "I hope you don't think I interfered, but you looked as if the top of your head was going to blow off if you didn't get out of there," he said as they crossed the causeway onto the Airport Expressway.

"Don't apologize," Belle said. "I think you saved my sanity." The temptation to tell Evan what was really going on was enormous, but she didn't dare take the risk. She didn't know him well, and he might insist on driving straight to the FBI or to the nearest police station to get help, which would put Tony's life seriously at risk. Citizens from law-abiding backgrounds tended to have what Belle considered a naive faith in the ability of the police to right wrongs and punish criminals.

"Dave meant well in arranging that dinner, but he's so concerned about Carole that he doesn't always consider other people's feelings," Evan said.

"I wasn't in the mood for a family dinner," Belle admitted. "Since Tony didn't have the courtesy to stick around when he knew I badly needed to consult with him, I guess I'm feeling grouchy and out of sorts. Add a case of upset stomach, and I have to confess I was one unhappy camper."

Belle wasn't sure how she managed to speak her brother's name without faltering, but she must have pulled it off, because Evan responded exactly as she'd hoped.

"Dealing with family can be a real pain in the rear end," he said. "I love my family, but what I love best of all about them is that they live in Hawaii. Every last one of them is still resident on Oahu, right down to the eccentric maiden aunt and a pair of slightly sleazy second cousins. God bless 'em all. Believe me, Belle, I understand completely why you chose to live in Chicago."

He surprised a genuine laugh out of her. "I don't believe your family could be as hard to cope with as mine. No other family could be as difficult as the Jouberts."

"You've never met my parents." Evan spoke with feeling. "My mother is an artist—a painter—and when she's in the throes of creation she isn't eccentric, she's flat-out nuts."

"Your mother's an artist? How interesting. What does she paint?"

"Landscapes, mostly, but some portraits if she finds a face that appeals to her. She does a roaring trade with the tourists, and takes her art much too seriously to have time to attend to mundane details like cooking meals, or cleaning house—so we pretty much grew up in a state of semi-controlled chaos. Fortunately, now that my dad is retired, he doesn't seem to mind being relegated to the role of chief cook and bottle washer. It wouldn't suit me, that's for sure. I guess I'm really glad Marisa decided to give up her career and stay home with the baby."

"Wait 'til Spencer turns into a teenager and starts behaving as if one of the Pod People has taken over his body," Belle said. "You'll regret every unkind thought you've ever had about your parents, and realize what wonderful people they were just to get you through the teenage years with all your limbs still attached.''

''I'm sure you're right. I was pretty wild back then.'' Evan launched into a hair-raising story about a teenage adventure with his sleazy cousins, the Neanderthal Twins, as he called them.

Under normal circumstances, Belle would have been captivated by Evan's knack for entertaining chitchat. As it was, she felt depleted by the strain of finding appropriate responses, using the tiny percentage of her brain cells that wasn't consumed with worry about Tony. Fortunately, she seemed to do a good enough job that their conversation kept ticking over, despite minimal input on her part. It was a great relief when they drew up alongside the entrance to the check-in level of the airport. A covert glance at her watch showed that it wasn't even seven o'clock. Thank God, she still had a full hour to get to the hotel and find the appropriate hotel room.

823.

The number popped into her head with sudden clarity. 823. Yes! Thank you, God. She'd finally remembered the room number Tony's kidnapper had given over the phone. It had to be a good omen, Belle thought, clinging to a fragile thread of optimism.

''Thanks so much for the ride,'' she said to Evan, trying not to show her eagerness to be rid of him as she jumped out of the car. ''But please, don't even think about parking the car. I can manage just fine from here.''

Evan lifted her satchel out of the back seat. ''At least let me carry this inside for you.'' He jumped out of the car, almost bumping into an elderly white-haired woman being dropped off just ahead of them.

"There's no need to come into the airport," Belle said, taking the satchel and draping it over her shoulder. She fixed her mouth into a frozen smile, hoping she didn't look as frantic and insincere as she felt.

"It's no trouble," Evan said.

"No, really, you've been more than kind. Why risk a ticket? Honestly, there's no need. This overnight bag is as light as can be, and the check-in counter is just over there."

Evan, thank goodness, didn't seem to feel any need to prove his machismo by pretending that she was incapable of checking herself in for a routine flight to Chicago, more than an hour before flight time. He gave her a quick hug, wished her a safe journey, and was driving away less than five minutes after they first pulled up at the curb.

Had she done the right thing in sending him away? Belle wondered. He was such a practical, down-to-earth sort of man. Maybe she'd missed out on a chance for help in rescuing Tony by not telling Evan the truth. Maybe she should summon him back...call the restaurant...or leave a message on his answering machine at home.

Too late to revisit that decision now. *Move on.* There was at least one bright spot in her situation. She had left her overnight bag locked into the trunk of her car at O'Hare airport, along with the printout of her father's disk. Now she was deeply grateful that she hadn't wanted to lug her case around with her. Even when she handed the original of her father's disk over to Tony's kidnappers, she would still have a record of most of the material Marc had prepared.

Not in quite such a compelling form as the one that included snippets of film and lots of color photos, but at least enough for law enforcement officials to bring indictments against most of the people her father had bribed. With luck, she would be able to ransom her brother and still fulfill her promise to "make it all come right."

Belle found the shuttle stop, took a minivan over to the hotel, and was standing in front of the hotel elevators by seven-eighteen. After the stress of getting away from the restaurant, things seemed to be going almost too easily. She was so tense, she almost expected to *twang* as she walked. Part of her brain was parked on a mental sideline, observing her actions and waiting....

The elevator arrived and Belle stepped in, along with a young man and a middle-aged woman. "What floor?" the woman asked politely, her hand poised over the buttons.

"Eight, please," Belle said, inspecting them covertly. It might be paranoid, but she half expected everyone in the hotel to be a kidnapper.

"Seven," the man said. He sounded bored.

The woman pressed the buttons for floors seven, eight and nine. The doors slid shut and the elevator started its ascent. It was the glass-walled type that always made Belle feel giddy, although from a hotel-security point of view the glass probably prevented a lot of unpleasant incidents and accusations of sexual harassment. Belle turned her back to the dizzying view, her gaze skimming past the man and coming to rest on the woman, who was carrying a large, nondescript purse that looked vaguely familiar.

She'd seen it before, or one just like it, only a few

minutes earlier. Evan had bumped into an elderly woman being dropped off at curbside, and the woman had carried a big, useful black purse identical to this one. But that woman had been old, Belle thought. This woman was no more than forty.

Had the other woman really been old? Or did she just have snow-white hair, which was so conspicuous that it was the only thing about her that Belle had noticed? In fact, Belle hadn't even glanced at the woman's face, and she would never have paid the slightest attention to the woman's purse if she hadn't been so fixated on Evan, watching his every move because of her frantic need to be rid of him.

There was an odd tension in the elevator. She was being followed, Belle was sure of it, and the tension emanated not just from herself, but also from the woman. Perhaps the woman sensed that she'd been recognized?

The kidnappers must have followed her from the restaurant, Belle thought. Were they going to try to steal the disk without releasing Tony? Belle grew very still, bracing herself for the attack she was sure would come. What were they waiting for? The elevator's glass walls suddenly seemed to offer very sparse protection. Were the man and woman working together, or was he an innocent bystander? Was the woman just waiting for him to get off the elevator before whipping out a gun?

The elevator stopped on the seventh floor, and the man got off without speaking. At the last minute, Belle slipped through the sliding doors after him, and waited with her back pressed flat to the wall, heart pounding. She wanted to get away from the elevator as fast as she could run, but that would send her straight into the arms of the young man. Was he going to turn and attack her?

The elevator doors didn't burst open and, far from attacking her, the man seemed unaware she'd gotten out. Totally ignoring her, he strolled down the hallway and turned the corner. Belle sucked in great gulps of air until she got a grip on herself. Then she sprinted toward the neon-lit Exit sign, and found the stairs. She ran up them two at a time, panting more from fright than from exertion by the time she reached the carpeted hallway on the eighth floor.

Maybe stress was causing her to overreact, Belle thought. The purse had been nondescript. Could she be sure she'd recognized it? Probably not, she decided, finding the arrows that pointed in the direction of room 823, and heading that way.

In retrospect, she realized that it had been mighty trusting of her to come to this hotel exactly as instructed, but she'd instinctively assumed that Tony's captors would keep their side of the bargain. In some ways, her reaction had been conditioned by experiences she'd had while working for Joubert Corporation. Her father's negotiations with his criminal customers hadn't exactly followed the Sears' salesman's handbook, but, nevertheless, a twisted sort of honesty had prevailed within the smuggling community. It had to, in order for the system to work. Smugglers like her father weren't going to invest millions of dollars buying contraband weapons if their customers refused to pay their bills. Conversely, dictators weren't going to hand over millions of their ill-gotten gains unless they were sure the weapons they bought killed and maimed with superb efficiency. Coming from that mind-set, Belle had simply assumed that if she handed over the disk, the kidnappers would hand over Tony.

The incident in the elevator—or maybe she should call it a nonincident—reminded her that she had been way too gullible. There were dozens of reasons why criminals might take the disk from her by force, and not surrender Tony. They might demand a cash ransom, since the Jouberts were known to be rich and this would be an easy way to acquire some spending money. They might think she had access to valuable technology that they could squeeze out of her without paying a fair price, now that they didn't have to contend with her wily father.

Last, but far from least, the realization dawned on her that she had no idea if these people were telling the truth when they claimed to be holding Tony captive. She'd heard his voice on the phone—but had he answered a specific question she asked? Not really. Those phrases could have been recordings made any time and any place. In fact, for all she knew to the contrary, Tony could be landing in Bangkok right about now. Come to think of it—and thinking seemed to be something she'd done too little of for the past couple of hours—Tony had personally called Dave this morning to say he was flying to Thailand. So if the kidnappers really did have Tony, they must have seized him in the narrow window of time between his phone call to Dave and the scheduled departure of Tony's flight to Bangkok.

Before she marched into room 823 and handed over her father's disk, she needed to stop and reconsider her options, Belle decided. Hearing footsteps approaching from behind her, she dodged into the alcove that contained soda machines and an ice maker, tucking herself as much out of sight as she could manage between the two machines. It was paranoid to assume that every human being on the eighth floor was out to get her, but right now Belle was more than willing to show respect for her most paranoid fantasies.

The footsteps passed by, fading into the distance. Suddenly realizing how she could tip the odds in her favor, Belle removed her father's disk from her purse and slipped it under the soda machine. From the dust she encountered, it seemed safe to assume nobody had checked under there in months.

Relieved that she'd finally shown at least a smidgen of foresight, she walked quickly down the remaining stretch of hallway to room 823. Now, if she was searched, she wouldn't lose the only bargaining chip she possessed before she even checked out that the kidnappers truly had her brother. She was much more likely to win his release if she refused to tell the kidnappers where the disk was until they agreed on a way to exchange custody of Tony for custody of the disk.

Room 823 was located in a corner and had double doors leading off its own mini-hallway, suggesting it might be a suite rather than a normal room. Belle knocked at the door and discovered that it was unlocked. The door gave way, swinging open at the first touch of her hand. She hesitated on the threshold, afraid that she would walk straight into a trap if she went inside. She was damn near volunteering to get bopped on the head, or worse. This situation was a setup if ever she'd seen one.

Belle knocked again, rapping on the side panels, but when there was still no response, she decided she had no choice but to go in. She kicked the door open with all the force she could muster, springing back so that she could dodge any hail of bullets that might be aimed in her direction.

There were no bullets, no shouts—only silence. Shielding her body with one of the doors and peering cautiously around the rim, Belle discovered she was looking into an empty room, with drawn curtains and only a single low-wattage lamp switched on for illumination.

"Hello?" she said. "Is anyone there?"

Nothing. What had she expected? Belle asked herself grimly. A bunch of people jumping out from behind the furniture? *Surprise! We're your friendly neighborhood kidnappers.*

She stepped through the doors and edged slowly forward. She'd guessed correctly. This was a suite rather than a standard room, and the sitting area where she found herself was crowded with rattan furniture— but empty of people. The drapes were floor to ceiling and looked as if they might conceal sliding glass doors leading to a balcony. In a minute, when she felt a little more courageous, she would open the drapes— and hope that the bogeyman wouldn't be waiting behind them.

Inching forward another foot or so, Belle could just discern a narrow archway that framed the entrance to a bar and mini-kitchen on the left. A door on the right presumably led to the bedroom.

The silence was oppressive. Still, she wasn't going to rescue Tony by lurking in an empty room. She walked over to the closed inner door. The sound of voices drifted out into the sitting room, but when she strained to make out individual words, she concluded that she wasn't hearing live speech, but a television news report about a forest fire. Had the kidnappers fallen asleep? No, that was too ridiculous even to imagine. It was much more likely that they were using the TV to cover up the telltale sounds of people waiting in ambush on the other side of the door.

It didn't take a genius I.Q. level to work out that the situation looked highly threatening to her health and well-being. Either she'd been stood up, or the kidnappers were clustered right behind the bedroom door, licking their chops as they waited for her to walk through. At which point, a thump on the head was likely to be the least of what they had in store for her.

Belle backed away from the door and eyed the furniture in the sitting room. She picked up a chair and hefted it in her hands, calculating her chances of being able to wrench open the closed bedroom door and simultaneously defend herself against the people on the other side. Her odds were somewhere between zero and none, she decided. If there were men with guns behind that door, rattan would be a poor defense against bullets.

Maybe she should just call hotel security. If Tony was being held right here in the bedroom, that would be far and away the best plan. But if he was being held somewhere else—which was much more likely—then his guards might well have orders to shoot him if anything at all went wrong with their ransom plans.

Belle realized she was waffling helplessly. She felt as if the events of the past three days had piled up until they'd finally consumed her capacity to make decisions. Ambivalent to the point of paralysis, she wandered over to the phone on the bar.

As she walked through the archway, she tripped over a foot sticking out from behind the counter. Belle stared stupidly at the tasseled leather loafer and the triangle of sock poking out around the angle of the bar. She stepped over the obstacle with exaggerated care and peered behind the counter.

Donald Gates was lying facedown on the floor of the kitchenette, his one visible eye rolled up in the rictus of death. Blood was splattered on the surrounding cupboards, and had oozed out of a gaping wound in his midsection.

He was obviously very dead.

Twelve

For a long time Belle couldn't move. Then a fly buzzed past her, brushing her cheek before settling on the floor by Donald's chest, its proboscis dipping hungrily into the congealing blood. Sickened, she instinctively moved to shoo the fly away.

That simple gesture seemed to break some internal logjam, and her stomach started to heave precipitously. She plunked herself down on the nearest chair, gripping the seat and breathing deeply until she was sure she wouldn't throw up. Poor Donald! Poor, *silly* Donald, whose desire for easy money had apparently gotten him involved way out of his league. If he'd only been honest with her and acknowledged up front what he really wanted from their relationship, she could have warned him that amateur crooks tangled with the Joubert family at their peril.

She couldn't bring herself to examine Donald's body more closely, but she found a towel in the half bath next to the kitchen and threw it over him, covering his wounds. Donald might not have been the honest, good-natured person she'd once imagined, but he hadn't deserved to die in such a horrible way, and she couldn't bear to think of insects dining on his remains until officials got here and took him away to the morgue.

She ought to call 9-1-1, but as soon as the thought entered her head, Belle realized that she wasn't going to notify the police about what she'd found. Donald was past human worries, so nothing she did now was going to make any difference to him, but her actions could have a very big impact on Tony's safety. Her loyalty had to be with her brother who—please, God—was still alive. Until she had a better fix on where Tony was, Belle didn't intend to do anything that might offend his captors.

It was so damn difficult to think clearly. Had the kidnappers ever really planned to trade Tony for her father's disk, or was her summons to this hotel room part of some bizarre and complex setup? She couldn't imagine any reason why somebody would have gone to so much trouble simply to have her find Donald Gates's dead body, so—unless her battered brain was overlooking the obvious—the fact that Donald had been shot and left lying on the floor behind the bar must mean that something had gone very wrong with the kidnappers' plans.

Belle wasn't cheered by that thought. Criminals whose plans went awry tended to behave stupidly. In her experience, stupid and criminal were *really* bad characteristics to mix. Add in violent, and you were looking at a disaster in the bud. If Tony was a captive of the same people who had killed Donald—and probably Marge—his odds of survival seemed frighteningly low.

Belle clung to the hope that the kidnappers wanted her father's disk badly enough to keep her brother alive. If she was right, and they really did intend to strike a deal with her, then the only smart thing for her to do now was get the hell out of here, retrieve her father's disk from its hiding place, and wait for the kidnappers to contact her.

She would leave just as soon as she'd checked behind the ominously closed door that loomed threateningly from across the room. Belle no longer feared coming face-to-face with armed gunmen, but she did fear opening the door and finding her brother lying dead on the other side.

Overcoming a cowardly desire to turn tail and run, Belle strode across the sitting room and flung open the shuttered door. To her huge relief, she was confronted by an empty room—a standard hotel bedroom with a king-size bed and attached bathroom. The TV was tuned to CNN; otherwise, there was no sign of human occupation, dead or alive. Belle checked the closet and all the drawers to see if she could find any clue as to who had been here. Every closet and receptacle was empty. Even the Gideon Bible and the phone directories were missing. Because Donald's killers had been afraid of leaving fingerprints and had meticulously cleaned up? Or the opposite—they'd left in such a hurry that they'd simply swept everything into suitcases and run?

The bathroom had a wet counter and there were damp towels on the floor, but no personal items had been left behind to provide insight as to who had used the facilities. Either Donald Gates had flown down to Miami carrying literally nothing in the way of luggage, or his killers had cleaned up his belongings along with their own.

Belle wished her exploration of the hotel suite had yielded a few concrete clues about the people who'd been here and who, presumably, still held her brother. But at least she didn't need to worry about how she was going to track down the kidnappers. She was sure they would be in touch with her, and sooner rather than later—

On cue, the phone rang. Her palms instantly turned sweaty, and her heart started to pound. For a craven second, Belle contemplated letting the phone ring, but then she realized she had no choice but to answer. If the kidnappers were calling with fresh instructions, she couldn't afford to ignore them, however reluctant she felt to negotiate with the people who had most likely just murdered Donald Gates.

She picked up the receiver. "Hello?"

The person at the other end made no sound at all, but she felt a sudden sharp tension in the silence. Whoever it was recognized her voice and was surprised to hear it, Belle thought. "Who are you?" she demanded. "Where's my brother?"

She hadn't really expected an answer to her questions, but she was oddly spooked when a soft *click* told her the call had been disconnected. Who had the caller expected to reach, if not her? Why hadn't he spoken, not even to threaten her?

Definitely time to get out of here. Strange how silence could sometimes convey greater menace than the most brutal of verbal threats. Belle quickly made her way to the door of the suite and checked to make sure nobody was in the vicinity before she stepped out into the hallway. The last thing she wanted was to spend the next several hours explaining to police why she was in a hotel suite discovering her second murder victim in the space of two days. The Miami police would instantly recognize the Joubert name and, depending on who was heading up the investigation—honest cop or a graduate of the Joubert bribery rolls—she would instantly get thrown in jail on suspicion of murder, or find herself chauffeured home to her mother's house. Right now, either option seemed equally undesirable.

After a moment's indecision, Belle walked out of the suite, leaving the doors open behind her. A staff member would inevitably notice that the doors were unlocked, and go inside to investigate. She hoped Donald's body would be discovered soon, because she wanted his killers to be brought to justice, and she knew that speedy access to the victim's body was important for a successful murder investigation. On the other hand, she couldn't afford to have the police identify the body too soon. Kidnappers who felt the law closing in on them tended to kill their victims, so she needed the investigators to bumble around long enough for her to pay the ransom for her brother. She had to worry about Sergeant Brady, too. If he heard that Donald Gates had been murdered, he'd be on her trail in a New York minute.

Walking quickly along the corridor, Belle wondered why every decision she made always seemed to be tinted in multiple confusing shades of gray. What must it feel like to enjoy the luxury of dealing in moral absolutes? To be someone who took decisions each day and came home at night confident they were the right ones. She couldn't begin to imagine a life of such blissful moral certitude.

Belle fought the urge to break into a run. Unfortunately, there were people in the long corridor—a room-service waiter pushing a meal cart, and a woman waiting by the elevators—and she didn't want to draw attention to herself.

The woman finally got onto the elevator and the

room-service waiter turned a corner, leaving Belle momentarily unobserved. She dodged into the alcove that housed the soda machine and swiftly knelt down, patting her hand over the damp concrete in search of the DVD disk. She must have pushed it deeper than she'd intended; she had to scrunch down on her stomach and slide her arm flat along the concrete until she eventually managed to grasp the plastic case in a scissor-hold between her index and forefinger. She dragged it out from underneath the machine with a sigh of profound relief. It was only as she leaned back on her heels to slip the disk into the zippered inner pocket of her purse that she realized the transparent plastic case was empty.

"Looking for this?" Sandro Marchese asked from behind her.

Belle twisted around so fast that she banged her head and both elbows. She rose to her feet slowly, which would have given her time to think of a snappy answer if her brain hadn't given up on the whole idea of functioning. Perhaps if she'd had any mental capacity left, she would have felt astonished that Sandro was here. As it was, his presence simply seemed inevitable.

He was leaning against the alcove entrance, feet crossed, the disk dangling from one hand, the other hand shoved into his pocket—the picture of careless indolence. But Belle didn't make the mistake of confusing appearance with reality. She knew she had zero chance of making it past him, and a less-than-zero chance of snatching the disk from his seemingly negligent hold.

She licked her lips, which were bone dry. "Please give me back the disk," she said. "I need it, Sandro."

"Do you identify it as yours?" he asked.

"Of course I do," she said wearily. "You know it's mine."

"Is it the Cronus disk?"

"I guess so. What does it matter? It's the disk my father entrusted to me."

"Then you must know I have to arrest you." He looked away for a moment, then turned back and spoke directly to her. "I'm sorry, Belle. You've left me with no choice."

Good grief, she couldn't afford to waste time being arrested, much less arguing with Sandro about what she had done that could possibly deserve arrest. She was too tired to think, too exhausted to find anything even marginally clever to say. Her chances of diverting Sandro's attention so that she could escape were nil. All that was left was to tell him the simple truth.

"I'll do anything if you'll give me back that disk," she said, clutching the empty case to her chest as if that would somehow magically restore its contents. She'd rarely regretted lack of brute physical strength as intensely as she did at this minute. "Let me go. Please. Pretend you never saw me." She swallowed her pride. "I'm begging, Sandro. Do the right thing for once and give me the disk."

His stance remained lazy, but his eyes were alert and watchful. When he replied, his manner was dispassionate, almost impersonal. "I couldn't let you go even if I wanted to. In addition to me, there are two other Customs agents who've been following you ever since you landed in Miami this morning. If I let you walk away, they'd stop you."

The woman in the elevator, Belle thought tiredly, with no sense of shock or outrage. Her brain's emotional center seemed to have gone numb. She'd been right to believe she'd seen that oversize shoulder purse twice. She'd suspected she was being followed; she'd just mistaken the source of her tail. Not the kidnappers, but Customs. The woman had been wired, of course, so that as soon as Belle told her she wanted the eighth floor, Sandro had known where Belle was going. He must have watched her dart into the alcove and hide the disk, and he'd probably removed it from its hiding place seconds after she put it there. Belle felt sure there was irony in the situation somewhere, but right now she wasn't capable of appreciating it.

"I've got to have the disk," she repeated. Like a beacon shining through the fog of her exhaustion, she clung to the knowledge that she could only save Tony if she had a bargaining chip to offer in exchange for his life—and her father's disk was that chip. She couldn't give up the disk voluntarily, even if she had no idea how she could prevent Sandro from taking it by force. She held on tightly to the empty disk case as the walls of the alcove started to ripple and dissolve.

"Belle? What's wrong?" Sandro's voice changed, becoming softer and more personal. She saw that he was walking toward her. Even though her vision had suddenly blurred, the outline of his body was starkly clear.

Belle remained where she was, not from choice, but because she knew she would fall if she took a step in any direction. She was too woozy to protest when Sandro's arms came around her. She ought to have felt repelled by his touch. Instead, she felt reassured. The room was spinning, whirling faster and faster, until her legs buckled under her. Almost abstractedly, she realized that she'd lost the knack of making them bear her weight. Humiliatingly, she needed Sandro's aid or she would topple over.

Her gaze remained fixed on his face. For some reason, she couldn't look away any more than she could make her legs support her. He stared down at her out of a halo of bright light, his expression a mixture of anger, frustration and concern. Odd how she could read all that so clearly when every other aspect of coherence seemed to be tumbling down the precipice to oblivion.

"They've kidnapped Tony," she said. With supreme effort, she shaped her lips to form another sentence, but the words slipped away from her.

She chased after them into the blackness.

Thirteen

He wouldn't put it past her to have induced a faint simply to provoke his sympathy, Sandro thought. And, dammit, she'd succeeded. He looked down at her pale face and the purple smudges beneath her eyes, feeling a spurt of mingled compassion and fury. She must be as exhausted as she looked. She'd been calling her brother half the night, and had left for the airport before dawn, so it was probably more than twenty-four hours since she'd slept. What had she been trying to tell him, anyway? Something about Tony. Belle had obviously been almost paralyzed with worry, although Sandro couldn't understand why she cared. Her brother was a chip off the old Joubert block, and had never done a damn thing to make her life any easier.

He took off his jacket to make a pillow for Belle's head, laying her on the ground so that he could get a cup of ice from the machine. She was still holding the disk case clasped against her rib cage as if even unconscious, she refused to surrender it. He took it from her, quelling an absurd feeling of guilt. The disk he'd taken from the case was identified as Charitable Donations 2000, but, despite the label, it must be the Cronus disk. The real, genuine article. Belle had been too determined to retain possession of it for this to be a decoy.

He got ice from the machine, then held the paper cup against her cheek and rubbed an ice cube across her lips until her eyelids fluttered and opened. She had the most spectacularly gorgeous eyes he'd ever seen, Sandro thought, hoping to immunize himself against their effect by acknowledging their power. For the past seven years, he'd thought about Belle more often than he'd cared to admit. Knowing that he couldn't afford to be emotionally tangled with the daughter of a notorious smuggler, he'd buried his feelings for her under layers of contempt for the Joubert family business.

Unfortunately, confronted with the reality of the woman, those layers were wearing mighty thin, mighty fast. Belle had always been something much more important to him than Marc Joubert's daughter, although this was one hell of a moment to start asking himself exactly what.

For about five seconds after she opened her eyes, Belle's gaze remained unfocused. Then awareness returned and her eyes darkened from hazel to a deep golden brown. She felt around for the disk, then seemed to remember that he'd taken it. Her expression conveyed desperation. Desperation at being caught by a federal agent? Most likely. Sandro put his arms around her to help her sit up, steeling himself to resist whatever ploy she might decide to aim at him.

It turned out to be a doozy. "They've kidnapped my brother," she said, her voice husky. "My father's disk is the only bargaining chip I have. Don't take it from me, Sandro."

God help him, but for a split second—half a split second—he actually considered giving her back the disk. Disgusted with himself, he spoke harshly. "I warned you what you were risking if you didn't surrender the disk to the proper authorities. Even if you're telling the truth and your brother really has been kidnapped, you have nobody to blame but yourself."

The last remaining dregs of color drained from her cheeks, leaving her chalk-white, and faintly blue around the lips. Her head was resting against his chest, and he felt the beat of his heart pulsing against her cheek. The intimacy seemed both warmly familiar and dangerously forbidden.

He was so angry with her—with himself?—that he lashed out with words, even as he cradled her more tightly in his arms. "It's too late for regrets, Belle. You should have given me the disk voluntarily when you had the chance. God knows, I offered you every inducement I could think of. If you'd done the right thing yesterday, your brother might never have been abducted, and you sure as hell would have saved yourself a jail sentence."

"A jail sentence?" Belle blinked, then shook her head as if dismissing his threat as trivial. "Yesterday's past and we can't go back," she said, her voice hoarse with fatigue. "I didn't give you the disk, and now my brother's life is in my hands. Can't you cut me just a little slack?"

A little slack? Asking him to betray everything that he owed to his conscience and his profession? Didn't she care that her neighbor's murder was just one death among many caused by her family? Sandro's sympathy disappeared in a flash of anger.

"No deals, Belle. No special favors. No promises of a suspended sentence if you offer to testify. This time you'll have to live with the consequences of your own decisions. Do you seriously think that I can put Tony's life ahead of the lives of thousands of innocent people? The Joubert Corporation isn't some rinky-dink operation smuggling cheap knockoffs of Cartier jewelry, or Barbie dolls on which they haven't paid import duties. In case you've forgotten what your father actually did, he spent thirty years dreaming up clever, sophisticated methods of evading the law in order to sell weapons to terrorists and dictators. Surely you understand why I can't let his network survive."

Sandro couldn't keep the bitterness out of his voice. "You should have walked away from your inheritance, Belle. I really thought you would refuse to take over the Cronus network."

She stared at him blankly—so blankly that he wondered if she was about to faint again. Then she wriggled out of his arms, holding the cup of ice chips against her forehead and propping her back against the wall. She drew in a couple of shaky breaths, looking as if she would keel over if the wall weren't there to support her. "What the hell are you talking about, Sandro? What has the Cronus project got to do with thousands of people dying?"

An impartial observer would have sworn she really hadn't understood. Sandro refused to allow himself to be taken in. "You can't act your way out of this one," he said curtly. "Your phone call to your brother last night was monitored. You told him that you had the Cronus disk, so there's no point in denying it."

"I'm not denying it. Why would I bother to deny my father gave me the disk, when you've already taken it from me?" She rubbed her forehead, massaging a spot above her eyebrow as if the pain really bothered her. "Look, Sandro, I'm desperate. I'm willing to do a deal. Give me back the disk, and I promise I won't—"

Sandro cut her off, getting angrier by the moment. "No deals, dammit! Jesus, you're such a typical Joubert! Convinced you're above the law and that you can pull everyone else down to your own level."

"I've never thought I was above the law," Belle said, her voice shaking. She dragged herself to her feet using the wall as a support, and Sandro resisted the urge to help. Or push her down again. Or do something—anything—that would give him an excuse to put his hands on her body and pound some remorse into her. Or just put his hands on her body.

"You, of all people, have no right to accuse me," she said. "I didn't choose my family, or my father's way of life. At least I've never taken a bribe—"

"Christ! Are we back on that again?" Sandro slapped his hands flat on the wall on either side of her, forcing her to look at him. "Enough, okay? I've had it with your constant accusations, as if I'm the bad guy and you're Ms. Purity. We'll do the rest of this conversation downtown, with witnesses, so that your lawyers can't claim that I beat you up. You can come willingly, or I can arrest you right here and now—"

She kneed him in the groin. The oldest trick in the history of the world, and he was so distracted by her nearness that he would have fallen for it—if she hadn't still been a bit clumsy in the wake of her faint. As it was, he barely managed to sidestep in time.

Seething, he reached for the cuffs hanging from his belt. "That does it. Isabella Joubert, you're under arrest—"

She knocked the cuffs aside. Far from appearing worried, she looked furious. The meekness induced by her faint seemed to have vanished. "Don't even think of arresting me," she said hotly. "In the first place, I've done nothing wrong, and you'll be a laughingstock by the time Dad's lawyers finish with you. In the second place, *you're* the person who appears on that disk, not me. Do you think I'm going to keep quiet about that if you arrest me? You may have the disk, but it's no use destroying it. That won't protect you. I have a hard copy of everything that appears on it, and I'll give the copies to the police in a heartbeat."

She was accusing him of being on the Cronus disk? What the hell was she talking about? Sandro stopped his Miranda warning, with the handcuffs still dangling open. "Wait, backtrack a little. What did you just say about me appearing on the Cronus disk? Are you serious?"

She looked puzzled. "You must have realized that you're on it. Why else are you so anxious to get it back? You must have known that you're one of the people my father included on his list."

He was understanding less and less. Sandro drew in a long, slow breath. "Let's start this conversation over. From the top." He held out the disk he'd taken from her. "Is this the Cronus disk?"

She shrugged. "I guess so. That's what you called it. I'd never heard of the Cronus network until you mentioned it. Remember? You said an informant had told you I was in charge of my father's final project—''

"And you agreed that you were."

"Yes, I did. Because I am. But you were the person who called it the Cronus project. That was your name, not mine."

She'd never heard of the Cronus project until he mentioned it? Sandro looked at her in amazement, and she glared back. He expelled his breath very carefully, afraid to trust his reactions when he so badly wanted Belle to have an excuse for what she'd done.

"It seems we, both of us, need to stop assuming things," he said. "Have you personally checked out the contents of this disk? Do you know what's on here?"

"Of course I do."

"Tell me. Use nice short sentences, and real easy words."

Her eyes flashed scornfully. "As if you didn't know. It's a list of all the people my father bribed over the years in order to keep the Joubert Corporation safe from prosecution. There are photos, film clips, scanned copies of documents, transcripts of bank records. Everything an honest law enforcement official could need in order to prepare indictments that even expensive defense lawyers aren't going to be able to beat."

The first ray of enlightenment began to dawn, along with a relief that shocked him by its intensity. "All right, Belle, humor me. Let's be real clear and very specific. This disk contains documents pertaining to officials and other people Marc Joubert bribed during his lifetime, and the 'final project' your father asked you to take care of has something to do with this list?''

''Yes—what else?'' She flashed a cynical smile that didn't begin to conceal her desolation. ''I'm sure you're wondering what my father said about you on the disk. Don't worry, Sandro, you have a very nice section all to yourself. There's a full-color movie record of that memorable day when my father canceled the Zauriac deal, and you sold yourself for a quarter of a million dollars.''

He was too stunned to speak, and she misinterpreted his silence. Color flared briefly in her cheeks, then she turned away as if she couldn't bear to look at him anymore. ''However much I beg and plead, you're not going to give me the disk, are you? You can't risk letting it out of your hands. Whether I trade it to the kidnappers in exchange for Tony's life, or turn it over to the FBI, you're screwed. One way you get blackmailed, the other way you get tossed in jail. Either way, you're ruined.''

Sandro felt as if sunbeams exploded inside his head, leaving behind crystal clarity where everything before had been dark and murky. *The disk Belle's father had given her wasn't part of the Cronus project, much less a disk that laid bare the structure of the Cronus network.* He almost laughed out loud with sheer relief. If only the real Cronus disk hadn't still been missing, he probably would have. No wonder Belle had been so angry with him. No wonder she'd been so reluctant to hand the disk over to him—she thought he would destroy it in order to cover up evidence of his own crimes!

In retrospect, it was easy to see how they'd misunderstood each other. Belle had refused to hand over the disk because she didn't trust him. He hadn't trusted her because she refused to hand over the disk. A comedy of errors with disastrous consequences.

"Listen up, Belle, because this is important. I never accepted any bribe from Marc Joubert." He took her hands, cradling them in his, as if by physical contact he could compel her to believe him.

"I swear to you that I reported your father's attempt to bribe me at the time it happened. The entire episode is already on record, which means that my ass is well and truly covered. Nobody's going to bring corruption charges against me, because there's a piece of film showing that seven years ago I said and did exactly what I told everyone I said and did."

If he'd hoped that Belle would smile and melt into his arms, he was doomed to disappointment. She clearly didn't believe him, and her tension level didn't decrease by a single jot. She withdrew her hands, not angrily, but slowly, as if she was almost too tired to care anymore. "That disk represents my father's belated attempt to make restitution for all the wrong he did while he was alive. Why would he have included a record of the Zauriac incident unless you'd taken the bribe he offered?"

"I don't know," Sandro admitted. "I wish I could think of a clever answer, but I have no explanation, except that your father died unexpectedly. It's possible—likely—that the disk was still a work-in-progress as far as he was concerned."

"That's not a very compelling argument in favor of your innocence."

"If I really had taken the bribe, maybe I'd have a more convincing story already prepared to share with you. Given the family you were raised in, you should know that appearances and truth often have very little to do with each other.''

She hesitated, and for a moment Sandro thought he'd won her over. Then her gaze slid away again. ''This is too important for me to risk accepting your word and then finding out afterwards that I was wrong.''

''You're right. So I'll agree to go with you to the FBI office of your choice and hand over the disk. Does that convince you?'' Belle didn't answer, and Sandro pressed his advantage. ''Your father's dead, and you have to accept that we may never know why he left that piece of film on this disk. But I do know that I never took any money from him, and I can show you the records to prove that I reported his attempt to bribe me as soon as it happened.''

''Then why did you pretend to my father that you could be bribed if you never intended to take any of the money?''

''Events were moving fast at the time, and circumstances changed from moment to moment. When he canceled the Zauriac deal, I felt I had no choice but to do what I did. But the case against your father was already collapsing, and once my boss committed suicide there was no point in continuing the pretense that I could be bought. My boss had made sure that the investigation was so effectively sabotaged from within that even if you'd stayed in Miami and agreed to testify, I don't believe we would have had enough hard evidence to win a conviction. The Zauriac incident was the last flicker of life in a dying investigation.''

Sandro was almost relieved to see some of her unnatural lethargy disappear, to be replaced by anger.

"You still went straight from making love with me to a motel room for a tryst with Bimbo Boobs. If you're such an honest, caring kind of guy, what was that all about?"

"The stupid behavior of a man who realized he was in way over his head," Sandro admitted.

"Translated, that means what?"

"That I seduced you because I thought it was a good way to have an inside track to your father. Somewhere along the way, I realized that the joke was on me. I was falling in love with you."

Belle made a small sound, and Sandro realized he was gripping her hands so tightly that he was hurting her. Loosening his hold, he stepped away from her. But at the last minute he swung around and finally made the apology that he knew was seven years too late in coming. "I understand why you find it so hard to trust me, Belle. My record is lousy where you're concerned. You were young and naive, and I exploited your vulnerability. You have every right to be angry with me, but not because I betrayed my oath of office and took a bribe from your father. You should be angry with me because I took my job much too seriously and betrayed you in the process. I can only tell you that I'm sorry for what I did."

She turned so that her face was to the wall. "I am angry with you for that," she said. "I wasn't just young and naïve—I was a virgin. I could forgive you for the sex, even though it's humiliating to know you were making love to me as part of your job. But I can't forgive the fact that you took my emotions and deliberately made me fall in love with you. You could at least have spared me that."

He put his hands on her shoulders and twisted her

around to face him. "I wish I had," he said, looking down at her. "Then maybe I would have spared myself, too."

She didn't answer, but they were standing so close that he could feel her tremble. He only realized how badly he'd been wanting to kiss her when his mouth touched hers.

"Don't," she whispered, but she didn't move away, and Sandro gave in to the urge that had been building hard and fast for the past three days.

Kissing Belle had always been different from kissing any other woman. It still was, Sandro realized. He'd forgotten how incredible her lips were, how soft they felt, and how instantly arousing he had always found any physical contact with her. Between one breath and the next, what had started out as a nostalgic gesture toward the past changed into a passionate confirmation of the desire he felt in the present.

When they finally broke apart, Belle looked as confused as he felt. "That was a mistake," she said. She touched her fingers to her lips, looking bemused. "Wasn't it?"

"Maybe. I don't believe I'm going to apologize."

"I should at least have stolen the darn disk while you weren't paying attention," she muttered.

Sandro laughed. How had he managed to forget that when he was with Belle, laughter had always come at the most unexpected moments?

His reply was drowned out by a piercing scream, followed by the sound of running feet. He stepped out of the alcove into the corridor and saw a woman in a maid's uniform running toward the elevator, babbling in an incoherent mixture of Spanish and English.

Belle peered over his shoulder at the maid and then

glanced back at a pair of double doors that stood open at the end of the hallway. "Oh, my God," she said. "She's found Donald Gates."

"What's Donald doing in Miami?" Sandro asked.

"Er...nothing. At least right now. Actually, he's...dead."

Fourteen

Sandro swung around, dragging Belle back into the alcove, out of sight. "How do you know Donald Gates is dead?" he demanded.

"Because I found his body."

"It figures." To her relief, Sandro sounded resigned rather than suspicious. "How did he die? I'm assuming it wasn't peacefully in his sleep."

"He was shot. Several times, I think. I didn't examine him too closely, but there was a lot of blood."

Sandro's brows drew together in a ferocious frown. "Tell me you called the police as soon as you found the body."

"Er...no. Actually, I didn't."

"Of course not," he said with heavy irony. "You walk into a hotel suite and discover your lover shot to death on the floor. Why would you even consider calling the police?"

"You wouldn't," she said hotly. "Not if your name was Joubert and your neighbor in Chicago had been murdered the day before. And Donald Gates isn't my lover. He was already an ex before he died. And don't say one word to me about my rotten taste in men. I've already given myself the lecture."

Sandro looked ready to explode, and she tried to reason with him. "I only found Donald's body by chance. I have nothing to contribute to a police investigation—''

"Sure, I can see that it was pure coincidence," Sandro said. "The fact that Donald Gates is your lover—excuse me, *ex-lover*—and the fact that he might have been involved in the abduction of your brother, is clearly irrelevant to any investigation of his murder—''

"We don't have time for sarcasm," Belle said. "Whether or not Donald was involved in abducting Tony, he's dead now. But my brother may still be alive, in which case I need to find somewhere to go so that the kidnappers can contact me to set up a new time and place for the ransom drop-off.''

For once Sandro didn't argue with her, and Belle took his silence as a bleak endorsement of her view that even if her brother was still alive, his life hung suspended by a frighteningly thin thread.

The maid had finally stopped her hysterical screaming, and Belle could see her sobbing out her story to two men wearing mustard-yellow blazers. Obviously hotel security. One of the guards pointed toward the suite, but the maid shook her head, refusing point-blank to go in again. Belle didn't blame her.

"Let's get out of here before the security guards cordon off this floor," Sandro said. "We'll take the fire exit and go down the back stairs." He took Belle's hand and propelled her toward the neon sign marked Exit, pulling a tiny, state-of-the-art communicator from the inner pocket of his jacket and speaking into it as they sped down the concrete fire stairs.

"Pete, I have Isabella Joubert in custody. I'm bringing her in. She insists she has no knowledge of the Cronus project and that she is not involved with

Joubert Corporation smuggling operations in any way. Tell Ken Oliver that he can expect a full report from me shortly.''

"Yes, sir. What's with all the screams? They're coming from the vicinity of the elevators on your floor. You ordered us to stay away from the eighth floor, so we didn't investigate."

"It's a maid. It seems she ran a routine check of suite 823 and discovered a dead body. Donald Gates, to be precise. He's been shot."

The unseen Pete sputtered into his communicator. "Donald Gates? In room 823? Jesus! That's where the Joubert woman went—"

"Yes, I'm aware. Hotel security has arrived on the scene already, so I'm getting out of here with Ms. Joubert before the guards start asking questions we don't want to answer. You and Wendy should do the same. We don't want any jurisdictional arguments with local law enforcement. Take the rest of the night off, and I'll brief you tomorrow morning."

"Do you need backup to bring her in?"

"No. Ms. Joubert is cooperating." Sandro disconnected before Pete could ask any more awkward questions. "Come on," he said to Belle, stuffing the communicator back into his pocket. "We need to get out of here."

Belle clattered down the stairs in his wake. "Sandro, I can't let you arrest me—"

"I'm not arresting you. I'm taking you into protective custody."

"Been there, done that, and it didn't work out too well. If I come with you, Tony is doomed. If the kidnappers can't contact me on their first or second try, you know they'll probably cut their losses and...kill my brother."

"Then we have to make sure the kidnappers can reach you." They arrived at the ground floor, and Sandro stopped in front of the heavy fire doors leading to the hotel lobby. "You have a potential problem, though. Has it occurred to you that you may not have anything to bargain with?"

"I will have as soon you give me back my father's disk."

"Maybe not. The kidnappers probably heard the same rumors everyone else did. Most likely, they think you've taken control of the Joubert smuggling operations and that what you have is the Cronus network system disk. *That* could be what they want—"

"Oh, my God." Belle sank down on the bottom step, appalled. When the kidnappers had ordered her to bring *the disk,* she had simply assumed she had what they wanted. But now that she knew her father had left two disks, she realized that she might not have the all-important one.

"We got interrupted by the maid screaming, and you never told me what the Cronus disk really is," she said. "If that's the one the kidnappers want, I need to know why it's so important. At least that way I might be able to run a bluff."

Sandro, thank goodness, didn't retreat behind the screen of the Official Secrets Act and refuse to answer her. "The Cronus network is the name your father gave to his personal record of every system he had in place for conducting illegal business. We've been informed that the missing system disk contains shipping routes, preferred carriers, names of dealers and overseas contacts, employees who've stolen commercial secrets from their employers, and complete details of your father's tactics for avoiding interdiction both at airports and on the high seas. In fact, everything anyone would need to carry on the Joubert family's smuggling tradition with barely an administrative hiccup.''

Belle had been wondering why Sandro was willing to stick around and help her find Tony. Understanding dawned in an unwelcome flash. ''You're helping me ransom Tony because you want to arrest him. You're assuming that if I'm innocent, he must have taken over from my father—and that he has the Cronus disk.''

''It's a logical possibility,'' Sandro said. ''If you aren't your father's designated heir, then Tony is the most likely alternative candidate. If there's one thing we can agree about in regard to your family, it's the fact that Marc Joubert didn't trust outsiders. The reason the Cronus system disk is so valuable is that Marc never shared more than the bare informational necessities, even with his closest partners. He compartmentalized everything. Dave Forcier managed the company accounts and dealt with tax stuff. Ray Hillman took care of legal problems and set up dummy corporations to launder illegal profits. And neither of them knows a single thing more than they need to for their specific assignments. Even your brother wasn't much better informed about the big picture, at least until very recently. Tony may have done a lot of international traveling for the past few years, meeting your father's most important clients, and building relationships, but Marc remained at the heart of every major deal, keeping all the most vital details a secret.''

Sandro knew exactly how her father operated, because he'd spent eight months unraveling the details of the Joubert Corporation's byzantine structure. Belle had to acknowledge that he was right, not only about the way her father had operated, but also about the fact that Tony was the logical heir to Marc Joubert's empire. And much as she wanted to rant and rave at Sandro's assumption that her brother would be willing to step right up and continue their father's illegal activities, she couldn't. She had harbored the same fears.

And yet, Belle couldn't shake the feeling that she was missing something. After a while, she identified the problem that was nagging at her. In the hospital, her father had been quite alert for a man on the brink of death. Since he'd been sufficiently aware to give her instructions on how to find the disk hidden behind the photo in his study, wouldn't he have realized the significance of what he was asking her to do? Even on his deathbed, a smuggler as wily and experienced as Marc Joubert would surely have recognized that nobody could continue to operate the Cronus network once the names of the officials on his bribery payroll had been revealed. Belle couldn't believe that her dad would send her in search of the disk if he wanted his son to carry on the family business.

Sandro reached up and tucked a strand of Belle's hair behind her ear. "What are you thinking?" he asked. "Talk to me, Belle. There's no chance of a decent outcome to this mess unless we're honest with each other."

Belle hesitated. As far as she was concerned, the concept of sharing problems and cooperating to solve them was something entirely theoretical. In real life, trust and cooperation had been luxuries she could never afford. On the other hand, the people who had kidnapped Tony weren't college frat boys on a lark. She had to accept that they were ruthless killers. If Sandro was willing to help get Tony back, she ought to grab his offer—and worry about the consequences later.

"I was thinking that if my father gave the Cronus disk to Tony and this one to me, then I don't understand his motives," she said. "I'm sure he was sincere when he said he wanted to make restitution. His last words to me were about the regret he felt for the past."

"If you're trying to convince me that your father genuinely regretted a lot of what he'd done, you don't have to. I often thought Marc was ambivalent about the path his life had taken. Even aside from that, last-minute deathbed repentance isn't unusual. In fact, it's the norm."

"I know, but here's my problem. I guess it's possible that my father only expressed regret because he'd realized that he was about to meet his Maker, and he had some hefty sins that he needed to atone for. But he was lucid almost to the end, and I think he was smart enough to have grasped the ramifications of what he was asking me to do. My father must have known that in the process of exposing the officials he'd bribed, he would also destroy the Joubert smuggling operation."

"Why do you say that?" Sandro asked.

"Marc Joubert may have built the Cronus network into the most efficient smuggling enterprise in the history of American civilization, but the Joubert Corporation can't succeed at home or abroad unless dozens of officials right here in the States are being paid to look the other way."

"You're right," Sandro said. "Damn! I can't believe I didn't think of that!"

"Then we have a dilemma," Belle said. "Why would my father give Tony the Cronus disk—and simultaneously give me another disk that's going to make the Cronus disk worthless? One gift canceled out the other."

"I have an answer, but you might not want to hear it."

"Try me."

"Okay. My best guess is that Marc only decided to give you the disk, literally, at the last moment of his life—"

"You already suggested that."

"So, here's my point. Let's assume Marc had given the Cronus disk to your brother before you arrived in Miami. But when he sees you again, your father is overcome by remorse. He changes his mind about allowing the Joubert smuggling operation to pass on to a third generation. Knowing he's already given the Cronus disk to Tony, he tells you where to find the list of officials he's bribed. Bingo! Tony is stymied. Later on, Tony discovers what his father has given you and he's furious."

"Because he realizes that the second I go public with my list, the Cronus network is useless."

"Yes." Sandro looked at her steadily. "I guess we have to face the fact that Tony would be highly... motivated...to get the disk back from you."

Motivated enough to kill her neighbor? Belle shivered. She wanted to protest Sandro's conclusions, but she couldn't. Tony had still been a young college student when she fled to Chicago. Conflict over the Joubert Corporation had kept them apart ever since, and she really had no firsthand knowledge of what kind of man he'd become.

Belle followed her train of thought, unpleasant as it was. If Tony knew what their father had asked her to do, it would explain why he'd been so angry when he came into Marc's study on the day of the funeral. At the time, she'd assumed it was just her brother being his normal anal-retentive self. In hindsight, his behavior seemed more sinister.

As for how her brother had found out about the existence of the disk, that was no mystery.

Their mother had been in the hospital room when Marc was dying. At the time, Belle's attention had been fixed on her father, and she'd simply assumed her mother was dozing. But it was more than possible that Carole had overheard her husband's dying request. Marc had spoken softly, and some of his words had been a little slurred, but after thirty-five years of marriage, every cadence of her husband's voice would be familiar. Carole could easily have repeated Marc's final words to her son, perhaps even in the context of discussing her husband's will. And once Tony knew that his father had instructed Belle to find a disk and "make it all come right," it was possible—even likely—that he had jumped to correct conclusions about the importance of the missing disk.

Belle saw no point in refusing to admit the logic of Sandro's suggestion. "Tony may have realized what my father asked me to do," she conceded. "And if he knows, then he's certainly smart enough to realize that the Joubert smuggling operation is doomed the moment I publicize the contents of the disk."

Sandro's expression was sympathetic, but his voice remained cool. Which was fortunate, because Belle was hanging on to her self-control by a very fragile thread, and sympathy from Sandro would have sent her crashing over the edge.

"There's one final point," Sandro said. "If Tony knows what you inherited from your father, there's every reason for him to stage his own abduction. Has it occurred to you that this supposed kidnapping may be a scam? That it never really happened?"

"What?" Belle jumped to her feet. Her level of tension ratcheted up a notch, leaving her nerves stretched so taut that she wouldn't have been surprised to see sparks flying as she paced.

"Why would Tony fake his own kidnapping? How can you suggest that he'd put me through this torment—" She broke off abruptly, not wanting to hear Sandro's response to that particular question. If she could contemplate the possibility that Tony was involved in the murders of Marge Bruno and Donald Gates, then she surely couldn't reject the possibility that he was willing to cause her some anxiety.

Belle glared at Sandro, stoking her anger to conceal her fear. "I should have known you'd leap to the conclusion that the Jouberts were up to their old, dishonorable tricks."

"And I should have known you'd leap to the conclusion that law enforcement officers are always hounding the Jouberts for no good reason." Sandro grabbed her hand, forcing her to stop pacing backward and forward over the same five-foot patch of concrete. "Hear me out, okay?"

She spoke through tightly clenched teeth. "Take your hand off my wrist."

"Give me your word you won't run. That you'll stand still and listen to what I have to say."

"The word of a Joubert?" she said bitterly. "Why would you trust that?"

"Not the word of a Joubert," he said. "Your word."

The fire of her carefully fed anger flamed out. Once again, Sandro had found just the right words to disarm her. Belle dropped her gaze and found herself staring at his throat and the strong pulse that beat there. Memories rushed in—memories of long-ago nights when they had made love in the tropical warmth of a Florida night. When the sex was over, they would lie close enough to feel the throb of each other's hearts as they talked and laughed in the languid contentment of physical fulfillment. The lightest scrape of a finger across hot, naked skin had invariably been enough to reignite the desire that lay between them, dormant but never extinguished.

The memories might be made up of wishful thinking and treacherous illusion, but they were too powerful for her to ignore. She looked into Sandro's eyes and saw her own reluctant desire reflected there.

"I won't run," she promised.

"Thank you."

His voice was husky and he'd lost the air of cool detachment that was his trademark. Belle had a sudden clear vision that they stood on the brink, and the suspicion dawned that she'd already moved too close to the edge to avoid disaster. In a last-ditch effort to dodge the fall, she backed away from Sandro and kept on going until she bumped into the wall. Given the accelerated thump of her heartbeat and the crazy rush of hormones pulsing through her body, the resulting five feet of space didn't seem wide enough to guarantee sensible behavior.

"What were you saying...before?" she asked. "I've forgotten."

"I don't remember what I was saying." Sandro's voice deepened. "What I was thinking is that you're still the most beautiful woman I've ever met."

Trying to ignore the melting sensation in the pit of her stomach, she made her reply deliberately mocking. "Tone down the compliments, Sandro. It would make them slightly more believable."

"Okay, how about this? Seven years after the last time we made love, I still get aroused just thinking about it. Sex with you was the best I ever had, and I want us to make love again. I want it real bad, right now. Up against the wall would be just fine." His voice took on a note of irony. "Does that sound more believable?"

It sure did. When Donald had said how much he enjoyed making love to her, all Belle had ever felt was a faint quiver of impatience. When Sandro told her the same thing, she came unglued. Reason, self-preservation, common sense—they all dissolved in a hot rush of desire.

But she had to be sensible. Even if she could trust Sandro to be sincere, her brother's life was on the line. Belle splayed her hands flat against the concrete wall and held on tight. As if that would restore her missing brain cells.

"My brother's been kidnapped," she said. "We need to keep our attention focused."

Sandro advanced toward her, a sense of purpose glittering in his dark eyes. "Trust me. Right at this moment, I'm feeling real focused."

"But you're focused on the wrong thing!"

"This isn't the wrong thing." Sandro spoke against her mouth. "This is just about the rightest damn thing I've done in seven years."

Belle closed her eyes—a really great way to show resistance, she thought sarcastically. Sandro had always been able to arouse her with a simple kiss, and the years since they'd parted hadn't changed their chemistry. She resisted the touch of his lips for all of ten seconds before pressing her body against his and returning his kiss with all the heat and passion that had been missing from her life for the past seven years.

It was a very long time before they broke apart. Sandro drew back, his expression somber. "It isn't over for either of us, is it?"

"No," Belle admitted. A part of her stood to one side, watching her fall off the cliff. "It isn't over."

He kissed her again, with passion, a trace of anger and an underlying sweetness. Belle understood his anger, because she shared it, and the passion would have been easy to resist. It was the sweetness that left her without defenses. Needs she had suppressed for too long rose up and swept over her like a tidal wave, destroying her carefully constructed defenses, and leaving the truth of her feelings for him brutally exposed.

Belle pushed him away, desperate to hide the truth from herself as much as from him. She couldn't cope with loving Sandro Marchese. Not here, not now.

"This is insane," she said. "We can't stand here kissing, with kidnappers maybe waiting to catch sight of me the moment I walk through that door! We have to concentrate on finding my brother."

Sandro didn't say anything, and she forced herself to continue in the same practical vein. "We've been speculating for the past fifteen minutes, but we don't know if a single one of our theories is true. And while we're theorizing, Tony's life is on the line."

For a moment Sandro looked as if he'd forgotten who her brother was. Finally, he dragged his hand through his hair, visibly refocusing. "You're right," he conceded, reluctantly moving away from her. "We need to get you someplace with a phone, so the kidnappers can call you. Whether the ransom demand is for real or not, we still need to receive it."

"I can't believe Tony would be cruel enough to fake his own kidnapping," Belle said. "Suppose I'd told my mother? He must have known there was a chance of that."

"Yes, but he may feel he has no choice, whatever the consequences."

"Of course he has a choice—"

Sandro shook his head. "Not if he's determined to stop you publicizing the contents of your disk. Tony grew up with you. He knows you won't hand the disk over to him voluntarily. That would not only betray your father's dying wishes, but would go against the grain of everything you believe in. However, he also knows that you're a sucker for family. He's counting on the fact that if you receive a ransom demand, you'll do whatever it takes to get the disk to his supposed kidnappers and save his life."

Belle wanted to deny Sandro's words, but they carried the ring of unwelcome truth. Suddenly bone weary, she sat down again on the bottom step and assessed her options. "What if you're wrong?" she asked. "What am I supposed to do when the kidnappers get in touch with me next time? I can't just ignore them. Suppose Tony really is being held against his will?''

''You should respond exactly as you would if you were convinced the kidnapping was for real. It's up to me to make sure that when you go to deliver the ransom, I have the systems and people in place to arrest the kidnappers—whoever they are and whatever their motives might be.''

Belle's mouth was so dry that she could barely speak. ''If I agree to keep you informed, can you promise me that Tony won't be killed?''

Sandro met her gaze steadily. ''You know that I can't.''

''My mother will go insane if she loses Tony as well as my dad.''

''So I have to work damn hard to make sure my people understand that Tony must be taken alive. And you have to work damn hard to convince your brother to surrender without a fight.''

''That's easier said than done.'' Belle jumped up and resumed her pacing. ''Tony doesn't exactly make a habit of following my advice.''

Sandro put out his arm, stopping her in her tracks. ''You can only do your best,'' he said softly. ''You aren't personally obligated to compensate for three generations of Joubert family members who screwed up.''

''Funny you should mention that. Tony said more or less the same thing the last time I saw him.'' Her sentence ended in a hiccup that was dangerously close to a sob.

''Just keep telling yourself that you aren't responsible for other people's lousy choices," Sandro said. He grazed his knuckles across her cheek. "Okay?"

She drew in a deep breath. "Okay," she affirmed.

"Ready to move on?" he asked.

She nodded. "We need to make some practical arrangements. How are we going to keep in contact with each other? I can't afford to be seen with you, in case someone recognizes that you're a government agent. The kidnappers—genuine or fake—will never call if they see me with you."

"We need to decide something even more basic than how we keep in touch," Sandro said. "It's eight-fifteen. Where do you plan to spend the night? I suggest you take a room here at this hotel, or else go to your mother's house. The kidnappers should have no difficulty finding you in either one of those locations."

It was only eight-fifteen? Belle couldn't believe that it was barely an hour since she'd been waving goodbye to Evan at the airport, and only a couple of hours since she'd left her mother and sister at the restaurant in Miami Beach. She felt as if half a lifetime had been crammed into the week since her father died, and several years' worth of living into the past couple of hours.

Sandro's suggestion that she go to her mother's house triggered the overdue realization that she ought not to make these life-and-death decisions concerning Tony without consulting anyone in her family. In theory, her mother had more right than anyone else to decide what should be done to rescue Tony. But Carole was still so emotionally fragile in the wake of her husband's death that Belle couldn't imagine how she would bear the news that Tony, her only son, had been kidnapped. Better, perhaps, to wait another few hours and hope that Tony would be released before Carole ever had to know.

Marisa, however, was built of sterner stuff than their mother. The kidnappers had warned Belle to say nothing to anyone, but she couldn't remain silent indefinitely. Maybe she would be smart to go to her sister's house and ask for help. The idea felt right, and Belle experienced an immediate surge of relief at the prospect of sharing the burden of decision-making with her sister. Marisa might be deliberately blind to the fact that the Joubert Corporation had continued its fifty-year tradition of criminality right up to the moment of their father's death, but she was smart and savvy about life in general. Anyone who'd entered the New York modeling scene at age sixteen, made the cover of *Vogue,* and emerged free of eating disorders and drug addiction had to be an amazingly strong woman. Plus, Marisa had spent a lot more time in Tony's company during the past seven years than Belle had, and must know their brother fairly well. She would be able to provide insights into Tony's character that Belle couldn't.

"You're right. I need to let someone else in my family know what's going on," Belle said, feeling more cheerful at the mere prospect of talking with Marisa. "But not my mother. I don't want to worry her."

"Your sister, then?" Sandro asked.

Belle nodded. "Yes. I'm going to call Marisa and explain that Tony's missing, and I need a place to stay for the night."

"I'll have to stay with you," Sandro warned.

"You're going to need me around when the kidnappers call."

Belle didn't protest. The truth was, right now she welcomed the prospect of having Sandro close at hand. After twenty-four hours of almost constant stress, she was running on empty, and Sandro's presence replenished her. She'd explore the ramifications of that later, when she wasn't on tenterhooks about Tony.

"Marisa and Evan have a live-in nanny for the baby, so they may not have a spare bedroom," she said. "But they must have a sofa or two where we could rest."

"Fine. None of us will be sleeping much, I guess. And, with luck, the kidnappers will call us quite soon after you get to your sister's place."

"I hope so. God, I hope so."

"Give me your sister's address." He cupped her face with his hand. "I'm trusting you to go where you say you're going, Belle. Am I being a fool?"

"No." She rummaged in her purse, glad of the excuse to look away. "I have my address book in here somewhere. Here we are—354 King Palm Drive, and that's her phone number."

Sandro copied the address and phone number into a small notebook. "Here's the plan," he said. "Go outside and use a public phone to call your sister. Don't try to hide. When you've alerted Marisa to the fact that we're coming, ask the doorman to get you a cab. Make sure you tell him you're going to Boca Raton. When the cab pulls up at the curb, give the driver your sister's address before you get inside. That way, if Tony's kidnappers have a tail on you, they'll have three chances to hear exactly where you're going."

"And what about you?"

"I have a departmental car," Sandro said. "As soon as I see you get into the cab, I'll drive to your sister's. It'll take at least forty minutes to get to Boca Raton—long enough for me to call my boss and warn him to put some agents on standby so that they can move quickly when you hear from the kidnappers. After the cab drops you off at your sister's house, I'll circle the block to check out who and what might be on your tail. Then I'll park the car a few houses away and walk back to your sister's place. I don't want to come in through the front door in case it's being watched, so I'll find a back entrance. I should be there no more than fifteen or twenty minutes after you."

Belle held out her hand. "I need the disk, Sandro."

"I can't give it to you."

Her expression must have shown her feeling of betrayal.

"It's not that I don't trust you," Sandro said. "I'm keeping the disk because the kidnappers are more likely to cheat you than they are me. Tony isn't my brother, so in a crunch it's easier for me to think with my head instead of my heart. Besides, it's what I've been trained to do."

Right now, Belle suspected that Tony might be in desperate need of a few people who were willing to give him the benefit of the doubt. But Sandro had agreed to act as if the kidnapping were genuine until they knew for sure that it wasn't, and nothing in his plan suggested that he was willing to put her brother's life at risk for the sake of retrieving the Cronus disk. She would have to be content with that.

"Sandro..."

"Yes?"

"Thank you for what you're doing."

"You're welcome." He touched his finger to her lips, hesitating for a moment before cautioning her. "Don't count on me, Belle. When the chips are down, you'll want to save your brother, and I'll want to retrieve the Cronus disk and arrest the bad guys."

Perversely, she was more reassured by his warning than she would have been if he'd vowed that she could count on him through thick and thin. Belle was all too familiar with split loyalties and half promises, and knew exactly where he was coming from. Her father had been the master of smiling promises, delivered with charm but broken almost before the words could dissolve into the ether. The conflict between loyalty, duty and love sometimes made for such unbearable conflict that a truthful warning was the most an honest person could deliver.

"Well, I guess I'd better get going." She realized that she was gazing up at Sandro, wondering why he hadn't kissed her again. She was instantly annoyed with herself for wasting time and mental energy on something so irrelevant, when her brother's life was at risk.

"Yes, you should be on your way. Even if the murder of Donald Gates was unplanned, the kidnappers should have regrouped by now."

Belle walked over to the door, rummaging for change to make her phone call. She wanted to ask whether there was any hope that Tony would avoid a jail sentence if he survived the kidnapping, but she suspected she knew the answer already—and she didn't want to hear Sandro put it into words. In the end, as so often happened, there was nothing she could safely say, and so she remained silent.

Sandro held the heavy fire door open for her. At the last minute he dipped his head and kissed her swiftly on the lips. "Good luck," he said. "I'll see you at Marisa's house."

Fifteen

"Come on in," Marisa said, opening the front door and drawing Belle inside. "You made good time. Heavens, you look beat, you poor thing, and no wonder. I can't believe you missed your flight. What went wrong? Evan said you got to the airport in plenty of time. Did the airline cancel?"

Marisa looked distressed on behalf of her sister. She also looked ravishingly beautiful. She had changed since leaving the restaurant, and was now dressed like a vision from a thirties' movie in a full-skirted white satin robe with long narrow sleeves that covered her wrists, and contrasted with a neckline that plunged just low enough to be provocative. She even wore high-heeled slippers, decorated with puffs of swansdown. The illusion of intimate domestic glamour was complete.

Confronted by her sister's elegance, Belle realized that she was not only exhausted, but also sweaty, grimy, and probably rancid-smelling. She was wearing the same linen slacks and tailored cotton shirt that she'd put on at five that morning. Her slacks looked as if they were part of a consumer test designed to see how badly fabric could wrinkle, and her shirt clung limply in all the wrong places.

"You said you had something really important to

discuss with me," Marisa said, leading the way into a brightly lit kitchen with gleaming counters and a glossy tile floor. She opened the refrigerator and pulled out a crystal jug with a silver lid—a very up-scale version of the plastic juice jug Belle kept in her fridge.

"Something to drink?" she asked, holding up the jug. "It's mixed fruit juice, mostly grape and apple. I squeezed it myself. Or we have iced tea."

"Juice would be great." Belle didn't even want to sit at the spotless kitchen table, she felt so grungy. "Actually, Marisa, we really need to talk. I have a problem—"

"Sure—I hope I can help. Would you like to go out on the patio? I always prefer to escape from the air-conditioning at this time of night."

Their conversation was taking on the surreal over-tones of a social call. Belle realized that in her effort to avoid alarming her sister when she'd phoned, she had ended up totally failing to convey the urgency of the situation. Her sister obviously hadn't the faintest clue that Belle was the bearer of bad tidings.

Debating whether to plunge straight in with the news of Tony's kidnapping, or to hem and haw in an effort to soften the blow, Belle's train of thought was interrupted by a squawking sound that seemed to come from directly behind her, followed by a cough and an odd wail. She jumped, looking over her shoulder.

"Gosh, that startled me," she said sheepishly, when she realized the weird noises came from a baby monitor. "I hope it wasn't my arrival that woke Spencer."

"Oh, no, I'm sure it wasn't. He's been having trouble falling asleep just recently. He's been teething and running a fever.'' Marisa set the jug on the counter and hurried toward the stairs without stopping to pour any juice. ''I need to catch him before he gets worked up and pitches a fit. I'll be right back. Help yourself to a drink, okay?''

Belle caught her arm as she rushed past. ''Wait, Rizzie.'' The childhood nickname slipped out unthinkingly. ''Before you go, I've got to tell you some really bad news. I'm sorry, but I don't know how to make this less awful. Tony's been kidnapped.''

Marisa stopped with one foot poised over the bottom step. Without making a sound, she set her foot down, then swung around, eyes glassy with shock, the full satin skirt of her robe fluttering to stillness around her ankles. ''Kidnapped?'' she repeated, as if she'd never heard the word and didn't understand what it meant. ''Tony?''

The baby monitor squawked again, and she jerked back into motion. ''Sorry, I've got to go,'' she said, running up the stairs. ''He gets so angry if he's left.''

Belle frowned at her sister's rapidly disappearing back. Marisa seemed on edge tonight, and her reaction to the news about Tony's kidnapping had been…odd. Belle poured a drink and put the jug back in the fridge, hoping she'd chosen the correct spot. The shelves were sparkling clean, with every item lined up in orderly rows, the tallest containers at the rear so that everything was instantly visible. The door racks held neat rows of condiments, and there were no mystery leftovers since each Tupperware container was labeled with meticulous care.

Belle wasn't sure whether to be awestruck or horrified. Their mother was a terrific cook, but a slapdash homemaker who couldn't keep things neat despite a full-time housekeeper and cleaning crews that came in twice a week to take care of polishing the floors and washing the windows. Marisa looked as if she was suffering from a major overreaction to their mother's casual attitude to domestic organization.

Glancing around, Belle realized the kitchen counters were as pristine as the fridge, and the family room looked as if it had been tidied for a photo shoot in *House Beautiful*. Belle considered herself an organized person, but she hated to think how much time and effort it must take Marisa to keep the house up to this immaculate standard. And how miserable for Spencer. She hoped to goodness there was at least one room set aside where the poor little kid could run around and make as much mess as he pleased. She suddenly remembered Horatio, the new puppy. Where was he? There wasn't a sign or sound of him anywhere. No water bowl, no blanket, no chew toys.

Evan came downstairs as Belle was carrying her drink out onto the porch. "Marisa just told me the terrible news about Tony," he said, sliding the patio door open for her to go through. "Jesus, Belle, this is awful. Horrible. Explain to me what happened and what ransom the kidnappers are demanding. How did they contact you, by the way? You're supposed to be on a plane flying back to Chicago."

"I was contacted while we were at the restaurant this afternoon."

"*What?*" Evan looked both shocked and annoyed. "Belle, I can't believe you didn't tell anyone! I can't believe you let me go through the farce of dropping you off at the airport without saying a single word about Tony! For heaven's sake, why didn't you ask me for help? I have some experience with this sort of thing, you know. Doing business in the Far East like I do, you have to be prepared for the worst. I've even attended a seminar on how American business people can minimize the risk of being kidnapped and having their companies held up for ransom.''

"I'm sorry I kept you in the dark,'' Belle said apologetically. "I know you must have a lot of useful advice to contribute. That's why I'm here now. I was desperate to tell everyone the truth when we were at the restaurant this evening, but the kidnappers insisted that I couldn't tell anyone or they'd kill Tony.''

"Well of course they threatened you! What did you expect? That they'd recommend you should call in the FBI?'' Evan drew in a deep breath and pulled out a chair, waiting for her to sit down before taking his own seat across the table. "Sorry, the sarcasm was uncalled-for. I guess I'm still in shock. Don't look so disheartened, Belle, I'm sure you did your best in a very difficult situation.''

"I tried. But I guess the bottom line is that Tony is still missing, so my best wasn't good enough. I'm sorry to dump on you and Marisa but I don't know where else to turn. I didn't want to bring Mom into this mess. She was so devastated by my father's death that I was afraid she would break down completely if we told her that Tony's been kidnapped.''

"You're right. Although Carole is never going to forgive any of us if something happens to her son and she discovers we didn't keep her informed. How the hell are we going to justify keeping quiet if we can't arrange a ransom and the kidnappers dump Tony's body on her front doorstep?'' Evan stopped abruptly, flushing bright red with embarrassment when he realized what he'd just said.

"I'm sorry," he said. "That was real tactless of me."

Belle noticed that he didn't apologize for suggesting Tony might get killed, only for having spoken the unforgivable out loud. "You don't have to apologize for being honest with me, Evan. I need to hear what you really think. So, do you suggest we tell Mom what's going on? I need to ask Marisa's opinion, too."

"Hmm...now you ask me directly, that's a tough call," Evan said. He pulled a face. "It's a lot easier to criticize than to make decisions, isn't it? I guess if we can get Tony back safely, the answer is obviously no. There's no reason to alarm Carole if it's going to be a case of all's well that ends well."

He had to speak loudly because the sounds of Spencer crying and Marisa trying to soothe him were blaring out of the baby monitor through the open patio door. Then a soft, pleasant voice with a British accent spoke over Spencer's yells, offering to hold the baby if Marisa wanted to join her husband and sister downstairs.

That must be the nanny, Belle thought. Anita somebody-or-other. From the fuss Spencer was putting up, he was not a happy camper, whoever was holding him.

Marisa rejected Anita's offer, sounding rather snappish. Evan got up and slid the heavy patio door shut. The voices from the monitor faded to an almost inaudible murmur, and he slumped back into his seat. "Phew, that's better. I don't know what's been going on with Spencer for the past couple of weeks. Marisa loves him to pieces, but she fusses too much. I keep telling her that healthy kids like Spencer aren't fragile. He isn't going to break if she doesn't run to him the second he cries.''

"Well, she had two miscarriages before Spencer arrived, and that must make him extra precious,'' Belle said. ''She just wants to make sure she does everything right. If you have another baby, I expect she'll be a lot more confident.''

"I'm not sure Marisa could cope with two babies, even if she could manage to carry another pregnancy to term. She already complains that the days aren't long enough for her to get through everything she has to do.''

"She'd soon learn to cope. Marisa was one of the most efficient teenagers I ever knew, and that sort of basic personality trait doesn't change.'' Belle glanced up as her sister came out onto the patio. ''Hey, that was quick. Has Spencer gone back to sleep?''

Marisa shook her head. ''He's still wide-awake. I left him with Anita.''

"Is Anita okay with that?'' Evan asked. ''This is supposed to be free time for her.''

"It's fine. She's reading him a story. In fact, she came almost before I could lift the baby out of his crib.''

"We're real lucky to have Anita,'' Evan said, pulling out a chair for his wife. ''Not only does she manage Spencer beautifully, but she's also a very low-key, easygoing sort of person. And she likes living in Florida, thank goodness, so we don't have to worry that she'll get homesick and rush back to England.''

"You have to tell me about Tony,'' Marisa said to Belle, cutting in almost before Evan had finished speaking. "I couldn't even grasp it a few minutes ago when you said that he'd been kidnapped. While I was with Spencer, I kept thinking about what you'd said, but somehow I couldn't make the idea of a kidnapping seem real. It's impossible. How can Tony have been kidnapped? I just saw him yesterday."

"It's real," Evan said grimly. "You'd better believe it."

Marisa appeared on the verge of tears, and Evan put his arm around her. "You've got to be strong," he urged her. "Your brother is going to need you to keep your head straight and act smart. He's going to need that from all of us. Can you keep your cool, Marisa? For your brother's sake?"

Marisa drew in a deep breath. "Of course I can keep my cool," she said, although Belle could see her sister was having to fight hard for control.

"How much do the kidnappers want as a ransom?" she asked Belle. "Why did they approach you and not Mom? Did you actually talk to them? When was Tony kidnapped? How—"

"Wait!" Belle said. "Let me answer those questions before you ask any more."

"Slow down, Marisa. Give your sister a chance to speak," Evan admonished gently. "Okay, Belle. Start with when and how you found out your brother had been kidnapped, and we'll go from there. Until we understand what happened, we can't make any sensible decisions about what to do next."

"The kidnappers approached me while we were at the restaurant," Belle said. "You remember, Rizzie, when you came into the ladies' room and asked me why I was taking so long? I was in shock, I guess.

One of the waiters had just passed me a note instructing me to call a certain phone number.''

"The kidnappers managed to track you down at the restaurant?'' Marisa asked, astonished. "But how did they know you would be there? We only made the arrangements at the last minute. Are they psychic, or something?''

"I don't know how they found out—''

"My God, they must be watching us.'' Marisa shivered. "It's creepy to think they were right in that restaurant—''

"We're getting off track again,'' Evan said. "I know it's difficult, Marisa, but you have to try not to interrupt. We need to hear what happened, not how awful it is.''

"Sorry,'' Marisa said. She was so overwrought that her shoulders were visibly shaking. Evan stroked his hand gently down her arm, and laced his fingers through hers. Belle was relieved to see that this seemed to calm her sister down.

"You were explaining that somehow the kidnappers found you and passed you a note,'' Evan said to Belle. "What did the note say exactly? Do you still have it, by the way?''

"Yes, right here. For what it's worth.'' Belle spread the crumpled note out on the table so that they could both read it.

"But this isn't from the kidnappers!'' Marisa exclaimed, pushing the crumpled slip of paper toward Evan so that he could see it. "It's from Tony. Are you sure he's been kidnapped? That isn't what the note says. He just asks you to contact him.''

"I know. But when I called that phone number, a man answered and told me that they were holding

Tony prisoner. He said that if I wanted to ransom my
brother, I had to get to the Tropicana Hotel at the
airport before eight o'clock. He promised that he
would release Tony in exchange for the disk.''

"A disk?" Evan queried. "Not money? How
weird. You mean, a computer disk?"

Belle nodded. "Yes, they wanted a computer disk
my father had instructed me to take from his study
right after he died.''

"It must have some very high-tech programs on it
for the kidnappers to go to all this trouble," Evan
said. "What is it, some sort of military technology
disk?"

"Actually, it's not a program disk at all," Belle
said. "It's a DVD disk that contains detailed information about all the people my father bribed in order
to keep the Joubert Corporation operations safe from
prosecution."

"But what use is that to anyone? And how did the
kidnappers know that you had the disk?" Evan asked.
Marisa made a small sound, and he glanced ruefully
at her. "Okay, Marisa, you don't have to tell me. I'm
sounding just like you—asking questions Belle can't
possibly answer."

"I don't understand why the kidnappers haven't
asked for money," Marisa said. "Why do they want
a stupid computer disk, whatever it says? Dad had
been running a strictly legitimate operation for the
past five years, so the information he prepared must
be pretty old. Why would anyone care enough about
an out-of-date list to kidnap Tony?"

"Your father *told* us his activities were all legal,"
Evan pointed out before Belle had to say the same
thing. "But how do we know the truth about what he

was up to? We're, neither of us, involved in the running of the business in any way, so it's just hearsay."

Marisa was looking increasingly anxious, and he rubbed his hand up and down her arm as he spoke, soothing her. "Think about it, honey. There are probably several important people whose names are on that disk. Any one of them might be willing to go to extreme lengths to save his career and reputation from ruin."

Marisa bowed her head. "I can't believe you were going through all this, and I never noticed," she said to Belle. "I'm sorry I was such a rotten, unobservant sister. I was worrying about Mom, and how much she was missing Dad, and I guess I wasn't paying attention to anyone else."

"You weren't rotten at all. I was trying my best to appear normal, precisely so that you *wouldn't* notice anything was wrong. The kidnappers warned me that I wasn't to tell anyone what had happened, or bring anyone with me to the hotel, or they would kill Tony."

Marisa shook off Evan's hand. She pushed back her chair and stood up, radiating nervous energy. Belle sensed the approach of a typical piece of Joubert melodrama. "I can't stand this sitting around and talking!" Marisa exclaimed. "We should be doing something. Tony is in terrible trouble, I can feel it in my bones. I've always had an almost psychic ability to spot trouble—you know that, Belle. We have to take action now, before something awful happens."

Belle suppressed a sigh, and refrained from pointing out that nobody needed to be psychic to work out that a man who had been kidnapped was in big trouble.

"We all want to take action," Evan said patiently. "But before we can do anything constructive, we need to know what happened. Belle hasn't told us yet what went wrong when she tried to ransom Tony."

His calm logic seemed to reassure Marisa, at least a little. She stopped pacing and leaned against one of the patio columns, shredding a paper napkin. "Evan's right," she said. "Tell us what happened next, Belle."

"After Evan dropped me off at the airport, I doubled back and went to the hotel," Belle said. "The kidnappers had told me they would be waiting in room 823, but when I got there, the door was ajar and the suite was empty."

"Did they leave behind any clue as to who might have been there?" Evan asked.

"Absolutely none. The suite had been cleaned out. There were damp towels on the bathroom floor, and I think the kidnappers may have used those to wipe away fingerprints. The furniture looked pretty much dust and debris free. A really detailed forensic sweep might reveal something useful, but there was no way for me to tell just by looking who'd been in there or how long they'd stayed."

"So we're at the mercy of the kidnappers," Marisa said. "We can't go after them, so we have no choice but to hang around and wait for them to contact us. That's great. Just great."

"It's true that we don't know anything about them. Except..." Belle drew in a deep breath. "Except the room wasn't exactly empty. I—I found a dead body lying on the floor behind the bar. It was a man I know. His name is Donald Gates."

Evan looked too stunned to speak.

"Oh, no!" Marisa said. "This is—this just keeps getting worse and worse. What did you do?"

"Stood still until I was sure I wouldn't throw up," Belle said dryly. "Then I turned tail and got the hell out of the room."

"How did you know this Donald Gates person?" Evan asked, recovering his voice.

"Donald and I had dated for a while," Belle said. "He lives in Chicago, only ten miles away from me, so I was really shocked to find him lying dead on the floor of a hotel room in Miami. I mean, what was he doing there?"

She massaged the spot on her forehead where a headache had begun to pound with ferocious power. "That sounded horribly callous, and I didn't mean it to be. But was Donald Gates involved with the kidnappers? I guess that's a stupid question. He must have been or he wouldn't have been lying dead on the floor of that hotel room."

"But if he was in cahoots with the kidnappers, then why was he dating you?" Evan asked. "That can't be coincidence."

It was humiliating, but Belle admitted the truth. "He knew Dad was rich. I think he assumed I would be rich one day, too, and he wanted my money."

Tears trembled at the ends of Marisa's lashes, making her look more than ever like a movie star playing a tragic love scene. "I'm sorry," she said, wiping away the tears. "You're the one who's been through all this crap, Belle, and I'm the one who's crying."

"Trust me, I would have cried buckets by now if I hadn't been too busy panicking," Belle assured her.

"It all finally seems real to me." Marisa took a paper napkin from the stack on the patio table and blew her nose. "I have to accept that my brother has been kidnapped by people who are willing to kill. I keep visualizing Tony lying...looking like Donald..." She couldn't bring herself to complete the sentence.

Evan broke the silence that followed. "Did you notify the authorities that you'd found Donald's body?" he asked Belle.

"No," she said, and cut off Evan's protests by explaining, "I couldn't risk it. I'd dated Donald for quite a while, and I had no excuse for being in that hotel room. At least, no excuse I was willing to share with the police. I was afraid they'd haul me in for questioning. And if I was in police custody, I knew, the kidnappers wouldn't be able to reach me."

"Good thinking," Evan said, revising his objections. "You kept your head in a tough situation, Belle. Well done."

"Thanks. But my smart thinking doesn't seem to have gotten us very far. Nobody's called with a new ransom demand."

"Give them time. The kidnappers have to track you down."

"Our phone number is unlisted," Marisa said, sounding anxious.

"They found Belle in a restaurant in Miami Beach, as you pointed out," Evan said. "Somehow, I don't think an unlisted phone number is going to defeat them."

"Are we going to tell the FBI what's happened?" Marisa asked.

"How do you think your Mom would feel about that?" Evan asked. "The FBI certainly has resources we don't. On the other hand, once they're involved, they'll insist we do everything by the book. Their book, not ours."

For reasons she hadn't examined too closely, Belle had managed to recount the events of the day without once speaking Sandro's name. But the time had clearly come. She could no longer avoid mentioning him.

"Actually, law enforcement is already involved. But not the FBI. U.S. Customs."

"Customs?" Marisa was enough of a Joubert to sound appalled at the mere mention of the word. "Belle, for heaven's sake, why did you involve *Customs?* You know those people won't lift a finger to get Tony back. They probably think he deserves anything that happens to him."

"I didn't have much choice," Belle said. "Unfortunately, it seems that Customs has been keeping the Joubert Corporation under surveillance. They monitored a phone call I made to Tony last night, and followed me once I got to Miami. When I came out of the hotel room, Sandro Marchese was waiting for me."

"Sandro Marchese?" Evan said questioningly.

"He's a Customs agent," Belle said. "I've known him for quite a long time." She waited for Marisa to jump in with some exaggerated comment about Sandro, but, mercifully, her sister remained silent.

"I'm getting to be like Marisa," Evan said. "I'm getting a very bad feeling about all this. What part of the story are you leaving out, Belle? What is Sandro Marchese planning to do?"

"Nothing that we wouldn't do ourselves."

"That seems unlikely," Evan said.

"Well, you can ask him for yourself. He should be

here any moment. He, er…wants to spend the night here so that he can monitor any phone calls that come from the kidnappers."

"He's coming here? Are you crazy?" Marisa was white. "Belle, you have to send him away. Get rid of him. As soon as the kidnappers realize we have a federal agent working with us, they'll get angry. Or frightened, which is even worse. For God's sake, do you want to get Tony killed?"

"I can't get rid of Sandro," Belle said tersely.

"Of course you can," Marisa snapped.

"No, she can't." Sandro spoke from outside the patio door. "I have the disk the kidnappers want as a ransom. I took it from Belle at the hotel."

Sixteen

At midnight they were still waiting for the kidnappers to call. The two hours since Sandro's arrival had passed with agonizing slowness, in an atmosphere that was strained to the breaking point.

Sandro had been polite but implacable in his determination to remain at Belle's side until Tony was free, and Marisa had eventually subsided into a hostile silence, accepting his presence only because she couldn't prevent it. Neither a career in New York, nor marriage to a toy salesman seemed to have overcome her Joubert-nurtured loathing of anyone connected to Customs.

Evan had at first been no more tolerant of Sandro than had his wife, but as time wore on and the kidnappers failed to call, he seemed glad to have another man around to share the waiting. They played chess and managed to concentrate well enough to get through an entire game, which was more than either Belle or Marisa was capable of doing.

Marisa hadn't budged from her seat next to the phone. She hunched on the edge of the chair, her hand curled over the receiver, ready to snatch it up at the first ring. It had already rung once, and Belle's nerves had snapped at the sound—but the caller turned out to be a friend of Marisa's, and her sister had hung up with a terse explanation that she and Evan weren't free to talk.

The abortive phone calls drained the final dregs of Belle's stamina. She retreated to a corner of the living room and filled the century-long minutes by blindly turning the pages of various glossy magazines that happened to be stashed in a caddy beside the chair where she was sitting. When the grandfather clock in the hall finished chiming midnight, Sandro came over and prized a copy of *Bon Appétit* out of her hands.

"Time to get some rest," he said. "You've been reading the same page long enough to learn how to cater a wedding banquet for two hundred."

Belle glanced at the magazine he'd taken and saw that she'd been staring at a picture of a multitiered wedding cake. She didn't move, because the only signal that could trigger movement in her body at this point would be the sound of the phone ringing.

Sandro took a strand of hair that was falling into her eyes and gently looped it behind her ear. "Go and take a shower," he said softly, pulling her to her feet. "I know it's useless asking you to sleep, but you look just about at the point of exhaustion, and you need to do something."

She remembered that a thousand years ago when she'd first arrived here, she'd felt grungy and disheveled, but she'd long since passed beyond that. "I can't shower," she said, impatient that Sandro would make such a silly suggestion. "Suppose the kidnappers call—"

"Then one of us can bang on the shower door to get you out. Or Marisa can bring the phone in to you. Come on, Belle. You're going to collapse if you don't do something to help you relax."

"He's right, you know." Evan came and perched on the arm of her chair. "There's no point in all of us sitting around, pretending we're not going out of our minds with the waiting. I'm going to persuade Marisa to come to bed."

He walked over to his wife and lifted Marisa's hand from the phone, just as Sandro had taken the magazine from Belle. "Come on, honey. Your sister wants to take a shower and she needs something clean to change in to."

"What?" Marisa stared at her husband.

"Your sister needs a change of clothes. Can you find her something comfortable to wear?"

"Oh, of course. Sorry, Belle, I should have thought." Marisa rose to her feet, but she didn't actually move toward the stairs.

"I'll come up with you," Evan said. "I guess there's no hope of sleeping, but we need to lie down for an hour or two. I do, anyway. I'm beginning to feel more like a zombie than a person."

"I couldn't sleep," Marisa said with total conviction.

"Maybe not," Evan said. "But we're, none of us, going to do Tony any good by staying up until we're too exhausted to think straight." He touched her very gently on her arm. "Come to bed, honey."

"I guess I am a little tired..." She turned to Belle. "I'll be right back with some clothes for you."

"Thanks." Belle yawned, which was about the most active thing she'd done in the past half hour. She hugged her sister. "Try to rest, Rizzie, even if you can't sleep. It's annoying when the men are right, but this time they are."

"I'll try," Marisa said. She tried to smile. "Right

now, I feel so wired, I'm not sure whether I want to fall on the bed or run ten times around the block.''

"You need bed," Evan said. He gave her a quick hug. "Husband's orders."

Anita, Spencer's nanny, came down the stairs just as Marisa and Evan started to walk up. Anita was carrying Horatio, as she had been two hours ago when she'd come down and been introduced to Belle and Sandro. She was wearing sweats, and her face was scrubbed clean, ready for bed. Belle had found Anita rather nondescript when she'd been wearing a tailored linen dress, but the lack of makeup and formal clothing suited her, making her appear almost sexy.

"I'm going to take the dog for a last walk," she said.

"Thanks." Marisa would have carried on upstairs, but Evan stopped her so that he could have a word with the nanny.

"I hope the puppy didn't wake you, Nita? He's really taking up far too much of your supposed time off."

Anita shook her head and patted the fur between Horatio's ears. "It's a pleasure. You know, we Brits are always suckers for dogs, especially puppies. In fact, he was snoozing peacefully, so I got *him* up, not the other way around. He can't last more than five hours between walks, and I didn't fancy being woken up at four in the morning to supervise a call of nature."

"He's doing quite well in the housebreaking area, isn't he?" Evan scratched the puppy under its chin, and Horatio licked his hand in a slurpy, grateful kiss. "Hey, fella, are you being a good boy for your nanny?"

"He's being a very good boy. Aren't you, pet?" Anita smiled. "Trust me, after potty training so many children, Horatio seems quite easy by comparison!"

"Marisa and I really appreciate the extra time you're giving us, don't we, honey?"

"Yes." Marisa made no effort to look either at the puppy or the nanny, and she showed no sign of wanting to scratch Horatio's chin or pat his head. "It's very good of you, Anita, and the dog seems to be settling in quite well." She hadn't touched Horatio the last time Anita had brought him down, either, Belle remembered. Odd. Her sister had always loved animals, especially dogs.

But not Horatio, apparently. Marisa continued up the stairs without a backward glance, and after a brief apologetic murmur to Anita, Evan followed his wife.

"I'll be right back with your clothes," he said to Belle, turning at the top of the stairs.

"Thanks." Belle's body ached in places where she had never realized she had muscles, and now that she'd given herself permission to halt her vigil long enough to shower, she was suddenly longing to step under some hot pounding water and scrub herself with scented soap.

"Oops, Horatio seems a bit impatient. I'd better hurry up and take him out," Anita said. She dangled a key chain. "I have my key, so I won't disturb you when I come in." She hesitated for a moment, checked that Evan and Marisa had gone into their bedroom, then spoke quickly. "I hope I'm not intruding, but there's obviously something wrong, and I can see Marisa's very upset. She's such a wonderful mother and a great employer, so I wondered if there's any way I could help."

"Thanks," Belle said. "Unfortunately, this is strictly a family problem. But I'm sure my sister would appreciate your offer if she knew about it."

"Well, let me know if you think of anything I could do. In the meantime, I'd better walk Horatio before we have an accident. He's such a sweetie. I hope Marisa gets to like him better as she gets more accustomed to him."

"I'm sure she will," Belle said.

"Do you want me to walk with you?" Sandro asked. "It's quite late to be out alone."

"I'll be fine, thanks. I come from sturdy Scottish stock, you know." Anita grinned. "Besides, I have a black belt in karate."

"Now I know why Marisa's so intimidated by her," Belle said as the front door closed behind the nanny. "Good grief, it's bad enough that the woman has all those child care qualifications. Now she's Ms. Animal Trainer and a black belt in karate, as well. Not to mention the British accent, which makes her sound twice as smart as she probably is."

Sandro, who was looking abstracted, didn't reply. Evan came downstairs, carrying a neatly folded pile of clothes. "Marisa's glued to the phone again," he said, the corners of his mouth turning down. "I can't seem to convince her that it's going to ring whether she hovers over it or not."

"I guess we can't force her to sleep if she doesn't want to," Sandro said.

"But how long is Marisa going to keep this up?" Evan asked.

Sandro shrugged. "The problem will solve itself, because this situation can't go on for too long. If the kidnappers haven't contacted us by tomorrow morning, I'll have to notify the FBI, and then the waiting won't be your wife's responsibility anymore.''

Belle was horrified. ''You can't just unilaterally call in the FBI,'' she protested. ''I have to talk to my mother first. If the kidnappers don't call tonight, it's *her* choice what we do next. Not mine, and certainly not yours.''

''Not from my point of view,'' Sandro said quietly. ''I'm sorry, Belle, but once I've been made aware that a kidnapping has occurred, I'm obligated to report it to the proper authorities. I'm only able to get away with keeping it secret for a few hours because I've convinced my boss that there's every reason to believe that this is a case of extortion—with your father's disk as the target—rather than a genuine kidnapping. We're, both of us, way out on a limb here.''

''You're taking a mighty big risk with Tony's life if you bring in the FBI,'' Evan said.

''I could be taking an even bigger risk by not bringing them in. When the kidnappers call, they might insist on a rendezvous that's too close timewise for me to summon backup. Then we're screwed.''

''Not necessarily,'' Evan said. ''I'm sure Marisa and Belle, not to mention Tony's mother, all care a great deal more about getting him back alive than about capturing the people who've taken him. I can't believe the family of the victim has no say in what happens in a situation like this. It's not right.''

''It's the law,'' Sandro said.

Evan snorted. ''Well, that sure convinces me to pick up the phone and call the FBI right now.''

''It should,'' Sandro said. ''The FBI has experts who are willing to work closely with the family of the victim. They're not going to move in and follow some rigid plan that isn't appropriate to the situation. Anyway, we're not to that point yet.''

If Sandro was trying to inject a note of cheer, he didn't succeed. Evan looked about as angry and helpless as Belle felt. "I guess this is an area where we'll have to agree to disagree." Evan was visibly struggling to be polite. "Fortunately, we still have every reason to hope that the kidnappers will call us tonight. The night's young, and they may well still be regrouping after Donald Gates's murder.''

Belle couldn't stand to listen any longer. "I'm going to shower." She was tired of going over the same ground, endlessly trying to second-guess the kidnappers, tormenting herself with images of Tony suffering at the hands of brutal captors. Or—far worse— wondering if he was sitting in a hotel room somewhere, drinking a beer and debating how much longer he should wait before picking up the phone to set conditions for his ransom.

She took the clean clothes from Evan and fled down the hallway to the guest suite, pursued by the demon of her own imagination. The shower, Belle decided as the scalding water poured over her, was about the best thing that had happened to her all day, but, even so, she was too jittery to linger under the spray. As soon as she felt clean, she started to worry again about the phone ringing. Or not ringing. She toweled off quickly and sprinkled scented talcum powder over her skin, only realizing how truly awful she'd felt before, now that she was feeling almost human again.

In addition to a nightgown and toilet articles, her sister had loaned her a gauzy dress with a drawstring waist and a shirred neckline, vaguely Mexican in style. Unwilling to waste even a few moments if the phone rang, Belle decided against wearing the nightgown, and pulled on the dress instead. The fabric was soft, comfortable, and brightly colored, the sort of dress Belle had worn in the old days, before she ran away to Chicago and tried to pretend that her life as Marc Joubert's daughter had never happened. Marisa had probably selected it simply to accommodate the differences in their height and body shape, but Belle felt right at home in the dress. Like her feelings for Sandro, banished for seven years and now rushing back with all their old power, it seemed that her preference for flamboyant clothes had simply been waiting for the chance to spring to life again.

Anita and Horatio came in from their walk as Belle emerged from the guest bathroom. "Mission accomplished," Anita said, shaking her foot to stop Horatio from chewing the laces of her sneakers. "I'll see you both tomorrow morning. Spencer and I usually get up about seven, but we'll try not to disturb you. Good night." Anita scooped Horatio into her arms and ran lightly up the stairs, a picture of youthful energy, despite the late hour.

Anita might be annoyingly well qualified, Belle reflected, but she was polite and cheerful, and Marisa was very lucky to have her. Anita could have pursued any career that appealed to her, so the fact that she'd become a nanny suggested she must love children, which was great for Spencer.

Belle followed faint sounds of splashing out onto the patio, and found Sandro swimming laps with ferocious concentration. He completed five more while she watched, then pulled himself out of the pool and crossed to the lounger where he'd left his towel.

Belle's exhausted system had reserved just enough energy to react with hormonal overenthusiasm to the sight of Sandro's half-naked body.

He walked over to the phone and adjusted the volume control on the ringer. "I had it turned up so that I could hear it while I was swimming," he said.

"Why haven't they called?" Belle asked, as if he could possibly give her a definitive answer.

"Because they're disorganized." Sandro pulled on his shirt, but didn't fasten the buttons. "Because they don't know where you are. Because they want to torment you to the point that you do exactly what they say when they finally call. Take your pick of any of the above."

"If the kidnappers don't know where I am by now, there's no way for them to find out." The chill that slithered down Belle's spine had nothing to do with the night breeze. "Maybe they didn't think to leave a tail at the hotel. Maybe we credited them with way too much intelligence."

"If they've lost track of you, the first place they'd call to track you down would be your sister's home."

"Do you really believe that?" Belle asked.

Sandro looked away. "It's what they'd do if they have any smarts at all."

Belle wrapped her arms around her waist. "My brother's going to die, isn't he."

"Not if I can possibly prevent it." Sandro got up and came to stand in front of her. Water still ran from his hair onto his forehead and shoulders. Without thinking, Belle reached up and touched her fingers to the wetness, following the path of a water droplet down his body.

He caught her hand, holding it against his chest so

that she could feel the thud of his heartbeat against her fingertips. He looked down at her, his eyes dark and turbulent. "You should go to bed, Belle. It's more than thirty-six hours since you got any sleep."

The desire that she felt was powerful enough to chase away exhaustion, urgent enough to provide temporary anesthesia against the pain of her brother's disappearance. She leaned forward, resting her cheek against Sandro's chest. "Come with me."

His arms closed around her, and she felt the touch of his lips on her hair. "All right. I can understand if you don't want to be alone."

He accompanied her to the guest room, walking behind her and keeping his hand pressed lightly against the small of her back. Once they got to the room, he picked up the phone and held it out so that she could hear the dial tone.

"It's working, so you can relax." He pulled back the bedspread and waited for her to kick off her shoes and lie down.

Instead of joining her on the bed, he pulled up a chair. "Okay, rest time. Don't worry if you doze off. I'll be right here, and I'll grab the phone the second it rings. Do you want me to switch off the light? That might make it easier for you to nap a little."

Belle sat up, her fingers folding nervous pleats into the fancy, lace-trimmed sheet. This was a hell of a moment for Sandro to start behaving like a perfect gentleman. "I don't care about the light. I don't want to take a nap. I want you to come to bed with me."

"That might not be a smart move," he said dryly. "Right now, I'm not feeling real sleepy."

She sighed. "You're not making this easy for me,

Sandro. I don't want you to sleep with me. I want you to make love to me.''

He came and sat on the bed next to her, but on top of the covers. He reached out, cradling her cheek in his hand as he spoke. "It wouldn't be a good idea, Belle.''

She blushed painfully. "I'm sorry. I thought you wanted me—''

"Of course I want you. I've been wanting to make love to you for the past three days.'' Sandro gave a wry smile. "Hell, I've been wanting to make love to you for the past seven years. But this isn't the right time for us, Belle.''

"Why not?''

"The first time we made love, it was for all the wrong reasons. I was using you to get to your father, period. When I started to care about you, I always had to live with the knowledge that I would have made love to you that first time even if I'd hated and despised you.''

"Do you...care about me now?''

"I care a lot. And I don't want us to make love now because you're so upset about your brother that you want to do something—anything—to take your mind off the fact that Tony's kidnappers haven't called.''

She turned her head enough so that she could kiss the palm of his hand where it rested against her face. "For a smart man, you can sometimes be really dumb, Sandro. This has got nothing to do with my brother. Trust me, this is strictly between the two of us.'' She linked her hands behind his head, pulling him down until his mouth touched hers. "Kiss me, and then tell me again that this isn't the right time for us to make love.''

"One of us should show some sense," he muttered. "I know you're going to regret this.''

"Wrong again, Sandro.'' Her smile was as unsteady as her pulse. "This is one of the few things about the last few days that I'm never going to regret.''

His head bent slowly toward her until at last he kissed her. His kiss was hard, carnal, demanding. Her answering arousal was swift and powerful. Desire clouded her mind and shortened her breath. She reached for him, aching with a hunger that she only now recognized as having been seven years in building. He kicked off his still-damp swimsuit and pushed her back against the pillows.

Sandro had always been a skillful lover as well as a passionate one, but tonight she felt a raw urgency to his lovemaking that was new. Before, he had been her tutor, and she had been his willing pupil. Now they were equals. Two mature adults coming together by choice, with no pretense and no secrets to act as filters for the intensity of what they felt for each other.

When he brought her to climax, the sensations ripped through her, leaving her limp and stunned. Before she could come down, he drove hard into her and, astonished, she found herself trembling on the brink of another orgasm. Her hips arched off the bed. He moved slowly, then faster, bringing her up to the heights again, holding her poised on the brink before plunging into her one last time. They tumbled together into the dazzling void.

When Belle could think again, she discovered Sandro was still sheathed inside her, holding himself over her body. With one hand he pushed her sweat-dampened hair out of her eyes and tilted her head, compelling her to look at him.

He spoke very softly. "I love you, Isabella Joubert. I think I always did."

She felt tears shimmer on the ends of her lashes, and he kissed them away. She said the words she had never before spoken to anyone—not even Sandro. "I love you, too. I think I always did."

Seventeen

The sound of a dog barking woke Belle. She sat up in bed, instantly wide-awake. Glancing at the clock, she saw that it was only five-thirty. Still, she couldn't believe that she'd actually managed to sleep for more than four hours.

Sandro got up from the chair and came to sit next to her on the bed. "Hi," he said, running his hand lightly over her hair. "It's early. I was hoping you'd sleep a little longer."

"I'm not tired." She looked at him despairingly, needing him to answer the unanswerable. "Why haven't the kidnappers called, Sandro? It's been almost twelve hours—"

His reply was interrupted by a hysterical cry. *"Somebody please help me!"*

Sandro took off at a run, but Belle had to stop to throw on some clothes before she could chase after him in the direction of the screams. When she reached the family room, she found Anita Gillespie collapsed in a chair, sobbing wildly. Horatio, leash still dangling from his collar, ran around in circles, barking with a confused puppy mixture of excitement and fear. Otherwise, the room looked as neat and orderly as it had the night before.

Sandro was already kneeling beside Anita's chair,

holding her hands to prevent her from clutching in a frenzied fashion at the neck of her shirt. "Are you hurt?" he asked. "Did you fall? What's happened? Talk to us, Anita. Tell us what's wrong."

Belle went to the kitchen for a glass of water, which she managed to get between Anita's chattering teeth. Just then Evan rushed headlong down the stairs, followed by Marisa, who was tying her robe as she ran.

"What happened? My God!" Evan snatched the glass away from Anita's mouth as she started to cough and splutter. "She's choking on it," he said, handing the glass to Belle.

Belle set the glass on the nearest side table, feeling guilty that she hadn't noticed Anita was having difficulty swallowing. Since Marisa seemed too shocked to move, Belle took control of Horatio, who had given up on chasing his leash and had started to chew his way through one of the sofa cushions.

Evan knelt opposite Sandro on the other side of Anita's chair and grabbed her chin, forcing her to turn and look at him. "Stop this, Anita! Calm down and tell us what happened. Quit the hysterics, right now. *Now,* do you hear me?"

His severity seemed to work where Sandro's more sympathetic approach had failed. Anita drew in a shuddering gasp, and her eyes lost some of their panic. "They were waiting for me," she rasped, her voice cracking. "Lying in wait when I took the dog out for his morning walk."

"Who was lying in wait for you?" Evan demanded.

"Two men. They tackled me from behind and held me by the throat. I was choking, struggling for breath.

It was horrible. I still can't swallow. One of them put his hand down the front of my shirt. His hands were all over my breasts..." She broke off, shuddering, on the verge of losing control again. "Bloody bastard."

Sandro and Evan exchanged a quick, grim glance. "Did they rape you?" Evan asked, his hand tightening around Anita's shoulders. His voice was much more gentle than before.

"No. Horatio saved me." Anita gave a gasp of hysterical laughter that quickly turned into a sob. "The puppy was barking and jumping up on them. He might even have realized something was wrong, because he wasn't playing like he usually does. His leash must have twined around their legs, at least enough to distract them for a few moments. They were cursing, trying to untangle themselves, and when they started swatting at the dog, I was able to break free and run back to the house. They didn't follow me, thank God. I heard them run off down the street."

Sandro's eyes narrowed. "Did you see your attackers clearly enough to make an ID?"

Anita shook her head. "I could hardly see them at all. It's still quite dark outside."

"Where did they attack you?" Sandro asked. "Were you walking Horatio on the road?"

"No, I didn't go off the property. I'm trying to teach Horatio to recognize the boundaries. They must have been hiding behind the jacaranda trees at the entrance to the driveway. They sprang out at me. All those years of karate training, and the first time I run into trouble in real life, everything I know about self-defense flew clean out of my head." Anita continued to clutch frantically at the neck of her T-shirt. "They pushed something down inside my bra. I can't bear it. I have to get it out.''

Her voice rose, spiraling toward renewed panic. "Oh, God, I keep feeling his dirty hands squeezing my breasts. I want this damn thing out of my bra! It makes my flesh creep.''

"Wait, let me help," Belle said. Anita was so upset that it obviously hadn't occurred to her that it would be easier to reach under the hem of her shirt than to try to poke her hand down from the top through the narrow neck of her T-shirt. "Try going from the bottom up instead of the top down.''

"Oh, yes.'' Anita drew in a deep breath, suddenly calmer. "Why didn't I think of that?'' She fumbled under her shirt for a couple of seconds before pulling out a crumpled wad of paper.

A chill snaked down Belle's spine. Rapists didn't shove notepaper down the front of their victim's clothing—at least, not any rapists she'd ever heard of.

"Is this some weird sort of sexual fetish that I don't know about?'' Anita stared at the wad of paper in bewilderment before handing it to Evan. She looked puzzled, but sounded more in control now that she no longer had a physical reminder of the attack scratching against her breasts.

Evan smoothed out the crumpled ball. An angry flush darkened his face as he read. "The people who attacked you weren't rapists. They were kidnappers.''

"Kidnappers!'' Anita exclaimed. "Oh, my God, *Spencer!* I never checked on him!''

She was already half out of the chair when Evan stopped her. "Spencer's fine,'' he said. "Unfortunately, though, Tony Joubert was kidnapped yesterday, which is why Belle and Sandro are here. This seems to be a message from the people who abducted him. It never occurred to any of us that you'd be dragged into the situation, or we'd have told you what was going on.''

Evan handed the note to Belle. A hollow opened in the pit of her stomach as she read the brief printed instructions aloud.

"Isabella Joubert. Come to the intersection of King Palm Drive and Lake View Road. Come alone. Bring the disk your father gave you. Your brother has one hour to live.

Marisa made a small sound of distress, and Evan turned quickly, patting her on the arm in a calming gesture. "What are you going to do?" he asked Belle.

She tried to keep her voice steady. "Well, I guess the note is clear enough. Give me the disk, Sandro. I should leave right now."

Sandro grabbed her hands, forcing her to stand still. "You're reacting exactly the way the kidnappers want you to, Belle. Stop and think before you rush into this."

She drew in an angry breath, drumming her fingers on the table for a couple of seconds before saying, "Okay, I've stopped to think. And what I've decided is that I need the disk *right now*."

"Stop playing the kidnappers' game," Sandro said tautly. "You don't even know that Tony is still alive. Hell, you don't even know that these so-called kidnappers actually have him under their control. Before you go tearing off on a mission to save your brother, you need to get some guarantee that when you hand over the disk, Tony will be released."

"What guarantee do you suggest I get?" Belle demanded. "And how am I supposed to get it? Should I go stand on the front porch and ask any watching kidnappers to please step forward and promise they'll play nicely?"

"They've given you an hour," Sandro said. "You can spare five minutes to think through your options. Complying blindly with the kidnappers' orders isn't your only option. I could have backup agents out here in forty minutes. A police helicopter could be here in less than that."

Marisa spoke for the first time. "No," she said, her hand clasping Evan's, which still rested on her arm. "Tony is my brother, and I forbid you to do that. These people have already killed twice. Bringing in police helicopters would be the equivalent of signing his execution warrant."

"I agree." A sick feeling lodged in the back of Belle's throat. "You warned me that we could end up seeing Tony's rescue from different perspectives, Sandro, and I'm afraid we've reached that point. You want to capture the bad guys. Right now, I don't give a damn about that and neither does Marisa. Just give me the disk. We don't have time to stand here arguing!"

"What happens when you've surrendered your only bargaining chip, and your brother is nowhere to be found? Take a few seconds to mull that one over."

"It's easy for you to talk, because Tony isn't your brother," Evan said hotly. "You're gambling with a man's life. I guess Marisa and Belle have a right to decide that they don't want to take that gamble."

"Marisa?" Belle turned to look at her sister. "Do you think I should do what the kidnappers say?"

Marisa hesitated. "It might be dangerous for you, Belle."

"They have no reason to hurt me," she said with more conviction than she felt. "Bottom line, they want the disk. Once they have it, why would they have any reason to cause me harm?"

"To stop you talking," Sandro said. "To stop you identifying them. To see if they can squeeze another ransom out of your family. Let me count the ways."

Marisa flushed. "He could be right, Belle. I have no right to ask you to risk your life to save Tony's. Why don't I go?"

"Why would it be any less dangerous for you than for me? And you have Spencer to think of," Belle said quietly. "I'm not crazy, and I don't want to walk into a trap, but what happens if I don't go? How do I live with myself if they kill Tony? I can't go through the rest of my life, knowing that my brother was murdered because I was too frightened to go to the intersection of two roads and hand over a computer disk." She turned to Sandro. "I'm not going to change my mind about this. Please give me the disk."

Sandro started to say something, then clamped his mouth shut. "The disk is in the guest room," he said. "I'll get it. Belle, come with me. You have to put on sandals, and, at the very least, I'm going to send you to this meeting with an electronic tracking device inserted in your sandal. No arguments."

Evan followed them into the guest room, leaving Marisa to take care of Anita. "Are you going to be able to tail Belle without being spotted?" he asked Sandro.

"Yes, that's not a problem. The range on this particular device is thirty miles. We use them a lot in

Customs—for tracking freight more often than people.''

''Why are you assuming the kidnappers are going to take me anywhere?'' Belle asked. ''Aren't they just as likely to grab the disk and toss Tony out onto the sidewalk?''

''Let's hope so,'' Evan said. ''Jeez, I hope that's what they do. Isn't that what they're most likely to do, Sandro?''

''No.'' Sandro unzipped his overnight bag with excessive force. ''Give me your sandal, Belle. Left foot.''

She handed it over to him in silence, and he examined it critically. ''This should work, although sneakers would be better.''

Belle watched as he cut a small slit into the heel and poked a microchip into the resulting opening. ''Won't it be damaged when I walk on it?'' she asked.

''It's fairly well protected,'' Sandro said. ''Here— you can put your shoe back on.''

She did so and stood up, holding out her hand. ''I'm ready. All I need now is the disk.''

He took it from his bag and handed it to her without speaking. ''Thank you,'' she said, turning to go.

''Belle...''

She turned. ''Yes?''

''Take care. And remember, I'll be close by, even if you can't see me.''

''What car are you driving?''

''A white Ford Taurus. Florida's favorite sedan, so I won't be conspicuous.'' He pulled her into his arms and kissed her. His embrace was tight, and his mouth moved urgently over hers, but Belle had kissed him often enough to know that this kiss was all show and no emotion. She stirred uncomfortably in his arms, but Sandro just kissed her more aggressively.

"I'll check on Anita," Evan said tactfully.

As soon as they were alone, Sandro clamped his hand over Belle's mouth and spoke directly into her ear, so quietly that she strained to hear. "Don't say *anything*. No! Keep your arms around my neck. Look as if you're nuzzling my neck. Good. Your watch is on the bed. There's another tracking device stuck to the back of it. Pick up your watch and put it on. Don't ask any questions. Don't comment on the tracking device in any way." He suddenly raised his voice, although he kept his arms locked around her. "Jesus, Belle, I don't think I can do this. How the hell am I supposed to stand back and watch you walk into danger? Oh, Marisa. Hi. I didn't see you there."

Marisa looked briefly at Sandro before her gaze slid away and fixed on her sister. "Are we doing the right thing?" she asked. "I couldn't bear it if anything happened to you, Belle."

"Nothing will happen." Belle tried not to sound as disoriented as she felt. "Besides, Sandro will be following me. With any luck, this could all be over in a few minutes." Belle picked up her watch from the bed with a feigned casualness that seemed to her not only fake but also ridiculous. She slipped the stretch band over her wrist, feeling the tracking device press against her skin, making an almost imperceptible bump. She had no idea what was going on, but she discovered, to her surprise, that she trusted Sandro enough to do what he asked without understanding his reasons.

Anita stood up as the three of them returned to the family room. "You're very brave," she said to Belle, looking a little shamefaced. "I'm sorry I made such a silly fuss about the attack just now. Not much stiff-upper-lip about my reaction, I'm afraid."

"You thought two men were trying to rape you," Belle said. "That's enough to frighten any woman."

"I have to go with Belle, but Marisa will be right here with you," Evan said, giving Anita a quick pat on the shoulder. "I'll be back in a minute. Belle, I'll come with you so that I can take down the license number of any car that approaches you. We'd better leave via the patio. That way Sandro can sneak into his car while you make your way around to the front of the house. If the kidnappers have someone watching the house, we don't want them to see Sandro getting into his car."

"Fortunately, my car is parked around the corner, on the street that backs up to this one," Sandro said. "Give me a couple of minutes before you walk out onto the driveway, will you, Belle? It'll take me that long to get to my car."

"Yes, of course." She didn't point out that a tracking device wasn't going to offer her much protection against a bullet. They were all too aware of that already.

Sandro kissed her swiftly on the lips—a genuine kiss this time, full of tenderness and passion. Then he cut across the backyard, disappearing through the oleander bushes that marked the rear boundary of the property.

"He seems like a good man," Evan said, staring after him. "He's a lot more flexible than most of those Washington government types. To be honest, I expected him to ride roughshod over our wishes and simply call in the FBI."

"He's worked undercover ever since he joined Customs," Belle said. "I guess he produces results, so he's pretty much allowed to do things his way." She glanced at her watch, too nervous to register what time it said. "Has it been two minutes? I don't think I can stand still much longer."

"We could start walking slowly around to the front of the house," Evan said. "As long as I stop at the end of the driveway, I guess the kidnappers won't complain if I come with you."

"Thanks for the moral support." Belle's heart was beginning to hammer against her ribs. The sun hadn't yet come up, and the air retained the chill of night. She hoped that was why she was shivering as she walked.

"You know I'd volunteer to go in your place if it would do any good," Evan said somberly. "But I'm afraid the kidnappers might get spooked if they saw a man waiting for them when they specifically asked for you."

"Evan, you don't have to explain."

"I'm getting an attack of macho guilt for letting a woman face the danger. But at that seminar on kidnapping I told you about, one of the things they kept hammering into us was to follow instructions. Unlike political abductions and hostage situations—when you need to call in government assistance as soon as possible—if you're dealing with criminals who want to make money, or gain some business advantage, going along with the perpetrators' demands without involving law enforcement is often the best way to negotiate the release of the victim."

"Don't worry, Evan. Honestly, I understand why it has to be me delivering this disk," Belle said.

They had reached the point where the driveway joined the road, and Evan cleared his throat, obviously uncomfortable at being the one who was about to return to the security of the house while Belle carried on alone. "Lake View is to your left," he said. "We're on King Palm, and Lake View is the second intersection. Good luck, Belle. We'll all be praying that you come through this safely."

She turned left, stressed to the point that she forgot to say goodbye. Walking doggedly forward, she forced herself to pay minute attention to her surroundings, as if noticing everyday things like a rabbit breakfasting on a home owner's petunias would somehow ward off disaster.

At this early hour, the streets in this upscale residential neighborhood were deserted, and it took her less than five minutes to reach the intersection of Lake View and King Palm Drive. She stopped on the southwest corner, wrapped her arms around her waist in an effort to ward off the chill, and waited for the kidnappers to make their move.

An ancient Toyota rattled by, its driver throwing newspapers onto driveways. Half expecting the car to turn at the last moment and spew out kidnappers, Belle kept her gaze glued to the vehicle until it disappeared from sight. She tensed again when a man in a tracksuit jogged by, headphones clamped to his ears—but he carried on at a steady pace, showing no interest in her. The waiting was unnerving her, which was probably exactly what was intended. She peered into the dense thicket of tropical vegetation on the opposite corner of the street, but she glimpsed no lurkers waiting to ambush her.

Where was Sandro? she wondered. Even when she

strained to listen, she couldn't hear the sound of a car engine idling. That was probably a good sign. If she couldn't hear his car, then presumably neither could Tony's captors. She waited for two minutes, and then for another two. Time expanded and simultaneously contracted. She felt as if she'd been waiting for hours, and yet her nerves were stretched so wire-tight that the seconds seemed to race by. This was a great moment to finally understand Einstein's theory of relativity, Belle thought with a tinge of hysteria.

A silver Lincoln Continental turned the corner from Lake View onto King Palm Drive. It slowed and drew up next to Belle. The rear door opened, and Dave Forcier leaned out.

"Hi, sweetie. I think you have a disk for your Uncle Dave."

Dave Forcier! Belle felt weak-kneed with shock, but she refused to let him see it. "I don't have anything for you until I see my brother. Where is he?"

"Get in the car and I'll take you to see him."

She flashed him a look of utter contempt. "You're confusing me with yourself, Dave. I'm not the stupid one."

"No, you're just a typical, fucking Joubert," Dave said. "Arrogant to the last." He pulled out a gun fitted with a silencer, and aimed it at her stomach. "Get in, Belle."

"So you can kill me at your leisure? I don't think so."

She saw his finger move on the trigger. A muffled *pop* sounded in her ears as the bullet blew up a shower of gravel from the sidewalk. "Next time, it'll be your knee. Get in the car, Belle."

She did the only thing she could. She got in the car.

Eighteen

Marisa finished changing Spencer's diaper and sat him upright on the changing stand so that she could tie the laces of his sneakers. Usually the all-too-short time she spent with Spencer was the highlight of her day, and she treasured every minute, but this morning not even the gratifying routine of caring for her child could ease the terror that left her hands clumsy and her heart pounding.

Spencer finished banging the brush against his head—his effort to comb his hair. "Good boy," Marisa said, working to keep the tremble out of her voice. "You look so handsome now."

He grinned up at her, then pointed to the animal embroidered on the pocket of his T-shirt. "Tigger," he said. "Tigger-tiger."

"Yes, that's Tigger the tiger. I like Tigger, don't you?"

"Tigger," Spencer said again by way of answer. He wiggled around, indifferent to the fact that his squirming made it almost impossible for his mother to fasten his shoes. He gave a satisfied chuckle when his chubby toddler fingers succeeded in grasping a fat-bellied teddy bear that had been seated on the edge of the changing stand, observing the proceedings with a benevolent, glassy-eyed stare.

"Pooh," Spencer said, pointing to the teddy, which had long since been cuddled into a state of one-eared shabbiness.

"Pooh tookie."

Marisa had no difficulty translating this enigmatic comment. "Pooh wants a cookie?" She wiggled her eyebrows in mock amazement. "That bear always wants cookies. Do you want a cookie, too?"

Spencer nodded his head, his whole body moving with the force of his enthusiasm. He smiled widely, displaying perfect, baby-white teeth. "Me tookie!"

Marisa ruffled his hair, which was curly and still silky soft. "How about we have cereal for breakfast, and a glass of juice. Then you and Pooh can both have a cookie."

Spencer was an astonishingly good-natured child, and he accepted the slight modification to his plans without protest. He gave another body-wiggling nod of his head, and Marisa kissed him on the tip of his pug nose, her heart melting with love. Even today, when ninety-nine percent of her conscious thoughts were fixed on Belle and what might be happening to her, the wonder of being mother to such a cute and intelligent baby never quite left her.

She was just scooping him up into her arms when she heard the nursery door open behind her. Marisa's hold around Spencer instinctively tightened, and he gave a little squeak of protest.

"Oh, dear, you're hurting him," Anita said. "You really should have learned how to hold him properly by now, Marisa. Let me take him. I'll give him breakfast."

"No, thank you." Marisa strove to keep all trace of irony out of her reply. "I'm sure you need to rest after the horrible ordeal you went through this morning.''

''Thanks, you're so considerate. Fortunately, I have remarkable powers of recuperation.'' Anita smiled. ''Besides, Evan wants to speak with you. He's in the bedroom.''

''Whose bedroom?'' Marisa asked bitterly.

''Why, yours, of course.'' Anita held out her arms to Spencer. ''Come to Nita, you lovely boy, you. Let's go and give Pooh breakfast, shall we?''

Spencer went to her willingly, clutching Pooh by his remaining ear. Why wouldn't he go willingly? Marisa thought sadly. Her son spent far more time with Anita than he did with her, and Anita's genuine affection for Spencer was one of the few tiny sparks of brightness in the dark nightmare of Marisa's life.

Feeling as if her heart were being ripped from her body, Marisa handed Spencer over to his nanny. She made no overt protest, kept silent by a potent combination of pride and fear. Pride was pretty much all she had left to support her, and if she made Anita's life too difficult, there was always the monstrous possibility that they'd live up to their threats and take Spencer completely away from her.

She couldn't afford to keep Evan waiting. Giving Spencer another kiss, and forcing a smile as she waved goodbye, Marisa hurried along the upstairs hallway to her bedroom. She found Evan seated at her dressing table, pawing through her makeup drawer.

''I didn't like the lipstick you wore yesterday,'' he said by way of greeting. ''It was too dark. It made you look cheap and vulgar. I'd have thought that by now you would remember I don't like you to wear dark colors."

Marisa avoided looking at him when she replied by the simple device of keeping her gaze fixed on the floor. Evan preferred her to look humble, anyway. "I'm sorry," she said tonelessly. "Would you like to pick out a lipstick for me today?" She had long since stopped fighting battles about things that didn't matter to her.

"No, your drawer is too messy, and I've no interest in wasting my time searching for something you should be able to find yourself. Tidy up the drawer and find a paler lipstick. You're supposed to be worried about your missing brother. Make sure you look the part."

She summoned her courage. "I *am* worried about my brother. And about Belle, too. Are they going to be all right?"

Evan rose to his feet. She was a tall woman, and he was only of average height for a man, but when he loomed over her like this, she thought of him as a giant. "What precisely is that remark supposed to mean? Are you implying that I'm not worried about them? My own sister- and brother-in-law?"

"No, I'm sure you're worried." She never managed to sound quite as subservient as she should, and Evan instantly picked up on undertones she hadn't quite realized were there.

"Are you suggesting that I have a reason to be worried? That you think I've made a mistake in handling the goddamn mess your father left behind?"

"No, of course not. I'm sure you have everything under control. It just struck me last night that things didn't seem to be going as smoothly as they usually do for you."

"You're much too stupid to know when my business affairs are going smoothly. Since you have no idea what you're talking about, you should shut the fuck up."

"Certainly."

"Sarcasm isn't attractive in a woman," he said, gripping her arm with brutal strength. "Especially when their husbands are in the middle of an important business deal and need some moral support."

She winced as he applied pressure to the bruises, new and old, that decorated her arm from shoulder to wrist. But she didn't cry out or protest, afraid that he would punish her by taking Spencer away from her for the rest of the day. He got tired of hurting her surprisingly soon, a sure sign that he had a lot on his mind.

His cell phone rang, and he pushed her away hard enough that she fell down. He flipped open the phone. "Yes?"

He listened in silence, then spoke briefly. "Good. Take her to the warehouse." He snapped the phone shut. "If Sandro Marchese returns here, you can express horror and dismay that he has lost track of your sister. If he suggests summoning the FBI, you can agree, after some hesitation. Don't let him tell your mother that Tony and Belle are missing. Dave's got enough on his mind right now without having to keep that stupid old bitch under control."

Marisa didn't even wince at the insult to her mother. She had heard others, far worse, too many times before. "Why do you expect Sandro Marchese to come back here? Has he lost track of Belle?"

"Yes, of course he has."

For some reason, it was a blow to hear it confirmed, even though she'd known the answer. What use was a tracking device if her husband had already informed Dave Forcier that he could find it in Belle's sandal? Belle was incredibly smart, though. How long would it take her to figure out who Dave was working with and for? Marisa's fear had been growing exponentially ever since last night when she learned that Donald Gates was dead. Clearly, events had spiraled out of control since the death of Marc Joubert. Evan and Dave were operating under intense pressure to prove that they could deliver the goods as efficiently with Marc gone as they had when he was alive. But the way things were going, Marisa was afraid that her husband would soon feel so vulnerable that he would be left with no option other than the elimination of everyone who might be able to guess that he had spent the past three years in a titanic power struggle for control of the Joubert smuggling empire.

"Belle and Tony are my family," she said with amazing courage. "I can't help worrying about them. Please, Evan, I know I have no right to pry into your business affairs, but could you tell me when they're going to be released?" *Don't even mention the terrible possibility that they might be killed.*

"They'll be released when I say they will be." He walked into his closet and began to change into a business suit, her only clue that this was a day he didn't plan to spend at home.

She set about tidying her makeup drawer, which had been organized within an inch of its life until Evan rummaged around among her lipsticks. "Why do you believe that Belle has the Cronus disk? She never mentioned it last night.''

"Because her mother told Dave that she had it. Neither disk is important, anyway. I only want to get them back as a precaution. Now, get dressed and don't ask any more stupid fucking questions."

Evan was lying. For her own safety, Marisa had learned to read every nuance of his body language. He lied to her all the time, about where he was going, whom he was meeting, what he was planning. Most of the time he didn't lie for a practical purpose, but because it gave him a feeling of power to mislead her, to leave her totally unaware of the details of his life.

But this wasn't a trivial lie of the control-seeking kind, Marisa thought. Evan desperately needed access to the details of her father's smuggling operation, and he seemed to need access now. Why the urgency? It could only be because he was attempting to smuggle something especially profitable, dangerous and forbidden out of the country. Right now, in some warehouse, he was sitting on merchandise that could get him and Dave jailed for a lifetime. Marisa was sure of it.

What merchandise could that be? Presumably not something small and super high-tech that could be smuggled out of the country in the guise of a harmless component for one of Evan's Far Eastern toy manufacturing facilities. That meant the merchandise had to be something big, and bulky. Something that needed a guaranteed safe route, and dozens of officials paid off to look the other way.

The fact that Donald Gates had ended up dead suggested that what was being smuggled had something to do with military technology. The fact that they needed the Cronus disk with its invaluable route maps and overseas contacts meant that they were shipping out actual weapons, not just the specifications or design blueprints.

The phone rang, but Marisa ignored it. She wasn't allowed to answer the phone until Evan or Anita had approved the caller as someone she could speak to. Fighting back despair, she completed the rearrangement of her makeup drawer. Somehow, if only she weren't almost as stupid as Evan claimed, she ought to be able to come up with a way to reveal what she knew to the authorities, without putting her life at risk. In the past eighteen months, however, she had never found that way. And she really didn't want to die. Not that her current life would be much of a loss. But she couldn't bear to contemplate Spencer's fate if he were left entirely at the mercy of his father and Anita Gillespie. Spencer needed at least one parent who was capable of providing some ethical guidelines and moral boundaries.

Evan returned to the bedroom, carrying a portable phone. He held it out to her, smiling the smug smile that she had learned both to hate and to dread. "My dear, bad news, I'm afraid. But you need to keep your hopes up even so." He spoke close enough to the mouthpiece that the person at the other end of the phone line would hear every word.

"Who is it?" she asked, dry-mouthed.

"It's Sandro Marchese, and I'm sorry, but he's calling to let us know that he's lost track of Belle."

"Oh, no," she said woodenly. "How terrible."

"He wants to speak with you." Evan tossed the

phone onto the bed. "Whatever the two of you decide, you know I'll support you a hundred percent."

"Of course." She picked up the phone. Her hands were so slick with sweat that the receiver slipped, and she dropped it back onto the bed. She couldn't wipe her hands on her skirt for fear of leaving a mark— she was wearing another of her endless, hated, white linen dresses, selected by Evan—so she hurriedly found a tissue and dried her hands. Then she drew in a shaky breath, forcing herself to play the part expected of her.

"Sandro, this is just awful! How did it happen? Did the tracking device stop working?"

"Either that, or the kidnappers found it and crushed it. Bottom line, Marisa, we no longer have any idea where they've taken your sister."

"Oh, my God! What are we going to do?"

"We don't have much choice. I've already called in the FBI. My only regret is that I didn't do this yesterday."

Marisa allowed herself the luxury of a few tears. If she wasn't crying for quite the reasons Sandro would assume, at least her tears were genuine. "What do you think will happen to her, Sandro? Why have they taken her?"

"I don't know, Marisa. I wish I did. God knows, I don't seem to have any answers right now."

"I'm going to have to tell my mother." Marisa's tears flowed faster. "Sandro, keep the FBI away from her just a little longer, will you? Let me at least prepare her before federal agents go banging on her door."

"I'll do what I can. Right now, I'm not in much of a position to make deals with my superiors. Try not to worry, Marisa. I promise you, I'm going to bring Belle out of this alive.''

She hoped that he could live up to his promise, but she doubted that he could. Marisa was alternately burning up with panic and frozen by despair. In a minute, if only she got left alone, she would try to straighten out the whirligig of her thoughts and find a way to save her sister. Maybe, if she could find her brains and her courage, there was still a way. "Th-thank you, Sandro, for all your help. I'm really counting on you. Please, don't let Belle down.''

"I won't. You have my word. I have to go, Marisa. Sorry. I'll be in touch as soon as I can.''

"Yes, go. If I'm not here, I'll be at my mother's.'' She pressed the off button before handing the phone back to Evan. "Did I say what you wanted?'' she asked tonelessly.

"Dry your eyes,'' he said. "Your mascara's running, and you look like a wreck.''

Nineteen

Dave Forcier tucked the gun into his shoulder holster and settled back against the soft leather seat of the Lincoln. "Drive around for a coupla minutes, Ray, while I check her out for concealed weapons."

"I don't have any concealed weapons," Belle said.

Dave turned to her with a leer. "No, you probably don't. But your uncle Dave needs to see if you're wearing a wire, sweetie."

"I'm not," she said. "Take your hands off me, you jackass."

"Not a chance, sweetie. I've been waiting to do this for years. Besides, I really don't want any of your friends from Customs listening in on our little chat." Dave Forcier ran his hands over Belle's body with lascivious pleasure, barely pretending to search for a wire. Even when he found her father's disk tucked into the side pocket of her dress, he simply tossed it onto the seat next to him—and continued mauling her.

Belle stared out the car window, trying not to let him see that he was making her flesh creep. She couldn't stop him from touching her, but she wasn't going to give him the additional satisfaction of cringing and protesting. She could have kneed him in the groin, but, realistically, she knew the probable result would be to make him mad. And she didn't think her safety would be improved by making Dave mad.

With an effort of will, she fixed her attention on the problem of what to do next. Anything was better than registering his hands on her thighs, creeping upward.

Ray Hillman, uncommunicative as ever, was driving them south on 95, back toward Miami. He seemed oblivious to Dave's back seat activities, or perhaps he'd chauffeured for his old friend before and had learned not to watch. Belle wondered why she hadn't been blindfolded. Even more troubling, Dave and Ray were making no effort to prevent her from knowing where she was going, nor from knowing their identities. She asked herself why, then wished she hadn't. She disliked all the answers she came up with.

"Take your sandals off," Dave said curtly, when he finally got bored with feeling her up and getting no reaction.

"Why would I do anything that dumb?"

"So that I can get rid of the tracking device you've got tucked into the heel of your sandal, sweetie. Why else?"

"I don't have a tracking device in my sandal."

"Sure you do. That son of a bitch Sandro Marchese would never have let you out of his sight without a way to keep track of you. And it's bound to be in your shoe, because that's where they always put 'em. Don't you ever go to the movies? Good guys always hide the microchip in the heel of their shoes."

"Sandro isn't in the movies," Belle said.

"No, sweetie, but federal agents get all their best ideas from the movies. Now, give me your damn sandal."

He found the tracking device almost at once and dug it out from the heel of her sandal with his fingernail. He flashed a satisfied smile as he opened the window and tossed the chip onto the road, directly into the path of an oncoming truck.

"That takes care of that," he said, brushing dust from his hands. "I guess Lover Boy isn't going to be running to your rescue, after all."

It was instinctive to touch her watch, to reassure herself that the second chip was still there. Dave, thank God, didn't notice her gesture, although that was a piece of luck she didn't deserve. Reminding herself to be more careful in future, she muttered a silent prayer that the chip was sending out a powerful signal, and that Sandro was on their tail, no more than a few cars behind.

Moving as far away from Dave as she could, she twisted around to confront him. "Since you seem to be hung up on the movies, let's cut to the chase, shall we? What's the purpose of all these crazy shenanigans, Dave? What's been going on for the past couple of days is insane. When are you going to release my brother?"

"Well, that's pretty much up to you, sweetie." Dave pulled a portable computer out of the car's map pocket, and set it on his lap. "First things first. Let's get this baby up and running, and I'll see whether you've brought me the right disk this time."

He glanced at the label on the disk while his computer booted up. "'Charitable Donations 2000,'" he read. "I sure as hell hope this isn't another one of your little games, sugar. I have to tell you, I didn't appreciate sending one of my best guys to search your house, just to get rewarded with a disk of fucking bagpipes wailing in my ear.''

So Dave had been responsible for the invasion and trashing of her home. ''It's the real disk this time,'' Belle said.

''You'd better hope you're telling the truth, sweetie, because your uncle Dave is getting real frustrated with the way you've been carrying on.'' He waited for the program to load, then flicked from screen to screen, silently absorbing the contents of the disk.

Ray Hillman spoke for the first time. ''Did she deliver?'' he asked.

''Half of it.'' Dave closed out the program and shut down his computer. ''Okay, sugar, now we get to the really big question. What you've got here is quite nice, but it isn't enough. Where's the Cronus network disk?''

''I don't have it,'' Belle said flatly.

''Yes, you do.'' Dave's voice hardened. ''Your dear old mother told me all about the touching deathbed scene with your dad. She assured me that Marc gave the disk to you, right before he went to the great smuggling convention in the sky.''

''The only disk my father gave me is the one you have right here. The disk that contains a list of all the people he bribed, with evidence so that the prosecuting attorneys can convict them.''

''Why the hell did Marc need to make a disk like that?'' Ray interjected, with real hatred in his voice. ''What got into him these last few years? It was like he had a religious conversion, and had to screw up a perfectly good way of life that had kept us all rich and happy for years.''

"Whatever happened to change my father's mind about the business he was in, he never betrayed his friendship with you two," Belle said. "He left you and Dave off the list completely. There's nothing on the disk he gave me to compromise either of you. Not a single thing."

"Gee, that was real bighearted of him," Ray said. "Sorry I don't appreciate the gesture more. You know what? It's lucky your father died, because I was just about ready to kill him myself."

"But what had he done to make you so angry?" Belle asked. "I don't understand. You worked together for years—"

"You worked together for years," Dave mimicked. "Yeah, we sure did. Thirty-four years I worked for your father, busting my ass to keep the Joubert family rolling in money, and out of trouble with the law. Laundering Marc's dirty money through dummy corporations, and keeping him in solid with the IRS. So what's my reward? Hey, Marc gets some burr up his butt and decides he's going legit. Starts to close down a network and an operation it took three generations to build. But does he consult with me or Ray about what he's doing? No, he sure doesn't. He's fuckin' Marc Arrogant Joubert, so he just assumes we'll go along with his change in plans. He expects us to carry on being loyal serfs in the Joubert kingdom, just like we always had been."

"I was hired in 1963," Ray said. "Same year President Kennedy was assassinated. That's thirty-seven years. And in all that time we were keeping him out of trouble, Marc never made us partners. Never even talked about it. We weren't Jouberts, so we were nothing."

"I assume he tossed the occasional million-dollar bonus in your direction to sweeten the burden of your serfdom," Belle said acidly.

Hot color darkened Dave's face. "You really are your father's daughter, aren't you? You've got his manner down pat. The same snooty look, the same biting tone of voice. But I can't say hearing you talk makes me feel all warm and fuzzy and nostalgic. In fact, what it makes me is real anxious to beat the crap out of you. Kind of a substitute for all those times I stood there and took it from your dear old dad. So I'll give you a piece of advice, sweetie. Don't give me an excuse to play out my revenge fantasies. I could get real mean."

"Then let's just negotiate this efficiently, like the business deal it is. You have Tony. And you're right, I have the Cronus disk." Belle managed to produce the lie without a tremor in her voice. "There's no point in sitting here, trading insults. I've just given you one of my father's disks as a gesture of goodwill. But so far, you've produced no proof whatsoever that my brother is in your custody."

"Sure we did," Ray protested. "He spoke to you on the phone."

"When I called from the restaurant, you mean?" Belle shook her head. "He spoke two sentences. Generic garbage. You could have recorded that and then killed him." She spoke coolly, as if the prospect of her brother's death carried no emotional meaning for her. When Dave had complained that she was the true heir to Marc Joubert, she'd been hit with a sudden inspiration, realizing the comparison might work in her favor. Nobody knew better than Ray and Dave that her father was not a man you could mess with.

She could only hope that some of their awe for Marc's ruthless ability would be directed at her.

"Your brother is alive," Dave said. "You have my word."

She laughed.

Dave slapped her across the mouth with the back of his hand.

His ring cut her lip, and blood trickled. Belle wouldn't allow herself to acknowledge the wound, not even by licking away the blood. She waited until the sting died away and she could speak clearly. Then she shook her hair out of her eyes and raked Dave with her gaze. "If you want to see the Cronus disk in this lifetime, I need to see my brother. Take me to him. That's a nonnegotiable demand."

"Yeah, sweetie, I'm sure it is. All Joubert demands are nonnegotiable. But today, I'm the guy with the gun."

"And if I'm dead, you'll never see the Cronus disk. Stalemate, *Uncle* Dave."

"Ask me real nicely, sweetie, and I might be persuaded to reconsider." Dave leaned over her, pushing her into the corner of the car and nuzzling her breasts with his mouth. She could feel his erection pressing against her thigh, and the sensation made her nauseated. "Uncle Dave" might be a courtesy title, but she'd known him for so long that sexual contact with him felt almost incestuous. It certainly felt revolting.

"Get off me," she said through gritted teeth, but his only response was to grab her wrists and lift her hands over her head so that he had better access to her body.

She struggled to loosen her wrists. Suddenly she was free—and Dave was holding her watch. *Oh my*

God, Belle thought frantically. When he'd grabbed her wrists, he'd snapped the stretch band and twisted the watch inside out, exposing the back.

Dave looked from the microchip to Belle, his eyes turning opaque with rage. She stared back with a defiance she didn't feel.

"She's got another tracker," he said to Ray. "It's stuck to the back of her fucking watch."

"You mean, we've had some tail sitting on our ass all this time, and you never warned me?" Ray sounded more annoyed than panicked.

"Don't worry. We'll shake 'em. Turn left here. No, don't speed up. They probably don't have us in visual range, and we don't want to do a damn thing to make them nervous. I'll tell you when to stop."

Dave scanned the passing highway with intense concentration. "Here, this will work. Turn into the service station on your right."

"But it's closed," Ray griped. "Can't you see it's all boarded up?"

"What does that matter, for Christ's sake? We're not buying gas." Dave handed Ray the gun and jerked his head toward Belle. "Shoot her if she so much as blinks. If she sneezes, shoot her twice."

"If he shoots me, you'll never find the Cronus disk," Belle said.

"Good point." Dave spoke over his shoulder to Ray as he exited the car. "If she moves, take out her kneecaps." He leaned over and patted Belle's leg. "Excruciating pain, but low risk of dying. I'd keep still, sweetie."

Helplessly, Belle watched as Dave stuck the watch with its accompanying tracking device to one of the abandoned gas pumps. Less than a minute after pulling up at the service station, he was back in the car.

"Get a move on," he said, taking back his gun from Ray. "But don't break the speed limit."

He turned to Belle. "Now, sweetie, it's time for us to start the real negotiations." He raised his hand and swung the barrel of the gun at her temple, hitting with brutal force. "That's my opening offer."

Belle didn't have time to reply before she fell hard and fast into darkness.

Sandro clicked off his cell phone and watched the blinking green dot on his car's navigation system. He still wasn't quite sure how involved Marisa was in her brother's disappearance, but there were several things about the strange Connor household that he knew with absolute certainty. To begin with, Anita Gillespie hadn't been attacked this morning. The rape story had been sheer fiction, which meant that however she'd gotten the note from the kidnappers, it sure hadn't been from two brutal men lurking in the Connors' front yard.

In view of the strange ease with which the kidnappers had been tracking Belle's movements, Sandro had arranged for surveillance on the house last night. Knowing he had agents watching front and back, he'd been suspicious the moment Anita claimed that two men had jumped out of the bushes and grabbed her in full view of any passersby. The body of a woman with a black belt in karate would be trained to react reflexively to any attack, however panicked she might be mentally. So either Anita was lying about her expertise in karate, or she was lying about the attack. The latter seemed more likely, since neither Pete nor

Rick had buzzed his communicator to warn of an incident. And once he had reason to doubt Anita's story, the anomalies had just kept piling up.

Pete had since confirmed that Anita's story of being attacked was pure invention. She'd come out of the Connor house at 5:25 and had spent five minutes walking around the front yard with the puppy. She'd returned to the house with Horatio frolicking at her side, having encountered nobody at all, much less two rapist-kidnappers.

Sandro was also sure not only that Anita was Evan Connor's mistress, but that Marisa knew it. The signs of tension between the two women had all been there, transparent the moment you looked beneath the unnatural tranquillity of the surface.

He was less sure how Marisa felt about her husband. He knew her feelings were intense, but he couldn't make up his mind whether she felt intense love or consuming hatred. Last night, when Evan had stroked his hand gently up and down Marisa's arm, he'd felt waves of suppressed emotion emanating from her. Because she cherished the tenderness of the moment? Or because she resented her husband's touch? Did she stay with Evan because she had such a fierce attraction to him that she was willing to share him with another woman? Or did she stay with him because she was afraid to leave? He half suspected the latter. But what was she afraid of? Marisa was not some poor, illiterate woman, trapped by her isolation and inability to provide food and shelter for her child. If Marisa really wanted out of her marriage, how did Evan compel her to stay?

The signal coming from the tracking device attached to Belle's watch was still functioning perfectly, thank God. Sandro checked their location on the navigation system in his car. So far, they had been heading steadily south on Interstate 95. Now the flashing green light swerved sharply left, indicating that Belle and her captors were driving east, circling around the Fort Lauderdale Hollywood airport.

He dialed Pete's cell phone number, not wanting to use any of the radio bands in case they were being scanned. "They're taking Tenth Street," he said, reading off the precise coordinates so that Pete could close in. "They can't go too far in this direction, or they'll be floating in the Atlantic. What's the latest from Rick?"

"He reported in five minutes ago. He says there's been no activity at the Connor house."

"How many phone calls have they had since mine?"

"Six. We don't know what about, of course. We got the wiretap order from the judge fifteen minutes ago."

"How long before we get a tap on their phone?"

"Another hour," Pete said. "If we're lucky."

Sandro quelled a rush of impatience. "We're probably not missing anything we could make use of," he said, reassuring himself as much as Pete. "All the important calls most likely come in scrambled. The line of business they're in, they've got technology twice as smart as ours—" Sandro broke off. "They're stopping," he said. "I'm going to move in closer and try for a visual. Right now, the signal is stationary, and it's coming from the intersection of First Avenue and River Drive."

"You want me to call in backup units?"

"Yeah. Looks like they've reached their destination. Wait for my orders before you approach."

Sandro disconnected, then approached the intersection with care, homing in on the signal. It was coming from a service station that was, according to a giant sign, closed for remodeling. A beat-up Honda Civic accelerated away from the gas station, as if frustrated at finding no gasoline. Otherwise, the entire area was deserted.

Sandro was beginning to get a very bad feeling. The tracking control unit inside his car gave a warning *bleep,* indicating that he was less than twenty-five feet away from the source of the signal. But there were no other parked cars within a radius of twenty-five feet, and no other structures, except the concrete canopy over the boarded-up gas pumps. The prefabricated structure that housed the attached convenience store was boarded up, too, but even if the store had been open, its entrance stood a good forty feet away from Sandro's car, which meant that Belle and the tracking device couldn't possibly be inside. The signal, in fact, could only be coming from the deserted forecourt.

With a sudden spurt of speed, Sandro drove into the gas station and stopped by the abandoned pumps. The control unit inside his car immediately indicated that he was less than ten feet from the source of the signal.

Sandro abandoned any worries about remaining out of sight. There was obviously no need for caution. He got out of the car and walked down the row of pumps, knowing what he was going to see. Still, his gut tore when he found it.

On the middle pump, stuck with adhesive tape to

the credit card slot, was Belle's watch, the tracking device still attached to it.

Sandro crashed his fist into the pump, swearing long and hard. He'd been suckered. The bastards had beaten him at his own game. For an hour he'd been tooling down the highway in hot pursuit of a decoy.

Ironically, his phone call to Marisa had just come true. He really didn't have an idea in hell what had happened to her sister.

Pain. Hideous pain hammering inside her head until she wanted to scream. Except that screaming required a lot more strength than she could summon. Belle tried to crawl back into unconsciousness, but somebody was shaking her shoulder, refusing to let her slip away to a place where she could hide from the suffering.

"Belle, wake up. It's me, Tony."

Obediently, she opened her eyes, but the world spun so sickeningly that she closed them again.

The voice was kind but relentless. "I'm going to slide your head onto my lap. Tell me if I hurt you anywhere."

Tony, she realized, before her thoughts once again slithered away into confusion.

The mental fog finally thinned, and she felt her brother's hands grip her under the arms, his movements gentle as he slowly levered her onto his lap from the concrete floor where she had been lying. This time, when she registered where she was and who she was with, she managed to hold on to reality.

"Hi, little brother. Fancy seeing you here." Belle tried to smile, although her facial muscles were too stiff to function properly. "I've been looking for you."

"And I'm real glad you found me." Tony probed the wound on her temple, and she winced, cringing even though his touch was careful and delicate. "I think you'll live. It's ugly, but fairly superficial."

"It sure doesn't feel superficial. How long have I been here, anyway? And where is *here?*"

"Ray Hillman shoved you inside the door about half an hour ago. And we're in some sort of empty warehouse. Very empty, in fact. I haven't even seen a rat."

"That sounds like good news to me."

"It depends how long they keep us here," her brother said dryly. "Rat meat might start to look pretty good in another couple of days."

Belle's stomach heaved precipitously, and it was a minute or two before she could speak. "We don't need to worry about starving. Dave and Ray can't keep us here for very long."

"No, they sure can't," Tony said much too heartily.

Belle's head might be hurting like crazy, but it required very few brain cells to work out that the easiest way for Dave and Ray to solve the problem of two live bodies locked up in an empty warehouse was to turn the bodies from live to dead.

Needing to take some action to counter her gloomy thoughts, Belle levered herself off her brother's lap and arranged herself next to him, back propped against the wall. Her battered body was about as comfortable as it ever was likely to be in a warehouse devoid of even a discarded packing crate. The concrete floor was very hard, but at least it felt dry, and at this time of year the warehouse was stuffy, but not uncomfortably warm. She decided to get herself into a positive mind-set and to be grateful for small mercies.

Now that she could see him, she realized her brother's face was puffy and bruised, and one eye sported a virulent shiner. Despite this, or maybe because of it, she could never remember being so pleased to see him. "Do I look as pretty as you?" she asked ruefully.

Tony cracked a weak grin. "Let's just say that you wouldn't need any makeup to be a convincing ghoul at a Halloween party."

"Gee, you pay the most elegant compliments." Belle reached out and very gently touched the tips of her fingers to his black eye. "How did you acquire your bruises? Were they a gift from Uncle Dave?"

"No, this was all courtesy of Ray Hillman and his hired help. Although I have the impression Ray wouldn't change his brand of toothpaste without first getting permission from Dave."

"Yeah, he's not exactly the good ol' Uncle Dave we thought we knew, is he?"

Tony met her gaze briefly, then looked away, obviously uncomfortable. "You know Donald Gates is dead, don't you? I'm really sorry. I didn't mean for it to happen."

Belle stared at her brother. "You mean…*you* killed Donald?"

"Of course not!" Tony sounded outraged. "Donald and Ray started to argue about the way things had been handled since Dad died. Donald was furious about the fact that your house had been ransacked. He kept saying that he could have found the Cronus disk while you were sleeping, if only Ray and Dave had been willing to wait for another couple of nights. And Ray accused him of being incapable of handling you. That you needed someone to show you who was boss, instead of meekly accepting it when you sent him away with his tail between his legs." Tony cleared his throat, embarrassed. "Anyway, the two of them were going at it hammer and tongs, and while their attention was distracted, I managed to break free from the chair where they had me tied up. I tried to get the gun that Ray had put down on the coffee table, but Donald saw what I was doing and he went for it, too. We struggled…"

"And the gun went off?" Belle prompted when her brother's voice died away.

"No. Ray just walked up and shot him at point-blank range." The blood drained from Tony's face, leaving the bruises to stand out in stark contrast. "That was the moment when I realized that after thirty years of acquaintance, I'd never really known Ray at all."

"We both assumed we knew him. And Dave, too. We were both terribly wrong."

Tony shuddered. "I still can't believe how easily Ray could kill. Donald had become a liability, and Ray was able to murder him with no more emotion than I would have felt if I'd run over a squirrel on the road. With far less emotion, in fact."

"We should have known what they were capable of," Belle said quietly. "We knew they worked with Dad. We knew they had no qualms about doing business with terrorists."

"But Dad would never have killed Donald Gates,"

Tony protested. "He would never have committed cold-blooded murder."

"Dad did commit murder." The words almost choked Belle. "Just because he didn't see his victims up close doesn't make him any less guilty."

Tony rubbed nervously at the stubble of his beard. "You always did have such a black-and-white view of what Dad did, Belle."

"You've no idea how long and how hard I looked for gray." Belle drew in a deep breath. "Anyway, Dad's dead and beyond our judgment, so we should change the subject. Since I don't plan to stick around here long enough for Dave to use me as a punching bag, I guess we have some serious escape planning to do."

"I agree," Tony said, sounding relieved to move away from a topic he found as difficult as did Belle. "There's only one problem. I already searched the place from top to bottom, and there's no way out of here—unless you're real good at leaping tall buildings in a single bound."

"There are windows. There have to be. I can see sunlight."

"Yeah, but they're twelve feet above the ground."

"Well, don't give up hope. There's two of us now," Belle said. "Are you sure the windows are too high to reach, even if I climb on your shoulders?"

"I'm sure," Tony said glumly. "I thought of that myself, but we'd still be six inches or so from the bottom sill."

"Never mind. We'll pool our ideas and come up with something brilliant."

"Right now, I'm not sure if I can even come up with adequate." Tony looked away. "Sorry to sound so useless. You've been wonderful, Belle, and I don't deserve all the efforts you've made on my behalf. Especially after the way I've treated you for the past few years.''

"The situation with Dad screwed up all our relationships.''

"I guess. Anyway, I just want you to know that I am grateful for all you've done to rescue me.''

"You're welcome.'' Belle gave a wry smile. "Or you would be if I'd done anything worth being thanked for. So far, I seem to have totally screwed up. As far as I can tell, we only have one thing going for us.''

"Which is…''

"We have to remember that Dave wants the Cronus disk as badly as we want out of here.''

"That doesn't help much, since I don't have the Cronus disk,'' Tony said.

"Of course you don't. That's because I have it.'' Belle hadn't planned to lie, and she was shocked at how readily the falsehood tripped from her tongue. It was only because she wanted to protect her brother, she assured herself, not because she was turning into a congenital liar. Tony had always been hopeless at hiding his feelings, and he would never be able to carry off a bluff with Dave and Ray unless he truly believed what he was saying.

"That sure is a relief,'' Tony said. "Or at least, half a relief. Where have you hidden it?''

Damn good question. Belle hoped she could come up with a credible answer before Dave and Ray asked the same thing. "It's better if you don't know,'' she said. "That way, only one of us has to keep the secret.''

Tony frowned, then winced as his abused facial muscles protested the movement. "Well, okay. But if Dave gets vicious, I'm warning you here and now that I'm going to tell him you have the disk. It sure isn't worth being tortured to save it."

"Don't worry, I'm not in the least anxious to be a martyr. What we need to do now, though, is work out a really clever way to make the exchange."

"Dave and Ray aren't going to trust us any more than we trust them," Tony said. "Realistically, once they have the disk, how are we going to stop them killing us? The Cronus network may be the eighth wonder of the world, but Dave and Ray won't be able to use any of the information on the disks if you've kept a copy somewhere, ready to hand over to Customs the minute you're free. Obviously they're going to feel threatened."

"I don't have any copies of the disk," Belle said. "I wish I did, but there was never time to make one, and I didn't have the right equipment, anyway." This wasn't exactly a lie, she reasoned. Since she didn't have the Cronus disk in the first place, obviously she didn't have any copies.

"That's all very well," Tony said. "Unfortunately, the fact that you happen to be telling the truth about not having copies isn't going to convince Dave and Ray."

"I guess that's another problem we have to work on," Belle said wryly. "First, though, we need to pool our information if we're going to come up with the best possible negotiating plan. We have to find out where they're vulnerable, where they're amenable to reason, and then work on those two areas. So, how did they kidnap you, Tony?"

"It was real easy," he said with a slight lift of his shoulders. "Dave and I have had our differences in recent months, but it never crossed my mind that he'd go to these lengths, so I wasn't remotely on guard. We were supposed to be meeting yesterday to go over some of the IRS forms in connection with Dad's estate. So I called him first thing to let him know that I had to beg off because I needed to meet with you instead. Told him I'd be leaving within the hour. I got as far as the parking garage, and that was it. *Wham!* A slam dunk on the back of my head and that was the end of me. Next thing I knew, I woke up here with a raging thirst and a splitting headache. And Dave standing over me, demanding answers to a lot of questions about the Cronus disk, most of which I genuinely couldn't answer."

"But you told him that I had it?" Belle asked.

Tony started to shake his head, then stopped abruptly. "Sorry. Acute attack of spinning walls. No, I didn't tell Dave anything about our phone conversation. I never even acknowledged that I know what the Cronus disk is. Of course, Dave promised to let me go if I would only tell him where the disk disappeared to after Dad died. Even if I'd known, I would never have told him, because I didn't trust him." His mouth twisted wryly. "Turns out, that was a good judgment call on my part, I guess."

"Any special reason why you didn't trust him?"

"Several." Her brother looked away, staring into the distance. "I lied to you at the funeral, Belle. Everything hasn't been just fine since you left Miami. When you cut yourself off from the family, all the heart and fire seemed to go out of Dad. After I got through grad school and joined the company, I told him that I hadn't spent three years getting my MBA just so that I could help him apply the latest management techniques to a business that was dedicated to putting weapons in the hands of terrorists. I told him that if he participated in any more illegal deals, I'd make it my personal mission to see that he was prosecuted.''

"Dad must have been furious. He hated it when people questioned his authority.''

"That was the odd thing. He wasn't furious at all. That's what I meant about all the fire going out of him. Instead of fighting back at me, he meekly agreed to cease and desist from smuggling.''

"You don't sound as relieved as I would have expected,'' Belle said. "After all, that was what all of us kids wanted from the time we were old enough to understand what was going on.''

"Despite his promises, I didn't trust Dad—not really.'' Tony sighed. "You know how it was. Dealing with Dad was like trying to fathom a Chinese puzzle box. However many secret compartments you opened, you were never sure that you had a solid grasp of the whole picture. I couldn't shake the niggling doubt that maybe he'd pretended to quit smuggling simply in order to get me off his back so that he could go about his business just as he always had. Then, about a month before he died, I overheard an argument between Dad and Dave that seemed to confirm my suspicions. Even worse, I got the impression that Dave was threatening Dad, forcing him to participate in some deal that he would have preferred to reject. When I confronted Dad later, he blustered a lot but didn't actually deny what I was suggesting. I came away from our discussion pretty much convinced not only that the Joubert Corporation was still actively engaged in smuggling, but that Dad wanted to get out from under and couldn't find a way."

"If Dave and Ray were blackmailing him into smuggling, I don't understand why Dad didn't call their bluff. How could they coerce him into cooperating against his will? He could simply refuse to provide the necessary information. Or he could have gone the other way and called in law enforcement. All he had to do was make a couple of phone calls, and he could have gotten good ol' Ray and Dave arrested in a heartbeat."

"How could he get them arrested without putting himself at risk?"

"Dad could have offered them a deal," Belle suggested. "He could have agreed to open up all his files, reveal names, shipping routes, contacts, the works in exchange for immunity from prosecution."

Tony shook his head. "Prosecutors never would have gone for that. They couldn't, no matter how much they might want access to the information. Besides, Dad had such a fearsome reputation for cunning and double crosses that if he'd gone to Customs asking for help, I'm betting they would have suspected a trap. I think at the end of his life, Dad discovered that he'd outsmarted himself. He'd cried wolf once too often, and the help he needed just wasn't forthcoming."

Belle was getting more and more depressed as she listened to her brother. If Marc Joubert, the master negotiator, hadn't been able to find a way out of the pit he'd dug for himself, then what hope did she have of saving herself and her brother? Her head was aching badly enough that thought was difficult, and she decided that getting on her feet and taking a walk around the cavernous warehouse might make her brain function a little more efficiently.

"I'm going to walk for a bit," she said, trying to get up. Her legs were shakier than she'd realized, and she stumbled against Tony's chest, clutching onto a handful of shirt to prevent herself from banging into the wall.

"Careful!" He jerked away.

"Gee, I'm sorry. Have you hurt your ribs? You should have told me."

"It's nothing." Tony's gaze slid away. "Just a bruise. Honestly."

He was lying—hiding something from her. Was he trying to conceal a really serious injury? Her stomach plummeted at the thought. Leaning toward him, Belle tugged up his cotton knit shirt before he could stop her. "Tony, you have to level with me—"

She saw the flat, telltale wire running from the tiny microphone taped to the center of his chest. Belle ripped the mike away from his skin and held it up.

"Who's listening, Tony?"

"I...don't know. Dave, Ray. One or the other."

"How *could* you?"

"I'm sorry, Belle. Honest. I didn't want to, but they were beating up on me."

"So you decided to let them beat up on me instead?"

"No, it wasn't like that. They just needed to be sure that you had the Cronus disk and that you hadn't made any copies. That's all, Belle. Everything I told you about what happened was the truth. They just want to make sure that they can negotiate in good faith."

"They can't," she said cuttingly. "And apparently, neither can you. None of you would recognize good faith or honesty if it jumped up and bit you on the nose."

The sound of a heavy metal door opening came from behind her. Belle refused to turn around and look.

"Feisty little thing, your sister, isn't she?" Dave Forcier strolled into the warehouse, Ray trailing behind.

"I did what you asked," Tony said woodenly. "Now, you have to let me go."

"Sure. That fits right in with my current plans." Dave smashed his fist into Tony's chin, watching with detached interest as Belle rushed to catch him and cushion his fall.

Dave poked Tony's unconscious body with his foot. "He really isn't worth saving, you know. You should forget about him and move on."

"If the world only had worthwhile people in it, you and Ray would have been shown the exit ramp years ago."

"What's worthwhile?" Dave asked. "One person's villain is another person's hero. There are lots of places in this world where I'm considered the good guy—the man who provides the weapons that enable oppressed people to fight for their rights."

"But we both know the truth, don't we? You and Ray aren't heroes. You're scum."

Dave's eyes flashed loathing. "You don't know how lucky you are that I need you conscious," he said. "So let's quit with the verbal foreplay, exciting as it is. Are you ready to tell me where I can find the Cronus disk?"

It would have been infinitely satisfying to tell him to go to hell, but Belle prided herself on being a realist. "The Cronus disk is the only thing standing between me and death," she said. "No, I'm not ready to tell you where it is until I have some guarantee of my personal safety."

He closed in on her, taking her arm and twisting it behind her back in an agonizing hold. "Look, *sweetie,* you need to realize that my patience has run out. You're about to get hurt real bad if you don't cooperate."

"He means what he says, Belle." Ray piped up for the first time. He winced and looked away as Dave increased the pressure on Belle's arm.

"The two of you—need to—realize that I'm—Isabella, not Tony." Belle's breath came in small, painful gasps, and she could feel beads of sweat popping out on her forehead. "Your threats—aren't going to scare me—into handing over the one thing that's keeping me alive—*Uncle Dave.* But for a price, I'm willing to show you where—the Cronus disk is hidden. I'll give you a hint. It's here in Florida."

His wrenching hold relaxed a fraction. "What's your price?"

"My brother's life, and mine."

"Sure, it's a deal." Dave released his hold. "Now, where's the disk?"

Belle massaged her throbbing shoulder. Then she smiled, despite her swollen lips, aching head—and the fear churning in her gut. "Sorry, Dave. The dead bodies I've encountered over the past few days make me kind of nervous about relying on your word as a guarantee."

"So what guarantee do you want?" Ray asked.

"Several. First, Ray doesn't get to come with us, since I'd like to up my survival odds a little. Second, we take my brother with us so that Ray can't get any bright ideas about killing him off while I'm gone. Third, you don't carry any guns or other weapons, Dave. I'll trust you so much more if you only have your fists to enforce your point of view. And finally, you both need to know that although I told Tony I don't have a duplicate of the Cronus disk, that was only technically true. I don't have a duplicate, but I do have hard copy."

"I don't believe you would lie to your own brother," Dave said. "You're just saying you have hard copy to protect yourself."

"Wrong again, Uncle Dave." Belle directed a scornful glance toward Tony, who was just beginning to stir. "I've known my brother for twenty-seven years. Do you seriously believe that I would have trusted him with the full truth about something as important as the Cronus disk? You'd better believe that I spent most of Saturday making printouts. If I die, that material will automatically be sent to the director of U.S. Customs, and, trust me, that would mean your smuggling days were well and truly over. So if the two of you want to take over the Cronus network where my father left off, don't even think about arranging a neat contract murder to get rid of me after you take possession of the disk."

Dave and Ray exchanged glances. Dave eventually turned back and glared at her, but he knew he was defeated. "I'm not giving up my gun," he said.

"Your choice." Belle shrugged—a good way to disguise the fact that she was shaking. Of course Dave wasn't willing to give up his gun. It was a measure of how desperate he was to get his hands on the disk that he was even pretending to agree to her other terms. She pointedly turned her back on him as if his next move was a matter of complete indifference to her. She knelt beside her brother and felt for his pulse. He was beginning to stir, she saw to her relief.

Dave grabbed her by the shoulder and dragged her to her feet. "Okay, I accept your terms. No guns, and Ray gets to stay here. Now, where are you taking me?"

She shook her head. "Uh-uh, Uncle Dave. First, I frisk you. Then we get into the car—you, me and my pathetic little brother here. *Then* I tell you where we're going."

Dave thought for a moment. "The only way that's gonna happen in this lifetime is if your brother's tied up, and I get to drive. And don't even think about taking me to a crowded shopping mall and losing me, sweetie. Because the second I lose sight of you, I turn right around and go pay your dear old mother a visit. And for that visit, I'll take my guns."

The threat to her mother made Belle's blood run cold, but the deal they'd struck was still the best she could hope for. Dave was never going to allow her to sit behind the wheel of the car, knowing she'd drive straight to the nearest police station.

"Agreed," she said. She made her voice sound hard and commanding. "Face to the wall, Dave, arms and legs spread. I'm going to make damn sure I get all your weapons."

So far, so good, Belle thought as she searched Dave and removed two guns in addition to the .44 Magnum he'd been carrying, a Colt .38, and an old Soviet 9mm Makarov. Now she had him disarmed, which had to even the score at least a little. But where the hell was she going to take him?

There was no brilliant answer, no perfect solution that would take care of all the risks. For a moment, Belle allowed herself to feel real anger toward her dead father. Her true inheritance from Marc Joubert hadn't been a million-dollar trust fund. It hadn't even been a disk that indicted corrupt officials. What her father had bequeathed to her was this gut-wrenching, heart-tearing fear that whatever she did and however fiercely she fought back, she was never going to be able to protect herself and her family from the consequences of his criminality.

But since this terrible legacy was a Joubert family problem, perhaps the way to solve it was to stop fighting alone and to involve her family. Dave knew she had spent the previous night with her sister. He would find it quite believable if she claimed that she'd hidden the Cronus disk somewhere in Marisa's house. And once she was there, she would have Evan, Marisa and Anita to help her.

Was she putting Spencer at risk? Not really. Dave had no weapons, and he was going to be heavily outnumbered by members of the Joubert family. Evan, in particular, was young and strong, and not likely to stand for any nonsense from Dave Forcier. There was even the faint hope that Sandro might have returned to her sister's house. In fact, the more Belle thought about it, the more she decided that taking Dave to Marisa's house would provide the best possible solution. As long as she could solve the short-term problem of surviving the next couple of hours, the long-term problem of protecting herself and her family was taken care of. As soon as she got to Marisa's house, she and her sister and brother-in-law would join forces to overpower Dave, and summon the police. With Dave and Ray safely under lock and key, they would all finally be safe. As an added bonus, she would be able to reclaim her father's disk and turn the list of people he'd bribed over to Customs. Marc's dying request would be fulfilled.

For the first time in several days, Belle felt almost optimistic.

Twenty

After a brief search in the vicinity of the abandoned gas station, Sandro called regional headquarters in Chicago to report his failure to keep track of Belle. Ken Oliver was polite and sympathetic, which simply served to make Sandro feel worse. Even during the week, on one of his pinstripe-and-by-the-rule-book days, Ken was only sympathetic to underlings who had seriously fucked up.

Since Sandro had no more direct leads to follow and the case was now a double kidnapping, the FBI was summoned. Ken hadn't needed to point out that Customs would get its nose rubbed in the Joubert mess for months to come. The guys over at the Bureau always took a macabre delight in publicizing the failures of other agencies.

"Are you expecting to serve as the official Customs liaison to the Bureau on this assignment?" Ken asked Sandro. Since it was Monday, all trace of the folksy Southern sheriff had disappeared.

"I think Pete Hintz would do great as the liaison," Sandro said. "He's up to speed on what's happening, and he was working the tail with me."

"I will authorize Agent Hintz to act as our liaison, then. But if you are planning to pursue a separate line of investigation, I need to be so informed."

"Trust me, Ken. You will be the first person to know as soon as I have anything to report."

"Did I ever mention to you, Agent Marchese, that I never, absolutely never, trust people who tell me to trust them?"

"You're a wise man, Ken." Sandro cut off the call and switched off his cell phone so his boss couldn't call him back. Knowing that the FBI would conduct their search for Belle in a methodical fashion, he felt entitled to play his hunches.

His instincts were screaming that the Connor household merited further investigation. Since he knew Anita hadn't been attacked this morning, it followed that the note from the supposed kidnappers must have come from inside the house. It seemed pretty safe to bet that Anita wasn't acting on her own—but was she collaborating with Evan? With Marisa? Or with both? Sandro wasn't sure. He'd sensed acute tension in the relationship between the Connors, but he couldn't pinpoint the cause. It could be something as mundane as jealousy on Marisa's part because of Evan's having an affair with the nanny. Or it could be something more subtle, such as the fact that Evan was Marc Joubert's designated heir, and his marriage to Marisa was an old-fashioned dynastic arrangement that she resented. On the other hand, maybe the tensions arose because Marisa was the dominant partner in the marriage, and Evan felt emasculated. Marisa, after all, was Marc Joubert's daughter, and the fact that she looked pretty and had a cute baby didn't prove her innocent of complicity in her father's criminal enterprises.

What it all boiled down to, Sandro decided, was the fact that no matter who Anita had been working with this morning, somebody in the Connor household had written the ransom demand, and that same somebody must know where Belle had been taken.

Having finally reached a decision, Sandro swung his car around and headed north to Boca Raton.

Marisa blamed nobody except herself for the disastrous state of her existence and her marriage. Desperate to escape the complexities of life as Marc Joubert's youngest child, she'd seized the chance to go to New York and establish herself in an independent career. In no time at all, she'd succeeded beyond her wildest hopes—but had soon learned that success provided its own inevitable retinue of complexities.

As one of the most sought-after models of the early nineties, she'd invariably been surrounded by men who found her beautiful and who treated her like a princess. In fact, she'd been treated rather better than most real-life princesses. The men she worked with were nearly all gay, and they had an aesthetic appreciation for her appearance, even though they viewed her as little more than a beautiful object to be admired in their camera lens or on their fashion runway. Since she was an expensive object that needed to be cosseted and flattered, they pampered her accordingly.

The men she dated hadn't been gay, but they'd been equally inclined to treat her as an object rather than as a person. The fact that her dates wanted to take her to bed or show her off to their friends instead of photographing her hadn't helped to make her feel like any more of a real person. On the defensive after being hurt and disappointed once too often, she'd soon discovered that having sex was the best way ever invented to avoid intimacy. In a life crowded with men, none had ever bothered to find out that beneath the glittering surface of Marisa the Sexy Model lived Marisa the Homebody, whose major ambition in life was to be a suburban mother to a clutch of happy, well-loved children.

By the time Evan Connor had come into her life, she'd spent two years overdosing on increasing amounts of alcohol and chain-smoking Gauloise cigarettes to assuage the pangs of hunger caused by constant dieting. Models, she discovered the hard way, looked emaciated because they were starving, not because they were genetically predestined to have high cheekbones and protruding ribs. But even though she'd been pursuing a life-style that almost guaranteed self-destruction, her loathing for any activity outside the law kept her away from illegal drugs. Other models might float down the catwalk on a cloud of heroin. Marisa was supported only by willpower and a perverse pride that refused to allow her to admit that she had escaped from the destructive pathology of the Joubert family only to plunge headlong into the dysfunctional world of *haute couture*.

Going home was never an option. Like Belle, whom she admired so much, Marisa, once having broken free of the Joubert chains, had planned never to get close enough to Miami to be shackled again.

Evan, eight years older than Marisa and several lifetimes more cunning, had needed no more than a couple of dates to understand exactly how she could be conquered. He won her heart simply by treating her like the girl next door. Instead of taking her to the usual boring roster of fancy restaurants where she couldn't eat the rich food, and nightclubs where there was no room to dance, he drove her into the small towns and villages of upstate New York, showing her the natural beauty of the Catskills. He beguiled her into eating homey, forbidden wonders like mashed potatoes and gravy, and spending glorious nights in little inns where he always managed to make friends with the owners and elicit heartwarming human-interest stories that thrilled Marisa precisely because the dramas people recounted were so humdrum.

As far as sex was concerned, Evan came up a big winner in comparison to his predecessors. Their sexual relationship during the early days of their courtship constituted irrefutable proof that no genuine emotion was needed to produce magnificent orgasms—in Marisa's case, the first she'd ever achieved. Evan was smart enough to realize that she wanted to be wooed, and that she was shy about her powerful sexuality. He set out to provide her with precisely the lovemaking she had always craved: slow, gentle, traditional—respectful. By the time they'd been dating for a month, Marisa was head over heels in love. By the time he suggested marriage two months later, she needed no persuasion. Evan was her dream man. She eloped, and spent a blissful honeymoon fantasizing about the perfect home she would create for the two of them and their brood of babies.

The dream endured through two devastating miscarriages and painful surgeries to correct a variety of reproductive problems. It had ended abruptly the week after Spencer was born, when she learned the truth about Evan's real identity and why he had married her. By that time, she realized it was only willful blindness on her part that had kept her ignorant for so long. She also realized that it was typical of Evan's perverse patience that he had been willing to endure more than three years of marriage—three years of daily pretense, three years of pretending to love her—in order to achieve his goal of fathering the first Joubert grandchild.

Unfortunately, fathering Spencer hadn't won Evan the reward he sought. In Marc Joubert, he had finally encountered an opponent as strong-willed as he was, and every bit as ruthless. Denied the prize he craved, Evan's revenge had been predictable, given his true nature. He couldn't bend Marc to his will, and so he tortured Marc's daughter, knowing that she would never leave him as long as he controlled access to Spencer.

Marisa cut off her own train of thought—way too familiar to be useful—and shuttered her expression as Evan came into the nursery. She was tidying Spencer's toy box, both to placate her husband, who had a pathological need for neatness, and because it gave her something to do with her hands while she agonized about Belle and what might be happening to her. Anita had Spencer in the pool, and was giving him a swimming lesson. If Marisa was lucky, and if she obeyed all of Evan's orders without question, she would be allowed to give Spencer his lunch and put him down for his nap. Her days were made up of such small treats and hopes, and, even with Belle missing, she couldn't quite put aside her longing to earn a few extra moments with her son.

"Marisa, my dear, I don't think you heard the front doorbell. Sandro is here. You should come downstairs right away."

"Yes, of course." Marisa got hurriedly to her feet, hoping to hear news about Belle and Tony that she could actually believe. Evan, of course, was totally ignoring her questions, and deliberately tormenting her by refusing to offer any reassurance that Belle was safe. Thus far, she knew Evan hadn't got what he wanted, which was the Cronus disk, so she was reasonably optimistic that Belle wasn't in any danger of being killed. Yet.

As for Sandro, whatever news he brought, she knew he couldn't have found her brother and sister; otherwise, Evan wouldn't be looking so smug. Which meant that the dilemma she had been grappling with for two days was becoming more urgent to resolve by the second. How long could she wait before she took action and told somebody what she knew? Could she trust Sandro Marchese to help her? Belle obviously did, and Marisa suspected her sister was more savvy about men than she was. Still, Sandro was clever and charming and oozed sex appeal. Faced with such an enticing package, it was possible that Belle could be as bad a judge of men as was her sister. Was it safe to assume that Sandro would be on the side of the good guys?

Her tumultuous thoughts concealed behind the blank expression she'd first perfected as a model, Marisa entered the living room where Anita had enacted her early morning farce. Anita had only succeeded in tricking Belle and Sandro because she'd remained silent, Marisa recalled miserably. But how could she issue a warning when Evan had threatened to take Spencer away permanently if she breathed a word about what she knew? How could she consign her son to the exclusive guardianship of a monster?

Anita was in the living room again, reclining in the same white leather chair that she'd occupied this morning. Spencer sat contentedly at her feet, playing with his teddy bear and a big plastic dump truck. Quick to seize the opportunity to hold her son, Marisa crossed the room and scooped Spencer into her arms, taking care not to scare him by hugging too tightly.

She always felt more courageous when she held her child, and she didn't wait for a signal from Evan before speaking. "Sandro, I'm so glad you came back. I've been really worried. What news do you have for us?"

"Nothing exciting," Sandro said. "But I'm optimistic that we'll find your sister before too long. The FBI has sent in a full team. They're sweeping the area where I lost track of her, and they'll follow up on every possible clue."

"It's a great shame the kidnappers discovered the chip you'd put in her sandal," Evan said sadly.

Hypocritical bastard, Marisa thought.

Sandro directed a glance at her husband that she found hard to interpret. "The chip in Belle's sandal wouldn't have been a problem," he said. "I expected them to find that. Unfortunately, they found the other tracking device, too."

"The other device?" Anita asked, sounding startled.

Marisa was surprised, too. She hadn't realized that when Belle left the house, she'd been protected by two microchip tracking devices. She was sure Evan hadn't known, either. He'd made no mention of a second chip when he called Dave to warn him about the tracking device in the sandal.

"I attached a second tracker to the back of Belle's watch," Sandro explained. "Her watch with the tracking device still attached was found in a service station near the Dania area. However, I'm real hopeful that the kidnappers didn't realize we were on their tail until right before they discarded her watch, in which case we have a fairly good idea of the general area where they might have taken her."

Evan grimaced. "Miami's a big city with lots of places to hide. The FBI could take days—weeks—to find her."

"True," Sandro agreed. "However, the search of the Dania area is only one angle we're working on. There are others. For example, the FBI will be following up on the note that you gave me this morning, Anita. I'm sure they'll have a great many questions to ask about that. Some of them are bound to produce results."

"Are they hoping that I'll be able to identify the men who attacked me?" Anita asked.

"Oh, no," Sandro said. "We all realize there's no hope of you being able to do that."

"I wish I'd seen them more clearly," Anita murmured. "It's so frustrating that I can't help more."

"It's hard to see people who don't exist," Sandro said mildly.

His manner was so low key that it took Marisa a second or two to register what he'd actually said. When she did, she stared at him in blank astonishment, so surprised that she actually forgot to glance at Evan and check his reaction.

Anita looked scared. "Whatever are you talking about?" she blustered.

"Yes," Evan said, sounding more curious than anything else. "What *do* you mean by that strange remark, Sandro?"

"I've had this house under surveillance since the time I arrived last night," Sandro said. "There was no attack on Anita this morning. She didn't even have a friendly encounter with anyone, much less a confrontation. She strolled around with the dog and came straight back into the house, not having spoken to a living soul.'' He smiled bleakly. ''The way I see it, that means the ransom note was written by one of you three. Belle isn't very fortunate in her relations, is she?''

Anita started to insist that she'd been attacked, but Evan silenced her with a single command.

''If you knew the ransom note was written by one of us, why did you let Belle go to the rendezvous?'' he asked Sandro.

''Because Belle was desperate to find her brother,'' Sandro replied, his voice harsh. ''I figured that if I let you know your ruse to entrap her hadn't worked, the chances were excellent that Tony would get killed.''

''So you took a gamble with my sister's life, and it failed,'' Marisa said, so furious with him that she forgot to be scared of Evan.

Sandro turned, and the look he directed at her was filled with a humiliating mixture of scorn and pity. ''I didn't see you taking any steps to protect your sister,'' he said. ''Where is she, Marisa?''

Marisa buried her face in her son's soft curls. ''I don't know,'' she muttered, too ashamed to meet his eyes.

''If you have any ideas at all, you need to speak up,'' Sandro said softly. ''Are you scared of your husband? If you are, you need to realize that by remaining silent, you're playing his game and giving him the power he needs to harm your sister. If you speak up, you set yourself free, and Belle, too. Talk to me, Marisa. Tell me where Belle is.''

"I honestly don't know where she is," Marisa said despairingly. "I wish to God I did."

"But you know why she's been taken, don't you? The Cronus disk is missing, and they think that Belle has it. Is that what this is all about?"

"Don't answer that, Marisa," Evan said. "And that's an order."

Cradling Spencer against her breast, Marisa turned to look at her husband, and saw that he was aiming a gun aimed directly at Sandro's heart. She felt a fresh wave of despair. Evan never went far without his gun, but she'd expected him to try to bluff it out with Sandro. He must be truly desperate, she thought, to draw his weapon and thereby give up all hope of pretending to be an innocent bystander. Evan and desperation were a terrifying combination to contemplate.

"Evan is a crack shot," she said tiredly. "Don't move, Sandro, or he'll kill you."

"Thank you, my dear. I couldn't have expressed it better myself." Evan gestured with the gun. "Anita, check Agent Marchese for weapons. We don't want any nasty surprises."

Looking very uncertain, Anita stood up. "Evan, this is going too far. Put the gun away. Your son is in the room. He might get hurt, for heaven's sake!"

"In the unlikely event that I want your opinion, I'll ask for it," Evan said. "Otherwise, shut up and do as you're told. I asked you to check Agent Marchese for concealed weapons. Do it!"

Anita seemed both shocked and scared by Evan's attitude. What had Anita expected? Marisa wondered. For over a year, the woman had watched Evan abuse his wife in every way imaginable. Had she really been foolish enough to believe that his brutality would never be directed toward her?

"I'll take Spencer to his room," Marisa said, and turned as if she expected Evan to allow her to leave.

The ruse didn't work. "Come back here," Evan said coldly. "I haven't given you permission to leave."

Marisa turned, willing to humble herself in order to plead for her son, if not for herself. "Evan, please, he's your son and he could get hurt."

"Stay here. I want you where I can see you. You can't be trusted to behave as a loyal wife should." Evan never even glanced at her as he spoke, but Marisa knew he was perfectly capable of putting a bullet into her leg if she ignored him and continued to walk away. Keeping her gaze averted—she was afraid she might throw up if she looked at him—she came back into the living room and sat in a chair as far away from him as possible.

Evan snapped his fingers at Anita. "I'm still waiting for you to check Marchese for weapons."

Casting a worried glance at Spencer, Anita slowly approached Sandro. "I'm sorry, but I have to frisk you."

"Be my guest." Sandro obligingly held out his arms. Anita leaned in to pat him down, and soon found the gun holstered under Sandro's shirt. She held it gingerly, fingering the safety.

"Careful," Sandro said. "It's loaded and ready to shoot."

Anita didn't look at him or acknowledge his comment in any way, but apparently Evan had finally gone one step too far for her when he put his own son at risk. To Marisa's astonishment, the nanny suddenly swung around and aimed the gun at Evan.

"You told me nobody would get hurt," Anita said, her voice trembling with outrage. "You told me it was just a family squabble about your father-in-law's money, and that Belle was trying to stop you getting a divorce from Marisa. That was a pack of lies, wasn't it?"

"Don't threaten him! Don't make him angry!" Marisa screamed the warning, but she was too late. She didn't see Evan pull the trigger, because her gaze was riveted on Anita. But she heard the explosive sound of Evan's gun firing as she flung herself onto the floor, her body curved protectively over Spencer's. The baby cried fiercely, then fell abruptly silent, the air squeezed from his lungs by the pressure of her weight on top of him.

She unwound herself enough to let Spencer suck in a sobbing gulp of air, soothing him as best she could without getting up. When she was finally able to look up from her child, Anita was lying on the marble tiles, barely conscious, a wound in her shoulder gushing blood. And Sandro had a gun in his hand that was aimed straight at Evan's heart.

"I guess Anita didn't know that I never travel in the company of thieves and murderers without carrying at least two guns," Sandro said.

"Squeeze the trigger and you're a dead man," Evan replied.

"Possibly," Sandro said. "Or possibly not. In the meantime, it might be smart to discuss where we go from here. We can stand around playing who's-got-the-biggest-*cojones,* or we can put the guns away and talk about what kind of a deal I might try to work out with the federal prosecutor on your behalf if you take me to Belle and Tony. Right now, before they get killed.''

''Sorry, Agent Marchese. But as always with you feds, you're a day late and several million dollars short in your offer.''

''I'm the best chance you have of avoiding a life sentence in federal prison.''

Evan gave a snort of laughter. ''I don't plan to hang around to be indicted. Maybe I can't live happily ever after here in the States, but I can board a fast boat and disappear into the Caribbean sunset. Taking my dear wife and child with me, of course. One of the most rewarding aspects of a career as a smuggler is that you can build up such nice fat bank accounts in countries that refuse to release financial information to Uncle Sam.''

Sandro tipped his head to one side. ''You know, Evan, I believe you. I'm sure you do have money squirreled away in bank accounts overseas. Not as much as you'd like, maybe, but enough. And it's true that from the point of view of law enforcement, until yesterday you could have taken a boat out of Miami, sailed to the islands, and nobody would have lifted a finger to stop you. So why didn't you? Why did you hang around here in the States, practically inviting Customs and the FBI to come and find you?''

Evan shrugged, although the aim of his gun never wavered. ''Go ahead. You seem to be eager to tell me.''

''Yeah, I am. It has to be that you *can't* leave. You're obviously working on a deal so big that every move you make is being watched. Not by Customs, or the FBI, or any other law enforcement agency.

You've got customers who are as ruthless and immoral as yourself sitting on your ass, watching you so closely that if you sneeze, they catch cold.''

Evan looked bored. ''You're not making much sense, Agent Marchese. By your own logic, if I'm sitting on a huge deal, all I have to do is complete it, take my money, say thank-you, and sail for the islands.''

''Don't you wish,'' Sandro said softly. ''You can't complete the deal because Marc Joubert up and died on you, and you don't know how to ship the merchandise out. You're desperate to get your hands on the Cronus disk. Why would you worry about petty stuff like going to federal prison, or being chased by the FBI? You've got way bigger problems. If you don't find the Cronus disk pretty damn quick—like today, in the next few hours—you're going to be chopped up in bite-size chunks and fed to the alligators.''

''Well, it's an interesting theory. If you were right, then I would say it's very fortunate that minutes before you arrived here, I received a phone call from one of my associates to say that Belle was willing to show us where she's hidden the Cronus disk. The window is behind you, and I'm sure you don't want to turn around for fear that I'll shoot you. However, you might be able to hear that a car is just now pulling into my front drive. It's a white Lincoln Continental, and, yes, I do believe that Belle has arrived. I'm sure she's hoping to get lots of support from her sister and brother-in-law.''

Evan didn't actually look at his wife, but he smiled

the cruel smile Marisa had learned to hate—and dread. "What a shame that your sister misjudged the situation so badly, wouldn't you agree, my dear? Poor Belle is going to be so sadly disillusioned."

Twenty-One

To Belle's relief, the drive to her sister's house was accomplished with almost no problems. Satisfied that neither of his passengers could cause him trouble, Dave had been remarkably passive, his attention devoted to driving the car. Before leaving the warehouse, he and Ray had bound Tony's arms to his body and manacled his ankles so that he could only hobble. Tony had remonstrated weakly, but Belle had wasted little time in sympathy for her brother. She'd saved his life, she hoped. As for the rest, she was still mad at him and quite content to let him suffer a bit.

She didn't blame Tony for agreeing to wear the wire. Dave might be approaching sixty, but he was still strong, and she could imagine that Tony had been badly beaten up and in a lot of pain after twenty-four hours at Dave's mercy. But she wasn't yet ready to forgive her brother for the fact that he'd made no effort to warn her that their conversation was being monitored. It would have been easy for Tony to silently lift up his shirt and show her the wire. He'd chosen not to, and Belle was angry at the betrayal. Tony had tried to mumble an apology once they got into the car, but Belle hadn't been willing to listen. Her brother, it seemed, hadn't learned that taking the easy way out usually caused far more problems than it solved.

Despite feverish thought during the drive to Boca Raton, Belle's grand rescue scheme was still nothing more sophisticated than the hope that, with Marisa and Evan's help, she would be able to overcome any threats that Dave might present. The vagueness of her plan bothered her, but it wasn't until they were trooping up to the front door of Marisa's house that she felt her first really serious qualm.

Parading across the driveway with her brother hobbling in front and Dave bringing up the rear, she was struck not just by how vulnerable Dave was, but by the fact that he must surely *know* he was vulnerable. She'd been full of bluff and bravado in the warehouse, but why had Dave and Ray fallen for her bluff? Why had Dave meekly agreed to come here? At the time, she'd assumed he and Ray were so frantic to possess the Cronus disk that they were willing to accept any conditions she tossed at them. But now, faced with the practical reality of the situation, she was assailed by doubts. Why had Dave agreed to be disarmed, almost without protest? Why hadn't he realized that the moment she got inside Marisa's house, the odds would immediately switch heavily in her favor? Didn't he realize that he would be outnumbered by at least three to one, without any weapons to overcome his disadvantage?

The moment she asked herself the questions, she realized something: Dave would never have been stupid enough to walk into such an obvious trap. Therefore he had to know something that she didn't. What?

A yawning pit of desolation opened inside Belle. *Her sister.* The third Joubert sibling and the youngest heir to the disastrous Joubert legacy. Belle had blindly assumed that Marisa would be on the side of the good guys. Her side. But Dave must know better, or he wouldn't be strolling—unarmed and outnumbered—into her sister's home.

With a flash of despair, Belle realized that she—not Dave Forcier—was the person walking into a trap.

She turned to run, but understanding had come too late. Beneath his shambling, passive demeanor, Dave had obviously been watching her like a hawk. The second she made her move, he swung around, slashing his elbow into her rib cage with sufficient force to wind her. As she stumbled, he reached out and grabbed her, twisting her arm behind her again, so that her already torn shoulder muscles screamed out with pain. He pushed her along the last few feet to the front steps.

Evan or Marisa must have seen them arrive, because the door stood open. Dave shoved Belle across the threshold, and Tony shuffled behind them, stuttering ineffectual protests.

It was Marisa who greeted them, with Spencer in her arms. Until she saw her sister's horrified expression, Belle had forgotten how terrible her face must look after Dave's beating.

"Oh, my God," Marisa said, turning pale. "What happened to you?"

"I had to knock some sense into her," Dave said, shrugging. "For some reason, Belle was having a real hard time understanding my point of view."

Marisa shot him a look that was hot with hatred. "Like father, like son," she said. "If you can't win an argument, use your fists." She walked away without waiting for him to reply. But she didn't seem surprised to see Dave, and she made no attempt to rescue Belle from his punishing hold.

"What's she talking about?" Tony asked, his voice thick from the swelling of his face. "Which father? Which son? Is she saying that I'm like Dad?"

"Trust me, sonny boy, you're nothing like Marc Joubert," Dave said. "And of course your sister wasn't talking about you and your dad. She was talking about me. Me and my son, Evan Connor." Dave's voice was threaded with amusement, as if he relished the bombshell he knew he'd just dropped.

Belle's head jerked up and she stared stupidly at Dave. "What did you say?"

Dave's smile turned malicious. "I said, Evan Connor is my son. His mother was my first wife, and even more of a bitch than the other three. She ran off with Evan when he was just a toddler, and it took me twenty years of searching to track him down in Hawaii."

Belle heard what Dave was saying, but she had a hard time assimilating the incredible claim. Evan was Dave's *son?* She'd never realized that Dave had any children—just lots of wives. She was paralyzed by shock, and when Dave prodded her forward, she stumbled. Even when Dave hauled her back onto her feet, she couldn't quite manage to wrap her mind around the stunning truth that Marisa was married to Dave's son.

Which presumably meant that Evan was working hand-in-glove with his father, and that, at the very least, Marisa must be a silent accomplice to their plans. No wonder Dave had seemed so willing to be disarmed. Belle had proposed leading him straight where he wanted to go! How could she have been so trusting, so unquestioning of Dave's easy compliance? How could she have been so totally *dumb?*

She was taking too long to move, and Dave jerked on her arm. "Into the living room, sweetie. I believe that's where my son is waiting to receive us."

The sight of Sandro Marchese when she entered the living room boosted Belle's spirits several notches. He held a .38 revolver aimed directly at Evan Connor's heart—a fact that would have thrilled Belle if not for the fact that Evan was aiming a similar weapon right back. Anita Gillespie lay facedown on the floor, apparently unconscious, with blood seeping from a wound in her shoulder.

One down, three to go, Belle thought bleakly.

"Hi, Belle." Sandro's gaze was fixed on Evan, and it didn't even flicker in her direction. "I see you've managed to rescue your brother. Congratulations."

"Hi, Sandro." Belle figured that this probably wasn't a good moment to point out that she'd "rescued" her brother right into a trap. "I'm really pleased to see you. You look kind of busy."

"Yeah. I'm trying to save the world from assholes like Evan and Dave. It's a tough job, but somebody has to do it."

Evan's finger moved on the trigger of his gun. "Tell me why I shouldn't just pull this trigger and get rid of you, Marchese."

"Because if you do, I'm going to fire right back. And you'll be dead. Count on it, asshole."

Dave made an impatient sound. "Enough already with the macho-man contest. We're here for one reason, which is to get the Cronus disk. Okay, Belle, you said you'd hidden it here in your sister's house. Where?"

"If you want it, go look for it yourself, Uncle Dave." Belle tried to sound brave and unconcerned—no mean feat when her knees were knocking and her stomach was whirling like an old-fashioned butter churn.

"No, I'm not looking. You're going to take me right to it. I don't have time to play games anymore." This time there were no mocking undertones to his voice—just brutal impatience.

He took hold of her pinkie and bent it backwards until the bone snapped. She screamed, unable to stop herself, teetering in and out of consciousness as pain traveled in a tidal wave up her arm.

"Nice going, sweetie." Dave sounded satisfied. "You probably were too preoccupied to notice, but when you screamed, your favorite macho-man flinched. He managed to hold his aim this time, but you've got nine more fingers. How do you think he'll be doing by the time I get to number ten?"

"I'll be doing fine," Sandro said. "I'll be inspired by the thought of how much pleasure I'm going to get when I finally arrest you and this weasel excuse for a son of yours."

"Talk's cheap," Dave said. "Spout off all you want, Marchese. I know at heart you can't stand to see people suffer. An unfortunate weakness for a man in your position. Now, Belle, I'll ask you one more time. The last time before something real bad happens. Where's the Cronus disk?"

Through a red mist of pain, Belle searched for an answer that might offer some faint hope of survival. "It's upstairs," she said. "I hid it in Spencer's nursery."

"She's lying," Evan said. "She was never alone in Spencer's nursery."

"Yes, I was," Belle said quickly. She shook her head, fighting against a disabling wave of dizziness. "I went upstairs with Marisa when we heard Spencer coughing. You and Sandro were playing chess out on the patio, remember? Marisa went into the bathroom while we were up there. She needed to put more water and medication into Spencer's vaporizer. That's when I hid the disk."

"Where?" Dave asked.

Belle tried to ignore the pain that throbbed and seared in her finger. What was she going to say? However much she connived and invented, the truth was soon going to come out. And once Evan and Dave knew that she didn't have the Cronus disk, her life was going to be worth slightly less than bird droppings.

Sheer survival instinct forced her to come up with one more delaying tactic. "I hid the disk in one of Spencer's toys," she said. "It's inside his stuffed elephant."

"She's about to pass out," Dave said laconically. "Marisa, go up to the nursery and check the elephant."

"Spencer has at least half a dozen elephants," Marisa said woodenly. "Which one are you talking about, Belle?"

"I'll show you." Belle had to pin her hopes on getting help from her sister, although that hope looked pretty absurd right about now.

"Belle and Marisa can't be trusted to go alone," Evan said. "You go with them, Dave."

Why couldn't Marisa be trusted to go alone with

her? Belle wondered. Her sister had done and said
absolutely nothing so far that indicated she disap-
proved of the way her husband and father-in-law were
behaving. In fact, she'd gotten up from her chair,
where she'd been sitting with Spencer, the moment
Dave ordered her to go and look for the disk. And
she'd seemed not just willing, but eager. And when
Dave had curtly seconded his son's order for Marisa
to walk upstairs, she had obediently led the way.

"I have to put Spencer in his crib," she said to her
father-in-law when the three of them reached the
nursery. "I can't search for a disk while I'm holding
him."

"Go ahead. Be quick," Dave said. "It's better if
Spencer's not downstairs anyway. I wouldn't want
anything to happen to my grandson."

Marisa lifted Spencer into his crib, murmuring a
few words when he started to whimper. She handed
him his dog-eared teddy bear and a book, shushing
him until he settled down. His thumb went straight
into his mouth as he turned the stiff cardboard pages
of *Goodnight Moon.*

"Which elephant is it?" Marisa asked, keeping her
gaze carefully averted from Belle as if she couldn't
face her sister at this moment of betrayal.

"It was in Spencer's toy box yesterday," Belle
said, frantically trying to think of some way to get a
few minutes alone with her sister and at least make a
plea for help.

"I tidied the toy box this morning and put away
some of the stuffed animals he doesn't play with anymore. I expect the elephant you're talking about is in
the closet. I'll get it now."

Dave swung around to watch Marisa's progress

across the room. He was so tense that his hold on Belle's arm actually slackened, but she resisted the temptation to break loose before she had planned her next move.

Marisa emerged from the closet, holding a huge gray elephant. The animal Belle remembered had been much smaller, less than half the size, but since the disk wasn't in either toy, she supposed it didn't matter much which elephant her sister found.

"I think she's telling the truth about the disk being in here," Marisa said to Dave, pressing the elephant's belly. "I can feel something hard."

"Then open the fucking seam and take it out." Dave's grip on Belle's arm loosened still more in his eagerness to hold the precious Cronus disk in his hands.

"Okay. I'll get a pair of scissors from the bathroom." Marisa walked behind him.

"Make sure you don't get any fancy ideas about using the sciss—"

Belle felt Dave's hands drop, and she quickly sprang forward out of his reach. She pivoted and saw that Marisa had looped some sort of chain around her father-in-law's neck and was pulling with all her strength. Dave was clawing at his throat, and it was obvious that Marisa didn't have enough strength to keep him subdued. Sending a frenzied glance around the room, Belle snatched the first heavy object that her hand touched, and smashed it over Dave's head. He collapsed on the floor at her feet in a gratifyingly inert heap.

She and Marisa exchanged slightly hysterical glances. "I broke Spencer's Winnie-the-Pooh lamp," Belle said.

Marisa unwound the dog leash from Dave's neck, pressing her finger against her mouth. Belle remembered the baby monitor that was located in the kitchen but might be audible in the living room. Nursing her broken finger, and fighting waves of nausea, she couldn't offer to help when Marisa returned from the bathroom with a roll of tape, which she used to seal Dave's mouth and bind his hands. For good measure, her sister looped the dog leash around his ankles, pulling it as tight as she could and then clipping it shut. From the safety of his crib, Spencer watched their activities with interest.

"What the hell's going on up there?" Evan's angry voice floated up the stairs. "Did you find the disk?"

Marisa walked out onto the landing and called over the banister. "We found a disk inside the elephant. I'll bring it down. There's no identifying label, but I guess it's the right one."

Turning to Belle, she whispered, "I had to get Spencer out of bullet range before I could do anything. Evan keeps his other guns locked up, so we can't get one. I don't know what to do next."

Belle pulled a fleecy blanket from Spencer's crib. "With Dave and Anita already out of commission, it's three to one," she whispered. "Four, if we count on Tony. When we go downstairs, Evan's back is to the entrance and Sandro is facing us. That's in our favor. Distract Evan when you hand over the elephant, and I'll run into the room and throw this over his head. It'll give us a couple of seconds to wrest the gun from him. Sandro will react fast and help us."

Marisa rolled her eyes—which was a pretty good assessment of her plan, Belle acknowledged ruefully. Amazingly, considering the mess they were in, her spirits were starting to fly high. The knowledge that her sister wasn't cooperating with Dave or Evan was the best pick-me-up she could have had. Better even than drugs to kill the assorted pains in her finger, head and shoulder.

They walked downstairs, Marisa in front, clutching the elephant as if she hoped it would protect her from Evan's wrath. They arrived at the entrance to the living room. Fortunately, Evan couldn't see them, and because of his standoff with Sandro, he was in no position to turn around and check exactly what they were doing or where they were.

"Here's the elephant," Marisa said, standing off to the side, out of the line of fire.

"I want the disk, not the elephant," Evan said. "Are you just stupid, Marisa, or are you deliberately trying to annoy me? Why the hell did you put the disk back inside the elephant?"

While Marisa fumbled at the seam in the elephant's pendulous belly, Belle crept up behind Evan, the blanket stretched out, ready to throw over his head. Dave had broken the pinkie on her right hand, and she was left-handed, which meant that she had at least a slight chance of throwing the blanket accurately enough to blind Evan momentarily.

She knew that Sandro must have seen her, but he didn't betray her presence by so much as the flicker of an eyelash. Tony was less disciplined. He sat huddled on a chair in the corner of the room and didn't notice her at first, but when he saw Belle creeping up behind Evan, he half rose from his seat, then hastily dropped back down again, studiously looking away.

She and Marisa couldn't have devised a more compelling distraction if they'd rehearsed with Tony for hours. Their brother's actions plainly suggested that something hazardous to Evan's safety was occurring out of his line of vision. The unplanned diversion worked perfectly. For a crucial second, Evan's attention was drawn away from Sandro.

Belle threw the blanket over Evan's head just as he fired. Two shots exploded in quick succession.

Evan fell to the floor.

Sandro felt the sting of Evan's bullet slicing a shallow path through the flesh on his left upper arm, but he didn't have time to feel pain. Evan was wounded, but not dead.

"Keep back!" he yelled, diving for the floor and making a grab for Evan's gun. Jesus, he'd been so scared of hitting Belle that he'd fucked up his shot. Not only was Evan Connor still alive, but the bastard was taking aim at his wife.

Sandro brought his gun down in a stinging chop on Evan's wrist, and the gun skittered across the polished tile floor. For good measure, he slammed his gun against the side of Evan's head, and the man finally collapsed into unconsciousness. Panting, Sandro hauled himself to his feet and propped himself against the nearest stretch of bare wall.

Marisa looked down at her husband. "Is he dead?" she asked, her voice devoid of emotion.

"No," Sandro said. "Not yet. But he's seriously wounded and needs medical attention if we're going to keep him alive long enough to stand trial."

"Much good a trial will do us," Marisa said bitterly. "His lawyers will get him off somehow. The Evan Connors of the world never end up doing serious jail time."

Sandro's wound must have been making him slow-witted, because he didn't realize what Marisa was planning to do until she actually picked up the gun and aimed it at her husband's inert body.

"No, Rizzie, don't shoot him!" Belle quickly put herself in front of Evan, cutting off her sister's line of fire. "For God's sake, you're free of him now. Don't do something that will destroy the rest of your life."

Marisa didn't respond for several long seconds. Then she tossed the gun to the floor.

"You're right. He isn't worth doing jail time for," she said. "Belle, you need to sit down before you fall down. Sandro, too. I'll call 9-1-1 and get some medical help."

Sandro walked over to Belle and put his arm around her. She yelped in pain. Sandro smiled wryly. "Guess it's gonna be a couple of days before we can have mad, passionate sex again, huh?"

"Twenty-four hours, at least." Belle didn't quite manage to return his smile. Now that the rush of adrenaline was fading, she seemed to be having a really hard time standing upright. Sandro helped her to the nearest sofa and then sat there with her, watching numbly as the blood from his shoulder wound dripped onto her hand. If he'd had even a smidgen more energy, he'd have laughed at the picture they must have presented.

Marisa hurried back, carrying a tray equipped with water and clean kitchen towels. Tony finally emerged from his funk sufficiently to demand to be cut loose from his shackles, so Marisa slashed through the tape binding his wrists and, with evident impatience, handed him the tray. "Here, make yourself useful.

Try to see if you can do anything for Anita, and give
Sandro and Belle some water. I'll be right back.''

"Where do you think she's going?" Sandro asked
woozily, sipping water as he watched Marisa retreat
upstairs.

"To check on Spencer, I expect." Belle leaned
against the sofa, barely able to hold her water glass.
"Do you hear sirens? I'm beginning to think that a
very large injection of morphine would feel really
good right about now."

Marisa came running back down the stairs. In her
hands she held her son's much loved, but decidedly
shabby, teddy bear.

"You look like hell." Marisa reached out and
gently pushed a limp lock of hair out of Belle's eyes.

"Then I look just how I feel," Belle said ruefully.

Tears filled Marisa's eyes and she brushed them
away. "I don't know how to say thank-you. You
saved my life."

Belle started to protest. Marisa ignored her and
pushed up the sleeves of her dress, revealing arms that
were a hideous mass of bruises and contusions in
every state of healing and newness.

"This is how Evan kept me silent," she said simply. "He threatened to take Spencer and hide from
me if I didn't do exactly what he told me. How could
I possibly risk leaving my son with a man who was
capable of physical abuse like this whenever he got
angry or frustrated? But you showed me that no matter how impossible the odds seem, there's always a
way to fight back."

Belle stared at her sister's arms, then jerked her
head away, looking as if she were going to throw up.
Accustomed as Sandro was to seeing the evidence of

physical brutality, even he felt his stomach heave. He remembered the strange effect Evan's touch had seemed to have on Marisa, and now he understood why. She'd been silenced by sheer terror whenever it looked as if she might summon the courage to rebel. The lightest pressure from Evan against her bruised flesh would have been enough to remind Marisa that she needed to bend to his will—or face the terrible consequences. Not just for herself, but for her child.

Belle finally collected herself enough to speak. "I think it was the other way around, Rizzie. You saved my life by attacking Dave and distracting Evan with the elephant."

Marisa smiled—a little shakily, but it was still a real smile. "You were more clairvoyant than you could possibly have known, Belle."

"What about?"

"The Cronus disk and hiding it in a stuffed animal." Marisa held out Spencer's teddy and slit the side seam open with a knife. She pulled out a wad of soft fibre stuffing, and finally extracted a small, shiny laser disk.

"The Cronus disk," she said, holding it out to Sandro. "My father gave it to me."

Epilogue

"Marisa, I've been trying to call you all week! Now I know why I couldn't reach you." Smiling, Belle held the door open wide. "Why didn't you tell me you were planning a trip to Chicago? And you've brought Spencer, too. Come on in. This is a wonderful surprise."

Not wanting to intimidate her nephew, Belle bent down so that she was almost at eye level with him before reaching out to take his hand. "Hi, little guy, how's it going?"

Spencer's only response was to hang his head, so Belle tried again. "Sandro and I have a new kitty cat. Would you like to come and meet her? Her name is Dottie. She's very pretty and she has nice soft gray fur."

Spencer didn't answer. He clung to his mother's pants and buried his face against her leg, refusing even to look at Belle.

"He's a bit shy these days," Marisa said, and her hand curved protectively around Spencer's shoulders. "There have been a lot of changes for him to cope with. I thought he'd be too young to care about where he lives, but he seems to miss the house and the swimming pool."

"The past couple of months must have been really

tough for both of you. But give him a few weeks and he'll soon settle down and be his old self again.'' Belle was afraid she sounded annoyingly upbeat, but these days optimism seemed to be her strongest trait. With no effort at all, she managed to find the silver lining in every cloud that dared to scud across her sunny horizon.

"I hope you're right.'' Marisa bent down and picked up Spencer, carrying him into the living room. "He keeps asking for his father, and for Anita, too. That hurts.''

"He'll adjust, Rizzie, you'll see. What's happened to Anita, anyway? Sandro said she planned to go back to England. Did she?''

"Yes, as soon as she came out of the hospital.''

Belle squeezed her sister's hand. "Then you don't have to worry about either of them anymore, although I guess Spencer's bound to miss them for a little while.''

Her sister gave a laugh that held no mirth. "Sure he misses them. Why wouldn't he? Since his first birthday, Evan never allowed me to spend more than a couple of hours a day with my own child. So from Spencer's point of view, he's lost the two people who were his primary caregivers.''

"I can't believe you were going through such a nightmare and you had nobody to turn to.'' Belle felt a flood of bitter regret for the distance she'd allowed to creep into her relationship with Marisa. During all the years she'd been struggling to come to terms with her father's criminality, she'd blindly—arrogantly—assumed that her sister had somehow grown up un-scathed—and that Marisa had escaped into the glamorous world of high fashion with no need to battle the demons that peopled Belle's nightmares.

Belle was so angry every time she thought about what Evan had done to her sister that if her brother-in-law hadn't died of his gunshot wound, she'd have been tempted to murder him herself. Preferably after some long, slow hours of torture.

She hadn't realized that she was crying until Marisa reached out and squeezed her hand. "Please, don't cry, Belle, or you'll set me off, and I swore last week that I was done with tears. Two months of undiluted self-pity is more than enough."

"Okay." Belle found a tissue and blew her nose. "Let's talk about good stuff for a while. Sandro went into the office for a couple of hours to catch up on some paperwork, but he should be home any minute now. He was threatening to cook his world-famous manicotti for dinner—"

"I can't stay very long," Marisa said. "I've come to say goodbye. Spencer and I are going...away...for a while."

"For a vacation?" Belle asked. "That's great. You deserve one for sure. Where are you going?"

Marisa shook her head. "Not for a vacation. Spencer and I are going to start over somewhere new. The sale of our house—Evan's house—went through last week, and I've signed all the papers so that my share of the Joubert inheritance will go into the charitable trust you set up." She glanced toward Spencer, her expression worried. "It was so tempting to set aside some of the money for him, you know? It's scary to realize that from now on, I'm going to have to support him with the money I can earn myself."

"You'll do great. And even if the going gets rough

from time to time, you won't regret giving the money away.''

''I hope you're right.'' Marisa managed a smile. ''Although you know what Sophie Tucker said—'I've been rich and I've been poor, and rich is better.'''

''Yeah, but she earned her money with her own talents—that's the difference.''

Marisa took a coloring book and some crayons from her purse and set them on the floor for Spencer. ''Have you spoken to Tony recently?''

Belle hesitated. ''Not in the past couple of weeks.''

''He's trying to make amends for the way he screwed up,'' Marisa said.

''He has quite a lot to make amends for,'' Belle said curtly.

''He had a tougher time growing up even than us,'' Marisa said. ''If it was hard for us being Marc Joubert's spoiled little darlings, can you imagine what it must have been like to be the only son, trying to step into Dad's shoes and yet hating the family business? Whatever neuroses Tony may have, I guess he acquired them the old-fashioned way—he earned them.''

''I know how rough it was for him,'' Belle acknowledged. ''And I know he's trying to make up for the past by dedicating the next few years to getting the trust up and running efficiently so that Joubert money will finally be used to do some good. It's just going to take a while before I can forget that he always searched for the easy way out, and that he never cared if other people got hurt in the process of saving his own skin.''

''He cared, but he was afraid. You need to talk to

him, Belle. He needs your forgiveness before he can move on.''

Belle sighed. ''All right, I'll talk to him. Okay?''

''Yes.'' Marisa smiled. ''Thank you.''

''Turnabout's fair play. How did Mom take the news that you and Spencer were leaving Florida?''

Marisa shrugged. ''You know Mom. She complained that I was removing her only grandchild and that I didn't care how lonely she was going to be now that she was a poor, neglected widow. I don't believe she remembered to ask a single question about what I planned to do or where I planned to go, much less how I planned to support myself and her grandchild.''

''I know you feel Mom let us down, but there's not much point in being mad at her,'' Belle said quietly. ''In fact, you have much more reason to be angry with me than with her. Mom has lived her whole life never asking questions in case she didn't like the answers. I don't have that excuse. When you stopped visiting, and suddenly our relationship was nothing more than Christmas cards and a quick monthly phone call, I should have known better and pushed for an explanation.''

''You had your own problems to struggle with,'' Marisa said. ''I never expected you to solve mine. Besides, I would never have turned to you for help, however hard you pushed. Evan had me so twisted in my thinking that I was convinced you and Donald Gates were actively cooperating with Evan and his father.''

''You thought *what?*''

''Why are you surprised? I was dumbfounded when I found out after Spencer was born that Dave Forcier was Evan's father. But that discovery just confirmed my view that nothing is ever what it seems. If good ol' Uncle Dave could turn out to be hiding secrets, not to mention a clawing ambition to take over the Joubert empire, how could I be sure that your supposed aversion to Dad's business was genuine?''

"Good grief, you never told me any of that before!''

"I was too embarrassed. But the fact that we misunderstood each other so badly only proves my point about Mom. She should have been there for us, and she wasn't. She should have protested more, Belle, not just turned a blind eye the whole time. Dad loved her. He would have listened to her if she'd insisted that the thefts and the smuggling had to stop. Even at the end, when Dad was really trying to pull back, and Dave and Evan were forcing him to continue, Mom never came out and said to him that he should go to the authorities and get help. She really liked the social power she derived from having all that money, and she wasn't willing to give it up. You notice she hasn't handed a penny of her inheritance over to charity.''

"That may be true, but it wasn't just her social position she wanted to protect. She was worried that Dad would be sent to jail. When you get right down to it, Rizzie, we've, all of us, made decisions we regret because of Dad. I loved him, but we have to place the blame where it belongs, which is with him. I've never been convinced that Mom really knew how the Joubert Corporation made its money.''

"Then she should have,'' Marisa said fiercely. "She's a smart woman. If she didn't know how Dad made his money, then she must have been working mighty hard to remain ignorant. Didn't Mom ever look at us children—really look at us—and see what was happening because of her willful blindness?''

Belle placed her hand comfortingly around Marisa's kneading fingers. "For what it's worth, you didn't go through all that torment in vain. Everyone in Customs is ecstatic about your decision to hang on to the Cronus disk instead of simply destroying it when Dad gave it to you. Customs has been able to launch a massive sweep operation and basically clean up the entire Joubert smuggling network because of information stored on that disk and the one Dad gave me.''

"I know it's been helpful," Marisa said. "I guess it makes the effort to keep it hidden from Evan worthwhile—although when I think about the Brunos, I wonder…''

"Marge's murder was a terrible price to pay, but you couldn't have foreseen her death. Besides, you have to consider all the lives that have been *saved*. As for us… Just think, Rizzie. With the Cronus network out of operation, we never have to wonder if the bomb that blows up the next U.S. embassy was sold by a Joubert.''

"You're right, and I'm trying to focus on the positive. I'm grateful to Sandro. He's been really great about keeping me informed. Between the disk Dad gave to you and the one he gave to me, Sandro says, the courts may have to hire new judges just to process all the Joubert-related indictments.''

"And he wasn't joking," Belle said. "I thought I was too cynical to be shocked, but it's totally amazing how many people who should have known better got lured into playing Dad's game. There are some really big-name politicians and businesspeople taking a heavy fall.''

Spencer, who had been quietly coloring, suddenly jumped up, scattering crayons. "Kitty!" he exclaimed. "Mommy! Kitty!"

"Yes, honey, I see her. Remember, be gentle if you touch her." Marisa hovered anxiously next to her son. The kitten—too young to understand the feline rule that cats are not allowed to express interest in mere humans—pranced and gamboled across the carpet and landed in a splayfooted heap around Spencer's ankles. Spencer bent down and petted her, his eyes sparkling. When the kitten rolled onto her back and stuck all four legs up in the air, Spencer gave a little gurgle of delight.

"I guess Dottie is a hit," Belle said, smiling as she watched them play. "What's happening with Horatio? Do you have him in a kennel until you're more settled?"

Marisa looked down, her fingers plucking at her navy-blue twill pants. Belle already knew that Evan had forced his wife to wear white all the time, as a symbol of her purity and submission. In retaliation, the sweater her sister wore today was a defiantly bright mixture of greens and purple.

"I gave him away," Marisa said. "I made sure he went to a good home, but I couldn't bear to keep him. Horatio was Evan's dog, and Evan had already started…training him."

So much unspoken horror was conveyed by that brief statement. Belle knelt beside her sister's chair, fighting feelings of paralyzing anger toward her dead brother-in-law. She realized her anger was counterproductive, but contemplating the way Evan had abused her sister still reduced Belle to a state of fury. What her sister must feel was…unimaginable.

Spencer gave a surprised yelp when the kitten's claws accidentally dug into his knuckles, and Marisa was at his side in a second. She was reassuring him that he was fine when Belle heard the sound of a key turning in the lock. The door pushed open, and Sandro walked in.

Dottie abandoned her battle with a squeaky toy mouse and launched herself ecstatically onto Sandro's shoes. Belle felt almost as enthusiastic as the kitten, she thought wryly, hurrying to add her welcome.

Sandro shook off the kitten, tossed aside his briefcase, and tucked his arm around Belle's waist, all in a single practiced movement. "Sorry I'm late. I've been in a life-and-death battle with government forms all afternoon."

"Did you win?"

"Nah. I definitely lost."

"You look great for a loser."

Belle felt the inevitable sappy smile plaster itself all over her face at the sight of him. "We've got visitors. Marisa and Spencer came to tell us they're moving."

"Not too far away from here, I hope." Sandro gave her a quick, reassuring kiss before moving on to greet Marisa. He gave her a welcoming hug and then bent down to scoop up Spencer, holding him high over his head. "Hey, big guy, do you want to be a plane and go for a ride?"

"Plane!" Spencer gurgled with excitement as Sandro swooped him around the room, making zooming noises and swinging him past furniture with inches to spare.

"More," he demanded, when Sandro prepared to hand him over to his mother.

"No, you'll make yourself sick," Marisa said. "That's enough, Spencer."

"We'll play some more later," Sandro said, relinquishing Spencer to his mother. "Where are you moving to?" he asked Marisa. "Will you be able to make the trip back to Florida when Dave Forcier's trial starts next month? I know the prosecution considers your testimony really important to their case."

"I wouldn't miss it," Marisa said with quiet determination. "But it's easy enough to fly back. That's what you both did for Ray's trial, wasn't it?"

Belle nodded. "It was such a relief to see Ray convicted. I hadn't realized how much anger I'd been repressing about what Ray and Dave had done until the judge handed down a fifteen-year prison sentence and I just about danced a jig of joy."

"Fifteen years was a lot less than Ray deserved," Sandro said grimly. "I don't think that man felt even a slither of remorse—except that he'd finally been caught."

"Let's hope we get an even stiffer sentence for Dave," Marisa said. "I sure intend to do everything in my power to see that the jury understands exactly what he was trying to do, and how he was prepared to threaten us all to achieve his goals. But I didn't want to hang around in Florida, just counting off the days until the trial. For the past few weeks I've felt as if I haven't done anything except wait for the rest of my life to begin."

"You're right. It's time for all of us to move on," Sandro said. "But I'm impressed that you've managed to wrap up the practical details of the move so quickly.''

"The house sold more easily than I expected," Marisa replied, handing Spencer his favorite teddy bear, neatly resewn after its stint as hiding place for the Cronus disk. "Apparently stark white decor with mirrors and marble everywhere you turn makes for an easy sell. And the couple who bought the house bought all the furniture, right down to the salt and pepper shakers." She shuddered. "Jeez, how I hated that house."

Belle gave her a comforting hug, relieved when her sister managed to smile. "You'll never have to set foot in it again, Rizzie."

"Thank heaven. Anyway, last weekend I was moping around at Mom's feeling sorry for myself and I suddenly realized I couldn't stand being in Florida a moment longer. So I packed up and left. I haven't decided where I'm going yet, but Spencer and I are going to check out a few places in Colorado. There's no rush for us to make up our minds. It's not as if I have to get him into school or anything."

"Why Colorado?" Sandro asked. "Any special reason?"

Marisa gave a rueful smile. "Well, it's nothing like Florida, so that sent it straight to the top of my list of desirable places. But there was a slightly more practical reason as well. The economy's booming in Denver and I'm hoping it won't be too hard to find a job."

"Companies will be fighting to hire you," Belle said.

Marisa grimaced. "Let's hope. Anyway, I'll keep in touch while I'm on the road, and when I have a new home, you two will be the first people to know, I promise. But right now, I just want to head the car west and see what happens.''

"You don't want to go back to modeling?" Belle asked.

Marisa barely concealed a shudder. "No. Anyway, I'm too old. I want to find a nice boring job as a clerk or a secretary. Emphasis on boring.''

"Boring might be good, after the past couple of years," Belle acknowledged.

Sandro turned to look at her. "Did you tell Marisa our news?" he asked.

Belle shook her head, her cheeks turning pink. "There wasn't time. She only arrived a few minutes before you did. You tell her.''

Marisa glanced up. "Tell me what? It's something exciting, I can see.''

Sandro slid his arm around Belle's waist, looking about as self-conscious as he was capable of looking. "Belle has finally agreed to marry me," he said. "I had to get her pregnant before she'd say yes, but she finally agreed and we've set the date for next Saturday.''

"That's why I was trying to call you," Belle said. "We were hoping you'd come to the ceremony. It's going to be really small and simple.''

"You're expecting a baby?" Marisa's eyes filled with tears. "Oh, Belle, that's so wonderful. Congratulations! When is it due?''

Belle laughed. "The Fourth of July, so we have about another eight months to wait. We only found out for sure three days ago, and you're the first person we've told.''

"So will you stay for the wedding?" Sandro asked. "Belle and I would like that a lot."

"Yes, of course I'll stay," Marisa said. "My new life can wait for a week."

"Thank you," Belle said softly. "It means a lot to us to have you and Spencer there."

"I wouldn't miss it." Marisa's smile was only a little strained. "You know I wish you both all the happiness in the world."

Sandro's arm tightened around Belle's waist and he bent down to kiss her. "We already have it," he said. "And we're planning to hold on real tight."

The haunting story of
Marisa Joubert
unfolds in

THE REFUGE

by

Jasmine Cresswell

Coming in October 2000
only from
MIRA

Prologue

*Early June 1999, Stankovec Refugee Camp,
Macedonia*

The refugee camp was hot, dusty and stinking. In another few months the nights would turn bitterly cold. Snow would fall and the dust would vanish, but the smells would linger, the inevitable consequence of too many desperate people crowded into too little space.

Most visitors, especially those from the deodorized comfort of the United States, were overwhelmed by the sight of so much human misery, especially since the war was supposed to be over. Not Stuart Frieze. He had seen it all a dozen times before and he strode between the rows of tents displaying no reaction to the depressing assaults on his senses.

Despite his brisk pace and deliberate emotional detachment, he was aware of every detail of his surroundings. He dodged treasure cooking pots, tattered clothes drying on improvised racks, and cardboard boxes serving as makeshift cradles. He was careful to avoid looking into the eyes of the weary mothers who were struggling to bathe fretful toddlers in plastic bowls filled with tepid water, or provide other basic

services for their shattered families. Stuart didn't need
to look at the women to know the sort of bone-deep
misery he would see. He already had enough haunting
memories from his experiences at other refugee
camps to fill the nightmares of several lifetimes. He
had been a field director for the United Nations High
Commission on Refugees for almost a decade and he
didn't think there was any form of human misery that
he hadn't been forced to confront and deal with some
time during those ten long and frustrating years.

Scanning the camp for the medical tents, he strode
past a dozen young boys who were playing soccer
with a battered ball and improvised goal posts. He
knew better than to create chaos by handing out can-
dies to the lucky few who happened to be close to
him, but gave way to temptation and passed out the
sticks of chewing gum he'd tucked into the pockets
of his cotton pants earlier that morning. As he could
have predicted, he was instantly surrounded by what
seemed like a hundred waving hands. Mad at himself
for falling into bad old habits, he had to call a security
guard to free himself from the crowd of disappointed
kids.

Once a path had been cleared for him he marched
on, his brows drawn into a thick, angry line. What
the hell kind of world would let kids waste years of
their lives stuck on a barren hillside with no place to
go, and nothing to do with their time except plot ways
to find a gun, join the "liberation" army, and wreak
vengeance on their enemies?

He knew the answer to his question, of course. His
world. The rich, indifferent, successful world of the
great western powers. Shoving aside useless philo-
sophical ruminations, Stuart concentrated on his

search for the medical tent. He found it at last and flashed his United Nations badge to gain admittance. He didn't actually work for the United Nations anymore, hadn't for three years, but in this winding up of the conflict, security in the camp was laughably easy to breach for anyone with his years of bureaucratic experience. The checks on his documents at the entrance to the camp had been so cursory that a blatant forgery would have passed muster, and his forgery was pretty good. Once inside the camp, security fell off even more, and the few remaining checkpoints could have been circumvented by any enterprising twelve-year-old.

"I have a meeting arranged with Dr. Mark Yarfield," he said to the orderly posted at the entrance to the medical unit. "Please tell him that Stuart Frieze is here."

He waited less than five minutes before a woman of about forty came out of the tent, stripping off a pair of surgical gloves as she came. She wiped the sweat from her forehead with a face mask before tossing it in the trash.

"Mr...Frieze?"

"Yes. I'm Stuart Frieze."

"I'm Dr. Riven. Carole Riven."

He shook her hand, returning her smile, even though alarm bells were sounding inside his head. This woman looked smart, savvy and alarmingly astute. Not desirable qualities from his point of view.

"I'm sorry, but Mark Yarfield was flown out of here last week," she said. "A medical emergency. Didn't they notify you?"

Stuart concealed a tiny spurt of relief. His information about Dr. Yarfield's hasty departure from the camp had been correct. A first small step in the right direction.

"I'm real sorry to hear about Dr. Yarfield," he lied, sounding convincingly worried. "I hope there's nothing seriously wrong with him?"

Dr. Riven grimaced. "He was diagnosed with TB. Once he's back in the States, it shouldn't be a problem." She paused, barely disguising a sigh. "Is there something I could help you with since he isn't here?"

"Well, Mark and I were originally in touch because I wanted to make a donation to the hospital on behalf of the charitable trust I direct. The Wainscott Foundation, headquartered in Colorado. Under the terms of Mr. Wainscott's will, the trustees agreed that I could provide some medical equipment to the exiled Kosovars that would help pregnant women and their babies. Dr. Yarfield suggested an incubator for infants needing intensive neonatal care, so that's what I arranged to have shipped here. It only took about a hundred hours of pleading with bureaucrats to get it added to one of the aid shipments...." Stuart gave a rueful smile before allowing his voice to trail off into a modest silence.

Understanding dawned on Carole Riven's expressive face. "Oh yes, of course. The Wainscott Foundation—there's a plaque inscribed with that name on the incubator. It's already been a lifesaver several times over." She struggled valiantly to conceal another sigh. "We certainly appreciated the gift, Mr. Frieze, and I'd be happy to give you a tour of our neonatal unit since Mark isn't here. You'll be pleased to hear that I've made arrangements to have your incubator shipped to Pristina as soon as our medical facility here closes down."

"You're a lousy liar and you wouldn't be in the least happy to waste your time giving me a tour." Stuart gave her a cheerful grin. "You're cursing the fact that I've turned up in Stankovec and you're wishing you could get on with your work. You're also wondering why the hell rich benefactors can't just be satisfied with sending money instead of constantly turning up on site and expecting to be thanked."

Carole looked startled, then laughed. A genuine laugh this time. "You sound as if you've been on the receiving end of one too many well-meaning official visits yourself."

"I have." Stuart grimaced. "Trust me, I understand what you're going through. It got so bad on my last UN assignment that I literally broke out in hives whenever I heard that a delegation from the U.S. Congress was coming to visit one of the refugee areas I was responsible for."

Carole gave him a sympathetic smile, a bond of trust forged between them, which was precisely what Stuart had intended. "There's been an outbreak of chicken pox in the camp and it's pretty hectic right now, but actually I'm glad to take a break for five minutes," she said. "And since you provided the funds for the only reliable level three incubator in this entire region, I guess I'm happy to spend time with you. Do you want to see our neonatal unit? That's a genuine willing offer this time. For a field hospital, our facilities here aren't too bad."

"I'd love to see it, but I'm afraid I don't have time," Stuart said. "I have a busload of orphaned toddlers waiting to board a plane to the States, and I have to be out of here within the hour. The problem is, Mark Yarfield had promised to help me with another matter. I only stopped here because I need his help. Urgently.''

"Well, I'll help if I can....''

"I think you'll be able to. It's a good problem really. I've called in every favor I'm owed by the State Department and our immigration service, and I've managed to finagle temporary visas for two more adult refugees to come back with me to the States. Outside the regular quota, that is.''

Carole Riven looked startled. "That's great! At this point, given the devastation inside Kosovo, everyone we can get out of the region before winter is a blessing. How in the world did you manage to get two extra visas?''

Stuart grimaced. "Don't even ask. I licked so much shoe leather that my tongue still has sores on it. Anyway, the good news is that these two visas are valid immediately, and I have the authority to process the paperwork for the individuals right on the plane. Dr. Yarfield figured that if I took a couple of young women who were pregnant, then I'd be rescuing not only the mothers, but the babies as well. Four rescues for two visas, so to speak. The bad news is that I need to take the adult refugees with me on this plane, with the orphans, so they'll have to come right now. No time for us to make a careful selection, and no time for the women to indulge in long goodbyes to their families.''

Carole frowned. "I don't think there are many Kosovar women who'd be willing to leave their families, even for the sake of starting a new life in the States.''

"Dr. Yarfield told me about some young women who'd been raped by a group of drunken soldiers who were supposedly guarding the camp.'' Mark Yarfield hadn't actually told him any such thing. In fact, his correspondence with Dr. Yarfield had been strictly limited to e-mail notes about the incubator. However, Stuart had read a British newspaper report about the rape of the young Albanian women and his interest had immediately been caught. There had been half a dozen of them, terrified women who'd escaped from Serbian soldiers only to be attacked by the Macedonian guards who were supposed to be protecting them. Two of the women, virgins at the time of the attack, had ended up pregnant.

"I know the women you mean," Carole said, her voice hardening. "I was the doctor who treated them after they'd been raped. If they'd only come to me right away, I could have given them medication to make sure they didn't get pregnant. Of course, they were so ashamed of what had happened that they hid in their tents without seeking medical attention until we managed to find them a few weeks later. I offered them the chance of an abortion, but they wouldn't agree. Of course."

Stuart forced himself to sound casual. "They'd be ideal candidates for my emergency visas. They'd probably be more than happy for the chance to have their babies in the States and start a new life there."

"Yes, I expect they would," Carole Riven looked almost cheerful. "This is great news. One of the few happy endings I've seen around this camp. I'll see if I can locate the women for you—"

"Time is really of the essence," Stuart said. "How long will it take you to contact them do you think?" He glanced down at his watch and gave Carole Riven another of his rueful, appealing grins. "I can spare you about forty minutes if we're going to get them on the bus in time for us to make our plane.''

Don't give her time to poke holes in my story. Once the women were gone, she'd be so relieved that she wouldn't give them another moment's thought. This visit would be entirely forgotten in the crush of her exhausting, eighteen-hour workdays.

Carole glanced at her watch. ''Noon. Lunch time, so they're likely to be eating or preparing food near their family tents. I'll get right on it. We must have details of where they're staying in my records. Can you wait here—''

''Don't worry about me.'' He smiled reassuringly, knowing that he looked like what he'd once been. A do-gooder who tried hard to get things done, a bureaucrat with a heart of gold. ''I'll stay out of everyone's way so that your work isn't interrupted any more than it has to be.''

Dr. Riven disappeared into the interior of the medical facility. She proved as efficient as Stuart could have hoped. She'd tracked down the two women— they were really no more than girls—within thirty minutes. The two bewildered refugees arrived at the medical tent where Stuart was waiting and stood with downcast eyes, clutching plastic shopping bags filled with whatever it was that constituted the remnants of their worldly goods. Beneath their light summer blouses, their pregnant abdomens were visibly swollen.

Stuart assessed them rapidly. Brown hair, blue eyes, smooth skin. Quite healthy looking given the circumstances. They were just about perfect for his needs.

''Thank you so very much for your cooperation,

Dr. Riven,'' he said, smiling at the girls in warm reassurance. They blushed and looked away. Poor things, they had been browbeaten by fate to the point that they had zero self-esteem. He resisted the urge to pat them reassuringly on the shoulders. After what they'd gone through, physical contact with a strange man wouldn't be in the least comforting to them.

He switched his smile back to Carole Riven. ''We need to get going, but I believe you've helped to make the future brighter for several people today. These women are going to enjoy a wonderful new start to their lives, and their babies will grow up safely in the security of the United States. This is great. Thank you.''

For once, Stuart meant every word he said.

One

April 2000, Wainscott, Colorado

Five minutes into the interview, Marisa already knew she wasn't going to get the job. She'd realized she was aiming high in applying for a position as assistant to the general manager at the Alpine Lakes Ski Lodge, but after six months of temporary jobs with low pay and no benefits, she was desperate to find something permanent that provided both paid vacation days and a medical plan. Right now, she and Spencer were only one medical emergency away from destitution. And if medical disasters were too unpredictable to worry about, she could give herself a fine case of insomnia fretting about what would happen when her paychecks from the mortuary came to an end on Friday. Unemployment wasn't something that might happen to her one day. Unemployment was scheduled to drop its ax on her three days from now, on Friday the fifteenth.

"Thank you for driving up from Denver to speak with me, Ms. Joubert. According to your current employer, you're a hardworking young woman and you've been popular with his clients, but I'm afraid you just don't have the skills or the experience I re-

quire. I need someone who can maintain a financial
database and run spreadsheets showing projected oc-
cupancy rates and revenue generation in each major
profit center—'' He paused significantly. ''Let me
show you the way back to the main entrance. The
corridors in this part of the lodge can get a little
tricky.''

Marisa came out into the Alpine Lakes parking lot
to discover that the spring snow that had been threatening earlier was now falling in earnest. She picked
her way across the slippery pavement, trying not to
ruin her one remaining pair of good black shoes.
These were her interview shoes, that teamed with the
gray all-season fabric of her one and only interview
suit and, given the number of job interviews she had
to go on in order to get hired, she needed to keep her
outfit in the best possible state of repair. Remember-
ing the hundreds of pairs of expensive shoes she'd
casually tossed into the bags for Goodwill had the
power to make Marisa cringe—although sometimes
she wasn't entirely sure whether she shuddered with
embarrassment at her past profligacy, or regret for her
vanished wealth.

Her car, a two-year-old Saturn with snow tires still
in place, would make it down the mountain roads to
Denver just fine, but she felt defeated and incompe-
tent after her humiliating brief interview and in no
mood to battle snarled highway traffic. When she noticed a trendy-looking café on Main Street she decided to pull over for half an hour and give the snow
plows a chance to clear the interstate. Spencer's day-
care center didn't close until six, and it was now
barely noon, which gave her more than enough time
to drown her sorrows in a foaming mug of *café latte*.

She pushed open the door of La Cafetière, which was shielded by a jaunty red-striped awning and had some brave tulips out front trying not to look frozen in their window boxes. The restaurant's efforts to look like a Parisian sidewalk cafe were somewhat hampered not only by the snow, but by the hardware store next door, which sent out an earthy smell of grains and dried horse feed that battled with La Cafetière's aroma of freshly-ground coffee beans.

The café wasn't crowded, especially in view of the fact that it was lunchtime, and the lone waitress quickly led Marisa to a vacant table by the window. "My name's Kathleen," she said, handing over a single-sheet menu. "My husband's the chef and our menu changes daily. Everything's good, but the *calzone* are our specialty."

It had been a long time since Marisa had eaten out anywhere more sophisticated than a fast-food place, where Spencer could indulge his passion for eating French fries dipped into his carton of orange juice. She read the menu with unexpected interest before finally selecting a panini filled with prosciutto, artichoke hearts and sliced black olives. She gave her order and saved a few pennies by asking for water to drink with her meal.

"Where are you from?" Kathleen asked as she came back to pour ice water into a tall glass. She sounded friendly rather than nosy.

"I was raised in Florida, but today I just drove up from Denver. How did you know I'm not one of the locals?"

Kathleen flashed a smile. "Folks who grew up around Wainscott don't order anything that can't be served with ketchup. I never did find myself until I went to New Orleans and met my husband. Andre is

Cajun, and he thinks the definition of civilized means eating great food before spending the night dancing. He's going to transform the eating habits of Wainscott or go bankrupt trying.''

A group of three grizzled men in bib overalls came into the restaurant and Kathleen excused herself before hurrying away to get them seated. ''What newfangled rabbit food has your husband got lined up for us today?'' one of the men asked Kathleen, taking a pair of glasses out of his pocket, but not bothering to put them on to read the menu.

''There's a tasty arugula and Belgian endive salad with walnut oil dressing if you'd like it,'' Kathleen said with false innocence. She pretended not to hear the men groaning. ''Or we've got a real nice chili with melted provolone cheese if you'd prefer that by any chance. Of course, Andre'll make you all hamburgers and fries if you insist.''

Marisa smothered a grin as the men all opted for the chili as if they were doing Kathleen a personal favor by not ordering burgers. Her panini arrived soon after, baked and seasoned to perfection, and she ate it with fervor.

Kathleen returned later, after bringing the three men huge servings of apple pie and ice cream. ''Would you like some dessert?'' she asked Marisa. ''Andre makes a fudge torte that's to die for. Or I can bring you a dessert menu and you can choose your own caloric sin.''

Marisa smiled and shook her head. ''I've already exceeded my quota of sinning for today. I'll just have coffee, thanks.''

''Regular, espresso, flavored? We've also got hazelnut decaf.''

Marisa ordered a cappuccino to compound the indulgence of a lunch she couldn't really afford. It was depressing how her thoughts constantly circled back to money these days. Six months ago it had seemed so easy to give away the 7.5 million dollars she'd inherited when her father died, and even easier to put the money Evan had left her into an irrevocable trust for her son's education. But a few weeks in Denver had been all it took for Marisa to realize that she'd vastly underestimated the difficulty of earning enough to support herself and Spencer.

Her sister, Belle, had seemed to achieve financial independence so easily that Marisa had ignored the crucial differences between her situation and her sister's. First of all, Belle had a college degree and professional training. Second, Belle had no dependents when she broke away from the corrupting influence of the Joubert's illegal family business. And third, Marisa had a humiliating suspicion her sister was just more competent than she was.

"The snow looks as if it's clearing," Kathleen said, returning to Marisa's table. "That's the worst thing about living up here in the mountains, spring takes forever to arrive, and then you blink and it's summer. Still, the summer's gorgeous when it does finally get here. Lots of sunshine, no humidity, cool nights. And hours and hours of digging in my flower garden so that I have a good crop of petunias for the deer to eat." Kathleen laughed. "Sometimes I don't know why I bother, but I got hooked on the gardening thing when I was in New Orleans and now I'm not smart enough to know when I'm defeated."

"It must be beautiful up here in summer. I've often thought I'd like to live in the mountains." Marisa must have sounded more wistful than she intended, because Kathleen looked at her with sudden speculation.

"I don't suppose you're serious about moving, are you? Or looking for a job, by any chance. My sister's planning to get married and she just quit as assistant to the general manager at Alpine Lakes. He's so desperate for a replacement, he'd hire you in a split second. They have great benefits, too. Three weeks' paid vacation your first year. If you stay right through ski season you get a bonus. Lots of good stuff like that, you know?"

Marisa felt her cheeks flame. The general manager might be desperate but not, apparently, desperate enough to hire someone as unqualified as her. "I'm not looking for a job right now," she said stiffly.

Kathleen sighed. "The job market's really tight these days, and nobody seems to be looking. It's a shame, because this town is full of old-timers and college kids just passing through from ski resort to ski resort. We need a few more people in the middle who want to stick around, especially women."

"Are there a lot of jobs currently available up here?" Marisa tried to sound casual, although she realized that the idea of living with Spencer in this small rural town was beginning to seem very appealing. Maybe losing the job at Alpine Lakes didn't mean the end of her dream of finding a job and establishing a home for Spencer in the tranquillity of the mountains.

"There's lots of part-time and seasonal work," Kathleen said. "That's why we get so many college kids moving through. Wainscott used to be an agricultural center for the county, then Colorado Properties bought the old lodge and turned it into a really upscale ski lodge and the whole balance of the town started to shift. Then when old Mr. Wainscott died—''

"The town was named after a person?"

"Yeah. The Wainscott family owned all the land for miles around, but the old man lived so simply that none of us had ever stopped to figure out that he was actually the driving force behind Colorado Properties, much less that he had millions of dollars he was planning to leave to some weird charitable foundation.''

"I don't understand. Is Alpine Lakes a charitable foundation? It looks just like a regular, for profit resort—''

"It is. I'm talking about The Wainscott Refuge at the other end of town. That's the place that old man Wainscott left his money to.'' Kathleen bent forward, peering out of the window, and pointed to indicate a massive brick building that formed an impassable bulwark at the end of Main Street. "You can see the Refuge from here. See? If you can believe it in this day and age, it's a group home for unwed mothers.''

Marisa looked up, startled. "That's kind of a nineteenth-century concept, isn't it?''

"Sure, but you'd be surprised at how much need there seems to be for the services they're providing. It's always full to capacity, maybe because word's out that they do a terrific job at finding just the right adoptive parents for each baby. Stuart Frieze, the director, often comes in here for lunch and I know he prides himself on the services they provide to the mothers after their babies are born. A woman isn't just tossed out onto the street to sink or swim once her baby's been adopted. The mothers can stay at the refuge until they have jobs to go to, even if that takes a couple of months to arrange.''

The horrors of her marriage to Evan Connor had

left Marisa with a large fund of sympathy for women whom she would previously have dismissed as foolish at handling their lives. "It sounds like a place that's providing a real service," Marisa said.

"Yeah, it is. But they have even worse staffing problems than Alpine Lakes. I heard they had to hire on a janitor who's awfully slow and Stuart's been looking for office help for almost two months." Kathleen gave a wry chuckle. "So far he says the best candidate he's seen is a sixty-year-old woman who insisted on hanging up a banner behind her desk that said God Punishes Fornicators in the Everlasting Fires of Hell."

"Oh my. That must have gone over well with the unwed moms."

"Yeah. To Stuart's credit, she only lasted a day. Now he's back to using temps who can spell their own names, if he's lucky."

Marisa disguised a sudden rush of hope by opening her purse and searching for the money to settle her bill. The director of the refuge sounded desperate enough to hire almost anybody, even a high school dropout who was more than a little vague about the details of her past. Maybe her luck was finally about to change and she would be able to snag herself a permanent job up here in Wainscott after all. And working with mothers-to-be would certainly make for a happy change after three months of arranging to inter corpses.

She would pay a visit to Mr. Frieze and The Wainscott Refuge, Marisa decided. At this point in her life, she had nothing to lose.

If you enjoyed what you just read,
then we've got an offer you can't resist!

Take 2 bestselling
love stories FREE!
Plus get a FREE surprise gift!

CHRISTIANE HEGGAN

"A master at creating taut, romantic suspense."
—*Literary Times*

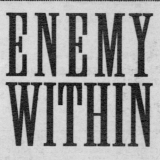

ENEMY WITHIN

When Rachel Spaulding inherits her family's Napa Valley vineyard, it's a dream come true for the adopted daughter of loving parents. But her bitter sister, Annie, vows to do whatever it takes to discredit Rachel and claim the Spaulding vineyards for herself. Including digging into Rachel's past.

What she digs up uncovers three decades of deceit. And exposes Rachel to a killer who wants to keep the past buried.

On sale mid-February 2000 wherever paperbacks are sold!

MIRA®

JASMINE CRESSWELL

66486	THE DISAPPEARANCE	___ $5.99 U.S.	___ $6.99 CAN.
66425	THE DAUGHTER	___ $5.99 U.S.	___ $6.99 CAN.
66261	SECRET SINS	___ $5.99 U.S.	___ $6.99 CAN.
66154	CHARADES	___ $5.50 U.S.	___ $6.50 CAN.
66147	NO SIN TOO GREAT	___ $5.99 U.S.	___ $6.99 CAN.
66040	CHASE THE PAST	___ $4.99 U.S.	___ $5.50 CAN.
66036	DESIRES & DECEPTIONS	___ $4.99 U.S.	___ $5.50 CAN.

(limited quantities available)

TOTAL AMOUNT	$_____
POSTAGE & HANDLING	$_____
($1.00 for one book; 50¢ for each additional)	
APPLICABLE TAXES*	$_____
TOTAL PAYABLE	$_____
(check or money order—please do not send cash)	

To order, complete this form and send it, along with a check or money order for the total above, payable to MIRA Books®, to: **In the U.S.:** 3010 Walden Avenue, P.O. Box 9077, Buffalo, NY 14269-9077; **In Canada:** P.O. Box 636, Fort Erie, Ontario, L2A 5X3.

Name:_____

Address:_____ City:_____

State/Prov.:_____ Zip/Postal Code:_____

Account Number (if applicable):_____

075 CSAS

*New York residents remit applicable sales taxes.
 Canadian residents remit applicable GST and provincial taxes.

MIRA

Visit us at www.mirabooks.com

MJC0200BL